The Donkey Cutter

a novel

Gregory Koop

GUERNICA EDITIONS
TORONTO · CHICAGO · BUFFALO · LANCASTER (U.K.)
2023

Guernica Founder: Antonio D'Alfonso

Michael Mirolla, general editor
Julie Roorda, editor
David Moratto, interior and cover design
Guernica Editions Inc.
287 Templemead Drive, Hamilton, ON L8W 2W4
2250 Military Road, Tonawanda, N.Y. 14150-6000 U.S.A.
www.guernicaeditions.com

Distributors:
Independent Publishers Group (IPG)
600 North Pulaski Road, Chicago IL 60624
University of Toronto Press Distribution (UTP)
5201 Dufferin Street, Toronto (ON), Canada M3H 5T8
Gazelle Book Services, White Cross Mills
High Town, Lancaster LA1 4XS U.K.

First edition.
Printed in Canada.

Legal Deposit—First Quarter
Library of Congress Catalog Card Number: 2022947266
Library and Archives Canada Cataloguing in Publication
Title: The donkey cutter : a novel / Gregory Koop.
Names: Koop, Gregory, author.
Identifiers: Canadiana (print) 20220435502 |
Canadiana (ebook) 20220435510 |
ISBN 9781771837729 (softcover) | ISBN 9781771837736 (EPUB)
Classification: LCC PS8621.O645 D66 2023 | DDC C813/.6—dc23

For Isa ...
Remember, your heart will be moulded with
care deftly inside the histories of the unseen hands
of many an amazing woman ...

Yesterday I held the breath of our baby in my hand
It fit inside a small three-ounce Jewel Jar
I just held it
Alone in the living room in the rocker,
I sat with our baby's breath in my hand ...

Historical statement here:

I N 1887, Claas Epp Jr. helped orchestrate, secure funding and resources for, negotiate, and lead an exodus of over 200 Mennonites from the Russian steppes of Crimea to the desert mountain plateaus of Central Asia or what is now present-day Uzbekistan. With permission from the Muslim clerics and the Khan, he and the Mennonite settlers established a community that would persist for half a century and that stands today, preserved by the surrounding Muslim communities. Why would so many men, women, and children brave a trek through thousands of miles of desert and mountains along the Silk Road? Salvation and a prophecy. Claas Epp Jr.'s motives—the exodus from Europe for central Asia, the coming of Armageddon, the End of Days, and a promise to be Raptured—secured the support of hundreds of families. What followed at best crushed the spirits of believers and at worst killed them. And for nearly a century and a half, it was shameful to discuss this element of Mennonite history. Many Central-Asian Mennonites and their families, lost in the disillusionment when Epp's prophecies failed to materialize, fled Asia for Canada and other parts of America, with many holding to the expectation that Armageddon was still upon mankind. But when?

Black Gully

MUTTA WAS DEAD. The Rapture never happened. And I learned how deeply Foda loved me.

THURSDAY, MAY 12, 1910.

Wapos County

W ITH BLOOD STILL on my hand, I shook it to cast the redness from my skin. I refused to wipe it off onto my dress
the way Jonah had. I didn't want to bring any of it home. Why was
this happening to me? My stomach felt pulled apart. He had only
touched me. I let his hand—no, I wanted his hand. Was it my fault?
Foda didn't believe in a god. Mutta had prayed to one every day. *For
God hath not called us unto uncleanness, but unto holiness.* I feared
Mutta had been right. The only other time I had bled from those
places was my accident falling onto the fence rails. I had fallen
again. Fallen for that boy and his sin. Was there sin? What was my
sin? It felt nice. He felt nice. My heart sang when he touched me. I
wanted his touch. But now I fled from the boy and the schoolyard.

I ran and ran through the silage field. The stubbed oat stocks
nipped at my ankles. I darted on angles, jumping the hollowed dried
stocks, trying to follow the fall of the swath. The morning sun at my
back pointed my shadow towards home. I thought it looked like I
was chasing after myself.

Spring came to Black Gully's prairie early. The budding branches
and limbs of the poplars, spruce, and birch rattled against warm gales.
The fields, having absorbed all the winter snow, were more ashen
than black, and fractured as if the ground had been dropped from
the skies. The soil billowed, disturbed by my pounding feet. I looked
over my shoulder and saw a soft, dull tail of dust. The fluttering

cloudy train fondled the edges of my white lace hem. Later I would notice it had left it a tea-stained colour.

What about Foda? Those thoughts slowed my legs. What about Foda? Where was he?

I stopped. I was in our oat field. The edges pulsed with long winding black veins of voles tunneling out of their hibernation. Chickadees chirped and hopped from pussy willows onto spilt oat seed, scattered like fallen stars atop the ground. The grassy roof of the *semlin*, already greening, was just over the brim. I pushed forward home. My breath plunged out of me, pulling the rusty taste of an idle winter from my lungs onto the back of my tongue. More blood. I coughed it up and spit it from my body as I kept going. An ache spreading across my pelvic bone tripped me up at the ankles. My hands tumbled over themselves against the prickly field. I kept upright and moved ever farther home.

I pressed my palm into my side. The cramps of piercing pain that had scared not only me but Jonah Wiebe were lashing my insides hard. I could feel a spongy sogginess swelling around my other parts.

"You made me touch you," Jonah had yelled. *Why did you say that, Jonah?*

But I could not have called him a liar if he had told on me. I had wanted to feel his hands, his soft lips, to comb my fingers through his hair. Every night for a year I had seen him—his big smile, his strong arms, and his glistening shoes, always polished. I always giggled in my dreams. And this morning, outside of my bedroom and away from my home, I had led Jonah way off from the schoolyard in the brush near the Wapos Creek's bank, a spot where the older children played. We came to the clearing, eaten down and pressed flat by whitetails, mule deer, and moose. It hung away from the last of the winter's wind and the schoolhouse windows. The sun had warmed the morning enough that I removed my jacket. I left it hanging from a broken branch.

I invited his hand to my body. His touch, his heavy breath melted the linger of winter from my nape. My body followed the strength of his wandering hands. I thought, *Oh goodness. Maybe I shouldn't.* But it felt so nice, a warmth pulsed through me. *He wants me. To be with me.* The hairs stood up on my neck and arms. I felt warm through my chest and ears and other parts. So my hips followed. I pressed back against him. I had liked the sweet butter and raspberry taste on his lips.

Then the stabbing came. I was confused at the pain. I thought Jonah had done something. When I saw him wipe his hand at the bottom of my dress, he left a smear of blood through the white hem. I reached a hand to him for help. Maybe the blood was his? The pain speared me again. His eyes bulged. And he ran from me. He ran back to the schoolhouse.

I reached between my legs. And with the scornful eyes of Mutta behind my mind I understood why she had said, "*He* sees all." I had not *abstained from fornication*. Mutta was right. The hot and wet blood all over my fingers, it was his warning. It had to be. He was killing me. I was to die for Jonah's touch. I had not fallen from the top of a splintered wooden rail. I had lain with Jonah.

I couldn't tell Foda, but I was running home. A sharp jolt stabbed through my hips and stomach. What had I done? If I could run home and find you, Mutta, surely you would have known what was happening to me. You would have calmed me. I could have confessed to you and be saved. But all I had of you were memories. I was left there in the clearing bleeding, dying, and remembering only your harsh warning.

"Men will hurt you," you had said. That was four years before you had left this world. "They are a selfish beast, caring only for urges, the urges that wake them, that cause them hunger. Men will no sooner slaughter a piglet after he's nurtured it into a hog."

"What about Foda?" I had asked.

You rolled away from me inside the bed that we shared, pulling the quilt over your head. "What about him?"

I could sense the quilt rising, ballooning with a deep slow breath.

"Foda is a good man, right?"

"John tried to save me."

"Then he *is* good."

"He's complicated."

Foda was complicated and the last person I wanted to see when I got home. An atheist Foda had left behind the Bible for books and magazines: literature, topography, science. He knew medicine. But the kind for his animals, his donkeys. I wasn't a donkey.

I saw the sod walls of the *semlin*, its fieldstone chimney with the rolling mossy grey and yellow stones rising out of the earth. I ran faster. The pain in my pelvis kept pace. I don't remember the first years of my life living in that earthen home dug into the ground. Most neighbours used these shelters the first years, while breaking the land, but let them fall back into the earth once their house and barn were built. Foda kept the *semlin* as a root cellar for our canning and his ales.

Down the timber steps of our *semlin* I plodded below the earth to the door latch, slid it back, and shoved inside. The planking door rattled the frame and pushed back against me. I crumpled down the rough-sawn face of the door not feeling splinters pin my vest and blouse to my kidneys. My arms squeezed around my stomach, wringing as hard as they could. I sat alone, my heart pounding inside my ears, and promised never to see Jonah Wiebe again, not to hold his hand, not to even look at his blue eyes, if I be spared. I promised to read Mutta's Bible. I would look for it if Foda hadn't thrown it away. I negotiated in the dark for my life back. Then I paused. Nothing.

I screamed into the root cellar: "It's your fault." I grabbed my mouth, but my cries were already free.

My own grip reminded me of our kisses. The openness of his mouth, his teeth clicking against mine, his tongue pushing inside like a lump of stew beef. I told myself it never felt like a real kiss. The kiss was missing the tenderness of Mutta's lips on my forehead at bedtime. It was missing the strength and stability of the peck on my cheek Foda had given me after we buried Mutta, the last time any such tenderness came from him. And his clumsy palms kneading my breasts like they were dough. The sharp edges of his fingers scraped along my skin inside my dress.

It was all wrong—all wrong. *He* was warning me, but I wouldn't listen. Jonah didn't feel the same as the version of him I imagined inside my bed. The length of my quilt rolled resting between my legs, and a second pillow across from my face with my hand just under its cool side, cradling it. I slowly rolled my hips focusing on the warm pulse spreading beyond my legs. My other hand became his, tracing up my thigh under my nightgown, his fingers wandering the canyons and plains of my torso, gracing the shadows cast upon my body.

"I'm so stupid," I shouted. I had to grab my mouth again.

Another resonant cramp curled me into a ball of tight muscles. It subsided, but a dull ache deeper than before haunted my stomach all across my hips, stabbing through my lower back. I moaned. And I thought to pray more to make amends for not having prayed since before Mutta died.

My genuflection steadied a newfound adoration to the world. "I promise, Lord, never again."

My prayer came from the same place in my gut as the prayers I used as a little girl for thunderstorms, the storms that broke the tops off the jack pines that lit my bedroom up before those lashes of lightning that cracked at my windows with thunder.

The musty earthen cellar air kept me searching for more breath. I rolled my chest nearly to the ground pinning the pain down—and spread my legs. In the darkness my hand crept under my dress. I hesitated, and my knuckles rattled against themselves. When I reached the silken hairs below my stomach, I held my breath and squeezed my eyes as tight as I could. I froze. No great wave of pain met me, so I slid my hands the rest of the way down. I sensed a cool wetness slipping down my thigh. I went to the trickle instead and followed it back to my underpants. They were wet and warm.

The darkness inside the *semlin* pulled up onto me. Images of the goat-headed creatures from Mutta's Bible washed over my wetted eyes. Something with horned crowns flashed grins from off behind the shadows of the cellar. There were no pickled beans or sauerkraut or baskets of sand hiding carrots, beets, potatoes. I wanted to flee.

The brays of donkeys came through the chinks in the door. Foda may have been in the barley fields picking stones or, worse, just off the *semlin* in the barn tending to the donkeys' hooves in anticipation of tilling the fields for seeding. "Here or Foda," I breathed into the cellar. What was more frightening?

Through a gap in the doorframe over my shoulder, dust sparkled floating upon a ribbon of sunlight sliding inside the cellar. I moved my hand out of the gloom and under the light, cutting my fingers through the glowing dust. My fingers, my palm, all were stained with more blood. I swallowed, tasting iron behind my breath. I rolled back towards the darkness and chopped my hands out in front of me at any demons sneaking upon me. My running heart pushed through my rib bones. I buried my hands into the root cellar's silty floor expecting the Devil's hands to take them. There was only soil. I pulled up sand, silt, and dirt by the handful. I rubbed it over and around my fingers, arms, threw it away from myself, hearing the filth tinker and chime off the preserves on the shelves I couldn't see. And then more soil up my dress onto my thighs. I threw that dirt, too, before scurrying on my knees to press my face against the gap in the doorframe, where I looked for Foda. The barn door was open. I didn't see him in the donkey pen. I yanked the door open and ran to the house hoping the chamber jug was still half full.

Eastern Reserve, Manitoba

EBECCA,

You are leaving and will be gone. So please know that a house is not a home alone. It is the family, and it is the friends. Your kitchen should give off warmth for those who gather. And always have a cup of coffee to offer. A home, it is love and understanding stitched together with a tender kindness that fills all hearts. Please make yours a place of happiness.

Please do continue your sewing. It will free you from the chore of everyday. The gardens, the kitchen, and prayer. The toil will leave pain and anger in your hands. Never leave that anger in your hands. The sewing needle, sharp, will rupture these feelings. Keep your needles sharp. Make a pincushion, and stuff it full of steel wool. This will keep even the finest fabrics free of snags because your needles and pins will be sharp.

I would also like to tell you that soap is your friend when sewing. Use it as another pincushion. The soap helps lubricate the needle and will make the sewing easier. The soap can also be used to mark your cuts and sewing patterns. It is better than ink or pencil because it will wash away.

When creating a quilt, special care and attention must be given, firstly to function, then to your creative expression. You select the fabrics, cut them into your desired shapes, and then you sew them together one by one, keeping mind to line and a strong stitch. So much care and attention will be spent until it is done. This is when you carefully fold it and store it away inside a chest or cabinet. Seems unusual to put so much time and passion into something that will spend most of its life stowed away. But it is not about the quilt, but those you present it to. Your quilt is to be brought out only for a special occasion, for special guests, to be placed at the foot of their bed.

The most practical stitch, especially when performed with a complimentary thread colour, is the blanket stitch. You simply bring the needle up from the back. Then make a stitch to the right. Finally, pull through, but let the thread run under the needle. Repeat, keeping the lines even and spacing equal.

Oma Katie Klippenstein

Winnipeg, Manitoba

Will All Life Perish? Ask Scientists
Earth to Pass Through the Tail of Halley's Comet

SCIENTISTS FROM ALL over America and Europe acknowledge that the spectra of the comet passing by the Earth later this month contain prominent levels of cyanogen.

Cyanogen, like other cyanides, is exceptionally toxic to humans. The introduction of the poisonous gas to the respiratory system results in headaches, dizziness, nausea, and convulsions before death.

A ghastly death, indeed. Such a presence of high levels of cyanogen has sparked concern with noted scientists such as French scientist Camille Flammarion.

Flammarion predicts vast amounts of cyanogen could not only penetrate the Earth's atmosphere but also impregnate the air and water, thus dooming all life on this planet. And if united with the prominent levels of hydrogen in our own atmosphere, states Prof. E. Booth, it "would form the deadly gas hydrocyanic acid, the deadliest poison known to science, which means death for all animals."

It's noted that most scientists disagree with Booth and Flammarion, insisting that the low levels of cyanogen combined with the mass and spin of the Earth will repel any and all dangers as we pass through the comet's massive tail on Thursday, May 19, 1910.

Wapos County

"**I** WANT A rocking chair," Rebecca said.

The stillness of the house ripped. John did not look up from his book. He sniffled, then turned the page.

Rebecca, she looked at John, focussing on his thinning, brown hair. She thought of old men as bald, but John had barely reached his thirties. "Could you get me a rocking chair?" She shuffled on the kitchen bench, her back straight as her hands guided a pair of scissors through an old sleeping gown that belonged to her daughter, Mareika, when she was a baby.

"What are you doing?" John put his book down, stepped up from the couch in the living room, marched into the kitchen, and straddled a small pile of material snipped into diamonds and triangles that mocked a pile of leaves that the autumn gales may very well have shaken off of Rebecca. She held the small white gown in her hands, her scissors poised at the collar for more cuts. He took the lace trim of the gown in a hand. "This is Mareika's sleeping gown."

"I know." Rebecca pushed the hungry scissors down the length of the gown—John jerking his fingers from the nip of the scissor.

"Why did you do that?"

"I'm making a quilt. That's why I need a rocking chair." Rebecca cocked her head as if to say, *Tell me when I can expect one.*

"My mutta made that. What if Mareika had wanted to give it to her children?"

"She wouldn't. I don't have any of my old sleeping gowns. Do you?" Rebecca continued the dissection, triangles falling between her knees to the hardwood. "A quilt makes a much better heirloom."

John escaped the table to the kitchen. He kept his back to his wife, and with a knife in his grip, he popped the seal of a jar of pears. He tipped the fermented syrup past his lips. A sip turned into a gulp. And he chewed a cored half of a tiny pear they had grown in the small orchard of fruit trees—pears, apples, crabs, cherries, and plums—hiding their homestead from the gravelled road that led to Black Gully.

"Well . . ." He held the jar for his wife.

Focussed, she continued dismembering the gown.

The winter cold flung open the door and seemed to blow not only flakes and ice but also a column of firewood stacked upon legs and stomping boots. John went to their daughter, Mareika. He took up the top three or four logs. Her face glowed red from the prairie winter. He checked her with his hip from the door, then kicked the door shut. The *kisinatin* hissed through the jamb. Mareika stomped her feet more. She stepped across the entry runner, an ornate Turkish pattern of yellow and bronze florals blooming from a bed of red that John's family secured during their days farming on the Russian steppe. She dropped her logs and kicked them under the wood stove. She squatted and arranged the logs below the cast-iron door of the wood stove inside a bottom knockout framed in brown bricks sourced from Medicine Hat. She loved the look of the knockout when full of firewood and tried to keep it always full.

The masonry stove was the heart of the home. It rose from the floor through the roof nearly two-and-a-half storeys, anchored to its own fieldstone foundation, a solid collection of boulders cemented in concrete, measuring three metres long by one-and-a-half metres. The monolith of stone and concrete acted as the exterior wall of the master bedroom, then elbowed down the east wall of the kitchen, shrinking from the full height of the rafters into a counter, topped with fir two-bys turned on edge, a dozen across. Several knockouts, also levelled with two-bys, gave the masonry stove function, keeping pots, pans, dishes, and woven baskets concealing anything from linens to preserves and potatoes. The potatoes and carrots were kept at the end near the cold of the entry. Shadows of fires smoked the mortar and sandstone mass the colour of charcoal above the cast-iron door and the brick knockout above the woodstove where stews could braise or breads bake. In the rafters a hidden second cast-iron door could be seen. This was where John hung rabbits and fowl, hams, and sausage to smoke. Oils from dripping fat brushed rusty brown streaks down the face of the chimney.

John opened the cast-iron door and tossed his logs onto the coals. Flames jumped over the barkless, silvered poplar wood.

Rebecca grunted to clear an empty throat that reined in the room with a tone saved for teachers or judges. "Excuse me—John."

Mareika froze. Her eyes widened and leapt from the stove, but with enough attention to survey her mutta's face, to her foda. His lips drew a false smile across his face, a straight line, and he nodded to Mareika. He took a deep breath and returned his attention to Rebecca.

She continued with her teacher's voice. "A quilt was all I wanted from my family." Rebecca took up a handful of large triangles from the mat. She shook them and tossed them to the floor. "I got nothing."

"You got a dish."

"A broken dish that you never glued."

John squatted and shoved three more lengths of wood into the stove. "I have a glue recipe."

"It doesn't matter." Rebecca stopped cutting and locked her gaze on her little girl. "Mareika, what would you rather have, a beautiful quilt that I made for you to cuddle in or a baby gown for an imaginary baby?"

The girl looked at Foda. Her eyes almost wide but restrained by an inkling of a frown instigated by her eyebrows. The look asked him to step in, to save her from her mutta's interrogation. She had not started this battle. She merely walked into it. The room pulsed with pressure to break the dead silence.

John nudged the air with his chin, an emotional push. Mareika would have to address this situation on her own. She couldn't handle the heat from her mutta's eyes. She looked at the Turkish runner, followed the twist and roll of brown vines to the dozens of large diamonds and triangles hiding Mutta's feet. Her gaze managed to scale the leg of the kitchen table to its top, covered in old shirts, pants, dresses, linens worn with holes, and a big shiny pair of scissors. Under the silver tool, her white gown lay slit up the middle.

"I ..."

"It's not hard. Choose one. You get a say. If you want a silly pair of pajamas—" Rebecca snapped up the garment, the scissors sprang onto the floor. The garment hung like a rabbit's pelt in Rebecca's hand. "—then I will stitch these back together, and you can take them."

Mareika again searched Foda for assistance.

He crouched and retrieved the scissors. "Go ahead," he said. His voice came soft as fog. It felt warm. But more importantly, it veiled Mutta's hard stare, her teeth clenched and grinding.

"Yes, go ahead. Don't be afraid. You get a vote. Did you read in the paper that women in Tasmania get to vote there? Perhaps we'll hop aboard a boat, and you can make the trek there where you can freely give me your answer."

"Rebecca." John wrung his hands around the scissors.

"What, John? It's not a hard question. I'm asking her to choose. I'm making her this quilt, and I thought it would be special to make it out of material that holds some sort of meaning." She yanked up the garments one by one with her free hand. "My wedding dress. Is anybody here upset that I'm chopping up this old thing? The bed linen and all those blouses you bought in Toronto. What else?" She pulled up a navy-blue dress drizzled with red and purple flowers at the end of arcing green stems. The flowers looked like the shadows of tulips swept over a puddle at dusk after a spring shower. The iron of her stare, rusted, flaked, and blew away. Her eyes softened, melancholic. She laid the garment over her lap and buried it under triangles and diamonds. She patted the table.

"Well." She held her hand out to John.

He handed her the scissors.

Mareika lifted her head and stared at Mutta's forehead. "Okay."

"Okay what?"

"It's okay. I don't want the pajamas."

John moved into the living room. He sat on the couch beside his glasses resting upon his book.

Mareika stood at the end of the kitchen until Rebecca nodded and freed her with a slim simper. Her steps stuttered around the far side of Mutta's pile of quilt fixings as she followed Foda into the living room.

Rebecca sat and continued cutting the gown into equilateral triangles, five inches each side, from a shiny template of tin John had made for her. She placed the metal triangle down and traced its edges with a stick of soap before she snipped them out. She didn't look at her husband or her daughter. She carried on.

Mareika moved to the couch and sat. John nudged her knee with his book. Mareika caught herself in the flicker of his lenses, two of her floating on either side of her foda's prominent nose. She tilted her head, and even though her lips remained tightly sealed together, their corners turned up. As did her eyes. His head fell back into the book. A hushed breath turned the blocked black-and-white syntax on those pages into whispers. The little girl shuffled down the couch and laid her head in Foda's lap to follow his voice into slumber.

"Mareika." Rebecca didn't lift her head from her cutting. "Come, please."

Mareika obeyed her mother, stood behind her chair.

"Come closer, please."

Rebecca sighed. The girl bent at her hip, draping her chin above her mother's shoulder. Rebecca continued with the scissors down one length of a triangle, sliding the gown ninety degrees and going through another soap line and placing the triangle into a basket sitting on the bench beside her. "This is a special quilt. You don't know this, because you are out here with us, but my grandmother used to sew. You would do this with all the other ladies. They would sit about and stitch together all these little pieces of cloth." She held up a triangle. "And they . . ." Mutta stared off as if following a butterfly. Her gaze peered through the walls of their home and looked somewhere in the past. When her voice returned, it was wet with a sadness and came slower.

"They would make all these amazing patterns and stitch them together with round curving lines. The quilts take much work. And because of that they are very special. I want you to have one. But I want it to be more than a lot of work. That's why . . . I cut up your gown. I know Foda's mutta made it for you, but I want you to still be able to use it. I'm sorry I got angry. I want you to understand that I am doing this for you with my heart. *Be ye kind one to another, tender-hearted, forgiving one another, even as God for Christ's sake hath forgiven you.*" She cleared her throat. "Do you understand?"

"I'm sorry, Mutta."

"Please don't . . . If you would like, you can pick something, and I will stitch it into the quilt. Anything."

Mareika stood tall. She looked to John. He held a finger folded into his book, looking at his daughter and wife. He nodded.

"I know what I want."

"Okay. Go get it."

Mareika danced off on the balls of her feet, and their patter lit the room up.

John, still beholden to his wife, got a look back. Rebecca exchanged a nod with him.

Their girl came out with a red shirt. She looked at John as she held the collared shirt to Mutta.

"That's Foda's shirt," Rebecca said.

"I know." Mareika's smile became John's smile.

He took his reading classes off, pinched the bridge of his nose, and walked to the pantry. He opened its door and stepped behind it.

"John, you still wear it. You use it in the fall."

"Can I, Foda?"

A yes came from the pantry, as did the cling and clang of jars.

"Okay. I will use Foda's shirt. Bring it here." Rebecca took the shirt and splayed it open like a deer hide. She drew triangle after triangle over the back of it.

John came from the pantry with a jar of pickled radishes and chokecherry jelly. Rebecca flashed him the scissors. The lamplight flickered over his glossy eyes. He nodded, moved past his daughter, turning his face from her and keeping his back to the dining room table. He set the preserves on the counter, went to the window, fished three pickles from their clay crock, and then took out a knife and sliced up the radishes and pickles with some bread. He looked over his shoulder. "I will go to Abraham about a rocking chair."

"Thank you."

"He was complaining of the coyotes and grey wolves last fall. He'll be calving in a couple of months, so . . ."

"Your neck looks fuzzy. Would you like me to shave it?"

John's face flushed with blood. His head tilted and swayed with hesitation. "It's late." John turned with a smile across his face, which he tried to drop on the floor as he carried a plate of pickled vegetables, jelly, and bread to the table.

"I don't mind." Rebecca kept to her task of plotting out her cuts.

He sat and pushed some of the material away to expose a corner of the table. Rebecca reached across to him, her fingernails dancing amongst the long curly hairs sprouting from his neck like alfalfa sprouts. He took up a slice of pickled radish and placed it onto Rebecca's tongue. She held it there as she sheared through his shirt. Her teeth crunched down, and she chewed. Mareika sat on the other side of Rebecca with a piece of bread and examined the triangles inside the basket.

Winnipeg, Manitoba

IBI **GIETZ, HIS** body long and lean from walking most everywhere, lay naked over the sheet of his hotel bed. He mopped his brow with the edge of the bedsheet. Sweat had risen from every pore and captured curls of his hairs and pasted them to his skin, a plain kissed dark by days under the sun shovelling grain out of railcars when he felt like it. Not many Mennonite men had great tufts of chest hair, and most shied away from the sun, evidenced by their usually white shoulders. Gietz had no such apprehension or farmer's tan, so in that regard he was measured the same as an Indian or an Irish. He ignored snarls of other men. He welcomed any kind of heat the prairies offered after his childhood spent in the hot mountain deserts of Turkestan. Besides, his body was never meant for the men he worked with.

He lay in bed most Thursdays in any number of hotel rooms around Winnipeg. This gave him the energy for what really mattered, Friday and Saturday nights. This room had been built only the previous year as the city exploded. Every floor had a shared bathroom at the end of the hall. Plus, the walls were brick and mortar and offered greater privacy for him and his guests.

He rubbed his palms against the throbbing behind his eyes. A woman dropped a glass of water on the bed stand. If asked in ten minutes to describe the woman, Ibi more than likely would have transcribed the curve of a chalice and the wetness of its contents. The water, cool, washed over the burrs of taste buds clinging to the roof of his mouth. He drank as if the water gave him life. He sat up straight, hunched, and moaned.

"You sound like you're enjoying that," the woman said. She poured more water. He stared up at the ceiling. The clack of hooves, the bleeps of automobile horns, and the barking of a dog floated into the room.

"You shouldn't have opened the window—I like that smell ..." He drank further before he gave his lips a lick.

She waved her hand in front of his eyes. "Bad boy. But it's too hot in here." She buttoned a white lace shawl over her soft blue dress and corset.

"Are you leaving already?"

The woman stood back, captured inside a smouldering glow filtered through the sheer amber curtain. It erased the edges of her body, made her float, because the floors, walls, furniture all ceased being independent objects. Ibi yawned and reached for her hand. She held herself tall. It was a physical confidence that had attracted Ibi to her. She had whispered upon his ear, *I've never done anything like this*, but he had heard all of them stake this claim. When she didn't take his hand, she and her beauty burned up.

Ibi scowled like a scorned little boy denied a toy.

The clock tower at city hall rang.

"It's noon, Ibi." She made for the door where she pulled a cloche hat over her parted brown hair, brushed back and braided. The brim of the hat, forced down by a team of short pussy willow twigs budding with grey and white catkins that Ibi had cut on their stroll along the Red River, ended at her eyebrows.

"Wait ..." He reached for a scarf from his duffle and held it out to her. It captured the late morning sun, which smouldered under the flow of purples and creamy whites. "I saw this, and it made me think of you."

"Did it?" She shook her head. The weight of thought, of contemplation tipped her forehead to the ceiling, and a sigh escaped. Her head still shook. When she brought her eyes back to Ibi, her eyelids were closed.

"What is it?"

"Nothing." She pulled the tail of an identical scarf knotted at her hip through an eyelet at the base of her corset. "Oh, Ibi. You're a good time. But ... but you're a distraction." She unknotted the gift and passed it back to him.

He held them both and stared into them, his brow furrowed. He stood to her. His size and flesh his invitation as he tried to dodge her goodbye. His face eased to her lips, but he only found her palms against his chest. She held all his weight—his lips parted slightly—until his balance returned to his heels.

"Goodbye, Ibi." She turned and grabbed the doorknob.

He spun, rolled, and rode atop the wake of her bouquet as last night pushed back into the room from breezes sucked in from the hallway through the door. He closed his eyes for ignorance and re-membrance. The click of the latch stabbed at him. He had had no issue walking out on a woman. For only one second did he consider if this dull strike perhaps could be what all the women before had felt when he walked out. But he had never said any goodbyes. He turned back to the door and stood where she had. The doorknob rested inside his grip. He held it much like a warm chicken egg—in-timidating, its fragility. His palm, followed by his forehead, found the sanded, whitewashed, and polished lacquer of the maple door.

He took a breath and let names fill the room. "Greer ... Gwen ... Gwendolyn, Guinevere, Geneviève?" He smelled the deep sigh of his morning breath soured by whisky. It cut through her perfume. In less than a twinkling as his muscles hesitated with the doorknob, Ibi heard the voice of the only other woman in his life, his neigh-bour, Mrs. Eunice Worth.

The muumuu-clad elderly lady, as tall and broad as most men, bore short, frayed, spiralling, intense waves of grey and white hair, a mat of steel wool. She usually only haunted the halls from eleven p.m. to three a.m. with a clutch of calicos. This was where she took hold of you and scoured your character with her Biblical mind.

Ibi pressed his ear to the door for her words. He needed her words. The hallway was her altar. She could ignite a revivalist talk for any man's ear from the cloudy intentions the Bible offered him. Ibi could see nothing but text, font, and serif. The Bible confused him. It had no voice when he used his own eyes. Before her, he had had a mentor, Claas Epp Jr. In the court of Ak-Metchet, he had filtered the text into something tangible, something real, an image he could smell, touch, see, course a compass. But with time away from his mentor, it had been easier to fall away from its text. But Mrs. Worth brought him back.

"The blood of the Lamb—the Lamb, His son—shall stain our doors, protect us from the words of the pretenders. Protect *You* from *The End*." Her voice stretched the ends of words as if they were saltwater taffy. "We feel it falling upon us like the beginning of night. Darkness! Darkness He shows us in every man's heart. And what of your heart? A vessel, a Station? Blood. Blood. Blood. The Lamb's blood pumps. It pumps! Washing through your heart. Your guilt reminding you of *His* sacrifice."

Ibi grasped for the door panels, fell down to his knees. His eyelids fell, too, and Ak-Metchet opened inside his mind. The breeze carried grit with it, this reality squeezing tears from his memory. The floor beneath him could have sprouted the brown stunted grasses and prickly blooms he'd long forgotten the names for. The wood casing surrounding the door, sprouted the limbs of the apple trees they had planted, which unfurled before they wrapped around his now weeping form.

Her voice chased after his lover, never fading as it moved away from his door to the stairwell. How her voice lifted him. Oh, she moved him, her sermon a dance.

"Isaiah 53:7." Ibi's lips moved along with hers. "'He is brought as a lamb to the slaughter, and as a sheep before her shearers is dumb, so he openeth not his mouth." Her voice burned inside Ibi's ears. When she spoke, he reached for the pale blue skies above that Central Asian plateau. Her fervour lifted his heart. He stood straight and true. He clapped from behind his door. He imagined she must have grabbed his lover's face as she had grabbed his and shaken that sin free as it seemed to have shaken off his skin.

"Yes!" he said, when she waxed and polished Revelations.

"Revelations warned us of Napoleon. It showed him to us, a head, one of seven, with ten horns, each with its own crown. Napoleon was one of those heads, snapping and snarling, devouring us whole when it crawled out of the sea and moved over Europe."

He lapped at her sermons that dripped from her brain. He understood her message of doom. He washed Eunice's feet that night. Claas had allowed him to wash his feet and Claas washed his. His reverie for Claas, for Revelations, and the Book of Daniel had been only matched by this Evangelical.

He dropped back onto the mattress as he had done on the day Claas led the second baptisms in the water of the Amu Darya, the weeks before the last of the believers made the final push to the "Big Garden," Ak-Metchet. The warm shadow of Claas's palm rested between his shoulder blades. Claas's voice poetic and gentle as the cold waters flowed around his thighs before it cascaded over his face and filled his ears.

"*Believer . . .*"

"*Believer . . .*"

A newspaper crackled under Ibi. As the blood rose through him, he felt Eunice Worth's finger pointing just as that first night, its nail chewed and chiselled blunt. She had found him still drunk and smelling of perfume sitting outside his room with no key. He thought he must have dropped it in an alley as he fumbled with a nameless and faceless woman for release, pressing up underneath her petticoat, who just as eagerly pressed into him. Ibi sneered as this unremembered woman's body seized his mind. Her soft curves, her thigh's heavy sateen, her eagerness, which relieved that temporary union. Young women had this pull on him. He felt snared by them like he was tethered to their bodies.

He pulled the paper from under his hip as a distraction from the dread of once again lying alone in an empty hotel room.

He sat up and stared into a tag line almost lost in the first page: "Will All Life Perish? Ask Scientists: Earth to Pass Through the Tail of Halley's Comet."

His eyes darted over the article. Maybe Mrs. Worth was Claas. Her words became Him or His words became her. Harbingers of the coming *End*. Mrs. Worth had been pointing at his face, his mouth smeared with lipstick. Her voice bellowed deep. That experience had been warm and fraught with passion. Ibi needed them for this day. Ibi tapped his own forehead.

The ripples raised memories from the sulci. Again they washed behind his eyes the brown sand and jagged stone of Ak-Metchet, Turkestan, the milk-paint white of plaster, the tree groves. He saw the large lacquered planks of the table they all gathered around to sing hymns, where Claas Epp Jr. stood upon his chair and reached his hands skyward to ask that He take the Bride Community.

"Blessed are the peacemakers." Claas preached of a place for refuge. That is why he took Ibi and hundreds of other Mennonite families from Russia east into Central Asia with the anticipation the world would end. Jesus would return. And they, the Bride Community, the followers of Truth, should have risen into the heavens at the Rapture.

Instead, that day in 1889 after hours of hymns and watching the sky, Ibi and the others sat hushed. Then Claas burst from his seat, abandoning the table placed in the court for the hovel of prayer and reflection for days, to readjust his math.

But this day Ibi saw that paper promising a comet—a poisonous comet.

Behind Ibi, a voice echoed off his walls. *"And the third angel sounded, and there fell a great star from heaven, burning as it were a lamp, and it fell upon the third part of the rivers, and upon the fountains of waters; and the name of the star is called Wormwood; and the third part of the waters became wormwood; and many men died of the waters, because they were made bitter."*

It was Claas Epp Jr.'s voice. Ibi heard Claas Epp Jr. He looked out the window and searched the streets. Grey suits moved along, eyes hidden beneath felt hats.

"Devils!" Ibi cried. "Oh, my Claas, what have I become?"

He squeezed his eyes shut, the trolley car's bell, ding, ding, came like a call. He squeezed his eyes harder. Claas's image sparked out of the darkness with edges fuzzy as if the man was formed of soot and ash and coal. His dark hair parted at the left. A bowtie gifted the meekness of his neck gravitas. Claas brushed the ash off the cuffs of his black coat and extended his hand toward Ibi. His mitts looked too large for his wrists.

Ibi shook his eyes open. He saw the street still full of devils hiding under hats and blazers. His chest felt torn open by a heart with vestigial teeth and nails. He grabbed the paper.

"A date, give me a date!"

His eyes scoured the article: "Cyanogen gas ... impregnate the air and water ... death for all animals ... Thursday, May 19, 1910."

Ibi looked out the window into the sky. The sunshine seared his gaze.

"It is the comet. The comet is the pale horse. Claas, the comet is the pale horse." He nodded. *I get it now, Claas.* Ibi called into the room feeling his voice merge with Claas's. It felt strong enough to move over the horizons to the east and to the west. *"And I looked, and behold a pale horse: and his name that sat on him was Death, and Hell followed with him."*

Ibi needed to flee. Ibi spun in circles searching for Claas Epp Jr.

"Where do I go, Claas?"

"Home."

He nodded and began throwing clothes over his naked body.

"I don't know where that is."

Ibi felt Claas shaking his head. *"It's Revelations, Ibi ... Remember ..."*

He groped his duffle for his Bible. He couldn't tell if Claas stood at his left shoulder or his right. But the intensity of these hushed words wrapped around his nape, constricted. Ibi threw everything but the mattress inside his duffle.

He paused and looked over the cover of *Heimweh*, the only other book he carried with himself besides the Bible. The leather cracked along the spine appeared as dry as Ibi's own flesh. He looked as the book blended into his own body. He thought it had just become a part of him. He remembered the German title, the title meant homesickness. This book had been with Ibi since Ak-Metchet. He had been carrying it around with him. *Heimweh*, Homesickness.

"Claas, this was your book."

Claas's voice came back. "*Blessed are they that long for home, for homeward they shall surely come. The afflictions of the Earth awaken a homesickness for the house of the father.*"

"I am homesick," Ibi said.

"*Go Home . . .*"

"But surely the Rapture happens in the world, the entire world, not one place. Turkestan is not my home anymore." He reasoned he could never make it back to Claas Epp Jr. and Ak-Metchet in fourteen days.

"We left Russia for refuge . . . Where do I find it now?" Ibi dropped to his knees. His hands trembled. His heart scurried from his chest up his throat. He coughed. He heaved.

"*We sought . . .*"—Claas's voice emerged once again—" *. . . a gathering place.*"

Ibi's Plattdeutsch, no longer dormant, gurgled from his lungs with the bile and water. "*Sammlungsort . . .*"

"We all stand on Good ground," Claas said. "Our Movement follows the Law of Love. Now go Home, Ibi."

"Is it west? I have to go west." He wiped the sick from his chin.

"*You have been called upon to bear witness.*"

"I can't go south."

Ibi thought about the Colonies south near and around Steinbach. He saw them as the old colonies his parents fled in Russia. They were what Claas said the Catholic Church was. Claas called it the black power of the Jesuits. In every colony, stationed much like the Pope, stood a man, assuming for himself the role of Son. These simple men lifted themselves above the Word. Turkestan was to be different. It had been. Claas had merely been a witness, but Ibi's parents had cursed Claas when the Rapture had failed to happen, not once but twice. They blamed Claas, but Ibi knew Claas had just made a mistake, a mathematical error. But his parents felt such anger for the danger Claas dragged them through. But there on the pages of today's paper, even the scientists were proselytizing what Brother Daniel had seen so long ago, and now Claas Epp Jr.

"It is here for all eyes to read, Revelations 3:10! The Word of Patient Endurance is to be the markings of this new church. This is how we are to define pacifism—with patient endurance," he called.

Ibi's parents and many others threw the blame for death at Claas's feet. It was true, some of the refugees who had started the trek from Russia to Turkestan didn't survive. But Ibi knew this would happen. Claas had prepared them all.

But Ibi's family fled to Canada, and the colonies of the East became the same. His father cursed the bishops who held power. They rose and stayed at their positions and the same fellows who grew rich in Russia became rich in Manitoba. And their word rose to replace His. His! The Father and the Son!

Ibi stormed about the room. He resisted his return to Steinbach. He said: "They are lost."

"Indeed," Claas said. *"And when he had opened the third seal, I heard the third beast say, Come and see. And I beheld, and lo a black horse; and he that sat on him had a pair of balances in his hand."*

"Yes," Ibi said. "This disloyalty to the true church, to God. These communities, they act as they, they, they force us to sing to and stare at a flag. A Queen, filthy and fat, she is full of greed and gluttony and harlotry. Here my father has nothing. Has nothing. He had been a horseman there and remains a horseman now. Every day, he rides somebody else's horse, managing their herds, their fences, to barely eat from their barley. My mother surely dies at this place."

Ibi massaged his temples. Then turned to the paper again. He flipped it over to the back. A huge advertisement for land west of Manitoba. *The Last Best West … Homes for Millions.* Ibi brushed his finger over the advertisement, an image of countless stooks, a distant homestead, men atop a team of horses as a golden sunset melded with a prairie larger than any ocean. West, to go west, meant a man could have land. The cost of this land, what your body could handle breaking for gilded and argent fields of barley, flax, oats, rye, and wheat.

"I have to go West. I have to go West." He knew of men shovelling coal and grain, saving their pennies to go farther west and take up land of their own. No church to answer to, just God and their own land. Then he was certain. He nodded. "To continue west, I would find the deserts and mountains of Ak-Metchet again. West . . ."

With his duffle barely over his shoulder, Ibi hit the hallway. His shoes filled with only his feet, no socks, moved faster than his body. He bounced off the opposite hallway wall. He halted and jammed his shirt, buttoned just at the middle, inside his opened pants, which hung from his shoulders by suspenders. Ibi's clothes looked like a flag blown free from its pole but caught by the naked branches of a limber pine stripped by wind and bleached grey by sunshine.

Home, home, home . . . His eyes turned to the stairwell. One of Eunice Worth's calicos wandered out of Room #7 and tripped him up as it rubbed a fuzzy cheek against his shin.

"Kitty, Kitty, Kitty," his tongue clicked a pleasant beat, not words but an invitation.

Ibi squatted to scratch under the cat's chin. This calico, a patchwork of oranges, blacks, and whites, was rare—almost male. A fuzzy pouch, sexless, bloomed about his haunches.

"Mrs. Worth?" Ibi called and pushed on her door. She never returned his call. The plaster and brick pulled in around the man as he ushered the cat between his shins, pinching its neck with a shaken tenderness a child uses to soothe herself during a thunderstorm. In the hallway Ibi called for Claas. No answer came. Had he left him behind in the room? He stayed in a crouch, hoping to hear a voice, Claas Epp's or Eunice Worth's. He shut his eyes.

"The Lord is writing to the church of Philadelphia," Claas Epp Jr. had said as their wagon train crossed over deserts and mountains to Central Asia.

"I am paying attention now, Claas. I see now. I see *It* coming. Please forgive me. I was young and sheltered. I never knew who had died. It was hundreds, hundreds of Mennonites crossing out of Russia into Turkestan. I never saw much of the strife. I only listened.

There were only your words and a land of men who wore many colours. I gleefully ran through the markets teeming with a thousand other tongues only to return to your words."

There behind his memories he saw the caravans of camels carrying him to the final leg of his trek into Turkestan. His body swayed with the same cadence as the *howdah* he rode in sitting upon his mother's lap. Every woman and child got a boxed-in, tented seat on either side of a camel, with an open window view of sky and stars. Heaven had felt closer to Ibi there. It felt over him and under him as the moon flickered off the black sand, sparkling silver and cobalt. He had asked his mutta if they were crossing heaven.

"Is this the Rapture?" She had shaken her head.

Ibi returned to the hallway, with a whisper. "Thank you, Claas." Then something stronger than he could describe forced him to scoop up that cat. Its fur, fluffy and smooth, pushed across his cheek as their chins met. The cat purred and wriggled content into Ibi's arms.

He called the cat Claas. "You will be my talisman and my compass."

Wapos County

"**I**t's best to** castrate before the flies, because the wound is left open." John, down on his knees, broke then dropped tinder and kindling over a small batch of used straw, green birch bark, and cow manure he had dipped in water and had crumbled. He lit the straw. He lowered his head, an ear almost touching the cold crusted snowcap hiding the spring earth. About his knees, his pants began to dampen from his body heat melting the crust still lingering from winter. "Always light a smudge. It keeps away whatever bugs are out. And Charlie told me to add sage." John dumped a mason jar full of the dried, insipid leaves atop the lifeless licks of orange flames flaying to reach the top of the smudge. Thick smoke ballooned like a storm cloud emanating from the earth. "Smells a little better, too." John crinkled his nose.

Mareika's nose crinkled, too, as an image of a baby donkey walking around with its separate parts left open as a dark gash swarming with flies and creepy crawly maggots invaded her mind.

"Doesn't it hurt?"

He spread his words out in front of her. "Maybe. But they don't seem to respond to it." He milled about the barn, a galvanized bucket in hand, dropping shiny metal tools into it. "Maybe it's because I do it before they're weaned …" He scratched behind his ear. "I think with their mutta … it's easier. That's why I don't castrate them before they are weaned. Yeah. Don't castrate before they finish weaning."

His words made his daughter miss Mutta. John carried the bucket into the pen with the young jack. He was bridled and had two lengths of rope draped over his front quarter. His mutta brayed, scratching her chin against the rough-sawn rail. The young jack's head twisted and turned trying to navigate its way through the rails to suckle.

"How do they not bleed to death?"

John put down the bucket and gripped a long, elegant, matte-silver tool that looked like pliers with one half of the jaws, shaped like the letter C, that folded inside the other half, shaped like a bar.

"These." He held the Emasculator out for Mareika. She took it for a moment but handed it back, shocked at how heavy it felt. He put the tool back inside the bucket. "Those will keep him from bleeding. I'll also tie everything off—but I'll show you."

He reached up the wall for a canvas sack. "This is filled with oats sweetened with some watermelon syrup." He held the sack to the jack's nose. The oats and sugar pulled him in. His lips twitched and flicked at the treat. The grinding of his teeth sounded like gravel crunching under a wagon wheel. John strapped the sack to the bridle. He reached under the young donkey and lifted his furthest hoof and pulled it towards himself. The feeding donkey resisted but soon lay down. With the first rope, John looped it around a post, which lifted and pointed the animal's nose to the fence. He kneeled on the neck of the donkey and cinched the rope. The other rope attached to the bridle, he stretched towards its hindquarters. He grabbed its top hind leg and lifted it across the animal's belly and cinched it with a quick double clove hitch. "Can you grab and toss that burlap piece over his face and sit right here on his front shoulder?"

Mareika nodded and followed the instructions. With the young jack's head secured and his hind leg, John grabbed his bucket and said: "Sit real heavy on his shoulder. And pay attention."

John moved with quickness and purpose and precision. His body language said he wanted to end this discomfort as quickly as possible. He used very few words. "I make one slit." He drew a straight razor he seemed to pull from the air over the middle of the jack's scrotum. Mareika almost looked away but followed his hands, watched them as they eased a testicle out. Everything he did, so precise, so fast, she couldn't imagine the sedentary beast under her could have felt anything. She leaned in, her chin tilted by confusion, but her discerning eye open for discovery and understanding.

"There isn't really any blood."

"Not yet."

Her mind erased the purpose of those strange fruits. They, in a twinkling, became a mass, a mass of silver skin wrapped about pink, wormy coils that her foda gripped. It held as much intrigue as a hen's egg, but she didn't want to eat these.

John pulled a large, shimmering white, silver, and red bulb away from the black underbelly of the jack, and, around a cord of flesh drawn out from the inside of that animal, he whipped threading—round and round. Several swift knots followed, then the emasculators. Mareika's face threatened to look away when blood spurt from the cord attached to the testicle as John's hands gripped down on the handles and freed the first meaty globe.

The jack twitched and tried bucking. The mother brayed. John tossed the first oblong orb. A tuxedo cat had crawled out from a corner somewhere in the barn under the fog of blood. She tipped her pink tongue at the mass, a toe into water, before she nipped and gnawed at the red and pink meat.

Mareika watched her foda's hands do the same thing with another fleshy orb, but as he finished his last knots, he passed the emasculator to her.

"*Schnell*—hurry."

The end of the emasculator dipped and plunked against the ground. Mareika lifted the tool's weight up. She rubbed the dirt clinging to the blood off the tool. John moved and sat upon the jack's shoulder and grabbed his daughter's wrist. A pull and push edged her to the exposed testicle.

"Pull the cord taut." John swung around and now lay across the animal's shoulder on his belly. He reached and pointed. "There. Cut just above where my finger is."

Mareika placed the jaws of the silver tool into place and squeezed the handles together as hard as she could. Blood shot over the animal's leg.

"Good. Strong grip. That was clean." John grabbed the testicle and tossed it to the cat, now joined by four of its kittens all lapping and gnawing. He then massaged the beast's tummy. His fingers, splayed but clenched, raked back and forth through the gelding's fur, his tips adding pressure, which chased the tension out of the hip. Churning creaks and gurgles below its hide rumbled. "Watch out." John pointed to the donkey's tail end.

Mareika tossed the tool away. "What?" Her eyes widened. She rose and sidestepped around its tail. Her glance danced all over the hindquarters as she searched for a twitch or ripple of muscle that would signal a kick.

"Did you hear that gurgling?"

"Yeah."

"It's nervous gut—borborygmus."

"That's a neat word." She scratched at her chin with the back of her hand and wrist. This smudged blood across her face. She tried the word, let her mouth and tongue play. The sounds passed over upon a whisper. "Borborygmus." The syllables drizzled past her lips. Her celebration didn't originate with its strangeness or its newness, but for its time, this moment. It had been a moment shared with her father. His knowledge, his patience, he offered them to her. And she saw on his face a lightness. His perpetual contemplative scowl lifted, replaced by a subtle grin. This moment under a new word, it led away the image of a bound animal, gory and sexless.

She said it again, "Borborygmus," but the intonation came wrapped with an atmosphere of gratitude. She nodded to her dad. Her lips returned his soft grin, and Mareika rocked from her heels to her toes.

The donkey's sphincter popped several times with flatulence. Its tail wafted against the ground with an air of anger, its ears pinned all the way back to its neck.

"Take away the burlap and take the sack of oats off." John untied the ropes, unclipped them from the bridle. The gelding slowly stood, its eyes wide. It stared frozen. John unbolted the pen's gate, exited and opened the neighbouring pen. When he moved away from the gate, the gelding rushed to its mutta's side.

"What do we do with the ..."

"The cats can have them."

Thursday, July 5, 1902.

Wapos County

"**W**HY DOESN'T **FODA** read with us?"

"He doesn't have time for God or religion. His mind doesn't need it." Mutta looked content. She didn't smile but her chin seemed higher. She looked up to the skin, tossing glances upwards as if fishing for hope. Her dress had been laundered and she pressed it with hot stones. Originally black, it had faded to a charcoal. And on this day, I remember she wore her bonnet. It was black, having been kept in a box inside the pantry above the flour bin.

"Is that why he doesn't go to church?"

"Yes."

"How come we don't go to church?"

"Because we study here at home. We do not need a building for God to see us."

"But everybody else goes to the church. Ruth goes to church."

"I cannot explain it, but we are too far away to go. We are outside and far away. And your father and Bishop Dyck do not ... agree."

"Why?"

"Because Bishop Dyck ... doesn't know the real Bible."

"How come?"

"It doesn't matter. Foda doesn't need the Church and we don't need to go, because God can see us here. He can hear us reading. All they do there is read this book just the same as we're doing now, but they don't get to do it outside, and they have to sit on hard benches."

34

"I like it outside. There are pretty butterflies and shiny dragonflies."

I remember cupping my hands, lowering them towards a sparkling blue dragonfly that had landed on the lace hem of my dress. His tail flicked up twice as my shadow fell over him. His wings twitched before fluttering as the black whiskers of legs lifted away from the lace. None of the other Mennonite girls had lace on their hems. The first day I came to school with the dress, we all squatted and pulled the lace up to our cheeks.

"Careful, Mareika. You don't want to kill the dragonflies or yourself. That would be a sin."

Mutta's soft, cool touch came around my wrists. Together, we lifted her hands.

"Where'd the dragonfly go?"

I felt her arms wrap me up, and we tumbled to the grass.

"Look at Foda over there cleaning the donkey's hooves."

The donkey kicked his leg away from Foda's hands. Draped in a heavy leather apron, he slapped the critter's hindquarters, bent over, backed his butt into the animal's back leg, and grabbed the furry knobby base above its hoof. He placed it between his thighs. He squatted down more and began jabbing and digging and pulling under the hoof with a wood-handled tool. He dropped the hoof, reached into the apron's pouch, and held his open hand under the donkey's chin. Its bottom lip flicked and jostled, its head turning sideways at the dark clump pointing into the air. Foda grabbed the donkey's ear with a wiggle. The donkey's ears tilted back towards his ass end. "Don't be mad." He slapped the donkey's butt. Foda stalked the yard towards us, but he didn't look at us. I waved.

"What are you reading?" he said.

"Shhh. Don't say." Mutta's words wrapped about my neck like a scarf.

I said nothing and looked up at him.

With the tip of his boot, he nudged the soles of Mutta's shoe. "You're in a good mood."

"The Bible," I blurted. I slapped my hands over my lips, one over the other.

"Couldn't find a better book, eh? Maybe I should head north to the city and look for some more. More fairy tales, I suppose, if that's what she likes."

"Yes. We read Aesop's tales in school—bad wolves and foxes. I saw a wolf in the field." I climbed back atop the fence and pointed to the field where the cattle grazed. The field grass reaching high at every post bowed to the summer gales. A good one pushed at me. I lost my balance. My arms twirled, and my body bent and swayed, but I righted myself.

"No, you didn't," Mutta said.

"Yes, I did."

"Those were coyotes," Foda said.

"No, wolves."

"No. They were coyotes. Puppies compared to wolves. But that's why we have donkeys. To keep the coyotes away—"

"And wolves."

Mutta, her eyes lifted to Foda, said: "Say thank you."

"How come I say thank you?"

"For keeping us safe."

"Thank you, Foda."

"Say thank you for taking care of us."

"Thank you for taking care of us."

He nodded. He reached behind his back and untied his apron. He lifted it over his head, rolled it into a scroll. His left hand took the scroll while his right took to the button below his collar. "I'm going in. You don't have to. I was going to wash up, eat, then I should walk the back fence." His smile was only a line he dropped into the grass. He looked to the house, to Mutta's legs, and back to the house. "Maybe you could shave my neck."

Mutta nodded. "I have to read this last passage to her. Can she go into the loft?"

"Yeah! Can I play in the barn?" I stretched and reached up for a cloud. I loved feeling so high. And the barn loft was about as high as I could get, and maybe cats and kittens would be there too.

A nod, then Foda walked to the house. He pulled his shirt over his head and used it to wipe his face and brushed it across his thinning hair. He disappeared into the house.

"Okay. Let me read to you about Lydia. She is a lady of purple. Did you know my favourite colour is purple?"

"No."

"What's your favourite colour?"

"Red."

"That's a good colour."

"Red is my favourite."

"Hmmm ..." Mutta took up her Bible. "Do you see that purple ribbon draping over the spine? Pick it up and slide the book open." She passed me the book.

I used both my hands, one at the top of the Bible's spine and one at the bottom with the book pressed to my belly. I wobbled, and Mutta put a hand at the small of my back for balance.

"If you're going to stay up on that fence, let me do it." She got the ribbon and she lifted it as high as it would let her pull it. She dodged my hands pulling the book open for her; her fingers filled in the gap the ribbon created whilst pulling the book open. "Okay, you can let go."

I looked below my toes to the grass. Ants marched over the dusty brown ground surrounding the fence posts.

"Are you ready?"

"Yes," I said.

"*Then came he to Derbe and Lystra: and, behold, a certain disciple was there, named Timotheus, the son of a certain woman, which was a Jewess—*"

"What's a Jewess?"

"Shh. A strong Christian woman," she said. She turned her head and coughed. She looked to the house. Foda's shadow moved past the windows. The chimney coughed a cloud of grey. "Okay, where were we ... *and believed; but his father was a Greek ...*" She held her chin and stared at the ground.

"Is Foda a Greek?" My body moved across the top rails of the fence, post to post, planting my foot and spinning on the pillars, turning around to race back.

"Shush, no." Mutta's chest rose and fell as she read. *"Now when they had gone throughout Phrygia and the region of Galatia, and were forbidden of the Holy Ghost to preach the word in Asia—"*

"Is Asia in Foda's books?"

"Yes, in his atlas, the book full of maps."

"Where is Asia?"

"Well ..." Mutta scratched her chin and stared off to the gardens. "If you were to start digging a hole below our feet, in one week's time you would dig all the way through to Asia, all the way to Lystra."

"Really?"

"Please, will you let me finish?"

She read on, as I slipped out to the middle of a rail on my toes. I turned and looked into the grass. Mutta was in her bare feet, the edges calloused and black with dirt, and under her nails, the soft peach flesh was buried under the same dirt.

"And on the sabbath we went out of the city by a river side, where prayer was wont to be made; and we sat down, and spake unto the women which resorted thither. And a certain woman named Lydia, a seller of purple, of the city of Thyatira, which worshipped God, heard us: whose heart the Lord opened, that she attended unto the things which were spoken of Paul. And when she was baptized, and her household, she besought us, saying, If ye have judged me to be faithful to the Lord, come into my house, and abide there. And she constrained us. And it came to pass, as we went to prayer, a certain damsel possessed with a spirit of divination met us, which brought her masters much gain by soothsaying."

"What's soofsaying?"

"Shh. It's saying the future."

"The future? Can you see the future?" The wind pushed me again as I stood in the middle of the rail. I had to flap my arms even harder to stay on.

"No. So listen." She opened her legs and bundled her dress up tight between her knees.

I folded some hair behind my ear so it couldn't be pushed in my eyes by the wind.

> *"The same followed Paul and us, and cried, saying, These men are the servants of the most high God, which shew unto us the way of salvation. And this did she many days. But Paul, being grieved, turned and said to the spirit, I command thee in the name of Jesus Christ to come out of her. And he came out the same hour. And when her masters saw that the hope of their gains was gone, they caught Paul and Silas, and drew them into the marketplace unto the rulers, And brought them to the magistrates, saying, These men, being Christian, do exceedingly trouble our city."*

"Do you get in trouble for believing?" I asked.

"What?"

"The story says, the people get in trouble. Is it wrong to believe? Is that why Foda doesn't believe?"

"No. No-no. When I get to the end, it will be the Christians that ... Just wait. You have to be patient ... *"Sirs, what must I do to be saved? And they said, Believe on the Lord Jesus Christ, and thou shalt be saved, and thy house."* She continued. I stopped hearing her world, lifting myself up upon my tippy toes reaching higher and higher. My legs felt tired, and I felt myself about to fall, so I hopped to the ground, landing square in front of Mutta as the word *baptized* sprang out her mouth. She clutched her chest.

And I asked: "What's baptized?"

"Careful! It's when you are old enough to accept Jesus in your heart. And when you are old enough, we will take you to Wapos Creek or maybe Black Gully Lake, and we will dip your head below the waters, and you will be accepted into heaven."

"Like swimming? I like swimming."

"Shhh." Mutta dragged her finger over the pages. Her voice was like wisps of the breeze over my forehead.

"And when it was day, the magistrates sent the serjeants, saying, Let those men go. And the keeper of the prison told this saying to Paul, The magistrates have sent to let you go: now therefore depart, and go in peace. But Paul said unto them, They have beaten us openly uncondemned, being Romans, and have cast us into prison; and now do they thrust us out privily? nay verily; but let them come themselves and fetch us out. And the serjeants told these words unto the magistrates: and they feared, when they heard that they were Romans. And they came and besought them, and brought them out, and desired them to depart out of the city. And they went out of the prison, and entered into the house of Lydia: and when they had seen the brethren, they comforted them, and departed."

"Lydia is a nice lady. She saved them."

"Yes, she did."

"You're like Lydia."

"No. No, I'm not. I'm more Hagar, but today I feel more like Dinah ..." Mutta looked all around the yard then to the sky. "Look up."

I followed Mutta's arm, past her fingernail. Below the clear blue sky, as soft white clouds streaked into and out of my gaze. I noticed a hawk floating above me.

"Do you see that hawk?"

"Yeah. How does it stay up there?"

The bird seemed to hold still, then, as if on a string, moved sharply to the right but hung at the same height. I watched the bird hover, its wings spread, and shift, hover and shift. It covered the expanse of the entire home field beside the barn. The shifting became dizzying.

The hawk dropped out of the sky. It sat sentinel in the field beside the *semlin* root cellar. It bent its beak to the ground and lifted and bent and twisted and lifted, up and down, up and down, the way Mutta sewed patches of cloth into a quilt. A dark glistening string rose from the ground drawn up by its curved beak.

"What's it doing?"

"Eating."

"Eating what?"

"It must have caught a gopher."

"Aw … Gophers are cute." My eyes blinked and blinked and blinked and blinked. I looked. I blinked some more and then lifted my head. I climbed the fence once again and started tiptoeing across counting my steps as I tried to see the hawk and gopher.

"I can't see it." I turned sharply to Mutta, angry or annoyed. In my frustration, I had forgotten how thin the fence rail actually was. And gravity grabbed me faster than anybody could react.

"Mareika!"

I had not crashed into the grass but landed squarely on the railing between my legs. The pain thrust up through my whole body from my bottom to my head. My earlobes and all my toes burst with the impact. I slipped off the rail and landed on the back of my shoulders. My thighs burned. I screamed. I felt Mutta's cheek pressed to my mouth and the brushing of her cool fingertips upon my neck. On the ground surrounded by her dress, my hips, my lap, my buttocks, my other parts felt cold and wet.

"Where does it hurt?"

I didn't know what to call it. I pointed down and pulled up my dress.

Mutta pulled my dress back down and ran to the house.

"No!" I cried.

"It's okay."

The pain was so bad I felt if I tried to touch my own body my legs would fall off.

Mutta came to me and lifted my dress. I looked at the chamber pot full of clear water and cheesecloth.

Mutta pulled my panties off and dabbed at me down there.

"Oh, Mareika." Her face twisted the way it does when Foda guts a rabbit.

I screamed with every touch.

I saw Mutta pull bloody rags from under my dress. Was that blood coming from me? From down there? The place we didn't give a name? Mutta kept pressing the cold, wet cloth against me. I thought she was cooking me. The pain seared. It was meat in a skillet and my body burned. I could not push air out of my lungs. In the pot the water turned pink.

"Don't tell Foda, okay? Mareika? We can't tell Foda."

"I promise."

"You can't be climbing the fence like that. Do you hear?"

"Can I still go in the loft?"

"No."

"But I want to see the kitties."

"We have to stay inside. You have to get to bed." She wrung out water from a cloth and pressed its coolness against me and pulled my panties back up. "We have to go to bed. What did I tell you about Foda?"

I wiped my face. "Don't tell."

"Good." Mutta scooped me up and carried me to bed where I would lie for several days as Mutta changed out cloth after cloth until they ceased being red, always wetting them so they didn't stick to my skin as she peeled them from my other parts.

Gnadenfeld, Molotschna Settlement, Crimea Khanate

HIGH INSIDE THE attic, a young John Doerksen sat cradled upon the sill of the rounded window, bathed in moonlight. His shadow warped over the attic joists and the beds of straw and sawdust insulation. Though late into night, the boy sat fully clothed in black slacks, suspenders, and white collar. The only articles of clothing missing were his shoes. The skin of his bare feet shone blue under the moonbeams. Ignoring the rustling and gnawing of mice hidden under the insulation between each joist, he let a leg dangle. He pinched at straw with his toes.

While his family slept awaiting the return of his foda, Martin, from a trading expedition with the Nogai, he had climbed a bookshelf and slid inside a hole between the joists into the ceiling. A leak, discovered the previous spring, had been responsible. Mortar, yellowed and soggy, had fallen away from the slats under the joists after a week of heavy rain. And when investigating the extent of the damage, Martin had fallen through the lathe slats that had rotted, which suggested years of leaks. Even though the roof had gotten repairs, the hole remained. His foda thought nothing of it and placed two short blanks over it.

John stared at the hole those first nights after the repairs. His imagination presented him with an escape. So much of his days he spent in the barns and fields of other men Martin had negotiated to educate him. "Doing will be your best educator."

Each mentor was introduced with a promise his knowledge would instill in John the character best fitting a man. But John only wished to read, even trying to write his own tales. But once Martin discovered a journal with John's meanderings, he sought help to end John's idle observances.

John had been learning to fire iron, which was a delicate technique for cauterizing a gelding. As John squatted watching the able hand of Everett Erberhardt, Martin chucked the journal at his boy. It struck him between his shoulder blades. The boy felt the pain pop in each of his toes, fingers, his other parts, and tailbone before the jolt jumped free from his body. John would have sworn to anybody he confessed this cruelty to that he could see the rye grass parting as the pain fled over the Crimean steppe. Martin then forced John to destroy his journal page by page in the smudge smouldering beside Everett and the horse being cauterized.

"Men work." He tore the book from his son's hand and randomly flipped the pages filled with ink. "Do not be an *observer*," Martin said. The lack of any tradeable skill dogged the senior Doerksen. In his younger days, he moved from job to job, and even though he had not been the only Mennonite not to own his own home or property in Gnadenfeld, he carried the shame of never learning a trade or educating himself. His only skill had been his tongue, which in turn inspired his only craft, brewing. Though nobody talked of this, it allowed Martin access not to just the highest peaks of the Mennonite communities, but of the Russian government. And once there, his gift for language and story allotted his communities many advantages, like getting young Mennonite men positions in forestry rather than military duty or being sentenced to gulags. But in Martin's mind and many others', to be a writer or artistic meant being idle, lazy, an *observer*.

The attic gifted John the freedom to hide away and read. Buried under the straw and sawdust, John smuggled books into his home. And under the cover of night, he enjoyed venturing into the attic, where he read under moonlight. Additionally, the aroma of smoked sausages, bacon, and hams from the smoker lingered in the space. Like for many other Mennonites, the smoker was hidden inside the ceiling of his home, in a cubby high above a heavy earthen stove notched out of the chimney, capturing the smoke at low temperatures.

The attic had given the boy much of the enjoyment he seldom got toiling for the landowners Martin left him with for months at a time. The hole was wide enough for John to slip one arm at a time through, where he'd grab the joists and pull himself clear. Once inside the attic space, he bounded from joist to joist, each time trying to do it faster and faster. He could make the trip from the hole to the window in six springs without losing balance.

This night was different. Martin promised to return from an excursion to the edges of the steppe to negotiate trade with the nomadic Nogai, a tribal society the Mennonites referred to as Turks, but to whom Martin gave a deeper respect. He had used his tongue to learn their language and some Arabic. He had even picked up their palate for horse milk and roast horse. The man usually returned in great spirits with many tales and gifts. During the last excursion, he had returned with a hat trimmed with fur and a top that protruded straight out, like a flowerpot, but made of an animal hide. Through the entire night the boy picked through several books, never settled upon one. He sat and cast glances to the roll of the dirt road, two clay-stained ruts spooling out over matted grasses.

He leaned into the windowpanes. Condensation formed from the heat of his body cooling against the glass. The dew seeped through his shirt, kissing his shoulder. He enjoyed the cold against his skin. Outside, the boy watched the fall air thicken like *Schmauntfat*, a creamy sausage gravy. Fog poured over the crops of silvered wheat. He tilted his head to the glass.

Off in the distance behind the roll of the road, he saw lantern light sway side to side. The soft glow swelled, borrowing some of the fog, turning it into a spirited amber orb. Behind the radiance a second orange orb at a much higher height dropped light to road. His eyes widened. As the first lantern swept through the mist, his father's horse trotted into view. The clouded path, bordered by mulberry trees, seemed to part for the animal. His father was not atop the mount, only a pole to which the lower lantern was tethered. The boy pressed his nose against the glass. Stretched out behind the wagon was a long rope with red tassels knotted every foot. The tassels dangled and blazed flicking the lantern light at his window seat. He followed the festive rope into darkness. The rope, not taut, swayed. Its curve draped and flirted with the matted dewy grass between the ruts of the dirt road.

The trailing, higher lantern—as it swayed side to side—swept the fog clear. Martin rose out of the clouded soup wading in the amber light. The hair on his head flickered like flames, and black shadows jumped around his face. He took on the appearance of an apparition. The boy saw that his foda held the long pole from which the higher lantern swayed in his hand, the pole's end nestled in a stirrup. But the man did not ride upon a horse.

Martin rode between two humps of a lulling, sandy-brown camel. About the beast rode rolls of carpets and large burlap sacks as well.

John dropped from the sill; his toes perched on that first joist. He stood straight and flexed his knees. He set his weight on the balls of his feet. Then after a deep breath, he bounded from joist to joist. "One, two, three, four, five ..." He stopped shy of the hole. His toenails dug into the wood. His arms reached out for the rafter ahead. Once steady, he lunged with one leg to the sixth joist. He stood like a star across joist and rafter. Between his legs he glanced at the candlelight coming up through the hole. He threw his weight to his right foot and with both hands grabbed some blocking between the rafters and pulled hard, lifting and simultaneously dropping his legs through the hole.

He let out a breath. His bare feet felt the top of the bookshelf for the edge. He heard the clunk of the wooden latch and the rusty creak of the hinges. He squatted fast and wriggled down. He kicked one foot at a time off the bookshelf, his butt plunking down hard. He walked his heels down a shelf at a time until he balanced above the floor on only his fingertips gripping the crumbling plaster. Then as the door connecting the barn to the house creaked open, he let himself fall to the living room floor. He landed on his feet but crashed hard enough that his legs couldn't keep his body from crumpling, his butt bouncing off the floor, and his own face crashing into his knees. The boy fell to his back over the floor.

He scrambled to his feet and ran to the barn door.

"Foda!" he said.

"John? Good." Martin didn't look at his son. "Open those barn pens." Martin turned back inside the barn. The alley glowed with a single lantern. John hustled to the first pen gate.

"Is that a real camel?"

"What?" Martin slapped John behind his ear as he passed to the second pen. The blow knocked the boy over. Martin ignored his son and took the horse by its bridle. "I don't think these beasts want to share," Martin said. He closed the horse's pen for the night.

"What do you have a camel for?"

"Aren't you going to ask about your mother's *kilims*?"

"*Kilims*? Is that those rugs?"

"Finally something intelligent out of your mouth. Yes. The Nogais call these rugs *kilims*."

"Who are the *kilims* for?"

"I already said they're for your mother. Do you think she will like them?"

"Yes."

He slapped John behind the head again. "Aren't you going to ask about the camel?"

"I did. What's the camel for?"

"I got it for you."

"It's for me?" John clapped his hands before he jumped with his arms wide towards his dad. Martin put up a hand, which caught his boy square in the chest and knocked him to the ground.

"It's a work animal. You have to learn how to use it. It's a tool." Martin stepped forward, took the camel's harness, and yanked down. The camel blasted spit between its lips towards John.

The boy wiped at his face and smeared the sticky sour spit into the grass growing at the barn opening. "How?" John sat on the ground, his hand back behind his hips.

"Get up." Martin gave a kick to his shin with the toe of his boot. "You're getting your pants dirty."

Jumping to his feet, John fell face forward onto his knee. "Ow. Sorry." He pushed himself up and limped after his dad and the new camel.

"You're going to learn to ride him." Martin unknotted the cargo, letting each fall into John's waiting arms.

"Okay." John moved from the barn's edge to the camel to collect each rug and each sack.

"Don't get too boastful, but you are good on a horse, as good as most grown men, and yet you are a boy."

John smiled.

"Stop it. Vainglory is the path to hell." He kicked his son's shin again.

"Yes, sir." John jammed his hands inside his pockets. He pinched his legs to keep from smiling.

"The Nogai children, they too are exceptional upon horseback. Better than you. Do you think you can outride the other Nogai children?"

"I outrode those Nogai on horse when we came back from Ohrloff." John almost bent in half burying his smile somewhere between the back of his head and his bare feet.

Martin stepped on John's toes, pinning them under his boot. John's smile fell from his face, and he stared into his foda's eyes. He tried not to grimace under the crush of Martin's tread. John's body instinctually pulled back, but with the foot pinned, fell onto his butt again.

"Where are your boots?" Martin shook his head and clicked his tongue.

"I'll get them."

"Don't. But don't you come out here again without them, not at this hour."

"Yes, sir."

"Hmm. Even though you aren't smart enough to remember shoes, I have to admit that you did, you did indeed, outride those

Nogai raiders. Do you know what they would have done if they had caught you?"

"Kill me."

"They intended to rob us, beat us, and maybe kill us—like the Schroeders in Hierschau. Remember?"

"Yes. The boy's face was skinned right off." John waved his hands over his face, a mock scrubbing before he slid his thumbnail across his neck. "Ughhh ..." He dangled his tongue out the side of his mouth.

"Enough! Do not celebrate. The Schroeders are dead. And Margarethe, the girl, she was never seen again," Martin said.

John stood and pulled some late mulberries from the tree growing up the side of the barn.

"But you outrode them, didn't you? You nearly outrode me. Yes, you did ..." Martin scratched the animal's neck, staring through the animal, seeing something John could not find. His father's pupils grew. He nodded his head. "You're going to learn to ride this camel better than that horse." Martin slapped his son's back. "You and I, we will make the next trek to the Nogais together. I will need you to race for me. But this will be our secret." Martin grabbed John by his ear and with a firm twist lifted the boy closer to his mouth. His words fell hot with a simmer of vodka from Martin's mouth. "You are not to tell a soul ..." He let go of his son.

"Yes, Foda." John stepped to the camel, his eyes still on Martin, his head still nodding. He slid his fingers amongst the matted hair dangling from the creature's chest. The beast spewed another blast of spit at the boy.

Wapos County

1 DID EVERYTHING I could to wash the damage my desires had caused before Foda came in for supper. Behind the door separating the house from the barn, I could hear his heavy boots, so I hurried my movements to scrub the blood from my other parts before he came through the door. My heart exploded upon every bang of the door against the jamb from the spring gales. He stayed busied only a breath and the thickness of those wooden planks, but he did so until I was clean.

I distracted myself with a fire, using willow and hay, as Foda was smoking sausage in the smoke chamber hidden in the ceiling. I used to climb the bookshelves and sit in the rafters during the winters as a little girl, sneaking the chamber door open to smell the smoky warm meats hanging. Hams, sausage, whole chickens and rabbits, and even pans of potatoes, onions, garlic, carrots, and beets beneath all the meat catching the drippings. I would peel slivers of the crispy crust from the ham or rabbits. I would chew them until the sharp crust was soft, push the peppery meat between my gum and cheek, and suck on the smoke.

The door between the barn and house opened. Foda nudged a cat with his toes back into the barn.

"How was school?" He whiffed at the warm kitchen air greeting him. Carrots, onions, beef filled the room. A deeper breath told him about the morning bread that still lingered, mingling with the stew.

His shoulders slumped as the muscles in his back melted in the warmth of his home.

I shrugged and kept to the stew in the large cast-iron pot on the stove. I reached around my back at the piercing pain through my kidneys. I flinched. But I didn't mind as that new sharp piercing pain distracted from the pulling aches through my pelvis, lower back, and stomach. I huffed and looked at Foda. He looked back.

"You're pale. Are you sick?" He moved towards me. I stepped back into the stove. He pointed. "There's blood on your apron."

I grabbed it and turned away to stir the stew.

"Are you hurt?"

"No!"

"You're bleeding."

How could he tell? I looked at the floor, my feet. The tension of tears burned inside my eyes at the reality that I may be dying. I hadn't gotten the bleeding to stop.

He joined me at the stove. "Mareika."

I froze. Foda touched at my kidney. I flinched.

"There's blood here on your blouse."

I sighed with relief when he meant my kidneys.

"Come here." I followed his hand into the western sun shining through the window across the dinner table. "What did you do?"

Jonah rose out of my memory. His back, his broadening shoulders running away from me to the schoolhouse. I ignored the tired muscle aches pulling down at me. I ignored the three layers of panties I was wearing with folded squares of cheesecloth in between filling with blood, my blood. I looked to the loaf of bread on the end of the counter.

"I have to cut the bread."

"Mareika, you're bleeding," he said touching again above my apron strings.

"I'm sorry I only made stew." I pulled away from his hand again. My eyes were wide, and I searched Foda's face, only a blank stare. Words sprung from me. I almost yelled. "I. I was in the *semlin*. I wanted beets."

"Take your apron and vest off."

"Why?"

"I need to see what's wrong with you."

I followed Foda's order. I looked to the ceiling to avoid his eye. A fly walked the groove between a wooden timber and the white plaster.

"You have a splinter shooting out your back. It's the size of dragonfly's tail."

I cried out when I felt the yank of his fingers. He showed it to me. It was a rose colour. It swelled with my blood. I wanted to know how much blood was inside me. He tugged and slid my blouse from my skirt. I unclasped the bottom couple of buttons.

"I am going to get the water and pan."

He found the jug and pan beside his bedroom. He also found a rag already flushed pink with blood. He came out of his room with the jug and pan and the rag. "Why didn't you tell me you were hurt?"

I stood with my back to the south window looking over my shoulder. My blouse was up around my neck, still buttoned at the collar. I had the sleeve pulled taut under my chin so that I could examine the splinter in the reflection of the window. I could see the rounded curve of a full breast rolling away from my armpit. I looked at Foda. He was looking into the pan at the blood-steeped rag.

I thought I had heard him say, "Damnit, Rebecca." Before he squeezed his eyes shut. I imagined he must have opened them trying to replace the image of his groaning daughter with the little girl he read to at night, leaving her to sleep upon the couch. Where was that little girl? She stepped away from him when she walked away from Mutta's grave, having dropped some of the dried sweet peas she had collected and hung upside down in the pantry from the highest shelf where the pickling pot sat alone and dusty.

Foda took a breath and followed his feet to the table. He sat. "Come here." He looked at the jug as he took it from the pan and placed it on the table. He looked at the rag as the water flowed over it into the pan. I moved to the table, turning my back to him. He crouched. His thumb hovered for a moment over my flesh. His fingertips were cold.

Foda's voice broke the silence. It came deeper than his usual tone.

"I think it's getting warm enough that we can get started on that room for you."

I craned my neck. I spend the last several years sleeping on the couch. We had traded. I used to share his room with Mutta, and he slept on the couch. Now that's where I slept.

He pushed against the skin around the wound. I sucked a long breath through my teeth, as the stab of splinters through my skin.

"I'm sorry."

Foda took the largest part of the remaining splinters with his thumb and middle fingernail.

"It hurts."

He pinched my ear using his free hand as he plucked the second splinter free and dropped it in the pan. He looked at the hole, wiping it with the rag.

"I'm sorry; we're not done. I can see three dark strips of fir still under your skin." He patted the rag against my back. "Where are Mutta's sewing needles?"

I pointed to Mutta's dark wooden box over the mantle. Foda nodded but looked at the rocking chair off the corner of the stove. Whenever he missed Mutta, he could be caught staring at that chair. The chair was still. Certainly he saw her there. Mutta had told me of the day she had asked him for that chair. She sat stitching while I was amongst all the triangles of fabric. Each one examined before I would pass another to her. She told me she was fixed by the image of her grandmother sitting by a fire when she was younger, sewing patchwork blankets. She had felt a responsibility to carry on the art because her mother had never learned. And she had refused to start sewing until he got her that chair. Fabrics had been chosen, cut, but she wouldn't go any further without a rocking chair. So Foda, he took an older gelding to Peter Hamm's father Abraham, who made them.

Mutta had always said, "An ass for a chair." Her only joke.

So with Peter Hamm's coyote problem solved, Mutta could sew. And my strongest memories were of her there when she sat for hours into the night with her scissors cutting diamonds, triangles and stitching them into my blanket.

He looked down into the chair. His hand took the rounded spindled back, and he stepped around something imaginary.

"Mareika, you used to ... do you remember when you sat at her feet, separating and picking through the patches of cloth for her to sew next?"

His hand grabbed the top of the chair, his skin chirped against the wood with his grip. He let go and watched the heels of the rockers lift and fall.

"I guess I should have remembered where I put that thing." He reached for the sewing box upon the mantle. "It hasn't moved since I put it here after we buried Mutta. Do you remember helping her make your quilt?"

I remembered the day after she was gone. He draped that first and only quilt over me while I slept. I have held that blanket between my legs every night sliding a corner up and over my shoulder and tucked below my hair.

"I remember," I said. "I picked the red triangles."

"Yes, you did. Is red still your favourite colour?"

It wasn't today, but I said, "Yes."

"Did you know the red triangles used to be my shirt?"

"Yes. I used to think I could smell you."

"Really."

"Yes."

"And what do I smell like?"

"Trees."

He opened the box. "There's a lot of needles in here." He held up a red pincushion stitched with green seams. It looked like a tomato or a red pumpkin. He pulled out a long, thin needle with a slight bend. The western sunshine glistened off it as he held it up to the light. He looked to the chair, following its slowing rhythm one last time. He pressed down on one of the rockers with his foot and stepped away from the chair, setting it rocking again. He came back to the table.

"I don't want to burn the bottom." I stirred the stew.

"Take it off the stove."

Foda turned me into the direct light and began picking under the skin at the remaining splinters.

ॐ

I sat in silence through supper and waited for him to finish and go to his books. As soon as the last bite entered his mouth, I took away his dishes. I felt the cheesecloth and material stowed away inside my panty heavy with dampness. I had hoped he would have retired to his room. Instead he sat back at the table, lit three candles, and took up Joseph Conrad's *Heart of Darkness*. His eyes crossed over the words and paragraphs. But I felt he was not really reading. He looked like he would turn pages back and reread them.

Why wasn't he in bed? He would always head to bed. Did he know? I didn't know. If I was dying, couldn't he see it? He had looked so mournfully at Mutta's chair. He had mentioned her funeral. I brought an air of death with me into our home. His heart was breaking all over again, but he couldn't tell it was me. Instead he spoke of Mutta.

I dropped another log into the stove. The heavy cast-steel lid of the stove slammed. He looked up at me. I turned my back to him and crossed my arms. My foot tapped. Then I broke the silence.

"You should go to bed."

"Thank you. Maybe I should."

I nodded. Foda's eyes tracked me as I heaved a large pot of water onto the stove top.

"Are you washing your blouse?"

"What? Yes. Why?"

He stared at me. Why couldn't I have said something? He knew how to tend to animals, save them. Surely I was becoming more animal. I saw Jonah every day and night. But maybe Foda, he knew what was happening to me. I didn't have to tell him about Jonah. I could say I fell. Like when I was little. But he wouldn't remember that, because I promised to never tell him. We never told Foda any of our secrets. It was better not to. He was a good man, a complicated man.

He looked right into my face, my eyes, cheekbones, forehead, and nose. He saw me completely. I winced.

"You look remarkably like your mother. You have her soft white skin. And your hair, the streaks of barley and wheat, Rebecca blamed you for stealing her soft blonde hair. You might remember her having brown hair, but it used to be blonde and wavy. But after you were born, it grew in brown and straight." He looked down at his hands. They were not young anymore, no. Soft white hair had replaced the brown at the edge of his wrist. Wrinkles covered every knuckle even when he made a fist. He looked at his palms too. They were thick with calluses that were not there on his wedding day. He looked at me again. I tried to iron my body into the straight stick-figure of a little girl, remove the curves about my hip and breast. He put his attention back into his book.

"Foda."

He didn't look again at me, his unsmiling face—the way Mutta always stared into her sewing, a downturn of her eyes, somewhere between a frown and a grimace. "Yes."

"Nothing." I stood up straight. I think I was angry now. I was angry I didn't know what was wrong with me. I was angry that he was still in my kitchen. I was angry that he couldn't see I was dying.

"Mareika. What is it?"

"I said it's nothing. Why do you always think there's something wrong?"

"But you said ... your face—"

"What's wrong with my face?"

"Nothing." He stared.

My anger seared over me. My eyes narrowed. "Where is the washboard?"

"Right there." He pointed behind the pickle barrel. He looked at me again as I took up a pickle from the barrel and bit into it.

"Rebecca loved pickles. They were her favourite."

"Mutta?"

"Yes."

"And you think I look like her. And I eat like her. Am I crazy like her?"

Foda grimaced. His look fell to his feet and a shake of his head trailed.

But he was right. I had seen a photo. I didn't have memories of her face anymore. I couldn't see her, but there was a photo. It was taken on the day they married.

He saw the photograph on only a couple of occasions. I saw it once when I was eleven because Opa, his foda, had it. Foda told me he thought the only reason Opa had it was so that he could show off. It was like being rich, and Martin E. Doerksen could say he had wealth. And Foda did not. The photo was pressed in a book of other photographs of people and places I didn't know or care to remember. All were on black pages and sat awkwardly in the middle. But I saw her. She was barely older than I was at the time I saw it. I thought it was me. Later I stared into a wooden pail full of water. I looked through my eyes and I saw her again. Then I smiled and she disappeared.

"I'm off to bed." He turned without another look to me. I heard only the drag of his feet and the click of the bedroom door latch.

I pulled my dress up and inspected the cloth. The rags felt damp and squishy.

What if I had confessed to him? Could he save me? I had never heard of a woman bleeding from the inside. From her other parts. Somewhere my blood was leaving me. Everything down there swelled with more and more blood.

I had seen blood. That year I had seen plenty of blood. But the blood I had experienced meant the end of desire. Desire was dangerous in a jack, unpredictable and dangerous. That early spring the studs would follow me up and down the fence line braying and kicking at the air, biting and tearing splinters from the fence posts. One even reared back, balancing one hoof atop a fence post. Its separate parts, long and fully extended, tight, and flinched against its belly.

When I was a girl, I remember Mutta being knocked to the ground by one of the studs, his separate parts dangling below his belly. I had laughed and spent the afternoon in the corner of the kitchen cutting eyes out of potatoes. Mutta never tended to the jacks after that.

But this bleeding now, perhaps Mutta was right. *For this is the will of God, your sanctification, that ye should abstain from fornication: That ever one of you should know how to possess his vessel in sanctification and honour.* There was a God and he was neutering that desire inside of me the way Foda castrated donkeys. Maybe I deserved to be cut. Mother warned me of desires, desires that would torment me, confuse me. What was forcing my heart, corrupting my hand? Maybe I deserved to bleed. I moved to the stove. Inside the water pot I fished out a stone. I wrapped it in a towel and cradled it to the pain tearing at my insides. Then I moved to the couch and curled up. I asked that I not bleed to death in my sleep. It hurt my heart to think of Foda having to bury me as well. Then I made a promise to never see Jonah again, to never let him touch my other parts.

It was God castrating me. I wished Mutta could answer me. She would tell me now. She would tell me if I were to bleed to death for lying down with Jonah, letting his hand ease inside of my other parts.

"Yes, there is a God. And he has chosen to castrate you."

But where is Mutta now? I was weaned years too early.

Wapos County

Boys always felt so hard. Their pushing pulling pushing pulling. I understand that. They have only two directions to go. Forward or back. Too much time thinking of either, and they'll let the anger get into their hands. It's so clear to them after their anger. Tomorrow or yesterday. They hate yesterday. They fear tomorrow. And in that room. In that room beside me is ... that little girl. She doesn't feel like she's mine. And every night she cries. She cries and cries and cries and John is there. Always there. Every night I cry. I cry and cry and cry. And John is there. I hear him humming to her. He keeps that silly red shirt. He wraps her in it and falls asleep in a chair there in that room. He needed a boy. What could he do with a girl? She will most certainly be sick as I am. I feel contained inside my own chest, my rib cage. Oh, John. You are trading every hair for a tear. I see it falling away. It's the autumn of this life. We pass by. And from your eyes—so stained by nights awake, your eyelids have taken the colour of spent tea bags—my gaze always falls to the ground. All you have is that little girl on your shoulder. You pulled her from me. I stood over you both last night. You don't know this. I stand over you so many nights. But this night as your eyes flickered like a dog's leg attacking an itch, I slid my finger into her hand. She took it. She squeezed. And there was nothing. Another night I saw you asleep upon the couch. She was up upon your chest. She held your ear with one hand and your nose with the other.

What was she getting from your flesh? You cannot feed her. I was a little girl and it was Sarah's hand. Two little girls holding hands and spinning, twirling and spinning, I felt as though I held a silk kite. Her skin so soft. And we twirled. Her smile rose from the edge of my grip. In the schoolyard I let those hands, I let that smile lead me, my feet following, running with a resistance. But Higher. Higher. Higher and higher. I rose with Sarah. She was the best part of the day. She was my Mareika, The Mutta. The first one. On the Red River, we were twelve. She washed my feet. The brown water slow and cold. Ravens sat in the trees watching gophers spring from the coulee's sandy walls, a thousand holes climbing from the river up to a steppe. There was this fir tree, too, growing from the sandy side. I washed her feet. Her soles almost black, I rubbed them until they were pink again. We splashed and let our dresses swell around our heads as we sank and bobbed in the waters. But with this child now. Always in your arms. Crying. I can't find direction in her hands. They feel cold. She rises and falls with your chest. And her hands feel cold. I want to ask you for help. I want you to teach me how to read her, read her the way you taught me English, the way you taught me German. There are words for this, but I don't know them. I don't know them. And I don't know if I will ever know them. Sarah, she treated me as if I were Hagar, but would hate me because of this child, this betrayal, hated the child, because there was nobody to take her. I was supposed to take her. Then this child took me. John, you took us both. And still you love me more. John, you took her. I did not take me. You tend to her in a way I never felt from my foda. The sting of his hand, belt, rod. Spare the rod. Spare the rod. My life was so much worse with a foda. I'm sorry. It isn't fair. Why am I angry? Why is my life measured for what this little girl will get that I never had before? I did not want you. I did not ask for you. With you was I freed? I am supposed to be free. Sarah held my freedom. Sarah. It was always Sarah. Her memories, a ghost, fit so perfectly around me. She feels like the atmosphere, the wind and the weather. And when my hairs sprout with energy, I know it's her. But this child. Did I not buy my freedom with this girl? Take her. I leave you there asleep, together. Free me. I cleansed myself from all the filthiness of the flesh ... I cursed Foda and Mutta for delivering me to the bed of that beast, to the Bishop. My head, it shakes trying to throw those memories, the images, the seeds of this nightmarish hate away, but they sprout, stabbing out, and petals opening in moonlight ...

Their roots. Deeper roots tangled and knotted. The Bishop's demon acts ... My chest swells with heated pain. Don't give so much respect to that beast. Push and pull. They are owned by impulse. Impulses more like greedy hungry dogs. Impulses. Impulses. There is no thought if there are no bigger dogs to nip and bite at their necks to keep them at bay ... I was not a thought. An impulse. An impulse. An impulse. O, the smell. How he left my body oozing with his smell. I know Sarah was taken to him. Held in front of the elders to repent, to admit, and to be forgiven. I do not feel forgiven. Betrayed for there is blood between my legs. And my own mother will not look at me. She opened a drawer full of cloth and rags. I took one. I reached for another. She slammed the door and turned her back. And between your legs there will be blood. I have seen the coyotes surround a calf. On wobbled new legs torn down before it could walk. That is the smell. The smell of sun-soured meat left for the crows and maggots to peck clean. Those bones to disappear, the earth having swallowed them. Sarah. O, Sarah. What did we do? Our flesh was clean. You so near to me, before your mother dragged you from your room by your hair. Were you tossed to the dogs? And now I stink ...

And it is not her fault. She is a door to those memories. So I must not deliver this child away. I will not be that way. I will not forget my suckling child. So I rose and gave her my hand. She took it, John. So now I take her back. She is Mareika. I gave her the name Mareika. I made her the Mutta. But I must be a mother. I am a woman. With the same finger leading my eyes over Timothy 2:11, these are the words I found again. This is my weakness before it is strength. It is the strength and courage Sarah gave to me, the strength and courage Sarah gave to me before I was cast out. It is these words I forgot: *Let the woman learn in silence with all subjection. But I suffer not a woman to teach, nor to usurp authority over the man, but to be in silence. For Adam was first formed, then Eve. And Adam was not deceived, but the woman being deceived was in the transgression. Notwithstanding she shall be saved in childbearing, if they continue in faith and charity and holiness with sobriety.* I forgot. I suffered and blamed. I hated this child for delivering me from Sarah, keeping me here. Her face has disappeared in her bright eyes and fat cheek. I have forgotten to forgive. It is my charge to be silent, suffer, but to forgive. I forgive you, Mareika. I forgive you. And tomorrow you will lie upon my chest. *For if ye forgive men their trespasses, your heavenly Father will also forgive you* ... Please forgive me ...

SUNDAY, AUGUST 10, 1890.

Steinbach, Manitoba

Rebecca didn't remember taking the flight of stairs to Sarah's attic that last time. She only remembered how they stared across the laundry tub, their tiny smiles, the flush redness of their cheeks, and Rebecca looking down the barrel's edge to the grass populated by red and orange ladybugs whenever their fingers touched under the warm soapy water. Her dress was wet from the laundry, and Sarah said she could borrow one of hers to walk home. Her chest felt warm, and how cool the damp cloth was against it, as Sarah's milk-white hand guided it up to her nape, down between her naked breasts. She pushed her slip off, too, not looking at the other young woman. Sarah giggled and tickled the tips of her fingers amongst the dark field over Rebecca's other parts. Rebecca giggled. And they looked into one another's eyes. Sarah's hands took hold of Rebecca's hips, stepping closer. They giggled again. Then Sarah hushed their lips. Rebecca's mouth parted. The tips of their tongues tracing the aperture from where their breath entangled. Sarah closed her eyes. Rebecca kept hers open. And when Sarah moved away for another breath, drawing it from deep inside Rebecca's lungs, she smiled. Her whole body smiled. Rebecca sighed and all her worry melted from her shoulders, her hand falling, sweeping up her friend's fingers into hers. They smiled.

"You feel nice," Sarah said. She tugged at a braid under Rebecca's prayer shawl.

Rebecca lifted the white hat above her head. Sarah caught the shawl ends with a pinch and led the long white cotton stoles over Rebecca's nipples. They giggled and they kissed again. Rebecca closed her eyes this time. She let her hands follow the flow of Sarah's hip as the path led into her torso, then her shoulders, her neck before those hands, awash in an exciting newness, came to rest upon Sarah's face. She held her as if she were a puff of alder smoke, sweet and full. She opened her mouth more and drew in a deep breath. The tenderness exchanged promised to turn them into a singular beating heart . . .

Then Sarah's teeth banged into Rebecca's. Their faces smashed together. Rebecca's eye snapped open. Sarah's mother, a stout woman with heavy breasts under a dark black dress, dragged Sarah by her hair down the stairs.

"Get yourself home!" Her scream ignited the room with rage.

Rebecca ran. She ran.

❧

The moon nearly full shone orange in the east, blazing behind Bishop Dyck's home. Its planetary body seemingly so close that, if Rebecca had decided to run from her parents, she could have reached it in a couple of hours.

"Hello, Rebecca." Bishop Dyck stood with his door open only enough to see the white of his collar and his jacket's black lapel. One foot hid behind a white door. A muted amber halo of lamplight floated behind him.

Rebecca's father shoved her towards the step. Neither he nor his wife looked at the Bishop. They stared at the ground. The Bishop disappeared back into his home, leaving the door ajar. Rebecca's father shoved her again at the shoulders. She tripped on the first step. Then clasping her fingers together entered the house.

"Close the door, please." Bishop Dyck drew his curtains in the living room. He pointed towards Rebecca. "Behind you, on the table is a jug of water, please bring it here." The room, lit with a lantern atop the potato bin and one on the mantel, was sparse with simple pine furniture. A square table in the kitchen, milk-painted cabinets, a couch with grey cushions, and a bare pine chair with flat spindles. "You can set it on this table." In front of his couch, between him and the stove, he had placed a table, one with spidery long legs. Its tall, curved spindled legs and lacquered pine top made it look like the table Rebecca's mother used in the kitchen when she rolled out dough for *kilkya*. This table wasn't covered in flour. It lay bare except for a thin switch of willow.

Rebecca brought the white ceramic jug. Bishop Dyck, seated on the grey couch, looked too small for his black jacket, like he borrowed it from one of the elders. He gestured with his hand at a metal basin beside his feet. Rebecca got onto her knees and unlaced his shoes. She tucked his laces inside so that they wouldn't touch the floor, saving them from getting wet if she should spill or splash water. She rolled his pant legs to his knees, his skin the colour of the white jug and wisped with frail brown hairs. There was a bruise high up on his shin.

"I slipped trying to hop out of the corral drum." He cleared his throat. "The socks please."

His socks were damp with warmth. She rolled them down, pulled them inside out off his toes, and then placed them under the table behind her.

"No," he said. "Turn them right-side out and fold them together. Don't be lazy, girl."

"Sorry, Bishop." Rebecca slid the pan under his feet. She took the jug and poured water against his shin. It was warm. Bishop Dyck passed her a bar of soap. She lathered her hands and, lifting one foot, glided her hands around his ankle, down under his sole.

"Do you know why you are here?"

"Yes." She set his foot back into the water.

"Please get between the toes." He coughed. "Genesis says a man leaves his father and his mother, and shall cleave unto his wife: and they shall be one flesh. Do you know what that means?"

"No."

"It means that someday you will be a man's wife. I see you are entering womanhood. How old are you?"

"Fourteen." Rebecca took up his other foot and began to lather it, around his ankle, under his sole. Her index finger slid between each of his toes.

"You are nearly a wife."

Rebecca kept her head down.

"You are nearly a wife." The Bishop's voice came with heat and gravel.

"I don't know."

"Are there any boys you like?"

"I don't know."

"Okay. Tell me what you and Sarah did."

"We were doing laundry, and my dress got wet, and Sarah said I could wear one of hers, so she took me and helped me change." She lifted his feet onto the edge of the basin and with her apron against his toes she splashed his feet with more water from the jug. Then she took his feet into her apron and held them, squeezed them, and patted them dry.

"That's not all, is it?"

"No. She kissed me."

"She kissed you? You never kissed her?"

"I kissed her."

"Sarah's mutta says you were in undress." Bishop Dyck hand caressed the line of his pant, easing to his knee and up the middle of his legs. With his other hand he straightened Rebecca's prayer shawl.

"Yes."

"And you kissed her." He pulled at the groin of his pants and shifted in his seat.

"Yes."

"Turn around and put your palms on the table." She turned and placed her hands upon the table. The wood felt warm as she grasped at its polished grains with anticipation of the remembered sting that willow delivered. Rebecca looked to the curtained window beside the stove. The table was high enough to rest just under the sill. She imagined it must have been in the sunlight all day until now.

Bishop Dyck stepped into her. He reached around her and picked up the willow switch. Its tip flicked her cheek. She flinched. His breath fell against her nape. He reached around her with his other hand and locked both his grips around the switch.

"You can look at it." His groin pressed up against her tailbone. "I don't believe in the rod. Boys are easier. Simple. They forget themselves; and a switch is in their vocabulary. I cannot do that to a young woman. In the beginning I was expected to. And one mere creature did get the switch from me. She was only six. She had wanted to make right her wrong. She wanted to make me happy. And she cried. I lashed her eight times. She only weighed twenty kilos. It felt so wrong to inflict such punishment on a creature so much smaller, finer than me. I cried when she was gone. And I repented. And I asked for forgiveness. And I never took a switch to another girl again." He placed the switch down on the table under Rebecca's gaze.

"Thank you."

"Chasten thy son while there is hope, and let not thy soul spare for his crying. Proverbs 19:18. I will not lash you, but there are things you must tend to if you are to be a wife, and it would serve you best if you learned to enjoy them." Bishop Dyck drew the air from the room with a gasp from Rebecca as he lifted her dress and reached between her legs. "Shhh." He squatted and drew her panty down to the floor. He dipped a hand into the wash basin and on the hinge of his thumb pressed against her tailbone, probed a cold wet finger inside her.

"No."

"Shh. You are to be a wife." He slid his finger back and forth. The soft edges of her body pinching and folding inside of her, the hairs pulling. "Drink waters out of thine own cistern, and running waters out of thine own well. Let thy fountains be dispersed abroad, rivers of waters in the streets." He dipped his hand into the basin of water again. He slapped it back against her flesh, his fingers probing, pushing, stabbing into her. "Let them be only thine own, and not strangers with thee. Let thy fountain be blessed: and rejoice with the wife of thy youth . . ." He grunted and shoved another finger inside. His fingernail felt like the edge of knife slicing through her. She gasped and dropped her head. "The loving hind and pleasant roe; let her breasts satisfy thee at all times; and be thou ravished always with her love."

"Please stop." Rebecca squeezed her eyes closed.

"No. These are your duties."

"I promise—" Rebecca heard the cold rattle of his belt, the thud it made against the wood floor, the sound of him spitting, then knobs of his knuckles between her legs. The table legs squealed against the floor after he begins stabbing into her. He wrested her hair with one hand as he pushed through her. She leaned back to follow the pull of her hair rising back up.

"Put your head down." He said. His voice sounded angry. And he pushed and pulled harder, his body clapping against her. "*Wives, submit yourselves unto your own husbands*!" He pulled away quickly and dropped onto his knees over the basin, his arm pushing down at his groin like he was slapping out a fire. He stood, pulled his pants up and sat on the couch. "Corinthians 7:2-5." He huffed out his mouth, drawing in a new breath through his nose. Rebecca pushed and pulled on her clothes. Her frantic hand organised them where they should be, but they did not feel right against her skin. She still felt exposed.

He panted a few times before he continued reading. "Nevertheless, fornication, let every man, every man, have his own wife. You are to be a wife, Rebecca. And let every woman have her own husband. Let the husband render unto the wife due benevolence: and likewise also the wife unto the husband. The wife hath not power of her own body. Do you understand?"

She nodded, her head quaking as a leaf would in fall, reddened and threatened by the wind to fall. She wanted to throw up but swallowed it, then swallowed more breaths to choke away her tears.

"Wasn't that nice? Didn't that feel good?"

Her body stilled. She refused to look at him. At the window the willow branches shuttered scraping at the glass.

"Then why all this foolishness?"

"May I go, please?"

"No. I don't think you understand. There is pleasure in a man. And if you want to be a wife—The head of the woman, the man—you have to be able to surrender yourself to his needs. And I suspect that you do not understand that yet, do you?"

She nodded. Her lungs held to the breath which would be a scream: *That was horrible!*

"Don't be dishonest. I want you to read of Hagar, Genesis 16 and 21 and 35. And tomorrow we will discuss it."

When he walked her home, he made her walk behind him. He made her knock on her own door, and then return behind him.

Rebecca's mutta had come to the door.

"Yes. I will need further study with Rebecca. She refuses to understand her transgressions."

"Yes, of course."

"Send her to my home tomorrow. In the mornings would be best." He turned to Rebecca. "Genesis, Hagar," and gave her a nod, then pointed to her mutta. She ran inside.

Canadian Pacific Railway Line Construction

IBI CLIMBED DOWN from the railcar in which he had stowed away. His duffle slung over his shoulder, he marched through the back of the railyard. He moved with a straight back, his gaze forward, willing not to look away if a railway operator should want to stop him. This new rail line stretched from one ocean to another. The idea of it seemed to Ibi to stitch patches of other nations together into one, the French to the English, the Protestant to the Catholic, Indian, Oriental, Russian, Swede, and even the Mennonites. Could this expanse of land belong to us all? He followed the empty line as it stretched out in front of him chasing after the hazy mirage of mountains defying the horizon line. The fullness, the immensity of grey rock pushing up out of the ground captured his imagination. Being held so long to the flatness of Manitoba had stolen his memories of the Tian Shan Mountains. More accurately, Manitoba had been so flat, it felt to him almost below sea level, explaining why it flooded so often, and thusly eroded Ibi's memories of Tian Shan's snowy peaks, green valleys, and the crystal blue waters of its lakes and rivers.

At that very moment, he wanted to see the inner sandstone walls of Itchan Kala of Khiva. If he could trust his memories, he could close his eyes and follow the train tracks not into whatever town he'd just arrived in but back to Khiva. Because it had been there he had felt most alive.

When he wandered Itchan Kala, its brick roads, he felt shrunken, like he had been placed inside a sandcastle, the beige walls rising at a slight angle as if formed by a child's hand. Barely any straight lengths ran around the ancient city, inside Khiva. The architecture of those century-old Muslim walls preferred rounded turrets that resembled the bottom chin and jaw of a skull with sharp, jagged, saw-toothed pinnacles. Dotting the city skyline, blue-peaked minarets stood sentinel. The most impressive had been Kalta-minor. It rose with several bands of blue tiles, white tiles, and brown tiles, but it lacked a peak and resembled a large, ornate clay crock. Ibi, as a boy, imagined it full to the brim with sweet pickles.

Ibi stumbled over a rail sleeper. At this moment, the present world called him back from Turkestan. The fall tore a hole in his pant at the knee. Without noticing, he had drifted to the end of the railway.

Stacks of sleepers about two-stories high promised the railway would continue through the mountains onward to the next sea. He looked at them again. He felt as if he could step into them if only he'd walk fifteen minutes longer. But he knew this was not the case. Their enormity was a deception. He'd heard of many a man who had never experienced great mountains to wander off to scale them only to freeze to death before even reaching them. From his experience, he estimated them to be still several hours away by horse, and that was just to the base.

They were magnificent. The south face overgrown with a verdant blanket of evergreens and pines, the peaks white with ancient glacial snow. Just ahead he spotted an onyx-coloured gully. He filled five moose bladders with water. Then he moved back up the ridge under the conifers to rest. There he erected a tent of heavy canvas sheets, rope, and pegs. It barely covered the long, lean man, but it promised to be cozy for him to share with his calico friend. Throughout his trek he managed to convince the critter to keep following with a line of yarn he pinned to the bottom of his pant leg. The cat lay on its side at Ibi Gietz's feet, pawing listlessly at the brown cotton tail. Ibi closed his eyes looking over his memory for Ak-Metchet, looking for Claas Epp Jr.

The part on the left side of Claas's head was combed flat, while the wave of his hair bulged out over his right ear. Claas's large ears with thick earlobes, and prominent sharp nose protruding over an insignificant chin made him appear to be chinless. His overall appearance was ignored and never played into anybody's opinion of him until after March 8, 1889. When the Rapture did not happen, when nobody in Ak-Metchet rose into the Kingdom of Heaven, the muttering began. That day his appearance—big ears, pointed nose, and weak chin—was likened to a rat. Surely it was Wilhelm Penner, that badger, who started the dissention.

Ibi and his family, like so many families, had followed Claas from the rich banks of the Volga River through a desert and into the mountains of Turkestan instead of the plains and prairies of the New World. Ibi was only a boy when he started the two-year trek to Ak-Metchet. And after March 8, after fasting, after sitting around the church's communion table outside in Ak-Metchet's courtyard, holding his mother's hand under the table, holding Claas's hand under the table, after watching the sky, after singing hymns, after the minutes turned into hours, after the sun sank behind the world, after nobody was lifted into the heavens, after Penner and others retreated back into the church, after Claas stood and spoke, "Christ has suffered for us all. This is a message. A message meant for me, a revelation that I have not suffered in the ways that our Lord has, and until I have, I must remain. We must remain," after Wilhelm's wife, Katherine, sneered, Ibi still believed in Claas—in his words and in the Rapture.

Inside the tent, the calico climbed upon Ibi's stomach. He dragged his calloused thumb under the cat's chin and scratched the orange, brown, white spots speckling about its cheeks.

"He is no rat. Neither are you, are ya?"

A decade after following his mentor, the Gietz family was preparing to leave Turkestan for the Americas. Ibi remembered sitting outside the courtyard crying, eating an apple.

He missed the sermons and helping Claas afterwards, washing the dust from the white walls of the mortared stone, building boxes for shipping cotton. It was there, toiling in the work needed to create a community, that Claas showed him what the others were slowly ignoring. It was that work, that toil, where belief and trust in the word given to him by God grew. Claas had been a rich man, owned a brick factory. But in Ak-Metchet he toiled. He built furniture. He showed Ibi stone by stone as they dug the community well. He showed him in the doorways and windows constructed in every building, every home, because in those moments, shared but ignored by the others, Claas became the Second Witness.

"And do not think I am not aware of the insults," Claas had said.

Ibi laughed remembering Claas flicking at his ears with his calloused fingers.

"No matter where rats travel—Prussia, Samara, or Ak-Metchet—they live and thrive. That is admirable, and I hoped my Mennonite brothers should demonstrate such characteristics," he said followed by a slap upon Ibi's back.

After those words, Claas took Ibi Gietz past the schoolhouse to the eastern corner of the settlement to the north edge of Ak-Metchet between the cemetery and the road to Khiva. Ibi could feel the day's warmth as spring soothed the torturous winter air with the coming of summer. He remembered the air smelled of mortar dust as new homes and barns were still being constructed as the population kept growing with new families arriving every month.

"Even though your family has lost their faith and chosen to leave, a part of you will be here for his return." Claas took the apple Gietz was eating and dug a hole where he planted the uneaten half into the ground. "I will not forget you, young Ibi. And soon we will see each other again." It was then Claas took a book from a satchel and handed it to the young Gietz. "Take it to the Americas." The boy had hesitated. "A piece of me to travel along with you. Not to worry, I have another." Claas patted the boy on his head, and he walked him home.

He wished Claas were here with him. His voice was so sure. He himself stuttered and never looked a man in the face, instead chose to talk around his figure. He never feared looking into the eyes of a woman; his words for them were like a sermon. He saw women as an altar to kneel down at, and they only returned his fervor with passion. His mind felt the derailing of his true purpose by his body again. The seclusion of the railcar had kept him from the softer sex. There the sway and clack of the track kept him to the word of the Bible. He could hear Claas again.

"If only Claas had gotten his calculation correct," he said, stroking his calico friend, now on his chest. Its paws lifted, patted, kneaded at his shirt.

On March 8, 1891, the day Claas had recalculated, Gietz left his family. He gathered only bread and water and an apple for the walk. In a satchel under his arm, only a set of clothes and a white ascending robe, pressed and folded, he alone walked to an open field outside Hoffnungsfeld. And surrounded by poplars naked of their leaves and knee-deep in crystallized snow drifts, he waited to ascend. Claas had said his calculations were not wrong but off. Inside his home, Claas had shown him a Mariner's clock. He said that the clock in the migration to Ak-Metchet had fallen to the side. That he had needed to readjust according to the leaning clock. Ibi did not understand, but with the new and correct date, he left and waited to see Claas again.

Time continued on as it always had. He stood in his white gown with half a moon peeking down on him. His eyelids froze and stuck between hard blinks of his eyes. He wiped his cheeks. He called for Brother Epp. Cold darkness met him back, cold darkness. He became afraid alone in the dark. The calls of coyotes felt close. They yipped and cried, obviously scrapping over something large and dead. The yips stabbed loud and clear into his ear. Then and there Ibi had felt the sins of his family: abandoning Ak-Metchet had sealed his fate to remain locked out of Heaven to fight the hell that had surely been scouring across the lands of all the Earth.

He began to shiver long before he found his way back home, where he slept in the barn before he left for good to wander the prairies to revisit Claas's math, searching for the variable that would correct his mentor's error. After days, then weeks, then months before years, the boy became a man who had fallen from Claas's word and the Bible itself. He drank. He worshipped women, especially the married kind. To Ibi, all they needed was to be praised, to be listened to. Under their Rapture, Ibi felt saved. To come upon the soft embrace of a woman meant something more to him than the act of love. But he didn't know what that was. He knew now he was only being distracted. The war, the battle for this world, was about to commence, and had he continued to ignore the signs, ignore Claas's prophecy, surely he would have been left behind to fight—and worse—to suffer. Surely the pleasures of the Kingdom were greater than the kingdom of woman. But Ibi did give thanks to her, Genevieve or Gwendolyn, for fetching that paper.

Today, Ibi Gietz grew positive that Claas's prediction of the Rapture was now upon the world, that he had found that missing variable that must have skewed Brother Epp's calculations. Claas, too, must know this, and Gietz saw the man preparing with the others back home in Ak-Metchet.

He rolled over. The calico jumped over his face and licked his paws in the grass near his head. Ibi pulled newspaper clippings from his satchel. On the top, an article slightly smudged showed a drawing of a comet. He read two sentences he had underlined. "Earth expected to cross through the tail of Halley's Comet ... Will cyanogen poisoning mean mass human extinction?"

Friday, May 13, 1910.

Wapos County

MAREIKA WOKE WHEN John came out from his bedroom. The moment he turned the knob, her ears used the creaks and clicks to tempt her eyes. They fluttered open but enough for a thrown glance. She kept them ajar to monitor him. She also maintained a heavy breath which aped sleep.

He lumbered under a short night. As his heavy gait thumped across the wood flooring, he moved and grabbed bread and smoked rabbit. He gnawed on a leg and thigh. He discarded the bones in a large pot continuously boiling upon the stove with the week's collection of meal bones, rabbits and chickens, simmering down into a jelly that would become next week's soups, stews, and broth for bathing roasted potatoes, beets, carrots, and other root vegetables that had survived the winter inside the *semlin*.

John, dressed for the pastures, squatted at the stove. He shaved tinder off a log with the kitchen knife and dropped it into the stove's belly with several twigs and branches. He blew breaths through pursed lips. Ash rose in a cloud over his face and clung to his stubble. The ashen look aged him twenty years. The crack of wood catching flame filled the home. John stuffed the stove full of slender wedges of wood. Flames lapped at the brim of the stovetop.

He sat at the table waiting with another piece of bread. He scratched his chin. He yawned. Then when the firewood crackled, crackled, and crackled more, he opened the stovetop and held his piece of bread with a fork over the heat. He turned the fork in his fingers until the bread was light brown, he closed the stovetop, and then he buttered the toast. He stepped into his boots and didn't chew into his breakfast until he was out the door.

The pull and tear inside Mareika's body still haunted her pelvis and stomach. In fact, it had worsened in the night; the bone of pelvis and hip felt as if it had been pried open and taken from her. Mareika pulled her covers up under her chin as the last winter wind pushed over her face. She opened her eyes all the way and stared at the ceiling. In the wood beams and plaster she tried not to find Jonah Wiebe, but instead Mr. Graham, the schoolteacher.

He always wore peat-coloured slacks and a vest. He had many vests, greys, navies, linen, and khaki. And dependent upon his belt colour, his shoes always matched. His dusty hair, always parted down the middle, was soft and smelled like cedar. In the school stove, during class he always burned cedar. She tried to recreate the firm, stocky command his posture held over her. She closed her eyes then opened them again, looking above, but his face did not stop her from seeing the peak and plaster of the ceiling. She would not see Mr. Graham until Monday.

She sighed. Then her legs pulled and flipped at the quilt, its sides folding, twisting around itself. Between her legs it had looked like a tornado. She trapped the end of the twisted blanket between her ankles. She stuffed her feet into the corner of the couch cushion, where she lay, pulling up at it with her arms. She rocked her hips against the taut coil. Mr. Graham behind her fluttering eyes, fluttering heart was reading. He sat upon his desk, one leg up, the other dangling. She followed the loose cuff about his ankle, his grey sock—always grey socks—up as it got tight over his knee, stretching around his thighs. His groin, bulging, was smooth with the peat-coloured pants. She would sometimes stare at his groin, the bulge separated into two mounds.

She knew about the donkeys her fathered raised. On hot summer nights, their long blackness draped well below their stomachs. Sometimes they'd twitch. But she'd never seen another boy or man, not even Foda, naked, except chests at the end of the day in late summer and autumn during harvest. Or in Black Gully Lake where all the town's children swam to escape summer heat. It seemed strange to her to even try to guess what Mr. Graham must look like compared to a large animal. But inevitably she switched her focus to his arms.

His vests were always taut. And even though he had a bit of a tummy, not like her dad, his chest, his shoulders seemed wide. His cuffs were always pressed and tight, making his hands appear so large, his fingers larger, as he turned the pages as he read.

In her thoughts he always invited her to the front of the school-house to read a passage. She eased out from behind her desk, marched towards the blackboard, stood at the corner of his desk, and put out her hand. Her invitation didn't happen with her out-reached hand but at her smile, a coquettish grin, and sideways glance. She further coaxed him with a shake of her hip. She admired how bold she could be inside her own mind.

He placed the leather-bound pages into her outreached hand. But he never let go. She tugged. He never let go. Their eyes met. Then he would bid her in with an upward tip of his chin that lingered with a, "Yes."

She would back between his legs, pressing herself against the bulge of his groin, and he would close his arms around her holding the book open for her to read. His warm breath caressing her nape.

She pulled the blankets tighter. She rocked her body against its twisted length faster. She sighed. Her body felt freed from the pain.

Then she let go of the blanket, slid a hand between her legs. When the tips of her fingers graced the padding of cloth, she flinched away, moved the pads of her fingers just high enough to avoid and ignore them. The previous rubbing had eased the pain somehow, so she chased it further, though biting at the back of her mind, again, guilt and fear that perhaps this was why she had begun bleeding in the first place. But it felt too late. She couldn't control her own mind or body. She closed her eyes harder, tried to wring the shame from out of her to chase the pleasure.

Behind her imagination, she made a mistake, a slip of the tongue. So Mr. Graham leaned forward. His chest pressed against her back. He would reread the sentence she had just read, his voice, warm, spilling over her ear. The tickle of words lifted the hairs on her neck.

"Continue," he said.

Yes. She couldn't help but to continue. Mareika leaned back against him. She licked the tip of her middle finger, pressed it against the page, and as she looked over her shoulder at him in a classroom now empty in her mind, drew the page back, curling it like a wave inspired by the gravity of the moon, and let it crash over his fingers. She'd then read the next line without looking at the page, lifting her voice over his lips. The tip of his nose graced the tip of hers. He read along, following her lips, their breath tangled.

Mareika, with her hand, pressed harder, rubbed faster following the soft roll of her pelvis. She drew long breaths and felt them with the grip of her other hand taking her breast. Her body felt a swell of heat, an expansion building behind her hips. Her body bowed. Her lungs drew all the air from the house inside her.

Then the stomping clumps of boots shook the porch. Her father coughed. He coughed. He stomped more. He coughed more. Then the front door rattled as if stuck in the jamb.

Her hand ignored the raucous and hurried her to a conclusion. She bit down on the edge of her blanket as a rush of warmth overtook her. Her body stiffened, the dream held her suspended as it rippled through her several times. Then as it let go, she shuddered. Her breath, spitting out the sides of her mouth. She choked on the inhalation. The cold morning air rushed into the house ahead of John, who still coughed, though more restrained, and still stomped, this time inside the threshold hidden behind the door.

Her hands threw the quilt from between her legs. And as she sprung up, she shook it out, before she draped it over herself. Her hands rode over the top of the blanket in eight wiggly pink fingers on either side of her chin. Her toes were wiggling too. She slammed her eyes shut as the morning sun burst through the open front door.

"Mareika," John said. "Time to get up."

Mareika shot up. She looked to the wall, the bookshelves across from the couch. *Heart of Darkness* was the only title she deciphered.

"Morning, Foda."

"Did you want breakfast? Let's go to The Café and grab some ham and eggs."

"Toast," Mareika said. She looked at the floorboards. She looked up. Her dad busied himself with the pots and stove. He picked up the fork he'd left on the table and swirled it into the pot several times. He retrieved one of his deerskin gloves and lifted the pot. He carried it to a large copper pot and dumped the water inside. From over the ledge above the stove he took a cast-iron pan, laying it upon the stove.

"Did you need to starch anything?" he asked. "Grab some potatoes and I'll boil them for starch."

"No." Mareika, as soon as John turned his eyes away, stood and marched into the pantry, carrying her quilt. She closed the door and bit into the corner. She stuffed her mouth full and screamed. She dropped her blanket and stood on it, her feet off the cold, dusty planks. She reached out and slid her fingertips across the edge of the shelves. She turned inside, looking from one corner to the next. She reached under the bottom shelf and slid the wash basin out. She lay on the floor with her feet where the basin had been and reached her arms back over her head and pushed her palms into the opposite wall. She looked up at the two shelves built across the window. The morning light came through but was muted by empty mason jars. Her dad always kept the empty glass jars in the window. Mareika remembers a time her mother put a basket of potatoes on one of the shelves, during fall, when they were jarring and pickling what was left in the garden: beets, carrots, beans, relish, strawberry and raspberry jams. Her dad got angry and scolded Rebecca.

"Where do the baskets of potatoes go?"

Her mother shook her head.

"Under the bottom shelf. Come on, Rebecca. Is this the first time you've put away potatoes?"

"No." Her mother looked away.

"If you put the potatoes in front of the window, then there's no light. Can you see in that room without light? No." He hefted the potatoes back into her mom's arms. "Put them where they're supposed to go." Later he would apologize for raising his voice, not just to Rebecca but in front of Mareika as well. Mareika admired that in her foda, his ability to bear witness to himself when he acted irresponsibly with her or Mutta's feelings.

"It's not just the message, but how you deliver it," he'd say.

Rebecca picked up a small potato. She took the spiny white shoots piercing the potato's eyes and snapped them off, one by one, leaving the top root. Then she lowered it into a mason jar in front of the window. A rapping at the door brought Mareika to her feet. She brushed her butt and picked up her blanket, folding it four times.

"Mareika?"

She grabbed the door handle and felt the knob wanting to turn for a moment.

"Foda."

"Yes."

"Do you remember when Mutta died?"

"I do," he said.

"That night that she was sick, she told me that this was supposed to be my room." She reached out and touched a shelf edge, she flicked the rim of a mason jar, and the chime rang for half a second.

"That is true. It was."

"I would like a room."

"Would you like your mother's room back?"

"No. I want my own room."

"Yes. You shouldn't have to sleep on the couch."

Mareika's head dropped, her forehead rapped the door. The door knocked, the latch clicking against the striker. She heard Foda's feet shuffling, his shadow pulsing under the door. She felt the weight of his body trying to enter. It threatened to push her back. She grabbed the knob again, her fingernails digging into her palm.

"It's been too long—I know. And it almost feels too late, but I can do this for you. I have some lumber, some posts and headers. They are in the barn. I'll build a loft. Off the west ridgeline. Maybe under the round window. Would you like that?"

"Thanks, Foda." Mareika's brows fell. She sifted those words and held to *it feels too late*. Her hand fell away from around the knob. She squeezed the quilt to her chest. The steady fall of her father's soles moved across the room.

"I'll be in the wagon. Get ready and we'll go to Black Gully for a breakfast." The creak of hinges and bang of the door closing followed.

Mareika exhaled.

∽৮৬

The town of Black Gully poked into view as John and Mareika's wagon rolled along the dusty beige ribbon of gravel—first the shake rooftops, then the white milk-paint walls. Most homes had gable or hipped roofs and no fences. Dandelions had started to poke out of the spring grounds. Scattered over the lawns, little girls gathered the yellow flowers while mothers picked their greens. John Doerksen used the dandelion's root as a way to preserve the ale he brewed when he was short hops.

John and Mareika were carried through town upon a cart pulled by one donkey to its centre between the three churches, Catholic, Lutheran, and Mennonite, each at a corner of the main square, a park with a gazebo and several trees, including a young weeping birch, its bark white and curled at the edges of its trunk where branches stretched skyward before drooping towards the ground like a ponytail. At one corner of the park lay an expansive flower garden, maintained by the Catholic priest and the three nuns. To the south of the downtown, a short succession of building fronts, two-stories high and squared off at the top, ran for only two blocks, north to south with a brick and mortar hotel on the southeast corner. Everything looked the same stacked side by side, but the trim and wood panelling changed colour from store front to store front. None of the fronts had any signage. You had to be from Black Gully to know which building was the hardware store and which was The

Café. Most around town called the hardware store Red's on account of its red paint. The boardwalk, rough-sawn fir, ran along the entire stretch of downtown on both sides and the road was gravelled. This stretch, along with the future Railway Avenue, had the only gravelled roads.

In front of The Café, Black Gully's only restaurant, sat troughs for horses or John's donkey to drink. Hopping along the edges of the water troughs, chickadees dipped their heads into the waters before looking skywards to tip their drink into their bellies. They entered The Café.

In the small room sat pine furniture with a solid shellac finish and a visible mortise and tenon. Eight tables made up two lines of three inside. The small café buzzed with chatter from the usual men, including Bishop Dyck, who had turned in his chair to look at the door as John and Mareika arrived. For years, inside the walls of his own home, John had cursed Bishop Dyck, painted him as an unholy man. Mareika, wide-eyed, stared at his hair, bone white, and a full wild briar of curls from his forehead that invaded his matching beard. His weathered face looked as if it were carved from limber pine, carved by chinook winds and the slice of gusting snow. When his gaze caught John, his thick square eyebrows nearly collided. He and John, locked by a tension, a pregnant anger, orbited outside of themselves as if separated by a shared magnetic pole, impossible to touch. John's hands took Mareika by the shoulder and guided her away from the Bishop. He pointed to the table closest to the far wall treading between the Bishop and her.

"Grab those chairs." He pulled the other two of the chairs away from the table and left them against the near wall. "Grab an end." They lifted the table and placed it right against the wainscoting under the café's frontage window. He then used his cuff and wiped the dust from the top of the chair rail before he sat. He scratched his stubbled chin.

The men at the tables who had stopped to watch them began chirping again.

"Well, who is he?" they asked one another.

Bishop Dyck got up from his seat and went to the door. He pulled the knob as if to make sure it was closed, turned the knob again and slammed the door giving it another good pull.

"He says he's a follower of Claas Epp Jr.," Bishop Dyck said, knocking the heels of his heavily scuffed boots over the floor. The tall, broad Bishop had a narrow gaze like that of a father holding a willow switch over a child. He scratched under his chin, the long white hairs of his beard rustled. The room kept still. Only a restrained cough and the sizzle of ham frying at the back followed his words.

"Who?" asked Paul Lee, a younger man of only twenty-nine, large, almost grizzled, but pink of cheek and tender. He was the only man in the group who came into this world English, having joined the community through marriage. Always with smile and a tool caddy, he became known as a friend to all people and all animals. Inside his barn, nearly overrun with cats, but no mouse or rat, he penned sheep, miniature goats, and collies, plus inside the attic he put up a series of swings, ropes, and ladders. The town children loved to show up and play with his children and all those critters.

"Hey, fella." Nancy Borden, The Café's proprietor and cook, walked with a limp given to her by a horse. She came from the back with a plate of toasted English muffins. "I baked these fresh because I just knew you were coming in today." She leaned in towards John. But really she baked English muffins every day. She leaned closer to John's ear and whispered, "Actually this is Bishop Dyck's order." She winked at Mareika. She filled their coffee cups. "Ham and eggs?"

"No, thank you," John said.

She looked at Mareika. "None for her, then too."

"But you said we were coming for breakfast," Mareika said.

"I changed my mind." John passed Mareika some bills. "I need you to go get the seed now. Just the peas. I'll be right there." Mareika got up and hesitated to go to the door as the Bishop still loomed there.

Nancy looked between the large white man and the teenager.

"More, coffee, Bishop?" Nancy said. She cut in front of the girl, placing a hand on the Bishop's shoulder to edge him back to his table.

"No. Thank you." He reached for the line of hooks on the wall beside the door and placed his black hat upon his head. He watched John again, his mouth agape. He stepped against Nancy for the door.

She held her ground. "Your toast, Bishop . . ."

"It's fine," he said.

"Go," John said.

Mareika bustled out of The Café.

The Bishop stared out the corner of the window as the girl went, then followed her image until it disappeared. Before his lips moved again, his eyes dropped to the floor in the opposite direction of Mareika as if to physically say he had not just watched her.

Then his voice rose as if at the pulpit. "I never heard of Claas Epp Jr., or this Ibi Gietz. But he says he came from Samara through Ak-Metchet." He gave the room a look to see the impression his words had given the other members of the coffee shop. All of the men held their ears and eyes to the Bishop save for John. The Bishop's head turned John's way once again, but his gaze bent around him like river water around a boulder.

He fixed his eyes back upon the other men in The Café and cleared his throat.

John folded his hands together, and his fingers, long and lean growing out of large square palms, mingled. His eyes focused on the large airy pores of his toast, as the butter melted and pooled into them.

"Does anybody know who this man is?" Paul said.

"He was at the Jantzen's dairy yesterday or the day before," somebody else said.

John shook his head as if his body disagreed with what his tongue was about to do. "Claas Epp Jr." fell out his mouth.

Bishop Dyck lifted his head and eyes to John. In fact, all eyes drew to the man. So seldom seen around town, his name felt more phantasmal, but here he was and about to talk. The Bishop's scowl softened. He nodded as if to give John permission to continue. A smirk crept from inside his beard.

John sighed, beholding his words in case they would help the Bishop. He picked up an English muffin. "Khanate of Khiva," he said across his toast.

Bishop Dyck had been holding onto his lungs before he puffed a breath free. He probably didn't realize it, but he was now mimicking John's words. "Khanate of Khiva . . ."

"Where?" Paul Lee said. "I thought you said Ak-Metchet, Bishop?" Paul looked back and forth between John and the Bishop. "I never heard of such a place. My grandfather—"

"Hush, Paul." The Bishop shrugged after a couple of strokes of his thumb over his eyebrow, still keen on John.

John's chair squealed and cried against the hardwood floor of The Café. He stood. He chewed a mouthful of toast, his teeth crunching down six times on the left side before his tongue pushed the toast to the right for six more chews. He swallowed his bite, tipping his senses into a sip of his coffee. Then he stared right into the eyes of Bishop Dyck. He held his scrutiny until the spoons clinking inside their coffee cups stilled. He steadied his words, the necks of his audience craning, eyes darting back and forth from John to the Bishop, who returned a glower, which bathed around John.

"Claas Epp Jr. was a false prophet. And he dragged hundreds of us from Samara into Central Asia with the promise of the Rapture. Families died." John cleared his throat and nodded to Dyck.

The Bishop turned and marched out The Café.

"Sorry, Nancy, no eggs today," John said before he dropped some coins onto the table for his toast. He nudged his chin at air in a modest farewell, making sure to capture Nancy's eye—she smiled—and he pushed towards the door. He reached and held the knob. He peeked through the window at the Bishop as he moved across the park towards the Mennonite church. Then he yanked the door open.

At the cart, he tugged at the straps of the yoke around his donkey. He scratched the animal's jaw and held what was left of his

English muffin out in his flat-opened palm. The animal's big black lips fumbled and his tongue swept at the buttered toast. Yellow and brown stains streaked the large front teeth of the animal. His lips grabbed the treat. He tipped his head up high and shook his ears. John listened to the grinding of the beast's molars.

"It's only bread. Go easy now."

The donkey flashed its brown and yellow smile. He patted its rump and threw his leg up in the stirrup and climbed aboard his wagon. He had made a wish today that if he was to come into town that he would not see Bishop Dyck.

John thought about his kitchen. There had been bread. He had made it last night and left the raw dough in a cast-iron pot over the stove. The fire burned out in the night and the coals baked it. His stomach growled and gurgled with borborygmus.

"Why didn't I eat breakfast at home?" He shook his head and sent out a silent apology to the memory of his wife. *I'm sorry, Rebecca . . .*

Paul Lee blundered out of The Café, missed the second step, and stumbled over the boardwalk. He tried to catch himself, but his worn soles slipped, and he skidded leg first over the walk. His heel jammed into the ground, jarring his hip. He fell onto his backside in front of the donkey.

"Wooo! That was a ride. What happened there?" Paul said.

John stared at him and readied for the fallen man to get up and go.

"John, do you have any them there shepherding donkeys? I was thinking of getting me one. Got a bit of a problem with some coyotes. Lost three calves already this spring. There was that blizzard, right? I heard them yipping and yapping all through the night. And boy did they sound close. I should have known better. But you know how it goes. Anyway, I was thinking if I had had one of your donkeys that maybe I wouldn't be down three head. So do you have any?"

John took a deep breath waiting for Paul to actually finish. When Paul spoke, he usually repeated himself but somehow slightly differently.

"What do you think? You got any?"

John chuckled.

"What's so funny?" Paul's smiled as wide as the mountain range that boxed Black Gully's prairie plain. "Is it that Gietz guy? Because he seems pretty crazy. Do you know him? How do you know where Ak Met ... Met ... Metchy?"

"No," John said. "I have a gelding if you want one."

"Oh. Okay. That's great. Could I trade for it?"

"Yes. Yes you could trade for it." John thought of his promise to Mareika just hours ago. "I could use some help building a loft at my place."

"I can do that. I ain't discing and seeding for a couple weeks, yet. Does tomorrow sound all right?"

"Sure."

Paul moved around the front of the donkey. He pulled on the bridle in its mouth, holding John to The Café's front. He whispered up to John, "Seriously, do you know this Gietz fella?"

"No.

"But you know—"

"I don't know anything about that man, who he is or where he came from. But if he's a follower of Claas Epp Jr., then this town better watch out. My father came from Samara, and so did I. I was only a boy when we left for Nebraska, but one of my uncles, he sided with that Epp. My uncle followed him and a hundred others into Asia, expecting the Rapture."

"The Rapture?"

"The Rapture."

"Did it happen?"

John looked up into the sky and looked around at the clouds before returning his look to Paul. He shook his head. "No, Paul. The Rapture didn't happen."

Paul still looked up into the sky as well. "What?"

"We're still here, aren't we?" John said.

"Yeah," he said laughing, "yeah, we are."

"If you're smart, keep away from that Gietz. He's no good. I can guarantee that."

Paul stepped away from the cart and donkey. "When can I get that ass from you?"

"Your son in school?"

"Yeah, he's only nine or ten." He scratched his nails over his scalp. "I stopped keeping track after number six. Kids only become helpful around fourteen, right?"

John didn't move at this emaciated observation. He sat still, feeling the spin of the Earth's axis. Everything spun away from him into a blur of white. He held four seconds of silence and eye contact to Paul. His gaze stretched the boundaries of that moment into what felt like an hour to Paul. John shook his words from behind his tongue. "I'll have Mareika bring you one ... Monday or Tuesday."

"Then what do I do?"

"Just put him in your field. He'll kick the legs off any coyote that's stupid enough to come bother your cattle."

SATURDAY, JULY 30, 1892.

Eastern Reserve, Manitoba

Sauerkraut

1–2 large heads of red cabbage:
3 onions
½ pound of carrots
2 sour apples, cored
8 sprigs of dill
6 hands of salt
1 tablespoon of peppercorns

PEEL FIRST **2–3** whole leaves of cabbage of head, set aside. Shred cabbage and onions thin, grate apples and carrots. Put everything into a crock and mash with wood spoons together until enough liquid releases to cover everything. Pack everything down and tight. Use the whole cabbage leaves. Then weigh all down with a large flat river stone for 21 days. Check after 1 week. Add salt if you have to. Skim any mould that may form on the surface. After 21 days, pack into jars, topped with the brine. Add a tablespoon of vinegar to slow fermentation.

Black Gully (Creamery Road)

"**H**E CAN SAVE US!" Ibi stood so tall and full as he referred to Claas Epp Jr. and his prophecy. Herman Jantzen, the nephew of Elisabeth Epp, Claas's wife, looked to his wife Lisa. They bowed their heads with chaste imitation, then traded confusion between looks across the kitchen planks. Herman scratched behind his ear. Mrs. Jantzen kept to the kitchen table. The tangled silence strapped the kitchen screen door closed. Ibi had barely been on their stoop five minutes before his excitement and warnings of a coming apocalypse beamed into the room.

"I do not know how we can help you, Brother ..."

"It's Ibi Gietz, Brother Herman, Sister Lisa."

"We can offer you lodging."

Lisa Jantzen cleared her throat. The volume almost shut the door and shuttered the windows. Herman looked to her to suggest duty and charity.

She ignored her husband. Instead the Mrs. stropped potatoes, dragged her knife over the tubers with deep, exaggerated whips of her hand. She stopped and threw the flowing ruffle of her dress between her legs as she tucked her feet under the lacquered chair. She looked at Herman and then looked at the door. She repositioned the potato pail to hold her dress in place. Her heel tapped the floor, she cleared her throat again—more urgency to free their home of this man. Then she began humming as she took up blinding the eyes of the wintered potatoes.

"I was *put* here for you. To reunite you with Elisabeth, dear Jantzens." Ibi, his hands shook. Every muscle struggled with his heart's will to not rope his arms around the nephew of Claas Epp Jr.'s wife. Ibi's resolve, his inspiration, his confidence swelled. "Across oceans and nations and, now, here we stand in your kitchen—you, Claas and Elisabeth's nephew."

"I don't know my aunt Elisabeth. I never have."

"That is not the point. I was lost. Do you understand? I was lost. Dragged from Brother Epp's ... genius, his glow. Held away from him and *His* word. Brother Epp could see things. He saw *The End* approaching."

Herman shook his head, his body telling Ibi he now could not help him.

Ibi watched the woman, then held to the hesitation in Herman. "Do you not know the word of Claas?"

"To be honest ..." Herman's eyes softened. His gaze draped over the stranger as if he looked upon a foal with a broken leg. The hardest moments—though he'd never confess to it—were those of mercy, when he had to free any young animal from suffering. The torment of seeing suffering hurt his heart, like many Mennonites, and now this concern fell to this visitor, to Ibi's feet. He didn't make any sense of the stranger's ramblings. What he heard was *Help*.

Lisa's eyes grew bigger, her impatience tightening over her lips. Her tongue held inside a clenched jaw as her husband, again, stumbled towards helping this lost man.

"What did you say your name was?"

Lisa coughed, her focus squarely on the door. As Ibi spoke, her hand stropped harder.

"Ibi Gietz."

"Mr. Gietz. I can offer you a bed and I can put you to work."

"There isn't time. Time is ..." Ibi crushed an imaginary leaf and blew through his fist. "*His* return is near. Our Lord's only Son. Can't you feel it?" Ibi pushed open the door. "These times, have you

ever known them to be so warm and dry? Your field has no snow—
and listen." Ibi nodded at his calculated assumption. "The frogs have
dug themselves from the frost. What May has this been possible?"
Then a pleasant ripple of a million croaks filled the room and
soothed the air between the outsider and the Jantzens. It was the
true call of spring, the amphibious refrains.

"I don't know what else I can do for you," Herman said.

"Believe." Ibi reached out a hand. Herman took it anticipating a
coming farewell. Ibi cradled his elbow and swallowed his breath
after these words. "Listen. Do you not feel it?"

"No."

"You are Elisabeth Epp's nephew."

"Yes. But I told you, I do not know this woman."

Lisa's head shook through the entire conversation.

"Exactly." Ibi stepped to her. She sat stiff. Her knees shifted
away from him. But he crouched. He levelled his eyes with hers.
"You are a reasonable wife and ... Mutta?" She shook her head. "But
you are. You are the Mother. You cradle this home's heart inside
you." The strain and discomfort melted, and a grin sprouted from
the corner of her mouth. She raised an eye to meet his and raised an
eyebrow granting Ibi a moment longer to explain himself. He
dropped to a knee and rested an easy hand over her wrist. He looked
back to Herman.

"Your aunt, I have been inside her arms. She hugged and held me
as a boy on that desert plateau in Asia. She sang to me, her voice sweet
and nourishing as watermelon. But *You* have not missed out on her
tenderness ..." Ibi's hands tossed about the air and he stammered as if
juggling words, searching for the right ones to piece together his intentions. "It's impossible for us to have ever met. Where are you from?"

"Beatrice, Nebraska."

"Born and raised?"

"No. Prussia, I was born in Prussia."

"Then Beatrice, right? And now here." He rose and twirled with
an opened wingspan as if to invite the Jantzens to take in their own
home, to look at it and find the blessings that held it together.

"Beatrice and then Laid with my brother."

"Beatrice, Laid, and now Black Gully ..." Ibi drank in the beauty of the Jantzen's fine home. He savoured the sounds of spring, pointed to the roof where the cheery tracks of spring fluttered above them. "I came here through Manitoba, Khiva, and Russia. We have been fired from a barrel like birdshot, scattered. So how did *We* end up here? Tens of thousands of Mennonite families scattered across Europe, Asia, and this new world. And *We* share the blood and warmth of Elisabeth and of Claas Epp."

Lisa's brow furrowed at the unfathomable nature of this encounter. She nodded, staring off into memory. "Claas Epp. Wasn't there a Claas Epp back home?" She looked to Herman. His nod, hesitant, came like a hungry stray. "Yes, I do recall a Claas Epp in Beatrice. But he was a quiet gentleman, not much older than us. And yes. I believe he came from Turkestan. Were you in Turkestan?"

Ibi clapped and rose. "Yes! Brother and Sister, if this isn't God's work, I invite you to explain it to me."

"I don't understand," Herman said.

Ibi squatted again. He scooped up Lisa's hands. "You said Claas Epp the Third was in Beatrice?"

"Yes." She looked at Herman. He scratched his chin, his eyes focused on Ibi's hands.

"Don't you see? Claas. Claas's son. He went to Nebraska ..." His smile spread to Lisa.

Herman slid a hand under Ibi's arm, encouraged him to stand. "I don't understand," he said.

"It's the *Father* calling us all home. Like birdshot, we were scattered, but we struck the same target. Think about that ... If God did not intend for us to be here now, how do you explain it? You were born apart from Elisabeth, but *He* tried to bind you together in Nebraska, but *He* missed you in Beatrice. And now on this day, just days before we are to pass through the comet, we are together." Ibi reached into his pocket and pulled out his newspaper clipping. Herman unfolded it. He read. He past it to Lisa. She read.

"I am here to warn you—to prepare you. Claas Epp saw *The End*.

Wormwood is upon us. The waters will stop and the comet's poison will brim the shores. A holy war will rage across all lands. But only True Believers shall rise." Ibi held a hand to Lisa. She placed the clipping inside his reach. He held the paper high, pointed to the date. "May 19. Instant death."

Ibi looked about the room. He tucked away his smile and turned to leave. He pressed the screen door open. Purring and rubbing at the jamb, his calico companion dropped and exposed its belly. Ibi dipped a disrupting hand into the black watery surface of a wood cask placed below the eaves. His hand disappeared into his own reflection before it came back up. He brought his cupped hand to his lips to catch a quick drink of the winter melt. It tasted mildly of the cedar wood from steeping through the shakes above. Ibi squatted. He held the same hand to the cat. It lapped the wet grooves of his palm and between his fingers.

"Herman. We can save this entire town. Please come to my sermon. I have so much more to share of Claas's visions."

He didn't meet Ibi's eye.

Ibi put an arm around his new friend's shoulder. "It's Sunday. I'll be outside. Please come. And bring anybody you love. We need to save as many of us as possible."

"Okay."

Ibi clapped for his converts. "Brother, may I return in two days to borrow a cart or wagon?"

Herman Jantzen shrugged. Lisa nodded.

FRIDAY, MAY 13, 1910.

Creamery Road Crossing
at Ketchamoot Road

1 FIRST SAW him down from Creamery Road. From the distance, the sun behind me seemed to catch him, this singular figure. He appeared to be so much more man than what I had seen, both his form and his presence. He stood taller and his chin rode high, regal, with a look of contemplation cast over our surroundings.

I, too, looked around. I saw and heard scaups joust. The pleasant click-clack of the imperceptible pastel blue bills seemed on this day not ritualistic, but quixotic. Between glances of this stranger, my imagination captured the chickadees that hopped about the pussy willows. Oh, how I loved the kitteny grey puffs that lined the crimson branches. When I was a child, Mutta told me that that was indeed where kittens came from. The fuzzy buds fell to the ground where excited mother cats waited.

"Mutta . . . did I come from the pussy willows?" I had asked.

"No," she said before she slipped back into her usually hard silence.

I knew right away that he must be a visitor to Black Gully. As he drew closer, I could make out a very large smile. The Mennonite men, the Scandinavians, the Germans, Ukrainians, and English, none carried smiles. You may find one in The Café over coffee, but none anywhere else in Black Gully. Even from so far off, it radiated from his face. My shadow stretched towards this warmth as if he were pulling me. The long waviness I cast over the gravel looked as if it were a taffy. He also captured my curiosity, as he lugged a horse cart, no horse, no donkey. Where would such a man have arrived from? The sunshine warmed my back and neck. But he seemed to warm my chest and face.

Then as we came closer, his smile seemed for me. As if he offered it to me. It felt like a gift. This stranger, so aware of everything around us, pulling a cart, seemed to say to me with no words, "Please, take this." I felt my lips part as the corners pulled up. His smile grew even larger—if that were possible. I tossed my eyes back to the chickadees and scaups, but only for a moment, because I desired to know if his smile, indeed, was meant for me.

Oh my, my inner voice blurted. I looked around to see if he had heard me. This man, I noticed, had a nice face. I wanted those words inside my head to be bigger, prettier, but *Nice* was all I felt. It flushed through me. My heart began beating faster as we were almost right in front of one another. And it just felt *nice* to be so close to him.

He had sharp cheekbones and a squared jawline holding a small dimpled chin. He had a mature and carved handsomeness. He was both poetry and art. I felt uncomfortable looking at him, but I didn't want to look away either. My eyes darted from his face to the road and the surroundings. I felt like a hummingbird stealing the nectar from a calla lily. His eyelashes, dark and as long as a donkey's, framed the polished granite of his irises, which crackled with gilded veins.

"Do you need help?" I said. My ears pulsed with warmth. I brushed my right eyebrow down with delicate graces of my fingertips before my hand carried my bangs behind my ear. Standing so near, I couldn't look right at him anymore.

He chuckled through a slight open smile.

I love your laugh ... I felt ridiculous. I felt every moment near this stranger who hadn't even said a word simmering my age away, leaving me an immature child.

I coughed to clear away this silliness.

"Well, how do you do?" He dropped the pull of the cart. It dug into the ground and braked. He reached out a hand. I reached for it. Then as if magic blew all around us by the spring gales, a calico bundle of whiskers and a half pink and half black teeny nose popped out of his jacket sleeve. I pulled my hand away, then gave it back to the cat. I scratched his soft chin.

"Oh, my goodness, where did she come from?"

The stranger lifted his friend to his face. Nose to nose, the animal offered its cheek. He gave his friend a nuzzle. "That's Claas."

"Calicos are girls."

"Not this little fellow. Claas is a boy, honest and true." He offered his sleeve back to me.

The cat crawled upon my breast. It had the softest, most imperceptible purr, a kind of secret it shared with only those it trusted. We rubbed chins.

"By the by, I'm Ibi Gietz." He offered me his hand. It was so soft.

I smiled. "Would you like help?"

"Sister, my lower back burns. But if I lack the strength in these legs and these shoulders to continue forth to share my message, this world would be doomed. For I ..." Ibi searched to borrow Claas's tongue. "I have not suffered in the ways that our Lord has, and until I have, I must remain on this path. But that doesn't mean I can't keep company with a beautiful companion."

I scoured his body with my eyes. Long and lean, he looked strong under his oversized jacket and pants, chiselled like his face. He let go of his grip and took his hand back. I blushed when instantly I longed to take his hand again. I wanted to raise it to my cheek, show him the heat pulsing inside me. I wanted to say, "You did this." I didn't know what he would do with my confession. But I could feel the heat radiate down my chest, ripple through my stomach, before it rolled upon the shore of my other parts. I wanted to run home, but not before I hugged him, let him pull me inside his jacket as if I were his kitten.

His body folded in half at the hip, the weight of his shoulders fell towards his ankles with a stretch. He teased the cart's shaft tips before he dropped them and rested his elbows upon his knees.

He whispered through cupped palms up to the cat. "Claas ..." He looked to the road ahead, measuring the distance still ahead. "What do you think? Should we take this elegant lady's offer?"

Elegant ... Beautiful ... I could not remember ever experiencing those words. But off his lips it felt like he had just wrapped around me the splendour and wonder of this spring day—the cheery chirps of songbirds, the easy croaks of frogs, the warmth of sunshine—and dressed me up.

We never had mirrors inside our home. I could find a glimpse of myself off a darkened windowpane. I discovered the change. The little girl had disappeared inside the shadow of maturity, swallowed by the swell and curve of my chest, my hip. My vest no longer steadied my breast when I ran. I held an arm under them when in the company of other girls and boys. Their stares searching me, judging me. "It was your fault," Jonah had said. But in this moment under that word, *Elegant*, where I met this man pulling an animal cart all by himself down a dirt road, I had forgotten my shame. Even the allure of Jonah Wiebe had only been fumbling. And it ended in shame and pain and blood.

The blood. I hid my face by pulling the cat to my cheek.

"No," Ibi Gietz said.

I peeked up at him. His gaze focused on his cat upon my chest. He shook a thought away from words. He stood turgid.

"I will tell what. I should not discourage you from my company." He smiled, but it felt bigger than that. He was giving me his smile again. His whole face drew me from behind that calico. His chin wrinkled, his eyes sparkled, and his eyebrows opened. *Ibi Gietz*, my imagination whispered his name. I smiled. Then he returned his eyes to the ground.

I followed them to the space between us upon the road.

"I have donkeys."

Gietz laughed. "Oh. You mean for the cart."

"Yes. I live up the road. I could run home and bring you one."

I never had the words to describe how I felt then. I stood there, and I did indeed feel elegant, but my words dropped like apples to the ground to rot. This handsome stranger, pulling a cart alone—such an introduction was unique. And I craved to help him. I didn't want to leave his side. I wanted to know more. Where did he come from? What brought him here? I kept dropping words into sentences.

"I do have donkeys. My father raises them. They pull cart and shepherd cattle."

"I must do this alone."

"My name is Mareika Doerksen, and I live up the road. Behind to the Jantzen's quarter. Did you borrow that cart from the Jantzens? It looks like a Jantzen cart."

"Great eye." He winked.

Ibi rose, the shaft tips in each hand, and threw his shoulders forward over his feet. The cart rocked. He followed the rolling momentum and thrust his shoulders forward again. The cart rolled onward. And he gave me his smile once again. My feet moved with him. The calico jumped free. It scuttled after his feet, pawing at a length of red yarn pinned to the hem of his pant leg.

"Please follow," he said, staring forward. "I'm offering salvation." His tone dropped with austerity.

"What?" I wrapped my arms under my breast. I cradled my stomach ache.

"I am here to offer you and the people of Black Gully salvation. Are you Mennonite?"

"Yes. No. It's ..." My hands searched their way about the top of my dress line, my fingertips kneading the ache still plaguing my other parts. I didn't know what I was. Was I allowed to call myself Mennonite? Mutta had. Foda denounced the Bible, he called us atheists, and he minded to let me know the *A* was not to be capitalized.

"Doerksen, that sounds Mennonite to me, Sister. What would make you say no?"

"Foda ..." My body shuddered with pain and I felt blood leak out from inside me. I wondered if it had been guilt. Foda or Mutta's faith. "He doesn't believe." I wanted my tongue to stop working. I scooped up the cat and buried my face into its soft tummy.

"Have you noticed the mounting despair in our world: the droughts, the famine, the disease, the war? Everywhere you look are the signs: the Russians fighting with themselves and the Japanese, the plague in India and typhoid in America—did you know there is this woman who has it but does not get sick? She's giving it to everybody she knows. But why isn't she sick? It is a sign. Volcanoes and earthquakes are destroying us. And look around you. Where is the snow? Our ground is cracked with thirst. And soon the comet will poison our skies, then the rivers and oceans. We are living in it—the End of Days. Do you sense it coming?"

The calico leapt from me. It bound upon the cart's mounting step before retreating into the back seat. I clenched my coat closed around my stomach. I looked up away from the clammy wads of cloth stuffed inside my panty. I returned a look towards home.

I heard the cart's shaft tips dig and scrape into the gravel road.

"You feel it in your stomach," Ibi said. "It pours out from inside."

"Who told you?"

"I can see it. It was Brother Claas Epp Jr. who told me. And I can see you are in pain and you are confused."

"Yes."

He nodded. Concern washed over him. He reached out to me. I let his easy touch take my face. His eyes glowed with care. My hands rose to his wrists.

"I feel like I'm dying." The words jumped out of me.

He nodded. His lips trembled. Then he said what I most feared. "We all are." He wrapped me inside his arms. I held all my sadness and fear with all my might. It wrung tears, warm, through my eyes. I couldn't remember the last time Foda had hugged me. Maybe a single arm over my shoulder at Mutta's grave with the slightest of squeezes. From that day, we walked separate into day after day, night after night into preparation. Meals, seasons, seeding, castrations, our time together was apart. After a supper only silence, reading, journaling, and then bed. Oh, how welcome I felt so close to this man, this stranger. My breath stitched the words, Thank you, with a whimper over his chest.

"Brother Claas Epp—my mentor and our saviour—he is in Ak-Metchet awaiting *His* return, and God revealed to him of the Second Coming. And I can prepare you." Ibi held me from him. His eyes held firm to my own. "In the coming days *He* is coming back for us, our Lord and Saviour. On Thursday morning I will be ready. Will you?"

I shook my head. "Mutta died." I looked into the ditch, wishing I could have sucked those words back into my mouth.

His grip intensified about my shoulders. He peered into me. His mouth opened, but he seemed to lose his words somewhere between his lips and my blue eyes. My thin lips parted. His gaze went to the tip of my tongue quivering against my teeth. His palm found my cheek.

"Your skin is smooth like the cream at the top of the milk can. When I was younger, my siblings and I would fight over it. I liked spreading it over bread dried above a fire with berry preserve on top. Your lips look like strawberries growing under the edge of a pea field back home in Hoffnungsfeld—a real red."

His lovely words took all the pain and fear away, but I couldn't look at his beautiful face any longer. It almost burnt my eyes. *Who was this man?* I wanted to ask him to hug me again.

"I can help you, Mareika Doerksen. Come to my service in two days. I will teach you what I have learned. I will take you home to the Kingdom of God."

"I have to go." I pulled myself from this man, from under the reassurance that radiated from both hands that rested upon my shoulders. His arms fell freely. But my steps felt muddied. Flashes of Mutta crackled between my blinks. I couldn't stop. Her stern eye, there on Creamery Road. I heard the ravens; I heard the crows. Then the ache shuttered my body. I grabbed my stomach.

"Mareika—" He reached out for me. An honorific calm, a gentleness to his reach stretched out to me.

"No." I pulled my feet farther from him. But he stepped to me. "I know your pain."

"I can't."

"Come on Sunday. All will be revealed through *His* glory"

I shook my head. "I have to go."

"I promise." His easy smile melted the headiness weighing down my feet. It became easier to step back towards him than home. I turned back and could not see Mutta's scorn. And I believed him.

He stepped away and bowed his head. His smile grew. "Come to the square Sunday. I will show you. I will show everybody. I am staying on the lake nearest to town. Before you decide, please come to me there. Just come. He is upon us and the Gates will open. Do you want to cross into *His* Kingdom?"

"Father doesn't go to service . . ."

"But I can help you. All you have to do is listen. Just come and listen. If I cannot convince you there . . ."

I gagged at the pain radiating over my pelvis. "Father doesn't follow the church. He's only a farmer," I said, repeating the words Foda gave when his neighbours tried to persuade him to return. "We do not practise such personifications." I felt afraid confessing this to him.

He frowned. "I don't understand."

Inside our home Foda built shelves around every wall, even framing in under the stairs. And he filled them with books. He took his wagon everywhere, travelling days to find books. He brought them home for us. He found encyclopaedias, dictionaries, thesauruses, and atlases. He found story books, picture books, adventure books. For entire summers after the firewood had been split and stacked, as we waited for the fields and gardens to mature, I sat alone with these books. He called them our salvation.

"This is the entire world," he had told me. "It fits inside our home. That's the true miracle." I sat with them, rearranged them on the shelves. This summer he promised to take me. We would travel all the way to the ocean searching out new books, new experiences. Books were the true documentation of a real world. And every so many nights, he would take a book down and read it. Every so many nights, I would take a book down and read it. One night he came to me. He shook me from my sleep.

"I need you to read this." He handed me a dark leather book, opening it over my lap. "Read the title." He pointed over the words and whispered along with me, *"Heart of Darkness*. Do you promise to read this?" I wanted to tell him that he was scaring me, but I only nodded. The next morning I put the book on a full shelf, trading it for an atlas. I put the book in backwards so the spine could not be seen. I didn't just fear that book but how it had charged Foda. He had quit the church but found a new religion. His zeal matched Mutta's intense readings of her Bible before she passed. He wanted me to study the world through the eyes of others. He never wanted me to leave the school like the other girls my age, to disappear inside homes and gardens. They were all done and taking care of their homes. Some of the girls only a couple of years older were getting married. But in our home, Foda baked bread. I plowed fields.

He told me: "Become a doctor, a nurse, a teacher, or a lawyer." He showed me newspapers with a woman who became a lawyer in Toronto and another studying medicine in Montreal. And closer to us were women demanding to vote and to join the legislature. There were books of animal anatomy and grammar books too. He told me to leave Black Gully. I began to feel as if I should hate this place. That I had to run away. I no longer feared being alone. Foda prepared me. And I prepared to leave until Jonah Wiebe's hands had stirred me. I ignored the taunting and whispers the other children threw at me. *She doesn't believe.* I followed the pull and urgency of my body. I stored away all Mutta had taught me and had decided Foda was right. All around us was chaos, birds and animals living without a god, and us. "Only animals ourselves." He showed me the works of Darwin and Franz Boas, heartbreaking stories about an Eskimo boy, Minik, alone in New York City after his foda and uncles died from consumption. But lingering somewhere inside I found doubts. How could Mutta be so staunch, determined, convinced?

So I followed the desires that plagued me. There was no god to judge me. If there were, why did it feel so good? But it opened me up, it split me apart. And now, slowly and painfully I moved around dying. For days I had been afraid and lost and ashamed.

And now . . . this man, Ibi Gietz . . .

It felt impossible to run home. And easier to follow his beautiful calm.

"How?" I said. His warm eyes and pretty skin shimmered with warmth and a glory I could not explain. Such ease he offered to me just by hearing me. Believing me. I looked into his deep olive complexion and wanted to touch it. The silence between us felt comfortable. He didn't talk through it. He waited. He was listening even without my words. His eyes—I had been wrong—were not granite, but they were not green or blue or brown. They looked like a quilt, a carefully stitched mosaic with gilded thread his mutta had fashioned. His full bottom lip, lush like a red plum, his thin, smart upper lip, whispered to me to listen. I didn't know what this encounter meant. But I knew I needed to hear more. I believed that he could explain it. Maybe it was the straightness of its line, the definitive edges that separate his skin, the colour of polished and waxed chestnut wood, from the deep pink of his lips. I nodded before he could persuade me further.

"Yes . . ."

He clapped his hands and offered to me another one of his big, beautiful smiles. "Tomorrow, Sunday, and beyond, we will be prepared. Together. I promise. I will share everything with you. We can calm all your fears. And we shall save you, Mareika Doerksen."

I held the cramps. A sigh so heavy fell free from me. The hammering thumps dulled and my heart rested. I wanted to cry. He stepped to me and again wrapped his arms around me. I began to remember how to hug. I wrapped my arms around his waist and allowed myself to cry when the stern look of Mutta behind my eyes inside my mind softened. And I could hear her humming a hymn.

He whispered, "Now go along home. We will continue tomorrow."

"At Black Gully Lake?"

He nodded.

I freed myself from his gravity. The striking swiftness as I ran rang up my shins and shook my other parts. I felt more of my life leak from inside me, and for the first time in years, since before Mutta's death, I started a prayer, but could not finish it. *Our Father who art in heaven. How will be ... thy name. Our Kingdom come, they will be done ...*

Eastern Reserve, Manitoba

"WHAT ARE YOU doing with that girl?" Martin Doerksen asked. A large, thick tree of a man, he shoved the door to the church office wide open. He set his hat upon a bookshelf to free up his hands.

The Bishop pushed Rebecca Klassen an arm's length from him, yet clutched her shoulder. "Who are you?" He straightened and buttoned his pants, tucked in his shirt. He reached and flipped the back of her dress down. "What are you doing in my church?"

"What. Were. You. Doing?" Martin said. "I won't repeat myself again."

The Bishop ignored Martin's voice, choosing to peer over his shoulder as the stranger's question echoed inside the empty church off the fir pews, the wooden pulpit. The uneasy hesitation, the loss of words in the man and the shame of eyes cast down upon him in the act of copulation. He squeezed Rebecca's shoulder harder. His blame piercing her flesh, manipulating her bones. He craned his neck for another examination of the church. It remained empty.

Rebecca freed her hands from the Bishop's desk. Her skin screamed over the polished wood. It left humid shadows the hot summer air stole. With her sweaty palms she pushed her dress down. Her bulging stare searched Martin's face. Did his gaze splash her with fault? He nodded approval as she corrected and fussed with her attire. She finally exhaled. She wiped at her nose. Then she stepped out from under the Bishop's clutch. She stepped away again. She felt the steps—heavy with chains—lighten under this strange man's presence.

She started to believe that maybe she was dead. She'd spent every day with the Bishop since wishing the Good Lord to take her away. This must be death, an empty church, a stranger with benevolence inside eyes as blue as the Manitoban skies. How she saw everyday items as implements to a deliverance, a damnable freedom. Rope, razors, knives and saws, streams, watering holes, and even broken crockery or glass.

Bishop Dyck took her wrist. Martin stepped to the Bishop. His eyes corralled Rebecca's tormentor into the corner, so Rebecca ripped her wrist from him.

This stranger now stood completely inside the office. His form filled the room like he could wear it. He combed his hand through his salt and pepper hair, then, with a swipe of that calm hand, he knelt and picked up Rebecca's bonnet.

Rebecca took the hat from Martin. She bowed her eyes to him.

"I came here for the debts owed to the government for these lands. I am Martin Doerksen. And I represent the Mennonite Conference. Now I said I'm not going to ask you again." Martin stepped between the two.

The Bishop turned his back to the stranger. He fussed more with his pants. He picked up his jacket from the desk, threw it on, and buttoned it from waist to collar.

"This child is my charge. She has been left in my company by her parents. And at their request, I am to edify her in the ways of a proper bride."

Martin turned to face Rebecca. "Are you getting married?" he asked.

She couldn't restrain that word. It was the no she held inside her primal brain from the moment she had started her education. It chittered at the base of her skull. And now, it had swelled. Bigger than herself. And exploded into the room. "No!"

Martin caught that short sentence but heard only its intended pronunciation: "Help!"

"No, she is not promised," the Bishop said, "but she got into some trouble some weeks back, didn't you?"

Rebecca lowered her eyes from the strange man. She took to examining his coat pocket. She imagined she fit, able to leave the inside of that room, stowed away.

"I didn't ask you. I am asking the girl." Martin's voice softened. "Young lady, are you to be married?"

Rebecca shook her head.

"Sir, I am the Bishop."

"It would appear to me that you were not conducting yourself in such a manner." Martin reached his hand to Rebecca. His eye caught pain and fear, not shame. He followed the tracks of her suffering down her fresh cheek and saw relief soften her stance.

Rebecca's instinct was to sabotage the Bishop's dominion, so she reached for Martin. Her eyes glistened with hope washing away her fear. Her face said, Please . . . Her hand shot back to her breast with a step forward from Bishop Dyck. Her chin fell.

Martin stepped to her, his arm like a warm shawl. And his stand broke Dyck's hold.

"Please, go home, dear. The Bishop and I have a matter to discuss."

Rebecca ran from the back room of the church. She never looked back. The door flung open with such ferocity, it could have killed John who sat upon the landing, where the sweep of the lock stile swatted the billow of his shirt. The young man watched her as she fled.

∾◌

The sun, intense as though burning a hole through the soft blue cloudless sky, hung high over the prairie. Under the shade of the chokecherry and pear trees of Rebecca's Oma's gardens and orchard, John sat between the rows of watermelons. He folded his legs neatly, pressing the seams flat with a sweaty palm. His black jacket and vest lay suspended over the milk-washed picket fence. Even though he was draped under the orchard's shadows, pools of sweat collected at the small of his back, under his arms, and about his chest. Rebecca sat on the porch under the furious sun. She sent her gaze away from John down Main Street towards Joseph Reimer's store. Once a month, dried goods and textiles showed up on wagons. How she imagined crawling into the back of one and riding away. But this was a Saturday. The wagons weren't expected until the first Wednesday. She was four days too late. She grew angry at herself for not thinking of this earlier, instead bearing the Bishop's abuse, wearing it heavy and avoiding the openness of the community.

She and Sarah had not just stopped seeing one another, but they had stopped looking at one another. Rebecca couldn't even remember what her shoes looked like. She wondered if anybody else knew. She wondered if her future husband knew. She didn't want to look at him. This Martin Doerksen had saved her from the Bishop; now she had been negotiated free, but to that stranger's son. She felt the slavery would continue under him. She had merely been traded to a stranger. She looked at the young man. He stuttered with his movements, like his body couldn't be sure if it should be moving. His narrow shoulders rolled forward, which kept his face directed to the ground. He guarded himself, did not stand tall. He hid in plain view. He could have been a part of the shadows cast over the watermelons.

John held some of the young watermelon leaves, rubbing them to feel their velvet against the pads of his fingers. He cast his eyes onto Rebecca's shoes. He could see they were washed, woven grain stock. His mother made similar shoes out of the swathed stock, crocheting them into a summer slipper. They were flaxen. He followed the crochet up to her ankles. The flow of her soft skin disappeared just below her calf. He lifted his eye to her neck, which, too, held an elegant delicacy. She swallowed. He swallowed. Her head turned back towards his. He looked down to his hands and rubbed at the velvety patch of fuzz disappearing from the crown of his head. He coughed. A cat's fluffy orange tail poked above the greens between the rows, twisting and turning. He gripped a larger melon, thumped it with his thumb.

"I think they'll be ready in a week, maybe ten days."

"What?" Rebecca stared not at him but towards him.

He thumped the melon again. "These watermelons. They're almost ripe."

"Oh." She bit at her wicks.

"They're quite big," he said.

"The Penners' watermelons are bigger." Her stare appeared allergic to the young man.

"But these are much bigger than the ones we grew in Russia. Were you born in Russia?"

"Here." Rebecca threw her thumb over her shoulder to the house.

"I remember the melons when I was younger were small and had a creamy yellowish inside. Mutta made them into syrup for baking and in summer let us drizzle it over *rollkuchen*. Do you like *rollkuchen* and watermelon?"

Her face held no emotions. Her mouth could have been carved into that small straight line. After looking over the garden, she nodded.

"I wish these watermelons were ready, then we could have *rollkuchen* and watermelon for our ..." John shot a look away from Rebecca. He stared down the entire community. His eyes bounced off every building, not taking any of them in. He looked back at his feet. Then he looked to her feet. "The wedding. Watermelon would be nice. Do you like watermelon?"

"You asked me that already."

A thump followed by a dragging rumbled at the inner edges of the home. Rebecca stood and went to the screen door. John, too, stood, wiping his hand against the seat of his pants. A hunched old woman appeared. Rebecca held the door, and the old woman came only to the opening. She held her eyes to two halves of a broken plate in each of her hands.

"It has appeared as though I have broken this plate." She held them to Rebecca.

With the back of her hands she wiped at her eyes and let the old woman pass the parts of the broken dish to her.

"It's a shame. They used to belong to my grandmother."

Rebecca fell into the old woman. The sunlight threw their shadows beyond the threshold into the home. They stood with arms that weaved them together into a single moment.

"She packed them in wooden crates filled with heated butter before she made the trek from Prussia."

John approached the porch. He let his middle finger poke into a chink in the wood siding. He looked at the dirt under his thumbnail as he stroked the silvered wood grain. "If you put the pieces back together and bound them with twine you could boil them together in a pot of sweet milk."

The women stayed attached, Oma's head over Rebecca's heart.

John said: "You'd only have to boil it for two or three hours."

"I know how to mend glassware ..." The old woman's voice pierced John. She stared. Her lower eyelids brown and spongy gave the reddened corners of her gaze a spark, a flare. She held her eyes to his as if waiting for John to answer a question he didn't hear.

"You have a good garden," he said.

"What's your name?" she said.

"John. John Doerksen. John Doerksen is my name."

"She knows how to mend glassware, John." Rebecca and her grandmother separate. Rebecca sniffled and used the edge of her thumb to push a tear into the hairs behind her temple. The old woman handed her a black pouch into which Rebecca placed the two shards.

"I just thought ..." John said.

"I know how to mend glassware." She handed the pouch to John. He looped it around his belt. "I'm sorry, *Frau* ..."

"Klippenstein." She rubbed Rebecca between her shoulder blades. "I'm sorry I cannot attend your wedding. Now you must be off." She grabbed John's thumb and tugged his ear to her lips. Her breath felt like a gale foretelling of a thunderstorm both warm and cold, humid and dry. "Promise to take care of her." Her voice crackled. "She is a good girl, my favourite. Please, take care of her."

John nodded.

"Now go. We don't want to get in any trouble."

❧

Inside Rebecca Klassen's family home, John stepped off the porch to the small sitting room. The lace window coverings wore the grace of time and care, filtering only the gilded streams of sunlight that passed through it. The hardwood planks, heavy with years of oil, smouldered with the afternoon glow because of a fresh vinegar wash. The room, modest, felt empty—like most sitting rooms—with only a broad pine daybed, milk-white with curved armrests, placed in the middle of the room and a waxed birch armoire placed off the corner of the outside wall and one of the neighbouring bedrooms. John touched that wall and wondered if the room on the other side had been hers, Rebecca's.

"Rebecca." He said her name with his eyes closed, spelling it, storing his future wife's name.

Rebecca and her foda moved inside from the kitchen. Rebecca kept her head down and sat.

"Rebecca," he said. The name fluttered off his tongue. He let himself stare at her for longer than a moment. His gaze erased her father, Everett Klassen, and removed the furniture, but kept the haloed radiance bathing the young woman. Her hair, now braided and swirled into a bun, was hidden under a black crocheted hairnet.

"Here—" Everett said. His small hand hid an enormous strength that shocked John when it grasped his wrist. John sat next to Rebecca. She shifted from him, all the way to the armrest. John sighed. His head fell, and feeling her eyes away from him, and the inches she moved, wrung the optimism from body. His stomach stung.

"Rebecca . . ." Her name barely caught his breath.

Anna Klassen, Rebecca's mutta, burst into the room. She made for the armoire and took out a patchwork quilt. She moved behind John and Rebecca, giving them both a tap on the shoulder. They leaned. She draped the quilt, a stunning sunshine and shadow pattern of various brown squares, over the back of the day bed. Then she exited as quickly as she came for the kitchen. She returned a moment later with the Bishop.

Rebecca sat up, then edged closer to John. She turned her knees from the Bishop. They nudged into John. John looked at the man, who seemed a briar of salt and pepper beard. He barely came into the sitting room almost tethered to the kitchen.

"Everett ..." Anna didn't look up. She never made any eye contact with Rebecca or John. She raised her gaze once to nod at the Bishop before she took her husband into the kitchen. The kitchen murmured with the clink of dishwashing.

"It is God's will, that marriage—taken with the highest of respects—should be regarded as a holy state and wholly monogamous and eternal," Bishop Dyck said. His sermon pushed Rebecca closer to John, until they sat side by side.

She looked at John, which felt like the first time, when she said, "I will." Her marital promise pried at John; it pleaded with him. Her two words could have been a speech. Her fear of this place, of this man, of her world clutched at him and begged him to not hurt her. John nodded, a slight tip of his chin, while he cradled her stare inside his. John placed his hand upon her knee, without a squeeze, just the weight of his hand, a shield, he promised to her. Her eyes watered.

"I will ..." John, his words and his promise, gave Rebecca relief, as if those two words continued onward, *Promise to be careful with your heart ...*

The Bishop spoke very little and marched out as soon as he finished the service.

Martin Doerksen, having stood outside, held the door for him and marched into the Klassen home as if it were his own.

"John. Rebecca. We should be moving along soon," he said.

Rebecca stood to John like a corner, he the other corner, forming

90 degrees. They both returned their eyes to their feet. John removed a blue leather-bound book that was tucked under his vest and belt at the small of his back. He wiped the pebbles of sweat from the cover. He cleared his throat. He passed her the book.

"I have a Bible," she said.

"It's not a Bible." His hands took the top corners, and he folded the hardcover open. They flicked at the first three blank pages. "You can write your name on those." On the fourth page was some writing. The blank pages fell back over the writing. "I thought you could use it like a journal. Do you already have one?"

"No."

"You can put anything in it you want. Your thoughts, keep track of the days, the weather. My mutta puts recipes and stuff in hers. I put the first entry in it for you."

Rebecca opened the book to the beginning.

"No. I put it at the back." She flipped to the last page.

Mix 1 ounce of beef gelatin with 2 tablespoons of cold water.
Boil ½ cup of milk. Cool. And skim the fat from the top. Boil
the milk again and let cool skimming the fat from the
top. Take about 3 tablespoons of the skimmed milk and
boil again.
Stir the dissolved gelatin into the hot milk and mix.
Use the liquid to mend dishes or glassware.

"It's a recipe for glue." John pointed at his writing. Small and tidy. "Then you can fix your plate."

"Thank you, John Doerksen." His name almost sounded like a question. She closed the book, traced her hands over its leather. She squeezed the spine and hugged the book to her chest before she raised her eyes to him. "Thank you."

"There's more ..." John said. He lifted his hand and held it out to Rebecca. She hesitated. His open palm seemed to ask her permission. He didn't just grab the book from her. He held it in the empty space between, a before and after. He didn't hesitate, when Rebecca refused, and retracted his hand. "It's all right. I went back to your oma. She put a clipping inside and wrote you some recipes. I didn't read them. This is yours. Just yours."

"Thank you."

"You are welcome."

"Let's go," Martin said, marching out the house.

Tuesday, August 2, 1892.

Winnipeg, Manitoba

H<small>E IS</small> L<small>EVI</small>. He is Levi to me. In name I am Mrs. John Doerksen but in heart Dinah. More my brother and defender of name than a husband. I want to give my life back—to be a good wife to this man—but I am not well. I am sick and have always been. This sickness makes me see him as he should not be seen. His large nose may not be bigger than the next man's, but it does not belong on the face that I should hold in my hands. I long to hold a face of small, slight features. Soft should be the lips. And pink. The color of the wild rose. White and pure the skin. Oh, John, you are Levi. Your skin is rough and cold. Your eyes are my brother's. Your hair cannot stand against the wind, slowly leaving you in such short time. But with my mother's only advice I must convince myself of my duty. I am a slave girl given to your desires. I know this harsh life. It is my charge. And I will forgive you. I will forgive you. You are the man who should never raise a hand to me. I see this in you. You can hardly look at me. You are afraid. I hope not of me. But you are gentle. I write only a page away from the glue recipe you filled upon the last naked page of this journal I now write. I know you shall not raise a hand to me as Foda, brothers, or Bishop Dyck. Bishop Dyck. My hand trembles with his name, John. Your name does not fall from my tongue the way Bishop Dyck's does. His name resides under my skin, burrowed deep. His name is a sickness. My hairs stand as the worms of his name burrow through me. His voice echoes inside the tracks left behind. "Repent, confess and receive forgiveness." He whispered over me that he could change my ways, cure my sickness. But what of his confessions? He does not have my forgiveness. We mustn't give it. Mutta told me to live for the urges of my husband, to tend to your desire or lose you. And after you spent yourself inside me this first night, you lowered your head and apologized. I saw no violence, not him, not inside you. But you were a different creature. Your only words, *Sorry*. Before me, your head lower than your shoulders, you pulled those suspenders over your naked shoulders, pulled on boots and returned to the outdoors. You said *Sorry* again. My only wish that you had looked at me. You never looked at me.

Wapos County

THE DARKENING SKIES at gloaming ate all the light inside the Doerksen homestead. Through the night John wanted no calving. But winds in from the eastern prairies promised storms. They shook the roof, howled down the stovepipe, and kept the moon clear of clouds for now.

John's eyes shut only long enough for him to dream of tripping upon his face. His body jerked and sprawled under his sheets. He grasped out to brace himself to see only ceiling. He stared confused into the darkness up at the slatted roof. The nails holding the home together creaked against the strain of the winds. John sat up and looked out the window. The first handful of the brightest stars began to pierce the sky, as the edges of clouds burned red before blacking out. He heard the coyotes yip. Their growls and nips sailed as a kite may against the gales and loomed over the home.

John answered their calls. He got up, dressed. He scouted his quarter for cow-calves. The thunder of hooves barreled down upon him. He didn't turn to greet a gelding. Its heaviness nudged past his shoulder. It was the elder, Marty. John held out an oat bag strung to his back. Marty sniffed, snorted at John's ear. He ignored the oats until he had the recognizable scent. Then he burrowed his nose into the oats. His body jostled, and oats crunched and ground under his sentinel's bite. John grabbed an ear and scratched the donkey.

John stopped, keen to the radiant passing of the day as it was snuffed out against the horizon. Buster and Marcus, the twins, pushed their way to the oats. Marty towered over the others. John did not know what made him grow so large, several hands taller. He studded him, allowed him to keep his sex. John moved about those donkeys as if he were a part of the air. He held the feedbag of oats for a moment or two to each before he turned them out into the night of the remaining winter.

"Keep us well," he said with a whack on Marty's hindquarters. He turned his ear away from the wind. He heard no cows. He looked ahead to the *semlin* and followed the push of winter inside his old home, now their root cellar.

John pushed the *semlin* door with his shoulder, an attempt to straighten its bow. The latch clicked. He took a deep breath. The lingering essence of ash inside the potbelly and sod upon the roof teased a contentment he rarely acknowledged. This contentment anchored him here below the frost. He moved to an east window. It shimmered the muted silver-blue of a moon that had crawled inside over his surroundings. He slid it open. Wind whistled until he had it open enough to reach his hand out to break an icicle hanging from the eaves. He dropped it outside.

"She should sleep." He nodded to himself, resolving to tend to tonight's calving by himself and not bother Mareika. He put his ear to the darkness for the call of cow or calf. The yip of coyotes swirled inside the arctic gales, which shuttered the door under the sod roof and timber walls. They sounded closer than most nights. The swollen other parts of the remaining cows clouding the air with ripe torment, seemed to be whetting the coyotes' anticipation.

John paced the *semlin*. "Wait for morning," he said to the cow-calves. Then he spoke to the blizzard. "Wait for morning."

He moved to a wall of preserves. Inside a Jewel Jar, one for jams, he took out a match, struck it, and lit the hurricane lantern on the old dinette. The amber light reflected off the vinegar brine of carrots, beans, cucumbers, watermelon rind. It reflected the lantern light all about the temporary home he fashioned for his new wife when he first arrived to break these prairie lands. The room, washed in a muted glow, swallowed John. If Mareika had wandered inside, she would not have seen the man. He reached to the middle of the highest shelf and parted several rows of preserves to draw down a jar.

Inside a rattle and clink of metal, not the slosh of liquid. He sat the jar on the old rough-sawn dinette. Then he grabbed three corked bottles. With the first cork popped, he did not drink, but gulped, as if thirsty for days. His body reminded itself what it felt like to be quenched. He took up the jar with the clinking rattle. He stared inside. John looked at a pocket watch. It had once been the marriage gift bought by Rebecca and given to him, ordered from a jeweller in Toronto and brought to Black Gully. When Rebecca had died, John put it away, unconcerned about the time ever since. If he woke with darkness, he waited for sunlight. He ignored the calendar when it said winter or spring because true winter brought snow and ice, and spring meant the ground had thawed. But only the air filled with the rippled calls of countless frogs that have dug themselves free would tell you that. Then the ground was ready to be broken and seeded.

He looked to the watch not for the time but for its past. It got here all the way from the T. Eaton Co. Limited at 190 Yonge Street. The building was enormous. Its entire entrance was glass from the top of the first floor to the sidewalk, and high above—nearly four stories—was a flag waving that read The Eaton's Company.

John found Toronto intimidating. He felt comfortable atop a horse, donkey, or camel. But he had followed his father, Martin, on behalf of the Chortitzer Mennonite Conference, to meet with H.H. Smith Esq., Commissioner of Dominion Lands, for a ceremony to celebrate the fact that the Manitoba Mennonites had successfully fulfilled their commitments and honoured all government loans and interest. But most pressing, the Mennonites, with the skilled negotiating of Martin Doerksen, had wanted the Government of Canada to help them stop the private sale of Reserve land by Mennonites to other nationalities. They, too, wanted more land, more opportunities.

The Canadians dreamt of a union crossing from Manitoba to Victoria and knew these industrious people could break the rolling brush across the prairies as they had on the steppes of Russia. Very shortly after successful negotiations, John would leave for land in Alberta because his foda had gotten some land clear of the Mennonite Conference, land he intended John to break and farm in under three years.

Martin had always impressed upon his son that owning land was the richest a person could be. But now time became the motivator. He pressed John with the importance of the next three years in which they had only to pay the paltry sum of $10 per quarter. He commanded John to start breaking his quarter before he could move onto breaking his own farm.

John arrived with Rebecca and got to work, her beside him toiling. Though privately proud of his farm, he felt Martin had been wrong about time. It wasn't a pragmatic measure. As he never felt richer than the days and nights he spent with wife and later baby Mareika in his arms, his voice pitched and reading adventures to her from pages of books he collected where he could find them. Or the moments she sat as a toddler and young girl in his lap. In those moments together, Mareika and John sat quiet and dipped toast into soft fried egg yolks.

That was how John experienced time. He shared it. It wrapped around him and those he loved. Yes, he had responsibilities. Yes, he had deadlines. And with Martin gone, with the Colonialist Brethren searching for better deals south of California, he not only had his quarter, but his foda's to slash, break, and farm with no resources, no income, and no community. The man, now free of any colony, could be his own man. And he could have a family.

He handled the watch. His thumb ran over the hinge, graced the engraving. It took him away from the *semlin*, from his farm.

He remembered the trolley dropped Rebecca and him off at the corner. And inside they went with money she had smuggled away, all coins, from odd jobs with neighbours and family friends. She had picked out what the salesman had called a "young man's watch, made of coin silver, stiffened." It was plain, smooth across both faces and around its circumference. All the other watches were carved gold, elaborate with cranes, shields, or foliage.

"Showy," Rebecca said.

It only cost $7.50, and as she counted out the coins, the salesman pointed out that she did have enough for a one-dollar engraving. She had nodded and told him, "John. J-O-H-N." And at his second guess, she reassured him that "Yes, only John, J-O-H-N" would do.

John held the watch like a book, his thumbs coming to the hinge and skating over the watch's glass and over his name. He folded the timepiece closed. He dropped it down the face of his coveralls. The weight tugged at his lapel. He closed his coat one button shy of his chin. He looked out towards the east. Midnight glazed the hill silver above the brush, but below, across the crusted snow, everything looked blue, throwing purple and black shadows. John longed for the gilded fields of summer. He stared at the ground in front of him and followed his blue shadow over the mounds, drifts, and chips of snow. Every flake seemed to have hardened into ice. The wind-whipped south peaks of the drifts sparkled with a shattered mother-of-pearl.

He envisioned his wife belonging there, Toronto. In the city, he heard women could live and thrive on their own. She could have done it all on her own. Maturity had tempered Rebecca. He knew of the circumstances that delivered her to his hand. It hurt his heart that he had brought her here because he thought he had needed her. But it didn't matter. John understood that if he could have summoned the deepest most meaningful words to express that his heart brimmed with her, that she was all he ever needed in his whole life, it could not change her heart. He was not for her.

He didn't want to pretend he could understand her heart. But he knew, any good farmer would, her desires were not unique. Bulls mounted bulls. Cows mounted cows. And he heard women, single women, they called them women adrift, could live and work and be. She could have just been. In spite of her tempered past, it would have prepared her for Toronto. She wouldn't have been adrift. Heavy hearted, Rebecca had to mature harder, sharper than her past. Her eye, her read of both room and character whetted by pain. She cut up those around her and rearranged their thoughts so she knew anybody's past and future. Yes. She would have thrived. But John dragged her here.

But for Mareika, she could go to Toronto if she wanted. If John now dreamt in English, the tongue of this new world, then he could fertilize new growth in Mareika. Through the years since losing Rebecca his library grew with their daughter in mind: *Pride & Prejudice, Little Women, Jane Eyre, The Awakening*, which John kept backward in his library along with *Silas Marner*, because he saw himself, saw Rebecca under and inside their covers. But these books served his mind patience and insight. She no longer had the mould of woman or mother. So amongst the words he searched for empathy and insight into what a man could expect of a budding, modern woman. As Mary Shelley built fantastical humanity of the dead in *Frankenstein*, John recovered an idea of the inner life of a young woman for this new world, because in this evolving society she had more places to go than a garden on a farm—university and beyond. John promised Rebecca at her burial to prepare their Mareika for the entire world.

John sighed, the tension in his lips changing. His fatigue rolled past his teeth and raced higher over his brow in a bending cloud as the cold spring air took hold and dragged his breath away, dropping it upon the ground. There had been no calving. He marched through the field, listened to the different crunch his steps made through the snow compared to the crunch of teeth. Marty rejoined him. He ground his teeth, too, and nuzzled John.

When they got to the barn, John hung the feedbag on a post. The donkey stayed outside hiding its face in the bag of treats. John squeezed his eyes shut, one at a time, letting the frigid ether skate over his eyeballs. He sucked the air in through both his nostrils, but still he wanted to sleep. The warmth of his skin and the cold of the air almost seduced him to curl up atop a snowdrift and close his eyes. If the promise of a morning sun hadn't been so sharp, he may have let the arctic air lull him to bed under the sky. Instead he marched to his home. Reaching the west side, he stopped at the windows and turned his face into the glass. He cupped his hands around his eyes and looked to the couch that was once his bed.

Mareika walked awake. Her hand touching the books upon their shelves. He knocked. She came to the door.

"I'm walking the fields."

She nodded and dressed.

Without words they walked. They stopped. They listened. Marty's ears twisted and alternated forward and back. The beast stopped, his ears pinned all the way back as he stared into the darkness. Mareika raised one hand to stop the crunch of John's feet while the other rested upon the donkey's hind hip. The animal raised its nose to the air. Billowing clouds of vapour floated away. Mareika turned her ear toward the boneyard. Marty looked back at them. His eyes wide, flashed an urgency. It stuttered on its hooves. Mareika felt the muscles tense in its legs. Then the chill ripped open.

They heard a cow call. It did not come low, like the tuba. It came pieced together by a shill trumpeted cry—the notes of pain and fear. Marty raced over the rising roll as the field turned to hillock and galloped toward the wails.

"You go. I'll grab the sled and irons." The gales, dragging a storm behind it, pushed him away from the boneyard, sliced his face with shards of snow.

John returned with the calving sled, which he pulled taking all precautions not to lose any tools. He heard Mareika before he saw her.

"Foda!"

Her voice crackled with the same distress as the cow. As he neared her, her arm rose and pointed to the fenceline. Two large coyote males marauded on the other side of the fence. Each darted under barbed wire but retreated when Marty charged. They hesitated and kept jetting farther apart to draw the beast away from the other. Occasionally, they'd stop, sit panting, before they would yip and cry to the stars.

"What do we do?"

"Ignore them—Marty's here."

Marty stomped his feet by the fence at a ducking dog. It withdrew but not without a nip at a hoof.

"What if they hurt him?"

"Grab some brush. We need a fire."

Marty turned and threw a kick. His leg rebounded off the barbed wire. But the blow landed. The coyote rolled ass over tea kettle four times before it limped off farther down the line. The other raced in but hooked back around and away into the darkness as Marty backed him off, too. It was their fear that became hesitation; this was where their failure lay.

Beyond the darkness crept the coming storm. Storms could mean days. And on the prairie if you didn't eat before a blizzard, you might never eat again. All animals felt this urgency to fill up. A flurry of yips and howls blew over John, Mareika, Marty, and the labouring cow.

"They're definitely looking for a meal."

"They sound so close," Mareika said with her gaze shooting beyond the onyx and silver twisted briar of brush, dead-naked wild rose stems, pussy willows, birches, elms, and poplars into the night.

John lowered his cheek to the ice and snow. And within three deep bellows of his lungs he summoned a great heat that could have come from the belly of the earth, which exploded towards the sky in glowing, warped flames. It devoured the dried brush. His deft hands tossed layers of tinder before dropping full branches over the blaze. He even dragged full fallen trees over the fire, which he would push along as the fire burned. He moved his tools beside the fire, then draped a blanket in the sled.

"Sit. Stay warm. It'll take her a while."

The flames threw shadows over the cow. She kept her backside from the wind. Mareika watched as blood and shadow seeped from behind her tail. It did not flick but writhed. She cried. The call pulled her head down and stretched her neck long and smooth.

"How do we help?"

John moved some irons under the wood, where coals began to glow radiant orange.

"We don't. She's a young cow. She'll probably pass her on her own, but if she can't, we'll pull it."

"When would that be?"

"When we see hoof and elbow."

"Elbow?"

"Sure. Cows have joints, right?"

Mareika nodded. She looked over the cow. She compared the anatomy to a person. She looked at the engorged, leaking other parts. She pulled her knees to her chest and crossed her ankles.

An hour or more passed before the first sign of hooves budded from her other parts.

"Foda!" Mareika stood and pointed. "The hooves."

"Give her time."

Minutes turned into forever while darkness and yelping of hungry beasts surrounded them. The wind came stronger, and the falling snow, now ice, threatened to mince them all into coyote feed.

The cow, exhausted, lumbered onto her side. Her cries wilted into weak breaths. John went to her and placed a palm to her hide. She didn't even lift her head.

"Bring me the rope." His tone, curt, pulled Mareika into action. She cared only for his voice, his instructions. "Okay, we're going to pull her. Are you ready?"

His voice seemed to nod her head for her. His instructions came in syllables, each word necessary, clear.

"The knots of the clove hitches at twelve o'clock. No, its leg is the clock, not your twelve. One loop mid-cannon, then at the fetlock joint. One on each leg."

Mareika draped the lines out from the cow as her tail limped about the tiny fifth and sixth legs jutting out over the reddened snow. John took one line and handed her the other. The fire tossed the baroque shadows of their bodies about the cow and frozen prairie.

"When I say, you pull. But easy. Follow the weight of your body. When we see elbow, stop."

Mareika nodded. "How will we know? It's kind of dark."

"We'll know. Listen for a pop." John placed his index finger into his cheek and gave it a flick. The pop mimicked a cork freed from a bottle.

John had not lied. There was a pop. Mareika didn't know if she should laugh or cry. After all it had been that cow's other parts that had burst with that sound, not a bottle of ale. Under John's instructions, they heaved at the same time, freeing the calf. The cow lay breathing low and slow.

The morning sun started to burn off the night. The sky abandoned its obsidian pitch for a deep navy. Clouds turned charred grey. The nighttime and the chance to feed escaped around them. That's when the coyotes returned, the tease of flesh heavier over the air. There were three now. They came at once, one from the front and two from the back. No yipping, no barking. three blurs of white, grey, and dusty brown.

But Marty, too, came fast—really fast. He bowled over and trampled one, threw a back kick out into another before finally he reared up and started dropping his front hooves down on the last coyote like a prize fighter's flurry. The coyotes didn't have a chance. The two wild dogs not under Marty escaped back under the fence. The pluck of contact sang down the wires. The barbs snatched souvenirs, tufts of fur.

Mareika in the confusion grabbed a hold of John. She watched the donkey destroy the remaining coyote. Marty came down on that mutt's front leg as it stammered sideways, confused. Marty got him high up near his chest. Mareika buried her face after the shuttering snap of bone. Yelps followed, more thudding stomps, and then silence.

Mareika thought the thing dead. Marty trotted to them and turned long as if to shield them as John moved Mareika from his side to tend to the pulled calf.

Afterbirth slipped from the cow's other parts. Mareika stepped away. She eased to the fallen coyote.

The beast twitched and pushed itself only inches away from her as she approached. He whined. His tongue dangled out his mouth, saliva dripped into the snow. The frozen bank melted as the dog's life dripped from its body. Mareika knelt. The coyote's upper lip spasmed, as it aped a show of teeth. Soon after crows cawed and circled above, perched upon the trees adjacent.

"We need to help him."

"No we don't." John lifted the calf into the sled. The cow rose onto wobbled legs. She mooed.

"Yes we do—he'll die."

John began to lug the sled to the barn and pens. The cow followed.

"Foda!"

"No, Mareika. Don't feed your enemies."

"But Foda!"

"I said no."

"Oh, my goodness, I can't believe you. You're just going to leave it here to suffer?"

"Yes."

Mareika stood looking between John and the wounded animal. Her face wrung with pain and confusion. She looked at the tools beside the fire, but her eyes flashed more confusion as if she were trying to read another language in one of the many books inside her home.

"Please ..."

John stopped. He turned to her, his face as blank as the prairie's winterscape, and said, "No."

She burst away. The cow spooked, exploded with a trot, but slowed again once the young woman had passed, headed for the house.

John watched her until she disappeared. He looked skyward with a heavy sigh. Then he walked back to the where he found his irons. He pulled a burlap sack from his pocket. A brazen crow hopped about outside the coyote's bite, surveyed its condition. John kicked snow at it. Then he draped the sack over the coyote's head. The beast cried. He stabbed the cold end of the iron into the snow beside him and the wild dog. And following a deep breath, in one quick motion, he kneeled on the coyote's neck, and with a pocketknife that had once been concealed inside his breast pocket, he sliced the broken limb off, scooped the brand and cauterised the wound.

Every muscle in the dog twitched, tightened, and exploded. The animal bucked back to life and bucked and bucked and bucked until John fell back onto his butt. He dropped the hot iron. The hiss and steam drew a curtain between him and the beast. When the veil rose, the creature sat in the snow across from John. It stared wild and wide-eyed. Its tongue hung free as it panted. The animal seemed to lower his head and bow. Then between them silence stood. They stared at each other. The coyote's tongue lapped up at its snout, cleaning the mucous dripping from the nostrils. John slid his hand into his pocket, palmed a ball of red cloth, and lifted the rag towards the animal. Its nose flared to the air. With his other hand he pulled back the corners to reveal a chunk of roast. The coyote's nostrils flared again. It hopped a few inches. John leaned forward onto his knees. He felt the snow melting and soaking through his pants. He reached his hand forward more. The coyote hopped closer. His snout huffing, gracing his gloved fingers. It turned its head sideways. Its mouth opened to jaw at the meat. John retracted his hand and watched the coyote chomp on the beef three times and stretch its neck out to swallow. The coyote hopped away to the brush on the other side of the fence.

The days that followed, unbeknownst to Mareika, John brought water, fat, gristle, and afterbirth to the dog. And on one occasion the beast allowed him to wash its wound.

SATURDAY, JULY 30, 1892.

Eastern Reserve, Manitoba

Farmer Sausage

Salt
Pepper
Pork

R EBECCA, ON THE days in the fall when you and your neighbours gather to butcher pigs, please let your husband be. Men will have the weight of the year on them. They will dispense with vodka and ales and any number of concoctions. His tongue will flutter like laundry on the line and he will laugh too loud. Farmer sausage is the heart of all great meals and in order to properly prepare it, your husband may need to free himself of his responsibility on this day. But that is after all the work has come to an end. He and his neighbours will butcher and carve pigs into hams, bacon, sausage cuts, and fat. Do not let any of the wives take more than her share of fat. You will render it, and take what you need for soap and polish and for baking. And when the butchering and the preparations are done, you should have enough fat, casing, and sausage cuts for winter. If your husband lacks a good recipe for sausages, know you need cold smoke. You can increase this smoke by burning hay and straw. And remember, all things in life have one end except sausage. It has two ends.

Black Gully, Town Square

1BI **GIETZ SQUINTED** against the afternoon sun as he pulled at the head block of the carriage. Shadows fell long behind him and the wagon. He lugged it into the town square. He slapped the hard tension stretching his pants taut over his thighs. He shook his feet and stretched his back. He looked around the square. The grounds, brown and dusty, sprouted with slithers of green grasses. He turned his eyes towards the south. Then he looked forward, the glare of the sun leaving purple blotches inside his sight. He blinked hard and pressed his palm into his eyes. He opened his Bible and blinked more. He turned his body north a quarter step. Then finally he cleared his throat and waited for the radius-top doors to open, releasing the Sunday services from all three churches, Catholic, Lutheran, and Mennonite Brethren, into Black Gully's wide dirt streets.

The radius-top doors were all the churches had in common. By far the Catholic rose above the others. It was big and fat—immense. Made of fieldstone and clinker brick, it actually had a bell in its tower, where the much shorter steeple of the cedar Lutheran Church housed only perching pigeons, though it did possess a bell, mounted on a humble concrete base in the side court and rung when stuck with a mallet. Both steeples towered above their porches. The Catholic and Lutheran, though differing in size, held the common footprint similar to the cross, with the sanctuary and altar separated by a transept. The Mennonite Church by contrast looked like a home, a simple rectangular wood home under a gable roof with a short brick chimney rising several feet from the porch. While the Lutheran and Catholic Churches had ornate stained-glass windows, the Mennonite had regular panes of glass.

The Catholic Church bell rang from behind whitewashed slats. Pigeons hopped from off the ledges. The flap of their wings lifted them to the stooked eaves. The large fir door swung towards him. A handful of men, their wives, and children came out, hovering around the church's courtyard.

Not long after, the Lutheran Church and Mennonite doors opened, and the near collected masses of Black Gully emerged into the cool spring day.

Ibi balanced the cart on its shaft rest and hopped atop the box seat. He cleared his throat again. His throat choked on the thousand syllables swirling inside his mind. He didn't know where to start. His head fell. He pinched the bridge of his nose, and with closed eyes, he searched for Claas. He searched all his memories.

"We are the pure bride of Christ … And never will we raise sword to another. Instead thrust these swords into the earth—make them our ploughshares." Ibi listened as Claas rationalized that he was there to plant belief, not set fires. "Share our knowledge. Tell them our story."

Ibi looked up, letting his Bible fall open in his palm. He felt blue skies fall over him and merge with the weight of the book splayed in his hands. He placed a foot onto the footrest and leaned into this moment. He eased his eyes open and looked for somebody, anybody, to speak to. And the moment he made eye contact with one of the wives, a plain brunette wearing a bonnet, who smiled to him, his lungs surged with the energy he remembered flowed through Claas. He slammed the book shut and raised it high letting his voice fill the air.

"Brothers and Sisters! God will rescue us and this, our little town. Yes, He is returning, and we can all be prepared, for the times of the last judgement when it comes upon us all. Do you feel it?" He pointed at the people milling about to wagons. "I know you can feel it.

Chased from our homes across oceans and great tracts of land. How did we get here, to this frigid, wintery prairie?"

Many churchgoers mounted horses and wagons and eased out of town staring at him. A small handful entered the square with baskets and blankets. Gietz turned his attention to them.

"Under this sun, such a beautiful spring, so early. Last year ice capped our lakes, and snow buried our fields. Where has winter gone? Dried up, burnt off.

"And the third angel sounded, and there fell a great star from heaven, burning as it were a lamp, and it fell upon the third part of the rivers, and upon the fountains of waters. And the name of the star is called Wormwood: and the third part of the waters became wormwood; and many men died of the waters, because they were made bitter."

The crowd stared at him after that word, *died.*

"That's right, Halley's Comet. Is this the Great Star, Brothers and Sisters? Our Wormwood?" Gietz looked through the crowds of people leaving the church grounds. Many stopped, but few wandered to the empty lot where he had stationed his borrowed buggy. "It was our warning," he shouted to them. "But there have been others. Why have we not taken heed? And closer and closer they have come. I remember as a boy riding across the Kara Kum Desert, a great comet, it was so bright that I could read my Bible at night—this Bible—as if by lamplight." He shook his Bible into the air.

Many practitioners stayed a distance, across the street or on the far side of the square. Herman and Lisa Jantzen walked to Ibi Gietz's sermon. They brought a handful of Brethren.

"The dark sands rutted as if God had reached down and combed the desert into a million little furrows sparkled under the flame of the great comet. It shed light upon the pages that ignited my awakening. It exposed the words of Our Lord and I heard his warnings. Let me say it again:

"And the third angel sounded, and there fell a great star from heaven, burning as it were a lamp, and it fell upon the third part of the rivers, and upon the fountains of waters. And the name of the star is called Wormwood: and the third part of the waters became wormwood;

and many men died of the waters, because they were made bitter. Halley's Comet. Halley's Comet. This is our warning. Did you all see it? Halley's Comet may have passed us by, but in days we all shall pass through its streaking tail. That's right, we will all pass through this Great Star, people. I'm not here to scare you, but I must admit that I am afraid. I am afraid. Who else here is afraid?"

Lisa Jantzen raised her hand.

"Sister Jantzen!" Ibi Gietz clapped. "This brave, brave woman. She isn't afraid to share her feelings. I am scared, too, Sister Lisa. And let me tell you, I do not want any, *ANY*, not one of your souls left behind. Luke had said *take heed, lest at any of your hearts be overcharged with surfeiting, and drunkenness, and cares of this life, and that day come upon you unawares. For as a snare shall it come on all them that dwell on the face of the whole earth.*

"We're here now, Brothers and Sisters. We are dwelling on the face of the whole earth, every plain and every mountaintop. How did we get here?" Gietz reached into his vest pocket and retrieved a folded envelope. From inside he pulled a white sheet of paper and read, "Free land." He showed the leaflet to the handful of people staring his way. "They promised us riches, a better life, where bitter winters never existed because chinooks stole the winter ice. All we needed was a plow and a horse and a sickle. You all toiled to break the earth, to fertilize it, to raise a field of wheat. You came here and like the Christians coming into Rome, you were told to speak their language, to leave your children with their philosophers. Do you know who their god is? My Lord is your Lord, Jesus Christ. When their servant comes around with his outstretched hand his fingers clutching at your coin purse, do you own any of this land? How much was the team of horses or oxen? How much was your plow? Was there a lumberyard? And while there still sits no railway here, how do you get your crops to market? Our granaries sit full to the brim. Is that home yours?"

The politics of his words drew the husbands into the square. Some whispered, *Who is he?* while most listened. Their arms crossed, their chins tucked, and their eyes squinted.

"We are a wagon train of servants. We served the Russian tsar and opened up the Volga and Crimean steppe. Then forced to fight, pushed into their wars we had to flee. We had to escape their wars. We came here to the Americas. And again with the promise of freedom. It came free, right?

"We were to break another land. To bake the breads that feed. But have we been invited to the table? Do we break bread? Our backs hurt, our feet ache, and our wrists are rusted. But with empty pockets. Fevers, disease, poverty. Fevers, disease, and poverty. We toiled, forgetting to watch. We are too busy to watch. This day of rest we truly do rest—exhausted—we have fallen asleep. *Watch ye therefore, and pray always, that ye may be accounted worthy to escape all these things that shall come to pass, and to stand before the Son of Man.*

"I know every one of your wishes when that day comes." Gietz stretched a finger high over his head and pointed into the sky. His gaze followed past his finger into the blue apex of his words rising into the atmosphere. "We have been at rest, broken and tired. But only days ago did I wake up. I have opened my eyes. And I am here to say that I can wake you …"

Ibi looked over the crowd. It had grown. But most stood apart, sparse.

"*He* has shown me *The End* is near. *He* is coming once again. The great comet came first—so bright like two suns in the sky—it ignited the desert sands as though it was daylight. Men read without candle, the sand below sparkled like stardust under our sedan chairs as our camels slogged through the desert. This was not the first. Dozens more have streaked across our skies, scrolls opening above our skies. We just need read them. See their message. One after another. Closer the next. Ancient celestial bodies trumpeting a warning.

"*The star is called Wormwood: and the third part of the waters became wormwood; and many men died of the waters, because they were made bitter.*" Gietz repeated again, but the bodies stayed distant. He held up his Bible. Black and white, dry and crumbling pages floated like ash out beyond the leather covers. His face burned the colour of the wild roses that filled the ditches and forest floors around Black Gully. He looked over the crowd, which had grown to several dozen farmers and wives, Mennonite, Lutheran, Catholics. He nodded to the Jantzens. Then as he peered past the crowd across the street, a smile ignited across his face, burning off the scowl from his brow.

Off on the step of the post office sat Mareika. She held a pale red shawl over her shoulders. She crossed her ankles and held herself against the cool of the breeze that lifted at her bangs. Gietz held her image as a child would a baby chick. He cherished the lightness, the softness of her image so close to him again.

He stammered and had to look away. He gave his focus back to the community gathering around him. "These are the words not of Revelations, but from the newspapers and the scientists. They too echo the warnings. The evidence is in print from every nation. From Russia, Tunguska. A great comet struck Russia. Did you hear what I said?" He waved the newspaper. "A great comet struck Russia. Siberia burned. Trees did not have time to fall before they burned. Forests as big and as wide as our own county fell in a great blaze. Think about that … An entire forest, a great forest, incinerated faster than a stricken match.

"Revelations 13:13, is this not? He performs great signs, so that he even makes fire come down out of the heaven to the earth in the presence of men. Wars, plagues, we have found our way here to escape them. Do we have a means to escape the end days?" He nodded, holding up his Bible. He looked to the steps. Mareika brushed her knees, her ear perched on his words.

Gietz wrapped his gaze around her every curve. His breath lifted his chin up and held his shoulders back. He shook his finger at the crowd and called: "And now have we not the warnings of Daniel?

"And he shall confirm the covenant with many for one week: and in the midst of the week he shall cause the sacrifice and the oblation to cease, and for the overspreading of abominations he shall make desolate, even until the consummation, and that determined shall be poured upon the desolate. Yes, people, requite here." He slid a puffy square from out of the book. His thumbs slipped and flicked at the corners.

He licked his thumb. He palmed the paper and rested his Bible beside his left foot. Sunlight shone between the steeple of the Catholic Church and the post office to land over his toes. His boots, scuffed, did not shine. A red cut of yarn twirled against a puff of warm air, a mention summer would come. The fold of paper opened. He moved it away from the light. His eyes jutted over the words. He put his pointer finger onto the page. "Camille Flammarion." He held the paper above his head. He dipped down and took the book under the article. "This is from *The Call*, Boston, Massachusetts. February 7th, 1910. 'Camille Flammarion, the distinguished French scientist says: "The cyanogen gas will impregnate the atmosphere and possibly snuff out all life on the planet".'" He folded the article. Stored inside the Book of Daniel, he let the weight of his Bible take it back. Another clipping left the trappings of his Bible: *"The Ogden Standard, February 9th, 1910. Professor Booth from the University of California, a ... spectrum analysis, a well known expert, he says, 'We'll all be snuffed out if a sufficient quantity of this cyanogen gas unites with the hydrogen of this planet's atmosphere.'*

"You need not call yourself a Christian to know what these atheists and agnostics are saying. They too warn us of what Daniel long ago told us to be true. Our Lord is coming back. We, the new Israelites, are upon Philadelphia. And upon us crossing through the tail of Halley's Comet, surely this world will end as we know it. And for those denying that we have a master in heaven ... Everybody here now." His hand cut over the heads of the two dozen or so people standing on the lawn, nearly green. "I am sure you know what their fate may be." He opened his book, his fingers flipped through the pages. He lifted a coin from the inside, pocketed it, and read: "Galatians 3:28, *There is neither Jew nor Greek, there is neither bond or free, there is neither male nor female: for ye are all one in Christ Jesus.* And in the days before Thursday when we cross through the comet's tail, that great serpent—and surely we will pass—who will be Raptured into the Kingdom and who is to be left in a heap of blood and fire at the toes of the seven-headed beast, the dragon and the serpent ..." Gietz looked from his Bible. He looked off over the square emptying. His audience began to shrink. Many scowled. They shook their heads and looked away.

Gietz hesitated. He looked over the square for his words, for his confidence. He looked for Mareika. She sat still. He got nothing from her body language. He turned his eyes and lost his gaze in the naked brush of poplars and birch behind him. He shook his head.

"Cyanogen gas!" He looked above, holding his hands. "It will poison our waters, but unlike the Lord turning water to wine, this comet, Halley's Comet, will turn our rivers into wormwood."

People spread farther apart, farther from Ibi. Ibi shook his disbelief at the apathy.

"Death awaits you all!" Ibi's voice began to lecture. His bark chased the crowd back.

Mareika stood and leaned on the post office. She smiled through a grimace as she watched Ibi lose his audience. She looked away. She scoured the green grass rising from under the winter mould. The dirt under the greenness, dark with wetness, creeped about the edges of her boots above her soles. She flicked her finger at her bangs dangling in her face. She licked her lips.

"Rebecca." The words came hot and breathy from over her shoulder, dampening her ear.

Mareika wiped her mutta's name off her ear and stepped away.

"Oh my, you look exactly like your mutta." The Bishop took in every inch of the young woman.

Mareika crossed her arms over her chest. Her head shook. She glanced at the streets for Foda. But John had not been there, anywhere. He hadn't even known Mareika had left for Black Gully. It was just her. She stepped towards the square. The Bishop grabbed her wrist.

"I said you look like Rebecca. She was a very stunning young woman." The Bishop followed the line of Mareika's jaw to her eyes. He reached with a finger and tipped her chin to meet his gaze. "I said I paid you a compliment."

She turned to march away. The Bishop's other hand, grabbed her at the bicep, and he yanked her to him.

"His words are handsome and convincing, but, believe me, that man is a heretic." He leaned in close. His nose buried into her hair. She felt him breathe her in then groan, his groin tilting into her hip. "His words belong to the devil. Nobody floats into town to save anyone. A stranger is either fleeing punishment or chasing a great deception."

Mareika thrust her shoulders to break his grip. She stumbled back but freed herself. She glared. He smiled.

"Don't let this charlatan fool you. You'll find your salvation with me." He pointed to the Mennonite Church.

Mareika turned and moved from him.

"My office is open to you whenever you need."

Mareika dashed into the square and moved her way through the remaining audience to the cart. She gulped, and when she saw Gietz smile, she urged her lips to mimic him. His brow fell under a weighty concern. This acknowledgment eased a small but genuine smile over her face. Gietz looked down the mall. The Bishop caught his attention. Mareika followed his gaze to the Bishop, who strolled the boardwalk back to the Mennonite Church, his hands clasped behind his back. He appeared to be whistling, paid no heed to the activities in the park.

The whistling spurred her memory of Bible study with Mutta. She thought back to the songs sung to her under the shade of the willows. The Mennonite girls loved to sing in the schoolyard. She stammered over words she could not arrange. She began to hum, then some words followed. Her voice, almost a talking tone, wavered. She held her own hands, folded them together at her waist. Her thumbs stroked a pleat on her dress. She could not look at any of the other people in the park, sending her song towards the lawn.

"Saviour, Saviour, Hear my humble cry. While on the others Thou art calling, Do not pass me by . . ."

The women in the audience picked up the lyrics and quietly, respectfully joined along. Their voices rose over Mareika's. This allowed her to retreat from the song and the lyrics she could not remember. The rejoicing in refrain attracted more to flock back into the square. Gietz had his audience again.

His voice rose and he sang louder, set his voice aflutter. He rolled up his sleeves. He coughed. His chin followed his strutting neck and he coughed again, letting a cloth marker drop between his feet upon the carriage deck halfway onto the shadows, halfway onto the slice of sunshine that didn't shine his toes. "And the third angel sounded," he mumbled.

Mareika shook her head. She stepped away from the wagon into the audience. She moved to and took Lisa Jantzen's hand. The two looked at each other as the hymn came to an end and the voices through the park trailed off.

Gietz nodded. "Brother Jantzen, Sister Jantzen, they can attest— they are here. They came from Elisabeth Epp's family. How can we all ignore this? Claas Epp Jr.'s wife's, her family is here. A part of Claas is here in your very town. Is this not True Jantzens?"

"Yes. I am Elisabeth's nephew."

"And you came from Beatrice." Ibi looked over his audience. "Who else came from Beatrice? Show me your hands." The crowd stayed.

Herman pointed. "Franz. Franz Abrahams, you were my family's neighbour." The man stood with slouched shoulders and thick grey eyebrows. He nodded.

"Do you know of Claas Epp the Third?"

Franz, again, nodded.

"You see! Claas is connected to this community. I was meant to be here. I was sent to save us all. Who else?" Ibi, his hand reached out to pull the rein of the crowd's growing attention. The rabble of "I, what about so and so" rose above them into his ears, sweet and nourishing. "What about the Trakt Settlements? Or Furstenwerder?" The rabble expanded into a rumble. "Yes. Yes. Do you all see? Do you feel it?" Some in the audience raised swaying hands towards the heavens. Ibi smiled. "We are all connected. And like the chain, forged and tempered strong."

Ibi jumped from the wagon to shake Franz's hand. Others confessed to him, pulled at him, took his hand. He turned back around and returned to his makeshift pulpit.

"It is clear. Do you see? It is clear. But what is more bitter than poison? The fruit of the tree? The roots we pull up and roast? Wormwood, most bitter, is a poison that has killed many a man. And the words of Our Lord are echoing in this new-world science, spilling from the tongues of atheists, that our waters shall run bitter, run with the poisons this comet will impregnate, turning our waters into wormwood. I shall be on the shores of Black Gully Lake Wednesday to baptize those who wish to be Raptured. I shall be there in those meadows listening to the whispers carried upon the winds, holding vigil, singing His praise, and waiting to rise above this world to His gates, crossing into the Kingdom. Will you join me? Will you join me? Will you all join me?" His head fell into the band of light stealing inside the wagon. His hair about the top of his head shimmered. His head began bobbing and nodding, his arms rose from his sides, parallel with his shoulder. His heels clicked together twice. "See me tomorrow. I will be back tomorrow at one o'clock. Bring your family and friends—let's save our community. That is your charge, Brothers and Sisters."

Several of the observers walked away to return to the town, to their schedules, while others, only three or four, approached the wagon. They reached for him with their hands, taking him by the wrists, thanking him.

❧

"You came." Ibi wrapped Mareika up in his arms. He squeezed and lifted her off her feet.

She squealed. "Yes." Her ruddy cheeks swelled with a smile. Mareika kept her eyes on him.

"I am so glad." He wrapped himself around her again.

She let her weight fall into his arms as she moaned.

"Pardon," he said.

She looked up to him. "Your speech reminded me of Mutta."

"My sermon? Wow. That's high praise." He squeezed her again and again. "I cannot believe you're here. I'm sorry—Your mutta. Go on—your mutta sounds amazing, so wise. Where is she?" Ibi turned her towards the cart. He kept an arm around her shoulder as they eased through the last members milling about the Square.

"Mutta has passed."

"That's right. I am so sorry. Devastating." Gietz shook his bowed head. A short aping of consolation. "Tell me about her."

Mareika froze, her mouth agape. "I . . ."

"Tomorrow. I shall have all your answers for tomorrow."

"What answers?"

"The Ascension. Revelations. The Rapture." They moved from the cart. Gietz strolled with quick long strides. Mareika jogged to catch up. "I don't want to lug this all the way back. Do you think it is safe to leave it here for tomorrow's sermon?" He didn't look at her for an answer. "I'm sure it is."

He spun around and threw himself around her yet again. He lifted her and they spun in the sunlight. He set her down. He gave the same hug to his books, his clippings, pulling them into his chest, taking in the fresh spring air through his nose. He looked down at Mareika. Her gaze fell away onto the grass.

"Walk with me to the lake," he said.

A sharp sting stabbed through her pelvis. She limped from his side. A groan escaped. She took her side with her hand as if to force the pain back inside. She rubbed her pelvis; she massaged her stomach. "I'm sorry."

"No. A walk will do you wonders."

"It hurts."

"I know. I know it does."

"I wish it would go away. I woke several times last night. Every time afraid."

"You needn't be afraid. I searched for your pain. I know it. Your pain is here inside these pages. For the Lord himself shall descend from heaven with a shout, with the voice of the archangel, and with the trump of God: and the dead in Christ shall rise first."

"I don't understand."

He took her hand, weaved his fingers between hers. He enjoyed their chill. She looked into his face. The skin around his mouth crinkled, his lips parted showing the white of his grin.

"The shouts, the pain, your pain are the shouts of the archangel, the trump of God. Inside you, you feel the rise of Christ, His rebirth. You are Mutta. Mareika. Mareika, your name means Mutta. It was not chosen for you, it was given to us, the world. And through you, a beacon, we hear the trump of God."

"Then why do I bleed?"

"Did he not bleed? Upon the cross, did he not bleed? Five wounds spilled into the Grail. You are his Grail, taken upon you his blood. It is his blood inside you."

"I'm scared."

He stopped and took her by the shoulders. His face fell grave.

"What you are feeling is his rebirth—labour pains." To her navel, his hands fell. He knelt. He caressed. His fingertips pulled at her flesh as if he looked to pinch a morsel of bread from an uncut loaf. He licked his lips before he whispered the Lord's Prayer.

She looked at his glistening lips. She wanted to touch them. Feel their softness.

He felt the weight of her hips push against his touch. "Mmm …" He let go, rubbing his palm around the warmth spreading over her blouse. She crossed her ankles. Her eyes fell and rose around his stare the way bees circle a flower's stamen.

Ibi smiled. "You have been chosen."

"Let's keep walking."

Gietz stood.

"Where is your foda now?"

"He is at home building a loft."

"And he doesn't mind you out on your own."

"No. I'm used to being alone. Mutta died when I was a kid, and Foda, he leaves a lot, he does work on the Métis lands, and sometimes he just leaves and goes fishing, hunting, or finds books."

"Why?"

"Mutta said it was because it was better for Foda to *dwell in the wilderness, than with a contentious and an angry woman."* She kicked a stone, watching it bounce across the dirt road into the grassy ditch.

"Proverbs. I can certainly understand that. I wouldn't need to be around a difficult woman." His winked, chasing a playful blush and smile over her cheeks.

"I wish I had other memories of Mutta. She always seemed to be yelling at Foda in low German. Her words rolled and vibrated and harsh letters sprang from the back of her tongue. She sounded like she was a hissing cat perched up on a fence post, swatting at the bloodied nose of a dog. Foda would nod and wander off."

"Sprechen sie Deutsch?"

"No. Foda does. We had to speak English. Mutta only spoke German when she was mad at Foda."

"That's strange."

"I have to speak English in school. All the kids have to. The Mennonite boys talk and laugh in German outside and pull at the Irish girls' red ponytails, but I don't know what they are saying. Foda says they are probably being crude, and one time Jonah Wiebe did toss up my dress and everybody saw my legs and undergarments. I gave him a boot in the shin. Did you have a wife?"

"No."

"Why?"

"I was too busy doing His work."

"Are you ever lonely?"

Gietz felt the smooth pad of Mareika's thumb stroke the last knuckle of his thumb. "Of course."

"I get lonely. I feel alone out there in the country. I liked coming into town and watching you. It was nice to hear other people's voices. I am almost always reading or doing chores. Foda reads a lot too. I go to school, but I'm only there for a few hours, then I have to come home and do chores. What was the desert like? I read about them, and sometimes in winter when it's cloudy but the clouds aren't very thick and sun is still bright and the snow is blowing and drifting and everything looks bright and white, the sunlight reflects off everything, off the snow up into your face. It's weird because even though the sun is overhead in the south and it's cloudy, it's still so bright that there's no shadows. If there weren't any trees you wouldn't really know what direction you were going, and the sun hurts your eyes. You can't look down because the snow hurts your eyes. Sometimes I think that's what a desert feels like, except it's hot."

"Yes."

"Was it scary going through the desert?"

"I was not scared, but I was young, I was ignorant. The Russian government, they gave us camels when our wagons could not go. Over dunes and valleys, it took days. Camels would travel back and forth dragging one wagon at a time. We buried a child in the desert. He died. The mother wept and never opened her sedan chair once after. It was strange digging the hole. The sand kept falling back in, and what should have been a small deep hole was very large and shallow. His father marked his grave, but I'm sure the sand has destroyed it."

"Children died?"

"Many died. Not just children." Gietz lifted her hand to his mouth and kissed it. He kept his eyes forward. "It was only into the first three days of our voyage, not even out of Russia yet, that we saw our first death. It took us two years to get from Russia to Ak-Metchet, but only a few days before death."

MONDAY, MAY 16, 1910.

Wapos County

THE LATE MORNING air inside the Doerksen home held a warmth, a welcome hominess. Lingering coals from a feast of seared rolled cheese curds and farmer sausage stung the maroon willow bark of budding branches as John dropped several handfuls into the stove. He blew down. A grey, ashy plume grew from under the orange glow before the smoke bit his eyes. He stuffed a wad of straw inside and closed the stove. He licked the bottom knuckle of his thumb, as it had grazed the top of the stove. It swelled red with a white crust where it blistered.

John moved about the house, pulled open all the window coverings, and opened a west and a south window only enough to let a cross breeze of spring air wash his home with a crisp earthy mineral tang of soil mingling with blue and jack pine. He returned to the kitchen and leaned over the stove pot. He clacked his tongue. Burred, it wanted to cling to the roof of his mouth. He ladled a warm serving past his lips and gulped. He swished the next ladleful between cheeks, through his teeth, swallowed, before he took another. He groaned at the sickness that chimed in his guts as the water hit his empty stomach.

He seldom took to drink. The ales he himself concocted and kept in the *semlin* were a medicine. They eased the tension and pain at his back and joints after long days plowing, swathing, or chopping wood. Plus a jar draped a veil over a brightened mind at bedtime.

However, the community of yesterday with Paul Lee and Charlie Gervais as they all constructed the bedroom loft for Mareika had unbound him.

The spirit of last night had reminded him of the pig slaughters of his youth. His earliest memories were of terror, the squeals of dozens of hogs as they met the edge of blades. Later, the children had to clean the open pens left a rusted, ruddy muck. He and the other children were tasked with washing away the mix of blood and shit from pen walls, gates, and chore boots. And he had hated it. However, now neither butchering nor blood had risen from his memory, only nostalgia.

On those day in late fall, the men, Martin, his foda, included, they changed. Something fell from them. Rising away from the usual pragmatism of chores—the preparation of fat for polish and soap, the binding of hams, and the grinding of pork for sausage—festivity glowed over everybody. Several small casks were rolled into the yard. Foam exploded free as a wooden mallet drove spigots into the barrels and sprayed the boys who always stood within the splash zone—their tongues wagged, hoping to catch the same ghost softening their rigid fodas. Repugnance wrung from the bitterness caught upon their tongues. Around makeshift tables of several long planks lain over sawhorses, the men stood, sawed through bone, carved, cut, and ground meat. Mugs rested within reach of every man scattered amongst the flesh and bone or upon fence posts. The men shed their black jackets, rolled up their sleeves. They smiled. They laughed. They sang. They acted silly. Expectations did not dog them on that day.

But the morning came. In his sleep he became riddled with guilt. He did not want Mareika to have to use the smoke chamber ladder, or the staircase to the granary inside the barn, to access her bed in the short time he imagined she had left at home.

John had pulled himself from his sleep and spent part of Sunday morning removing books from the north bookshelf. He had realized the shelf spacing was similar to the rise of a stair tread; therefore, he would need only a single stringer to fashion a staircase parallel to the north wall without losing functional space. He measured and emptied specific shelves from west to east, starting at the lowest shelf to the taller shelves just outside the pantry that coincided with the stringers tread and riser.

The books lay stacked upon the kitchen table and bench. He stood over them, reached over the fortress of pages and grabbed a glass beside a plate of toast crumbs and smeared egg yolk. John finished the ale still inside with hopes it would ease the headache and unwrap his stomach, a trick Martin used the mornings after the slaughter. He chased the beer with some pickle brine, also one of Martin's remedies.

The rest of the morning and afternoon, he stripped, sawed, cut, and planed the stringer and treads out of birch trees he felled years earlier and left to air dry in the barn, while planning to leave the risers open. The ruddy glow of effort washed his pores with acrid sweat. He kept drinking water from the stove pot, hoping it would wash the smell of alcohol from inside him. He milled planks for treads and hammered each into the stringer and then shivved the shelves for plumb. He also reinforced the shelves carrying a tread with a strip of lumber secured to the log walls of his home. Then ran planks over the log rafters above to create a short boardwalk that connected the stairs to the loft.

He felt spent. He re-shelved all his books, having to stack them flat where the treads rested because the shelves had lost too much height to place them as they had been across. But the aesthetic pleased John. It interrupted the clean expectations of the library he had built. The roundness of the felled tree, the raised grain of the rough-sawn treads, and the perpendicular juxtaposition of stacked books interrupting his library felt like a soft voice. His house whispered to him and seemed to say, *Look around*. John took in his home. He saw the immensity of the library, books from all over the prairies. Each one had felt like it had been saved. He knew, logically, it was silly to feel that way about a book. But he felt pride for every one. He knew every town they came from. Some held a salty nose from trips to the British Columbian coast, where he tried salmon, and others were baptized with a smoky nose, having been recovered from a burnt-down neighbourhood in Saskatoon where he travelled with Charlie on his way to Frenchman's Butte to fish Sturgeon on the North Saskatchewan, and—his true intention—to visit the location where Charles Dickens's son, Francis Dickens, had commanded a unit of North West Mounted Police at Fort Pitt.

He stood back and looked at his home for what could have been the first time. The place had been a location for sleeping and eating. But now he looked. He saw the craftsmanship in the staircase, mouldings, wainscoting, and chair rails, plus his furniture. All of it had once been the trees on his property. He felled them all. Turned them into lumber. He never considered this space. It sat empty for years for after the fields had been broken and grain seeded, swathed, stooked, after cattle and donkeys were fed, after the firewood, if he had time, he slowly added to the house. It had never felt finished. It did not take precedence. It had been warm and dry—the only conditions that were important. But today, his daughter no longer had to camp on the couch.

"What took you so long?" He shook his head. He sucked the air of that space into his chest. He held it. The savoury smoke of sausage and rabbit above in the smoking chamber, the sweet and bitter trace of tree oils from the stringer and the firewood stacked at the door. Pleasant, inviting, homey, adjectives fluttered about his mind at the scene laid out in front of him. He held it. And he held it.

His lungs collapsed under the weight of never feeling at home. That exhalation did not come from his home, but from the start of his entire life, a cry forgotten at his birth. His eyes burned.

"Don't be stupid," he said to himself. He tried to clear the pride from his chest, but it lodged in his throat. He choked on the lump, which stung his vision with salt. He grunted at the lump.

"Still needs a railing," he said.

He moved to the porch to see what lumber remained. He pulled the door open, and there, dismounted from a buggy pulled by a buckskin Standardbred—its silver tail swatting the efforts still pulsing in its haunches—stood Bishop Dyck. He stared straight at John, but kept silent. He straightened the lap of his slacks. He pulled the crisp, white cuff of his shirt out of his jacket sleeve. He re-affixed his black hat and stroked his beard.

John spoke first.

"What are you doing here, Dyck?"

"Please, John, do call me Bishop. It's a sign of respect."

"What are you doing here, Dyck?" John picked up a roofing hatchet. His knuckles popped and his skin cried against the maple handle.

The Bishop sighed. "John …" He looked at the tendons and veins that pulsed in John's wrist. "I came about Gietz." He patted the shoulder of his horse. Its buckskin fur glistened in the sun, gilded flashes rode over the peaks of its rippling muscles.

"I told you I don't know him."

"I understand, but what of this Epp you mentioned, who is he? You talked of the Rapture. And this Gietz was spouting off about him today in the square. He was ranting for all to hear as we left church."

"I have no idea."

"John, please. Anything can help. He was talking like a heretic. Telling the entire town that the Rapture was happening."

"When?" John picked over the lumber. None of it seemed fitting for a rail.

"Soon. Wednesday. Or Thursday."

"I can't help you. You should leave." John tossed the hatchet into the toolbox and turned on the Bishop to walk inside. He threw the door closed behind him. But it sprung back open and the edge of the lock stile rapped his forearm. John peered over his shoulder. The large dark silhouette of the Bishop loomed over him. He filled almost the entire doorway. John turned and looked his visitor over, following his dark coat and pants to the one foot crossed over his threshold, the dusty toe and heel of one black leather shoe inside his very home on his mutta's *kilim*.

"What the hell do you think you're doing?"

"John, I need to know."

"No." John's lip trembled.

The Bishop looked John over. He saw a quiver in the man's hands, too. His vainglory misread this tremble. He puffed out his chest and stepped inside John's home.

John stepped back. He desired more room. He did this not for his safety and well-being, but by the same means as a cornered weasel springs about to create space to react. He didn't know what his body was about to do with the testosterone and adrenaline sparking through him bouncing off his knuckles. His slow steady step, his unwavering eye contact, and his hands rolling up his already rolled sleeves should have warned this hungry coyote.

"Impunity." John bit down hard. "You and the old colonial way. You just march around with this arrogance, this authority, don't you?"

"I don't know what you mean."

"Are you kidding? After everything you have taken from my family, you don't know what I mean?'

"I don't."

"She was my wife. You don't think we talked about you?"

The Bishop looked over John's shoulder, stared off into nothing. He shrugged. His lips tightened long into a mock frown. "There's been forgiveness. I have atoned."

"To whom?"

The Bishop shook his head. "I came here about Gietz."

"No." John pointed into the Bishop's face. "Rebecca died out here alone without her family. I had to take her away—take her from you!"

"John, please. All young women have to leave their family and enter holy matrimony."

"What absurdity! She had to marry me because you were caught raping her."

"John. Enough. I did no such thing."

"Then what would you call it?"

"I did not come here to be condemned by you. It's all been settled. I have made my peace."

"Oh, you've made peace. Well forgive me." John bowed and curtsied.

The Bishop shook his head at the showy mockery. "John enough. I need to know about this Gietz and Epp."

"How many times?"

The Bishop shot his gaze into John's eyes. "Excuse me?"

"I said, Rape. You raped my wife when she was a girl. How many times did you rape her?"

"I ..." The Bishop didn't just look away, but his body turned to let the harsh truths dodge by him. He nodded and shook his head and mind. "I ... I have ... atoned for my adulterous past. I cannot save you or your wife if you choose not to forgive."

"That's right—the greatest importance towards absolution was that she forgive what you perpetrated against her. She was forced to forgive or choose to be cast out. It was more shameful that she didn't forgive you, right?"

"I was trying to help. She was a broken woman."

"You broke her."

"Please John ..." The Bishop shrunk back to the door. "What about the safety of your daughter?"

"Don't." John pointed his finger into the Bishop's chest. "She's fine. She will always be fine. She has grown into an intelligent and sensitive person. She can do whatever she wishes. She is so capable I do not fear for her. In this life a woman has to be on guard for beasts like you. And believe me—she's ready."

"I don't care for the way you speak to me."

"I don't care for the way you raped my wife. And I don't care for the way you've sauntered into my home."

"I am here for the community. There is danger in this Gietz. He can't be allowed to continue."

"What is he doing?"

"Spreading the End of Days prophecy. He is a chiliast."

"I don't care. We don't follow your church and we won't follow his."

The Bishop smirked. "No?"

John's glare melted, and his squint turned askew.

"How old is ... your daughter? Yes, Mareika ... She looks to be close to Patricia's age."

"Who's Patricia?"

"My eldest."

"She's not yours, Bishop, if that's what you're getting at."

"Oh, come on John, that's not what I was alluding."

"She's mine, she's my little girl. You don't have to worry about that. Even if she weren't, she's safer here with me."

"Stop it. I did not come here to be insulted."

"Why would you ever step foot here?"

"Gietz. He's spouting all over town the End of Days. He's stirring up fear. Citizens are listening. I don't like it."

"So?"

"You said you know him."

"I don't know him."

"Well, you said you knew where he came from. You mentioned a Claas."

"Claas Epp Jr.? I don't have time for this."

"You have to help us."

"What? I don't have to do a damned thing."

"John, he's a dangerous man."

"To whom? He's going to take a bunch of suckers out to the field and sing and chant to the clouds, and when God fails to materialize, everybody will wander home, embarrassed they stood and sang hymns in a field in a their pajamas. The problem, your problem, will solve itself."

"I don't like your cavalier attitude. What about Rebecca?"

"You mean Mareika?"

"Yes, Mareika. I'm sorry."

"I'm sorry? You do know those words. 'I am sorry.' I never would have imagined the Bishop Dyck standing under my roof uttering those words."

"I'm serious. I have seen your daughter aiding this maniac, standing alongside him. Just this afternoon."

"No. You're mistaken."

"John. She's with him now."

"Mareika is too smart to get caught up in some fantasy of imaginary people floating up to heaven."

"Then where is she?"

"This is ridiculous." John looked around as if she were on the chesterfield reading. "No." He glanced to her newly risen room. There had been no flicker of candlelight. John clenched his fists. He clicked his tongue through his teeth and shook his head for letting the Bishop inside not his home but his mind. This moment felt like it may turn into a fight. Then he imagined how Rebecca would feel with this man, her attacker, standing here, insulting her home, besmirching her daughter.

"Sometimes I wonder if I shouldn't have done more." John played with plate of toast crumbs. He spun it. He spun it. He stopped. Then he cocked his chin up, stared sideways at the man who had raped his wife.

"I don't know what you mean."

"Rebecca. You come in here asking if Mareika is yours. Then you insult her character. What did you do to her?"

"I didn't do anything to your daughter."

"Not her. Rebecca. What did you do to her? You can say. It's just us here. And I know everything. Everything." John continued to stare at the plate of crumbs he spun. Patience casted over his body melted from his limbs.

"Your wife had a responsibility to your marriage. The things, the abhorrent things she and Sarah ... I cannot talk about this. They were made right in the eyes of our Lord."

"Were they, Bishop?" John shoved his plate away.

The Bishop stepped back.

"Why shouldn't I do more?"

"What do you mean, John?"

"Why didn't I do more? I was there on the East Bank. Foda arranged with you and her parents everything. And in a moment—me a complete stranger—would wed her and take her away. I sat awkwardly beside her. We didn't even look at each other while you presided over our union. I never said a word. I thought I was saving her. That's what I was told. All I knew was that she needed to be free of you. But you sent her away from one enduring pain to a stranger's bed."

"Take heed to yourselves: If thy brother trespass against thee, rebuke him; and if he repent, forgive him."

"Stop hiding in your Bible. When did you repent? You got caught and traded her for silence."

The Bishop shook his head. His eyelids folded over his eyes, put to rest the charges being flung at him. "You have a child, a beautiful child. *She shall be saved in childbearing . . .*"

John stepped to the Bishop.

"John!" The Bishop held his hand to John's chest, used a tone saved for scolding children or a woman, a tone muscular and taut with authority.

"I'm not one of your Brethren." John slapped the Bishop's hand away. He stabbed a finger into the Bishop's chest. The cloth of his lapel, no longer black but a charcoal, felt scorched by years of soap and lye. "You don't get a stipend from the church around here do you, Bishop? You left Manitoba in shame, didn't you? Sarah, absolution? You got caught. Her belly swelled with a part of you poisoning her. It wasn't absolution. It was shame. Shame forced you, her rapist, to save her family's reputation. Then they caste you out, sent you west to save them from the shame and rumour of your trespasses."

Bishop Dyck swung from his accuser and marched for the door. John slammed his palm against the stile, leaned all his weight, and prevented the Bishop from fleeing.

"I demand you stop this. I'm leaving."

"I don't care. You have never asked me for forgiveness."

"I don't owe you anything."

"No, you don't. But you owe it to Rebecca."

"I have said—"

"Nothing!"

"John, I demand."

"What?" John grabbed Bishop Dyck by his lapels and flung him to the floor, mounting him. The Bishop's eyes squeezed shut, and he turned his cheek anticipating John's fists to rain down upon him.

"Are you afraid?"

When violence never came, the Bishop tried pushing up against his captor. The men tussled, but John's years wrangling donkeys, cows, and steers gave him, the smaller man, a clear strength advantage.

"Get off me." The Bishop's voice shot high with a childish whine. He tried rolling. The men tussled more, but John never lost his top position.

John slapped him. He slapped him again. His hands rose and took over his words. The Bishop tried to grab his attacker's wrists. He protested. Then John's fingers coiled, and his knuckles fell. The hammering of fists shocked the Bishop. His pleas fell back inside. He relented. He folded his arm over his face and hid behind his elbows. John held his fists. He saw the Bishop's chest rise in rapid bellowing thrusts. John stared at the arteries in his neck thumping with spent energy and fear.

"This is how Rebecca felt ..." He grabbed the Bishop by his beard. "Look at me."

"John, don't."

John raised a hand again. The Bishop squeezed his eyelids and cheeks. John let the moment stretch. "This is how Rebecca felt." John's voice softened with empathy for his wife's memory. "I'm not going to do a damned thing. I just wanted you to feel just a fraction of what Rebecca and your wife felt. What Sarah feels every night under you. There has been no absolution, Bishop." John poked the Bishop between his eyes in an attempt to capture his full attention.

"I confess to you and your Lord that I have sinned. I confess!" John cleared his throat and waited for the Bishop to open his eyes.

The man under him blinked and blinked and blinked, his eyes wild, glistening like a snared hare. John continued, "I repent, Bishop Dyck. Now forgive me."

The Bishop, his eyes fell off John. His frozen gaze looked nowhere. It cast off into oblivion. His mind removed from the humiliation of his helplessness by this assault, he seemed to refuse to acknowledge.

"You can't even look at me. Do you get it now? You can never expect from me forgiveness. Your absolution, it's horse shit."

"Please don't curse."

"Jesus Christ."

"And do not take the Lord's name in vain."

"Don't moralize to me. And don't use my swearing as a way to stop listening. You aren't safe here."

The Bishop froze. He swallowed.

What remained between the two men were a succession of wild blinks from the man pinned against the floor and a stern heat from John's eyes. John felt the man go limp.

"It is *you*. You have taken the Lord's name in vain. You preach his good words, while raping your parishioners."

"I—"

"Quiet!" John took the Bishop by his throat, cocked his fist. The Bishop tried to hide his face under John's knee, now weighing heavy down upon his shoulder. "You sold your community on the word of a god and stole those girls' hope. How many others were there?"

The Bishop, his stare fell off to the side, its focus disappearing through the walls of John's home. His ears rang and he ceased listening.

"How many!"

Nothing. There would be no answers. Every second and every shake, the man who destroyed Rebecca's mind disappeared further inside himself, contented to his incapacity. He was physically bettered but still held some power wrapped within the secrets he held.

Words, hot and heavy, grated through John's teeth, littered frustration and hate over the Bishop's beard. "And you got away with it." John's dominant hand jumped around his neck. He clenched the throat as he would a drenched rag dripping with cold water. "I don't know why I shouldn't kill you right now."

The strained notes of the Bishop's voice evaporated from his mouth, "John . . . don't."

"It would be right."

"It would be sin . . ." The Bishop opened his eyes. They bore into John's forehead. His pupils dilated. Then he smirked.

"You son of a bitch . . ." John saw it. That dilation was memory. That memory, exposed in the twinkling as nostalgia. "You forget, I don't follow your doctrine. Where I live—in this world surrounding us—I see only chaos. And we react and adapt to it. It's how we react that matters most, you see?" John bore his knee hard, but his hand at the throat relaxed just long enough to inspire the Bishop with optimism that he would soon be free.

But then John reached back with his other hand, clenched the man's cock and balls. "I just remembered. I have a whole bucket of tools in the barn."

He twisted. The Bishop screamed, but the cry turned into sputters and gurgles. He bucked his hips. That only strengthened the grip. His fear filled the house with a fog.

"Have you ever seen an animal castrated?" The Bishop's breath wrung through his lungs from under John's knee, past his grip, and burst out his mouth and nose. Tears, snot, spit oozed from him.

"No!" He fell limp again. John's knee pinned the man there to the floor through his stomach.

"Do you think you'd bleed to death?" John released the man's testicles. "I don't think you would. I leave the gelding's wound open."

John got off the Bishop and went for the door. The hinges squealed as he eased it opened. "There is no sin where I tread. There is chaos and I choose to be kind." He stopped looking at the Bishop. "You made your choice. You sided with cruelty and ruin and called it salvation."

"John . . ." The Bishop lay. His eyes wide and held to the ceiling. A fly walked upside down on a girder. The heat from the stove felt dry but colder than his own forehead. John looked at the former church leader. He lay as a man placed to rest at a wake without the pennies upon his eyes.

"Forgiveness ... Forgiveness ... you have it wrong, Dyck. Rebecca never needed to forgive you. What she needed was to forgive herself. She never did anything wrong. She was not born wrong. Nothing was wrong with her. Yet she learned to punish herself everyday—every joyless day for the rest of her life. Rebecca needed to love herself. Get out."

The Bishop rose; however, his eyes turned to the floor as he walked out the door. He bent for his hat. He turned it in circles, his fingers marching around the brim. On the threshold, he paused. "But what of Gietz."

"I don't care about him or you. Go and thank your god I didn't kill you today."

His chin tipped to his shoulder, but he buried his eyes away from John. He smirked. His smugness and contempt mingled behind his cold gaze. He collected himself before he dished a jab at John. "He does have your daughter."

John shoved the man onto the porch and slammed to door.

Eastern Reserve, Manitoba

Dill Pickle Recipe

100 small cucumbers
6 pints of water
1 pint of vinegar
½ cup of salt
½ cup sugar
dill
10–15 quart jars

LINE JARS WITH dill. Scrub the cucumbers and pack into quart jars. Boil the water, vinegar, salt, and sugar, then pour over the cucumbers. Fill the jars but leave ¼ inch. Seal.

Oma Katie Klippenstein

Black Gully Lake

THROUGH THE NIGHTTIME, winds shifted from the north to the south and eased. The midmorning, warm, full of sunshine and clear blue skies, gave Black Gully Lake the feel of noon. A breeze combed over the pasture, slid inside Ibi's tent before it passed through his mind and rustled the dust that covered his memories and insecurities. The calico followed the winds to Ibi's chest, circled, and curled into a ball. Ibi stretched from his sleep then shoved the cat out of the tent. He draped a shirt over his face to ignore the day. But inside his mind, away from sleep, the courtyard of Ak-Metchet manifested. His breath strained as he saw empty tables, Claas's chair empty, too.

"Claas, I almost lost them ..." Ibi examined the desolate image of Ak-Metchet. The well was dry. And the windows of the homes were black, matte black. "I stood like you would. Remember how you'd climb upon your chair. Stand above us and share your visions." He focused on his memories of Claas's chair at the head of the table. "I can see it." His voice echoed inside his visions. "They came, Claas. I was there over them all. I stood and showed them the proof—even the newspapers. They looked. They laughed. They turned their backs. I lost them ... But then this girl stepped out of the crowd. And she sang. She had the sweetest voice. She both brought them back and held them to me. An atheist, Claas ..."

Ibi's dreamscape, a swirl of memory, rose out of his mind. What remained: Mareika inside an ascension gown, her long brown hair parted down the middle, draped over each shoulder, resting upon her breasts, her skin radiant with a pink flush. Ibi watched her breathe out from glistening parted lips.

He wove the outside world with his memories. Ribbons of bird-song and the chatter of squirrels wrapped around the Mareika he saw. Nature's cadence joined the melody that rose from her. He desired to raise her gown off her, touch her skin, cradle her breast, take her hips. He reached for himself. But shame held him still.

He snapped the shirt off his face. He rubbed the image from his eyes. He marched to the lake and into its waters. The cold, still holding winter, stung his skin, pierced his joints and scrotum. He dove under the water and let only his head surface. The soak washed the sex from his imagination, but, oh, how he wished to find Mareika in those same waters. She felt the same static charge that promised lightning before thunder, tugged at the hair about his forearms, neck, and genitals. He crawled from the waters and lay upon the sand. The sunshine warmed him, and he whispered up to the blue sky: "Claas ... *Who is this girl?*"

The murmurs and prattle floating with the first poplar seeds of spring upon the breeze warped and twisted into intonation and a pronounced voice took shape.

"And the Spirit and the bride say, Come. And let him that heareth say, Come. And let him that is athirst come. And whosoever will, let him take the water of life freely."

Ibi sat up and looked for Claas. "Should I go to her?" He looked for his answer in the pasture and brushline. He saw and he heard nothing. "I don't know if she will come today." Ibi thought about abandoning his sermon. He imagined the residents waiting around the cart in the square. He saw them as the people of Ak-Metchet had gathered for the Rapture all those years ago. How they had waited. How he had looked into the sky. How he had wanted to be the first one to spot Jesus. How he had felt lucky to be so thin and short, wishing the lightest children would rise before the bigger, heavier adults. The only thing that rose away that day was joy and optimism.

Disappointment lingered. His parents would take him away across an ocean where he'd wandered empty and alone. He knew the disenchantment the people he inspired yesterday would feel.

"We cannot lose them." The shadow of Mareika's memory fell over his thoughts. She pulsed through his blood. He placed his palm to his chest. He counted the racing beats and stopped after twenty-six. "I promise you, Claas. I know she will return. But I promise that I will not abandon your flock.

"*I am the good shepherd: the good shepherd giveth his life for the sheep.*"

Wapos County

JOHN IS GONE. Gone. Off into the wilderness for lumber, provisions with that Métis boy again. I should have felt bad, but I don't. I feel lighter. That first night Sarah and I lay together, it washed over me. I threw my clothes off to feel the sheets. I laundered them for this very night. Then I crawled inside and waited for you, Sarah. Remember, Darling, remember how we trembled, how we giggled. We didn't know what we were doing, and you so patient. You said you wanted to show me something. Your lips searched my entire body. From my neck, where I tickled. You nibbled my ear. But it was your tongue. My lungs filled full of your breath the moment you took my breasts with your hands, kissing them before your tongue traced over them. You licked me. You licked me as if my skin was covered in milk and cream. It felt like the greatest truth. I moved through the world not knowing who I was. But you discovered me, unearthed me. Your hand firmly pressed to my inner thigh. You kissed my hip. And my knees folded open and I lifted my foot until the soled rest flat against the bed. Sarah, our giggles turned into hot breath as you traced your finger to the cruxes of my body, from between my big toe to my separate parts. Your body moved over me as if I were silk. Your leg snaked over mine and we lay. How natural your head lay gently upon the root of my hip. Your lips fell into my hair and you kissed me. You slid your hand, your fingertips painting excitement, from my middle down my leg. I gasped. You said,

"Hush." And your hand with a circular sweeping pressure lit my person on fire. I closed my eyes and saw only you. My skin, smouldering everywhere, the soft hairs ashen and brushed into the air by those kisses. I took another deep breath and tried to keep my smile from swelling over my face. My hand found yours. I held your wrist as if we were one. And followed. I felt my hips rise. And I followed your whispers. With another deep breath you reached closer to my heart. It was there for you to take. Your kiss upon my thigh burned. You kissed my thigh again. You kissed it again. I said stop, but I dropped my hand onto the sheets. And felt your mouth, your tongue, your hands take hold of my hips. I didn't mean those words. Words can lie, but my body could not. My hands found your hair, their brown looping curls mingling, tangling, capturing my fingers. You had total providence over my being. I couldn't see the planks, the plaster of the ceiling. I only wanted to pull you inside my body. I needed you to be a complete part of me. I saw the midnight skies, the stars twinkle behind my eyelids. You kissed me with your tongue as if to feed me. Then we stroked our hair until we fell asleep. Do you remember, Sarah? You whispered, "You're my angel."

Black Gully Schoolhouse

Τ HE INSTRUCTIONS: "Take the donkey in the third pen to Junior. It belongs to Paul Lee now."

I walked Paul Lee's donkey out of the yard. This beast, a gelding used for pulling brush, Foda called Bison, because he bit, nipped, and chewed on anything, especially shoulders and fence posts. Foda explained that another similar sounding word in Low German meant bite. All the donkeys bit and chewed the fences, but he seemed to do it more. He was brown, rather than grey like the majority of Foda's donkeys. He liked to walk before me. I had to stop and pull his harness as Foda instructed, but inevitably he would trot ahead, yanking my arm. I didn't mind this day. I was not taking him to Junior Lee, but to Ibi. I wanted to help, and he shouldn't have to lug that cart around alone.

The northern wind swirled around me, pecked my neck, my cheeks with a goodbye from winter. And dawn vibrated with the wooden glissando of a million-billion frogs thawed, awake, and free of the frostline. The paradox of spring laid over the prairie, desolately brown, dusty, and ashen, branches naked of foliage, the grass a fragile, crisp mat of forgotten beige. But overhead, the blue skies themselves were woven together with an imperceptible gilded thread. And under the sunshine, the gales warmed their whispers and promises that dusted off my anticipation of summer. Patience. Resolve.

Optimism. Like germinated seeds themselves, they sprouted inside me. I felt so aware of the springtime racing around me. And my pace allowed for me to notice the thorny buds, shy sienna pinning a fervent energy inside, ready to uncoil, ready to sprout leaves all over the poplar, birch, and elm trees. The fuzzy seeds of poplars and willows captured the sunlight. They glowed. Those trees looked cast in a blonde-silver. And underfoot, poking through the beige mat of dead grass, the points of new green stabbed through the dirt towards the sunshine.

I tied the creature to the tetherball post in the schoolyard. All the younger children came around to pet him.

"Stay away from his backside. If he doesn't kick you, he got into the cattle's silage." Almost on my words the donkey lifted its tail and splattered the ground with evidence.

The kids collectively groaned then laughed and giggled. The boys tried to stir the girls into the mess. I swatted their heads with my gloves. The mornings still held a crispness before the sunshine had enough time to burn off the last remembrances of winter.

I marched through the damp and matted wild grasses, returned to the clearing Jonah and I had shared the week before, the morning Jonah had tried to convince me we needed more than the touch of our hands. The chill, it became my reason for returning. My coat still hung from a branch somewhere in that clearing. I found it crumpled below the trees, kissed with frost. I shook it. The dashed droplets rained over me. I cleaned off the dead grass and draped it over my arm. The felt, cold, drew my pores closed.

"Mareika."

I turned. Jonah Wiebe came out into the clearing. He smiled, his eyes sparkled with joy and excitement. He stood tall and sure. But I put up my hands to him.

He stopped, his face wrung with confusion.

"I have to go," I said.

"I just thought that we could ..."

"I don't want to."

"But ..."

"I don't want to." I rubbed my stomach.

Jonah scowled. His face warped with revolt. He looked like Foda fresh after a donkey kicked him in his separate parts while he tried to trim its hooves. Aggravation. Frustration. Disgust.

"That's not fair."

I felt taller. I had always been. But Jonah felt ... unimpressive, dismissed. "Grow up, Jonah." What did I owe him? I turned my back. And I waited for the sound of that boy to fade. But I didn't hear the crush of field grass or the snap of twigs.

I refused to look at him. "Why aren't you going?"

"You're ..."

I could feel him looking around for an adult. Then he threw it, a word like a stone at my back.

"Jezebel."

Such an ugly word. It reminded me of the pain clawing at my insides. I touched the cushion of cloth wadded up near my other parts. I crossed my arms, squeezed myself, with a hope my tears would stay inside where my heart hurt. His voice was only sounds. Rearrange the consonants and vowels, and it became nonsense. He didn't know what he was talking about. He didn't respect that I could be dying. And he'd be sorry if I did die. I hope he would. Maybe it was his fault. I wanted to scream at him, *It is your fault. You forced me.* But he had not. I dreamed of him. I enjoyed the jammy sweetness of his mouth. I broke. I gave in to myself. And this is my charge. Suffer.

The ache wrung my pelvis. His blame aggravated it further. I didn't want him to see me get sick. "Go back to school with the other children, Jonah."

I listened to his body rattle field grass and break the branches of brush as he pushed his way back to the schoolhouse.

I gagged from the cramps twice, swallowed the spit pooling under my tongue, collected Bison, and then followed my way along the creek to Black Gully Lake. I needed Ibi's smile.

I saw his tented canvas hung from the branches of a large pine. It looked like a caterpillar's cocoon. Ibi lay upon his belly. He licked his finger and flipped a page from a large leather-bound book. I followed his lips fluttering as he read. *I love the way he reads* flashed inside my brain. My skin lit with heat. I became embarrassed even before I could hear him talk. I froze, hesitated to return back towards the schoolhouse. I looked back to him.

He was looking at me.

I turned my back and growled at myself.

I looked to him again. He smiled, turning another page.

He waved.

"I love this quote from *Heimweh*." Ibi showed me the page. "*The Bishop in Kaiserslautern was called to account, because he had permitted a Mennonite woman to be buried in the churchyard, and had attended the funeral.*"

He held the book out for me to take.

Bison nipped at Ibi's hand and shoved into him. Ibi pushed at the animal and danced to come around. The beast stayed between us, herded the man away. I tugged on his bridle. With his neck cranked backward to me, Ibi picked up the book and moved to my side.

I didn't recognize the language of the words, but I knew what it meant to hold a book. Foda, excited, passed me books and pointed to passages I should read. "Read them out loud," he'd say, as if my voice released the words like flutterbyes.

I moved closer to the crackling leather of the spine, breathed the deep odour of its hide. The book smelled like the expanse of a world I had never seen. I imagined those aromas hidden inside those pages were spices and flowers and grains not grown on this prairie, every one unpronounceable to me. That book smelled exotic.

"What's it about?"

Bison pushed at Ibi again. He shoved at the animal's face.

"A prince, Eugenius, and the love of his life, a Mennonite girl not unlike you, and the journey and struggle to gather ..." Ibi closed his eyes. He looked as though he was listening to the breeze.

"Sometimes, I listen for Claas. I wait for his voice to rise from my memories. Always his words would glow when he discussed this book. 'It's about the Prince and this Mennonite girl and how they and ...'" Ibi's finger tapped the air as he seemingly quoted this Claas or the book. "... a *small band of protected believers from all nations ...*" Ibi lost his translation. "*He led them until the Kingdom of our Lord begins.*" He smiled at me. "It's prophetic. It's us ..."

I loved how he looked at me, shared eye contact. But following Ibi's interpretation, silence stretched out between us. Could he sense my own disconnection? I did not want to confess I had not read that book, nor did I understood German. I cleared my throat.

"Ow!"

Bison bit Ibi's shoulder. I gave his nose a swat.

"No." I untied the lead and smacked the animal on his rump. He galloped to the long rye grasses growing at the edge of the brush.

I watched Ibi rub his shoulder before he removed a silk scarf he used as his bookmark from between the pages.

"What a pretty scarf," I said.

He snaked it over my shoulder around my nape. My skin danced. My heart raced. I looked down to my knees, knocking them together under my dress.

"You can have it. I got it when I left Turkestan. In Akhisar, Turkey."

The smooth face of the scarf lifted my pores as I slipped it from my neck into my hands. I raised it to my nose. There amongst the swirls of purple and blue, I sensed those pages laced with the silk. I traced my fingers over its surface, the pads following the amoebic chaos of purples, almost reds, which had seemingly dissolved into the dense blue that dominated the edges of the scarf.

"Have you ever seen the rain on the ocean?" Ibi asked.

"No."

"When I was leaving the Mediterranean for Canada, that was the first time I saw the ocean. It rained that day. And when the rain water mixed with the ocean water, it was like rainbows swam over the surface."

I looked askance at the description. "Rainbows?"

He nodded. "Imagine them bending and curling and writhing like an earthworm in a puddle. There were all the colours of a rainbow twisting and warping and changing shapes across the surface of the ocean."

"Like this scarf?"

"Yes."

"But this scarf is purple."

"I know, but the swirling of the colours, that's what I speak of."

"It's pretty. My mother loved purple."

"Then you must keep it."

"I can't." I took another smell of the scarf.

He took out his Bible and flipped the pages. Ibi cleared his throat.

"And a certain woman named Lydia, a seller of purple, of the city of Thyatira, which worshipped God, heard us: whose heart the Lord opened, that she attended unto the things which were spoken of Paul. And when she was baptized, and her household, she besought us, saying, If ye have judged me to be faithful to the Lord, come into my house, and abide there. And she constrained us."

"Acts." I stood straight and stepped to the man. His teeth so white, framed by soft pink lips, shone with the sunshine.

"That was *Acts*. I thought you said you and your foda were atheists."

"My mother used to read that part to me. Lydia." I pulled the scarf to my lips. I was almost dizzy from pages trapped in the cloth. I became awkward and more aware of myself in the space between us. I didn't know if I was standing right or if I should sit. Confused, I slapped his shoulder. I didn't know why I did that. I wished I could have disappeared in that scarf. I inhaled another breath from it. Ibi looked at his shoulder before he continued.

"Thyatira, which is where I was."

"You said Akhisar." I palmed the scarf, then dusted the silk like a wild rose across my cheek.

"Akhisar is Thyatira. When Saint Paul was there it was under Roman rule. Now it is not. And known as Akhisar. But the purple dye still flows." His fingers pinched the scarf. He led it from my fidgety fingers up my forearm.

He held his eyes on me. He just looked at me. I loved being seen, but soon I felt naked. I looked across Black Gully Lake. Foxtails and cattails rose from the mud of its shores.

He wrapped the scarf about my waist. It graced my behind before he cinched it about my hips. He fluffed the bow he created.

"The quote, why do you love it so much?"

Ibi's eyes left the scarf, floated from my waist over my chest, neck, cheek, and back to my eyes. I looked away.

"The Lydia quote?"

"No. The one from before, about the Mennonite girl buried in the church grounds." I pulled the bow, gathered the scarf back into my palm and hid in its aroma again.

"Because it challenged the traditions of the Mennonite leaders. It was never okay to bury a woman in the same grounds as a man, and now it is."

"Mutta said that when she was younger she sat on the opposite side as the men when they went to church. That the service was in High German, and she couldn't speak High German."

"Not where I came from. Claas let everybody sit in on his sermons. He let women sit with their children and husbands. Women are so very important to man …" Gietz smiled.

I smiled. Then, with the grace of his thumb, he moved a fallen strand of hair from off my eyebrow. My cheeks, ears, and chest pulsed with warmth, which radiated over my lap.

"Foda says he never liked the way my mother served the Church. He said she did more than Bishop Dyck. But she never got any of the recognition, because she was a creature less than man. And Mutta said you don't do service for praise. Foda didn't bury her in the cemetery. He burned her in a fire, collected the ash into our copper scuttle. He kept it in the barn. And in springtime when the winds blew eastward the strongest, he scooped her up and let me scoop up two handfuls. And we dropped her onto the winds. I saw the ash streaked over the grass on our back quarter."

Ibi took me by my wrists. His granite eyes took me; they scooped me up and cradled me. Anything could have come out of his mouth and it would have sounded like poetry. I knew it would.

"Your mother sounds like Lydia."

I couldn't control the smile that escaped. I dipped my gaze and veiled the beaming with a wrist. The aromas of the scarf had enveloped my skin. I felt my pulse race.

"She truly must have been better than the church elders. I know Bishop Dyck. I met him. So I know she must have been a better person than him, than *that* church. And so are you." He wrapped the scarf over my wrists. And with them bound, he gave me a tug. "Come to my sermon today."

"You're having another sermon?"

"I must. The End is near, and I must let everybody know." He pulled his shirt off. A mat of dark hair covered his chest. He smiled at me, brushing his fingers at a piece of grass that sat amongst his chest hair. My gaze felt shackled to his body. He stood in front of me for what felt like a day. When he finally pulled on a different white shirt, I shook my eyes. But when I looked away, I still saw him, his lean form. "I promise I can save you."

I nodded.

His lips leapt onto my cheek. His skin felt as warm and soft as a puppy ear. I wished I could have wrapped myself inside that touch.

"If only the End was not so near ..." He sighed. His eyes fell from me across the distances past the lake. "Do you promise to take up so much more work to help?" He knelt and took my hands.

"Yes, I will help you. I brought you a gelding. For pulling your wagon."

He looked around the glade for the donkey. "I need more than this ... donkey." He looked some more for the animal. "I need conviction. I need ..." He pulled me up and stepped into me and untied my wrist. "I need you to help convince our people."

"It's ..."

"What?"

"I cannot say."

"Why not?"

"I wish you had come unto me sooner." I looked down into his chest. He stepped right into me. With his arms wrapped about my shoulders, he held me. His fingers traced what felt like letters around my back. I imagined them to be the curve and loops of the sweetest words, a love note.

"After Wednesday the Rapture comes, and we will be guided away from this Earth. And I only hope that I know you in heaven."

I giggled.

"Don't laugh."

"I didn't ..."

"It's true. There is something special about you ... and I am so proud to have found you."

"You can keep the donkey to pull your cart. Do you have oats? He loves oats."

"You are so far from home ..." His voice fell into a whisper as his forehead met mine.

I searched Ibi's eyes after his words. His mouth held open, patient, waited for me to respond. "Um ... he can just eat grass and drink from the lake."

Ibi tipped me a smile, then took my trembling hands. I couldn't look him in the eyes.

"Will you join me in the square today? I'm having another sermon." He gathered my hands inside his, placed his lips upon our knuckles.

"Yes."

"You are a godsend ..." His kisses rode up to my wrists. I saw from the corner of my glance that he looked at my chin. I let escape the slightest of nods. And he followed. He led his lips once again to my cheek. He held them there off the corner of my mouth. I turned my lips to his, stole them, tugged free, and ran back towards the school. I held my hand high and let the purple scarf wave.

Wapos County

JOHN STEPPED FROM his bedroom. Behind him, the windowless room, pitch black, seemed to drop him into the world as an errant coin from a pocket set to bounce and roll away. He palmed the knob and eased the door closed. With no click of the latch, he pushed-pulled on the knob. His bedroom door was closed. He turned. He examined the sofa where he expected Mareika to still be sleeping. He saw no slow rise of sleep lift the blankets. It didn't move. He tiptoed on his socked toes and pulled the quilt back. Mareika had gone. He nodded and proceeded to fold the quilt, drape it over the back of the sofa, and put away the rest of the bedding. He glanced over the bundles of pillows and cushions and the patchwork quilt on the sofa again. He felt glad Mareika wouldn't have to sleep there another night after he finished the loft today, but he also felt ashamed that he allowed her to sleep there for so long without a proper bedroom.

He stepped back and forth across the room several times, all on a heavier tread, his heels almost hammering the plank floors. His shoulders fell forward with the fatigue of long days and short nights that resided inside his skin. After he dragged the birchwood sofa into the kitchen he acknowledged his lethargy.

He grabbed and shook the coffeepot, slapped its base. Then poured a mug and gulped the lukewarm brew back. A smile snuck across his face as he knew the pot wasn't yesterday's but a brew

Mareika must have done before she left. As a parent, he saw it prudent to look at the world, every setting, and determine what needed to be done to prepare for what's next, to put tools away after using them in their original place, to wash dishes after a meal, to weed when those little buggers were sprouts. "Get things ready. Keep things tidy. Don't put things off." His mantras. His chest swelled, which lifted his shoulders as he stood there nodding for his daughter, her preparedness, her thoughtfulness. Though every action was now a memory to her, it helped prepare John better.

He touched the pot again in an attempt to guess when she must have left. The heat said an hour. His face scrunched. "That's an early morning." He shrugged and gulped down the brew. Then he remembered the donkey for Paul Lee—of course—maybe she took him early, because he knows she can get uncomfortable around strangers.

He entered the barn through the joining door at the back of the home. One of the barn cats had a mouse, its jaws latched over the critter's nape. Its legs still pedalled with escape. He walked through the barn, opened a pen, and filled a feed bag with oats for the returning donkeys. He hung it outside.

The entire morning glistened. Green grasses dominated at the bottom of the ditches and at the lower frays of the pasture. The high points and the north and east still struggled with winter, brown with stunted green flecks. The crisp air lapped at John's skin. He drew in the morning. The sweet syrup of birch and poplar coming back to life rode the spring air. The frigid morn held his shoulders higher. John nodded for only a second to this day. But his shoulders collapsed when he gave up on the breath. He let their weight pull him over. As he reached for his toes, his lower back hissed and popped. He grunted as he stood upright. When the buzz of tension and pain muted from behind his ears, he heard the clop of hooves and the grind of gravel. He saw Charlie Gervais.

Charlie, a young Métis man not yet twenty-five, sat at the reins. His hair, blacker than coal, lay back from his forehead in loose, oiled waves. The hair below his temples tapered fast to a clean shave around the ear and down his neck. His dress mimicked that of John, black slacks and a black coat. Under the jacket he wore a grey woollen shirt that laced at the collar but remained loose, the laces tattered. Charlie had a universal look, which posed a problem for most people. It astonished both him and John how important it was for strangers to categorically label him. At best most strangers could say he was not European, at least not French or English. He heard during many casual conversations—at wood mills, railyards, river ferries, banks, and on streets and boardwalks—an abrupt, "What are you?" He was a description of nots. "You're not white, you're not red, you're not black, you're not yellow. Not. Not. Not. And not."

Most assumed he was some sort of half-breed, but because they could not tell, it frustrated them in the least and angered them at the most. Charlie, a sharp wit, played with these frustrations, backed up by his strong frame, his farming hands and back, and his emboldened youth.

"Why is that important?" he'd ask. He himself considered character most—a person's actions decided who you really were. That's what drew him to John. The man was upfront, honest, and respected a strong work ethic. He was a rare white man who seamlessly moved through any community he entered. They met when John travelled through his community. He had stopped for water and found an eleven-year-old Charlie struggling to pull a sturgeon from the South Saskatchewan River. After the two battled the giant fish, he helped gut it, fillet it, and break it down. Then he loaded it into his wagon and drove it back to Charlie's home, where he even helped set up the smoking of the fish. He did not try to confiscate it like so many other white men of that region would have. It was there that he noticed many of the horses needed ferrying, so he stayed on for three days and tended to horses, sheep, pigs, and cattle.

In that time, a French priest, a Father Pierre, had come to their village to save the *illegitimate offspring from their unfortunate class*. The intent, as John had later explained to Charlie, was to send the children in his community far off to St. Paul to the lousy confines of that church-run lodging to be re-educated. John had heard from cousins in the area that this St. Paul was being devoured by the Great White Plague he imagined would kill these people, his neighbours. But with John present, Father Pierre left them alone, because he witnessed their community *were living outside the Indian mode of life within a pure white existence*—even if it was with a Mennonite.

The entire time, he let Charlie tag along as well as other Métis men and women. John demonstrated his veterinary skills. He asked for nothing. He simply shared his knowledge. In return, he became a student. He took in methods of curing and smoking fish. He had never considered using birch wood. But the deep leathery tan and smooth, deep, sweet smoke it imparted on perch won him over. He would introduce his own smoking with this wood. And he came back several times throughout the seasons, year after year. Charlie, when old enough, took stints with John to continue a mentorship of sorts, when he learned about millwork.

He steered a single donkey cart. Charlie earned the donkey from his work around the farm, a bonus. Inside the cart, timber collected and seasoned on Martin's quarter, where John allowed Charlie to operate a mill. In fact, because the banks would not deal with Indians, John had loaned Charlie the financing to start up the mill. He helped procure the machinery and on slow days before the harvest and after, he'd go to work for Charlie. He never flaunted his age or experience, merely kept his head down and listened. When the mill yard needed sweeping, he swept. John respected the work of a hired hand, and Charlie respected his ability to remove his ego while he established himself in the region.

"There's no such thing as an unimportant job," John would say.

"Just unimportant people," Charlie joked back with a ribbing.

At present, Charlie had a contract for one-third of the sleepers the railway wanted to pass through the Black Gully region with an option for more as the railway made its way over the foothills to the mountains, which made Charlie very prosperous in this single year. The contract had the mill running seven days a week with nine employees and a dozen contracts to local farmers, ranchers, and lumberjacks to supply timber.

It should have kept Charlie too busy for a small project such as Mareika's loft, but Charlie felt respect for John. He had given so much to lift him up, and his community, that his presence and hands were a drop in a bucket of what he could ever return to this man.

"Morning, John."

"Charlie." John nodded.

"I threw in some timbers and planking from the railway job just in case."

"What do I owe you?"

"Don't worry about it. The railway rejected these." He winked. "Did you hear about the fires?"

The men set to work unloading the wood onto the porch.

"Yeah, Athabasca is burning," Charlie said. "If spring keeps coming down, we should get that smoke in a few days."

"Incredible."

"I heard entire villages burned to the ground."

"Well, let's hope monsoon June decides to show up—our crops will need the rain, too."

With the cart unloaded, the work created silence. They pounded timber posts into place and secured them to the floor and rafters. They stopped to discuss the strategy of running a boardwalk from a potential staircase on the east wall that John thought to blend into the bookshelf previously.

"We can just drop planks from the top of a stair over the rafters and build our way to the future loft."

The men kept their heads down and worked.

Charlie sawed through lumber, sweat raining into the piles of sawdust as John called back measurements. He tossed the planks towards the front door, where John snagged them to pound into place.

"John?" Paul Lee stepped around Charlie, slipped into the house. He looked straight back at Charlie. "Sorry I'm late. I see you got yourself a Bungi."

"A what?" John said.

Charlie finished his cut and carried the plank to John. They both faced Paul.

Paul stood and examined the men casing him. He held his tongue trying to untangle the events leading to the stern expressions on his friend's face and the stranger that writhed inside his head.

Charlie spoke first. "I am Métis."

"Yeah, a half-breed. That's what I said." Paul pushed a short laugh to ease his discomfort. "You're half Indian and half French."

"I'm Métis."

"Paul, this is my friend Charlie. He owns the wood mill north of here."

Paul stood rigid at the door. He looked at John as he spoke. "Nice to meet you, Charlie."

Charlie looked at John and gave him a nudge. "I don't think your friend here works with any Métis."

"Well ... I know lots of Indians," Paul said.

"I'm Métis," Charlie said.

"I don't get it." Paul stayed frozen in his spot at the door.

John said, "What if he called you Irish?"

"I'm not, though."

"And I'm Métis," Charlie said.

"What's that supposed to mean?" Paul cocked his head and cinched up his pants.

"Do you feel that? You're insulted, aren't you?" John said.

"Well, Yeah. I don't know where I'm being insulting."

"That's how I feel," Charlie said. "I feel put down. I have lost a part of my existence. A huge gap in my traditional knowledge leaves me feeling as hollow as a oskana ka-asasteki, your buffalo, your bison, a pile of bones. I don't have a natural tongue. I dream, but I have to use your words to describe these thoughts and experiences. Mr. Paul Lee, all I want is my ... what's the word you'd use— Humanity. You and your family left Europe for a better life, because *their* world was closing in on you. Are you losing your faith? Are you losing your way of life? We, too, have been fenced in. How am I different than your pigs and cattle? This man raises donkeys, but it is I who feels like an ass. At least you have a spot at the table. You can own land. You can own a business. On paper, my mill is owned by

John. But it's mine. It's my toil. The Upper and Lower gentlemen hidden in Ottawa, they feared the Americans. *54–40 or Fight*! So they stitched east and west. And when these plains needed broke, they used the back of your Mennonite neighbours, The Hutterites and Doukhobors. But me? We have been pushed to the fringe to toil with promises as flimsy as the paper they're written on. After we fought for them." Charlie paces. His words pool into his fists.

John, intent on pulling the charge from the powder keg, moved to the door and slapped Paul on the shoulder. "We are not having fun with you, Paul. This is my friend. He, like you, is here to help. He's a good man, a hardworking man just like you. His people, they went through a rebellion with this country to be recognized. They struggled for their land just like you toil for yours. One of your greatest gifts were those two big ears of yours …" Paul chuckled. He fluffed his arms, rolled his shoulders and let the puff of his chest deflate. He sat on the porch and let what he had just heard settle. His knee bounced and danced as he passed a look back and forth between the stubbled field and Charlie. John gave him another pat. Paul let the weight of his neighbour's touch roll his shoulders. He rested his elbows upon his knee.

Paul contemplated Charlie's words, though he was too young to have heard about the Red River Rebellion or North-West Rebellion or remember the hanging of Louis Riel. He did know the strife of his family leaving Europe for Canada and pushing bush and breaking land every day for nearly three years for friends, family, and neighbours in a tight timeline set by a Canadian government and the work to meet grain demands to repay back those federal loans. Most had been a stress and burden on his father. He got the farm but worked from the age of eleven to feel like he could finally breathe if the weather cooperated.

"You're treating me like my culture, my name, that none of it matters. I am Métis. I am not Cree or Nakota or French or English or Mennonite. I am Métis. I am Charlie Gervais."

Paul dropped his eyes from Charlie. His head nodded above his rolled shoulders. He looked Charlie in the eyes. "I am sorry. I never gave it thought. You're right. I'm sorry, too, John. I meant no disrespect."

Charlie reached out his hand, "Marsee. Thank you."

Paul took it and bowed his head.

"Let's get to work." John said.

The promise of nightfall came as Mother Earth seemed to sigh a cool breath that moistened the grass and budding leaves with dew. But daylight still hung around the farm and prairie well past the supper hour. Songbirds still sang and squirrels still chattered under an azure horizon while plumes of the first mosquitoes rose in lavaliere columns about the fields, and the mating calls of frogs took over the silence of the day and eased through the open window of the farmhouse.

The breeze felt nice over the men's necks. The home held a humid heat of hard work and a soaked volume of community. The men were well away from the thought of sleep as they dove into glasses of ale with the work completed.

"Charlie, that's one hell of a crazy story." Paul lifted a glass of ale and took a good drink. He sighed at the release it offered his muscles. "Charles Dickens, Buffalo Bill, Rupert's Land, and Frenchman Butte, are you kidding me?" Paul stopped. His lips tightened with contemplation. He looked at Charlie and John. They smirked and looked at each other, then gave Paul a nod. "So Gabriel Dumont led the Métis at Batoche where your mother was the postmaster's daughter. And she had an affair with him while he fought with Charles Dickens's son, who led the North-West Mounted Police at Fort Pitt. Is that all right?"

"You got it," Charlie said.

"Wait … If you were Gabriel Dumont's son, how come your name isn't Dumont?"

"I was just messing with you."

"I knew it." Paul slapped his leg. "That's funny." He laughed and gulped at the last two mouthfuls of ale before he tipped more from the clay jug into his empty glass. He moved around the table to Charlie' glass then to John's, filling them to the brim. "So you aren't named after Charles Dickens."

"No, that is true," Charlie said. "Maamaa was a resident at Fort Pitt. And she did have an affair with a Métis during the battles, becoming pregnant. My grandfather was able to negotiate her leaving with Dickens as he and the NWMP retreated, while he and the rest of the townsfolk were held as hostages by Big Bear. She escaped with Dickens to Battleford and later at Christmas I was born. And she named me after Dickens's famous father."

"Wait . . . Charles Dickens lived in Saskatchewan?"

John interjected. "Francis Dickens. Charles Dickens's son, and he did lead the forces at Fort Pitt during the North-West Rebellion." John walked to his shelf and pulled *A Tale of Two Cities* down. "It's interesting the parallels between Charlie and the Rebellion and the French Revolution and the settings of this book." He tapped the hard leather cover.

"Did you read it?" Paul asked.

Charlie shook his head. "I can't get into it. It's long with descriptions. And I can't relate to it."

"You should try," John said. "Or write about your revolution."

Charlie picked it up:

"It was the best of times, it was the worst of times, it was the age of wisdom, it was the age of foolishness, it was the epoch of belief, it was the epoch of incredulity, it was the season of Light, it was the season of Darkness, it was the spring of hope, it was the winter of despair, we had everything before us, we had nothing before us, we were all going direct to Heaven, we were all going direct the other way—in short, the period was so far like the present period, that some of its noisiest authorities insisted on its being received, for good or for evil, in the superlative degree of comparison only."

"*For good or for evil.* Hmmm." Paul tipped his glass into his lips. "Did either of you hear about that fella who just got to town? They say he's been saying the world is ending in a day or so and we're all going to hell." Paul took another swig to whet his tongue. "My wife said he stood outside the churches trying to drum up a crowd. Not many people gave him their time, but she said Bishop Dyck and him got into it of sorts."

"Who?" Charlie said. He flipped his eyes back and forth between the men.

"I don't want to talk about crazy people," John said. He moved to the window with his eye on the darkness. He imagined Mareika would have used the barn seeing the wagons.

The sun fell away, so John lit a lantern and raised it into the loft for Mareika's arrival. From his perch he looked at the Werder clock mounted to the wall between his room and the earthen fireplace in the kitchen. He looked again to the loft. The lamplight flickered and dashed the roof with pin light. Then he turned his ear to the rafters. In the shadows, he saw the white lace of his daughter's hem and the shiny black leather of her toe. She must be scavenging in the smoke box. He sighed with irritation at Paul's gossip.

"Didn't you say you knew this preacher? Yeah, the other day at the Café, right?"

John lifted a finger to his lips, gave them a tap and Paul a scowl. "I don't know him, so ... let's leave it at that." John pointed up to the ceiling before he drained his ale and filled his glass with more as his guest looked over their shoulders to the smoker. They nodded. "This isn't a sewing circle." He took his drink to a timber column and gave it a pat as he pulled at his drink. He raised his glass to the post and the men's work. Paul and Charlie raised their glasses. "Nice job. Thank you."

With the wagons in the yard, Mareika had snuck around to the barn and climbed into the loft where the seeds from last fall were stored, crawled through the hatch and into the house. She then stole along the rafters to the smoking chamber where she sat, privileged to have access to this secret society of men.

"So, what about it, John, tell us a story about you. Any rebellions?"

"No." John looked at Mareika's toes.

"Come on."

"He told me he used to race camels," Charlie said. He took a gulp of his ale.

A twinkling radiated over Mareika's face when she heard Charlie tell the room about the camel races. She knew nothing of John outside of their home. He seemed to be only work ethic. She gnawed on some smoked rabbit and listened to the men as if all were characters from books. Her toes wiggled with anticipation of Foda's tale.

"Is that true?" Paul said. "Don't hold out on me, John. If you aren't going to tell us the tale of the crazy preacher who headed into the desert mountains of Asia . . ."

"Yeah. Yeah. Please. Yes, I did use to race camels." John eyed the ceiling.

"When?" Paul asked.

"I was eight."

"Eight! Who were you racing against? Where did you race them?"

"All over. Never in Gnadenfeld. This was a secret. My Mennonites didn't gamble. Well . . . didn't admit to it. A lot of men participated." John winked and raised his ale. "We all hide fruits of a garden in the corn field, eh?"

"Here, here," Paul said.

John put his hands up. "First off, it was normal for any given person in the colony to have a camel. Everybody had one. They were used all the time the way we use oxen here or the big Scottish horses to plow fields. But every once in a while, when Foda caught wind of a race, we would head out towards Crimea. We never went that far, but if the races were within four days, Foda took me. Most of the time we were on the steppe north of the Azov Sea. So south of the village a couple of days. In Molotschna we had to share the steppe with the Nogai. They moved east and west through the season like the Cree or Blackfoot. They were nomads."

Paul said: "Like Charlie's people."

"I'm Métis," Charlie said. "And we farm."

"Sorry, Charlie."

John tipped his drink towards Charlie. "The Nogai, they were dark-skinned and they wore robes with swords, and big furry hats. They worshipped a god. They called him Allah. And they could ride. I raced against those boys. And they could ride. The one noble-man that my father raced for, he had said that he was the descendent of Genghis Khan. But anyway, every so often, especially at the end of summer before harvest, they'd hold little celebrations, like fairs. There were open-pit cookouts with goat, fruit and fruit and more fruit. We would eat so many grapes and berries. We would bring honey and firm white cheeses, and their women would cube the curds and fry it on all sides in scalding oil before finishing it with a drizzle of honey and nuts and berries. It was amazing. If I could eat anything from the old colony, I would eat that.

"But it was like a fair. There were all sorts of contests: wrestling, archery. There was singing and camel races. Word got around that I was pretty good, and Martin would get invited. So we'd head out, camping along the steppe for a few days, we'd then get to the festival, and for a few more days I'd race camels." John took a drink. His glass beaded with condensation that ran down its base whenever he set it down, where it left crescents upon the tabletop. He got up and took to the stove, plunking in three lengths of aspen. He took some honey from his shelf. He looked back to the table. Paul, who was shaking his head, topped up the glasses again. The hiss of a metal hinge fell over the room.

John looked up the height of the stove towards the smoke chamber. "Mareika?"

Silence ...

"We're making a midnight *Faspa*."

Silence ...

"Are you hungry?"

Silence ...

"It's fried cheese and honey."

Silence ...

"Okay then."

"Yes, please."

John, relaxed enough to feel relieved to hear her voice, didn't register the darkness swaddled about the farm or that she had never heard him talk of his racing days. He cared only for food and to show her her new room. "Do we have any cheese curd?"

"It's on the windowsill in the pantry."

"Oh, good girl. Can I take it?" John stalked to the pantry. The tinkling and chiming of mason jars filled the house. He came out with a clay bowl and a small jar. "I don't have fresh berries, but I have some jellies: crabapple, Saskatoon, chokecherry." He set a bowl and jars on the counter beside the stove. He took a pan and put it onto the stove. He headed back to the pantry and came out with a streaky grey, brown, and cream jar. He lifted it with a cheer. "Bacon fat." He stopped at the table and took a mouthful of beer.

A giant dollop of fat sizzled in the pan. He chopped square chunks of hard cheese and dropped them in the pan, and he flicked each side around the hot bacon fat for a several seconds until the sides were a caramel colour. He drizzled honey over them. Then he dropped those chunks onto a clay plate, dumped a heaping spoon of jam into the pan for a few seconds, then flipped the hot pan upside down over the plate, placed everything in the baking box above the stove and walked away.

"You have to give it a couple minutes so the middle gets warm and melty."

Mareika froze at John's use of the word melty. The word seemed too infantile for his mouth. He moved with a stumble, like walking with one boot on.

He grabbed a chair for balance and plopped himself down. He took another pull of beer. "Mareika, bring down some sausage and some rabbit if you'd like." John jumped up and moved the ladder from the loft to the smoker. Mareika appeared with a splayed rabbit upon a wire hook, golden and caramel, plus two coils of farmer sausage. He pointed her to the loft as she came into the room. "Go ahead and take a look."

She set the rabbit and a foot of coiled pink farmer sausage, flecked with black pepper, onto the table. John took it to the stove, and with another skillet, he snapped the sausage open and squeezed the crumbled grind out of the casing into the pan.

"So did you win?" Paul asked.

The meat began to hiss and John broke up the stuffing more with a wooden spoon.

"Not the first time. And boy was Martin mad. I didn't know it at the time, but he was betting a lot of his money on those races, especially the first one. After that first one he was playing catch up. If you asked me what he did for a living, butcher, carpenter, teacher, veterinarian, I couldn't say. He was always gone. That couple of years was the most time I spent with him. Then we came to Canada. If I had to guess, I think he's in Mexico now. He followed several other Colonialists who didn't like not being able to establish colonies here—presumably because he was a great negotiator. I haven't seen him, but once, since Rebecca and I left Toronto. I came here with a letter with both deeds, this farm and the land Charlie mills on, explaining I had three years to start farming it or the government would take it back. But he never came." John took another drink. He rose, then stepped to the pans. With one hand under the plate, one of the cast-iron handles wrapped with a towel, he flipped everything over again. He set the pan on the table, the plate beside, and grabbed half a loaf of bread. "Just tear off chunks of the bread and dip it into the pan or the plate, soak up the honey, jam, and fat." He added the skillet of crumbled farmer sausage, browned with crispy edges.

"These are delicious," Paul said.

"Mmmhmm." Charlie nodded as he pushed a piece of stained glistening bread behind a chunk of seared, honeyed cheese. He chewed with an open maw until he swallowed enough of the bite to close his mouth. "Tell him what your dad did when you lost."

"No. I've been carrying on long enough." John moved to Mareika. "Try some cheese and sausage." He went into the kitchen and tore cold-smoked rabbit from the bone onto another clay plate and put it on the table.

"Come on, John," Charlie said. "Your father was mean."

"Whose wasn't?" Paul said.

John lifted his glass to the lantern and squinted at the flame's glow through the wash of amber. He followed a bubble rising from the bottom, which collided and joined the white froth at the top of his glass.

"What's in this here ale? It's pulled my tongue out."

"Come on. What did your father do after you lost?" Paul asked.

"Tell him, John."

"He cursed me. He told me I hurt our family. Then he took me out away from the Nogai village and stopped. He told me to dismount from my camel." John laughed. Then he lifted a caramel-coloured ball of cheese to his tongue. He dropped it and held it. He savoured the flavours of his memories over his feelings. He looked to the new loft. Mareika lay back on her new mattress under her quilt with a book. The lantern threw her shadow all over the peak of the roof. She was on her side, her legs stacked and bent at the knee. "We should have closed in a wall or hung curtains up there."

"On with it, man." Paul laughed. He dumped more ale into everyone's glass.

"So Foda has me off my camel, and he takes up my wrists and tethered them with the camel's lead. He tells me that the Nogai used to steal Christians off the steppe, enslave them. At night, they would sweep into the Christian villages and take boys and men. And they would mark them, the way we brand cattle, by cutting their noses off. He asked me if I wanted to be a slave, pinching my nose between his thumb and index finger. I shook my head. Then he said the next time I raced, he would bet my life. Then he dropped my bound hands. And said: 'This is how a slave travels with the Nogai.'"

"He made you walk tied to the camel?" Paul said.

"I wasn't walking. I was jogging, almost running to keep up to the camel. I must have run for hours. My shoulders began to hurt from holding my hands up with the weight of the lead. It felt like an anchor. My head started spinning. I remember throwing up and tossing my head to the side so that I wouldn't get it on myself. I had tried so hard not to vomit, but I did. And wiped my thumbs like so." John cupped his hands together, holding his wrists together and dabbed at his chin with his thumbs. Paul and Charlie clenched their teeth, their lips seared with phantom anguish. They laughed, but the sound was that of a shattering plate, an attempt to ease the uncomfortable confessions of a boy abused. This was not a spanking or a whooping for boyish energy wasted on cruelty by tossing stones at pigs in a corral waiting for slaughter, when they deserved to be honoured for the sacrifice of filling a family's empty stomachs.

Mareika too listened. And understood his silence a little better. He was telling a story of being bound and forced to run after a camel on a desert plain for hours. Her stomach, pelvis, hips, and back ached listening. She wanted to not just hug him, but that eight-year-old, too.

"I'm running. And it's been ... who knows how long, and the lead line is getting tighter. My feet feel like stones. My arms start to rise up away from my body. I tried to heave back with my elbows almost like I was fishing and bringing in a big pickerel."

"Or a sturgeon," Charlie said.

"Yeah, a desert sturgeon." The men laughed. "Well, I guess you know an eight-year-old boy isn't stronger than a camel, a man, and his horse. So now I am stumbling and begging that man to stop. The lead slackened a lot, but it still felt like iron. I flopped down hard. My chin hit the dirt. When I hit the ground, my hands were above my forehead like I was praying, and I was. From the moment my beak started grinding against the plateau for maybe a whole second. Then I felt a deep pull and a pop, and my left arm feels like it's both on fire and wet. And now I'm being dragged through the hot sand. I'm screaming, but sand fills my mouth. Then finally everything comes to a halt. I'm spitting up sand and crying like a baby. Martin then comes to me, grabs me by my vest, and heaves me to my feet and yells: 'Quiet!'

"I'm still choking on sand and snot, but I shut right up.

"Then he continued. 'You have to decide between your head or your heart.' And I'm standing there, sucking wind trying to ignore my shoulder. And at the top of his lungs he screams right in my face, his breath hotter than the plateau: 'Stop!' His nose is right between my eyes. I sucked my bottom lip in and bit down. And I stood hoping he couldn't hear, see, or smell me. I felt like a mouse under the snow under the shadow of a coyote under a full moon, hoping my racing heart doesn't give me away. But he pounced and chewed into me."

"What did he do?" Paul threw the last cheese ball into his mouth. John tore a chunk of bread and mopped the plate clean. They all took a breath, a swig, and waited for John's words.

"The head or the heart. He poked me in the forehead and said: 'The head or the heart.' He said, and I remember vividly: 'You lost today because you thought with your head. You decided you were going to lose before you had a chance to win.' He untied my hands. He pointed behind me and asked me to point at the Nogai village. I turned, and all I saw was steppe. I looked all around. Martin pointed forward and said: 'Do you see how far your heart took you?' I sucked on the air and nodded. He stood tall and said again: 'You ran with the camel with your heart. Now ride with it.' I saw him smirk. I didn't know if he was proud of me or his own wisdom, but for a second that twinkle of pride evaporated the pain away, then he says: 'Why are you slouching and holding your arm like that?' He grabs my wrist, straightens my arm while he paws at my shoulder. All the while I'm trying not to cry, and then with a lift and a push of my shoulder down, he popped my shoulder back into place."

"You separated your shoulder?" Paul said.

"No, the camel did," Charlie said.

"'Learn to use your heart,' he said. Then he put me back up on the camel, and we rode until dusk before we camped. He never said anything to me the rest of the two days home. Then he made me practise for a month before he took me back to the Nogai for my next race."

"Did you win?"

"It's how my father raised enough money to come to Canada. We stayed with the Nogai in yurts, eating goat for three weeks, travelling from village to village. We were on a hot streak, and Martin never seemed happier. After, he used to joke that a Nogai nobleman had tried to purchase me, and whenever I was bad, he'd threaten to sell me."

"That's unbelievable," Paul said.

"Desert Moose Champion," Charlie said with a laugh.

"Sand Donkey," Paul said. They tipped their glasses to their lips and took healthy mouthfuls of ale. Their fingerprints turned purple against the glass through the caramel amber glow.

Wapos County

GOOD FRIDAY GOOD Friday. I hate myself. My heart hurts. It hurts for her, my Mareika. I abandoned Oma's warnings. I left the anger in my hands. It was so heavy. She so small. The hate. The anger. Everything that makes me wish I was never born lay red over little Mareika. How could she know that she would be poisoned by the same blood that pulses through me? I try to focus on the ink and the words. I don't want to look at my hands. She's only a little girl. She couldn't have known what she was doing. She looked so scared when I screamed to her to stop. And she begged and shrieked. She hugged my legs when I told her to get the spoon. I'm sorry, Mutta. I'm sorry. She felt strong. Her fear felt so strong. I shoved her to the kitchen. She shivered naked and wet from out of the basin. I don't know where so much anger came from out of me. Good Friday. We only meant to get ready. The wash water was warm. We hummed together. I crushed the oils from this spring's tulip petals and thyme leaves I plucked from the pots John keeps on the windowsill. Mareika had loved the smell over my skin. I rubbed the scents on my cheeks and neck. Her little nose sniffed my earlobe and we giggled. Rub them on me, she said. After you wash. After you wash ... Her little hand found her other parts. And she washed. She lathered with soap and washed. She kept washing. Her face twisted with a sick concentration. And my anger and fear fell upon her. Oh, her cries sting. I'm sorry, Mutta. I'm sorry. My little girl hugged and hugged me. I pushed her away and made her go stand in the pantry. She screamed, Mutta, I'm sorry. I would not hear it. How could such a young creature be drawn to her other parts with such focus if she were not poisoned with the same sickness inside me? John came in from the back, from the barn. He needed to tend to her. I fled through the barn to the brush. I checked rabbit snares. There was so much anger in my hands. They shook. The hare kicked and kicked. Its leg bloody. My hands twisted through its fur. I could not even hear it snap. And I collapsed. I am sorry, Oma —I forgot to scream into a pillow. So much anger from these hands. I looked into the dark sky above. I didn't see any stars. A fog left my lungs, dragging the anger from me. And I wept. I cried so hard I lost my stomach. The corner of my lips burned. My sickness. My legs and knees felt wet from the tears. And I felt weak. I looked at the dead hare. Then I prayed for Mareika. She must know the dangers of our other parts. She cannot turn into me. She cannot turn into me.

MONDAY, MAY 16, 1910.

Black Gully Town Square

IBI ENTERED THE Alexander Hotel. Nobody in Black Gully called the new hotel the Alexander. Like the Café and the Store, residents called the Alexander "the Hotel." In fact, the only moniker, a small hand-painted sign, which sat over a small, black awning over an innocuous wood-panelled door, read *Hotel*. As a Mennonite, Ibi enjoyed this pragmatic virtue of this fledgling town—it refused to impress itself even on its citizens. This respect and enthusiasm bubbled from him when he convinced the hotel manager to allow him to borrow the upright Steinway piano that afternoon for his next sermon. The manager even offered to help him place it outside up the boardwalk nearest the square.

"I have all the help I need," Ibi said. He stood straight up with a wide-open smile. The shorter man, in full suit, vest, and polished shoes, looked around the empty lobby. Then his eyes narrowed with a slow nod. Ibi read the man's confusion, and after snapping his black suspenders, he pointed up. The manager followed his point to the pressed tin ceiling and the new electric chandelier before he nodded, understanding the reference.

"Do you pray, my good sir?"

"Oh ..." He scratched his chin and shoved his mitts into his pockets. "I wouldn't say I'm not a holy man—raised Catholic—but I missed a Sunday some time back, and you know how it goes." Both men chuckled.

"Well, I invite all to my sermon. All are welcome and all can be saved. That is the gift of the Holy Spirit. We never needed the opulence, the showiness of a church. God is all around us, in our homes and in our hearts. The Church is the People." Ibi rolled up his sleeves. "Philadelphia, Brother—Amen." Ibi gave the manager another huge smile.

"That's a nice sentiment." The manager jogged to the lobby entrance and pulled open the door. "But I have my responsibilities here today." Daylight filled the lobby. The polished fir planks flickered the sunshine back up to the tin ceiling while the swirling florals of red over black upon the runner stole the sunlight.

"Fair enough." Ibi winked and readied his shoulder into the piano. "But another day, then another, then it will be too late."

Ibi Gietz's lips twitched and flapped with the rabble of conversation as he pushed the instrument, but he made no utterance. He eased the piano through the doorframe and onto the boardwalk.

As the small brass wheels thumped against the gaps of the rough sawn planks, the hammers tipped and the chords hummed. The low notes morphed and stretched before they poured into a memory of Claas. When it brimmed, Ibi started to hear words, splashes of former sermons.

"This one true God, this living God, Creator of both the heavens and the earth, he's perfect in love, he's perfect in wisdom, he's perfect in righteousness. He is Mutta, He is Foda, and He is Shepherd. We need all three, the Holy Trinity realized, given to nature and given to form, isn't it? It's perfect holiness. Just as our invisible God took form in his Son, Jesus Christ."

The dust of Ak-Metchet blew across the piano into Ibi's eyes. "Amen," he said. He shot a glance to the top of the Steinway expecting to see his mentor perched, but only the shadows of oration fell over him.

"There will be more death, but the sin and the guilt shall not prevail. This is our new creation, the Bride Community, Philadelphia, and to be present is to see the first signs of God's forgiveness through his son, Jesus Christ. This new creation on Earth will deliver us to

His new heaven. Let the grace of faith wash *His* blood over your sin—be baptized once again and rise to *His* side."

Ibi stopped. He looked away from the piano as his mind wrapped around the rolling curve of Mareika's hips, the smooth lull of her thighs. He swallowed the saliva building under his tongue. He licked his lips. He turned to Creamery Road, where they met, and licked his lips again, swallowed more saliva. He pulled at his pant, then smoothed the crease over the pulsing swell. He pinched his ear, marking an X on his lobe.

"All disobey, all sin, all face the eternal departure. It's a physical death. It's a spiritual death. The knell ringing in our ears forever. Disobey Him, be the tempter."

Ibi did not see the edge of the lawn as the two side brass wheels anchored into the dirt. He leaned back to stretch his lower back, and he shook the pump of blood and muscle from his thighs. He looked at the square and decided to let the piano hang off the edge of the boardwalk rather than push and drag it over the grass. He retrieved his cart, pulled it to the piano. He tried to capture the words fluttering around his mind left by Claas for his sermon, but the Catholic Church tower rang with the hour. Ibi thought he counted ten strikes. He stood at the piano—one foot in the greening grass and one on the boardwalk—let his index finger fall with the last two chimes and began to play the only hymnal melody he knew, "Christ Returneth." The basic keys vibrated on a rusted cadence.

Ibi took in a deep breath through his nose. The honeyed aroma of poplar buds inflated Ibi's confidence. He looked around Black Gully and wished he could turn back time to find this gem earlier. He felt a pang of disappointment that this place would cease to exist in a matter of days, only hours, really. He went back to the hymn "Christ Returneth." His fingers warmed, and he released a song with a sweet somber flavour. Ibi's voice smouldered from behind his tongue and he exhaled words amongst a cloud of melody: *"It may be at morn, when the day is awakening. When sunlight through darkness and shadow is breaking . . ."*

He played bouncier tunes, like "Red Wing" or "Meet Me in

St. Louis, Louis," that he had learned in the basements of Winnipeg under clock sellers and laundromats, and in the McLaren furnace room. His playing rang warm. And the square filled. One by one citizens, like frizzy, cottonwood seed flittering on spring air, fell around Ibi's piano. The Jantzens, and many like them, returned after his Sunday's confirmation. All brought friends, family and food, while several dozen more bounced into the park on the music—all drawn to Ibi and the upright Steinway. He switched back to hymns, and let the women ring welcome.

Ibi delayed the sermon, stirred the words Claas had given to him from the bottom of his memory. They all felt so elusive, his mind muddied. Ibi let his playing slow. The tune turned melancholy.

"This one true God," Ibi refrained. He let go of the sentences as they came to him. The pause seemed to draw the people closer to him. "This living God .., *Creator* ... of both, the heavens and the earth ... He's perfect in love. Isn't *He* perfect in love?"

The audience replied with a salad of confirmation: "Yes, Amen, God is Great."

"He's perfect in wisdom. Isn't he perfect in wisdom?"

"Amen, Yes, God is Great." The audience kept to his lead.

Ibi swelled with confidence as his crowd grew to several dozen citizens. His fingers flicked alive and the piano picked up tempo. He looked around for Mareika. He found her. He found her smile. He captured it as she stood back near the edge of the treeline amongst the caragana, washed under the lush radiance of its yellow blooms, which burst along its slender branches.

"He's perfect in righteousness." Ibi drew Mareika to the piano. His voice softened as if the next words were meant only for her. "He is Mutta. He is Foda. And He is Shepherd." Ibi, his fingers fell over deep notes and let them get absorbed into the atmosphere.

"We need all three. The Holy Trinity realized. Give us to nature and give us to form. It's perfect holiness, isn't it? And just as our invisible God took form in his only Son, He gave to us forgiveness— say it with me."

"Forgiveness ..."

Ibi tickled the keys, his fingers scurrying up the scales before they slid back down to dance out "Christ Returneth."

"God the Son ... through whom all is possible ... we are *His* children. But we are all weak. And we have all sinned. Do you feel like sin and guilt and death are prevailing, prevailing over ye." Ibi's mind trailed away. He forgot his words and moreover forgot where he was going. His hands became heavy and stumbled over the keys. He stopped playing. His mind returned to Mareika, but he shied away from looking back to her. His prick grew as his imagination dissolved her clothes revealing the smooth flow of a woman. He cleared his throat.

He reset. But a horrid image of a young woman in a black gown hung in his mind. She hanged dead from the posts of a Hutterite colony far off in his memory. Ibi forced his fingers to keep playing. Her shoe had slipped free from her left foot. Her body, faceless, twisted around as his wagon travelled by. Ibi felt the shove of his mutta's hand into the back of the covered wagon, but he pressed an eye to a chink between the tarpaulin of the bonnet and the side-boards of the bed. The memory felt outside of Ibi, like it had not belonged to him, as he saw the body as more like a doll, because it hung faceless and puffy.

He reset. He closed his eyes. He squeezed them and wrung all women clean from his mind. He perched his ear upon the air and listened for Claas.

"None of us are perfect."

He restarted the hym, "Christ Returneth."

The lyrics rose through him. The women joined.

He played the last note of the hymn, pressed the white key down, and held it. His voice followed.

"We have all been on a journey ..." He stepped away from the upright. Walked in amongst the gatherers in the opposite direction of Mareika. He tossed a look over his shoulder at her. "On the day I started my journey—this one that we are all on—I remember a dead girl." The crowd gasped, before murmurs rumbled above them all.

"Now, now." Ibi raised his hands. "I am not here to shock and scare you. This is a story of love. *His* love. You see this girl, a Hutterite from the Hutterite village of Johannesruh, she loved the wrong boy. It was the first Sunday of our great trek from Russia on our way to Ak-Metchet. I remember most the hospitality of the Hutterites, our Anabaptist brethren: cheeses, yoghurt, breads, and pies, cherries, blackberries, and apples. It was the kind of warmth you all have shared with me today. Thank you, Brothers and Sisters. Peace be with you...." He raised his arms out to welcome the group closer to his heart.

"Peace be with you." The crowd took one voice.

"This girl loved the wrong boy. And on the day we left it had been decided that he must leave with us. This became too much for the girl who would be left behind. So there she hanged on the gates leaving her village. The boy lost all hope. He suffered day and night as we moved east through steppe, mountains, deserts, and plains. How awful. Such a sad way to begin a journey, isn't it?"

The women listening dropped their heads and sighed.

"His heart ached and ached. It hurt all our hearts. But it gave way to love. Love is our doorway. Love humbles us. Love redeems us. It's our bond." Ibi rested his palm on the shoulders of the men and women he passed. He left his last word hanging as he moved through to greet those who joined him this day. He bathed in their gaze. Some asked to shake his hand.

"All human life belongs to God. And even though that girl lost hers, *His* love saved that boy. He made it to the end of this journey. We all made it through nights crossing over the crumbling and decaying open graves of Muslims, the gruesome grins of their corpses smiling at us, raided at night and held captive at end of rifles. We made it. The dysentery, the miscalculations finally come to the end. The End. Mutta, Foda, all manners of death. But through it all, love." The Hutterite boy had been a lie. He, too, took his life just a day after the girl, but Ibi needed his survival to instill hope in those around him. Nobody likes a sad story. Hope drops light in front of each step forward as we navigate life.

"I believe I have forgotten to introduce myself. I am Ibi Gietz.

And I thank you for your love. So in return I promise to open the door for you, a return home." Ibi pointed skyward. He continued to weave himself around the crowd. He came upon Mareika. He held his feet. Though she faced him, she kept her regard to the grass. He raised his hand to her chin as if to pluck an apple. Their eyes locked and they exchanged smiles. Ibi moved on back to the piano. His fingers danced a jaunty tune before they eased into "Christ Returneth" again.

"I am glad to see so many of you back. And you've brought friends. That's love right there. I brought you all terrible news yesterday. I started today with an awfully sad tale. So why have you all returned? Hope. H-O-P-E. We may not be long here on this Earth, but that does not mean we cannot return home. Let's allow this hope to light our way forward. Now some will say I'm wrong ..." Ibi lifted his fingers from the piano. He turned to his audience. He waded back in amongst them. He stopped at the Jantzens.

"What if? What if we aren't wrong? Doesn't it feel like we have no control? That Hutterite boy didn't. He fell into chaos. We have been warned. Daniel, Ezekiel, Claas Epp Jr. We don't have to fall in on our own weapons. God is telling us now. Don't let it escape or you'll regret it. What are the consequences? Fighting for your salvation over a wasteland. What are the rewards? That we rise through *His* door to heaven."

Ibi held his tongue. He listened for Claas once more. The answers were in The Book of Daniel. He made a mental note to read that portion of the Bible tonight. *Read Ezekiel, too*, he thought. He took a deep breath. On the nose of the westerly he caught the hint of smoke. Campfire? Very similar. He could make out the sweet hint of birch and the bitter bite of pine. *Hellfire*.

"Do you smell that?" He pointed to the sky. Everybody looked up. The trees could have rattled as they all took a deep breath. "It's fire. Fire and brimstone. The Earth opening up. The cracks and fissures bleeding magma, scorching the earth. Daniel 12.

"Multitudes who sleep in the dust of the earth will awake: some to everlasting life, others to shame and everlasting contempt.

"*Those who are wise will shine like the brightness of the heavens, and those who lead many to righteousness, like the stars for ever and ever.*

"We all feel a *time of distress*. Have things gotten any easier for us? For how many of you is this yet another land to call home? We have been chased from all corners of the world. This is the third country I have had to flee to. I have crossed oceans, mountains, deserts. All for my chance to get home." Ibi closed the Bible and hugged it to his chest.

"I want to open that door and step across that threshold and really go home. What about you?"

"Amen," the crowd said.

"Indeed. The comet is here and we have hours left. But eternity with *Him* will be our reward. There is no debate. We are going to pass through that comet's tail. The greatest human minds have told us so. But what the atheists and scientists have forgotten is there is a door for us to return. I know it. *He* had told us all how." Ibi used the keys of the piano to cast melodies over his prayer. The deep chords of the piano boomed. "We ask you, O heavenly Father, to show us your grace and your mercy. Together we have come from throughout the whole wide world for your protection. Carefully drawn under your guidance and under your protection. Here. Yes, here, we pray that unity, not division, blessings, not damnation and care, grace our community.

"Follow me."

He walked the crowd around the square, around the town. Ibi invited all to lead her favourite hymn. The group toured the entire town and sang. Then as he led them all back to the square, he spoke again.

"Please do all gather with me again. Thursday will come, the day we shall all rise to *His* Kingdom. I shall stop with the nightmarish image of the end of days. I promise. Amen."

"Amen."

Ibi felt a loss. He looked over the crowd, marvelled at its size. It was only Monday. He still had more than forty-eight hours. A member of the crowd approached him and handed him a basket of bread before she bowed and backed away. He took up a bun and chewed off a bite.

"Tuesday! Shall we do this again?"

The audience cheered.

"I agree. Tomorrow, Tuesday, let us all meet again. We have such a short time left for this place, and should not all days after be about love? And I do not know about you, but I feel most loved while I am breaking bread. How about it? What do you all say to a Love Feast?" Some in the crowd clapped. "A *faspa* for our souls. Here, tomorrow, we will eat, fill our souls with *Love*."

Ibi took Mareika by the hand, led her away through the crowd. People shook his free hand, patted his back as he moved back towards his camp.

Ibi pulled a blanket from his tent and stretched it out over the grass beside his firepit. Mareika lay on her back. Her eyes moved from cloud to cloud as they floated into view. Her mind played with the sky stretched out over the privacy they shared, as Ibi lay silent, propped onto his side upon an elbow. He ignored the clouds. He traced his eyes over the line of Mareika's face and body. His bare foot touched her ankle.

Her eyes flickered around Ibi's gaze. "What are you looking at?" Smiles bloomed between them.

Ibi sighed.

"What?" she giggled.

Mareika let the pad of his thumb trace over the line of her jaw from her earlobe to her chin. His thumb then lifted, and he withdrew it. His nail now riding the ridge of his own lip.

Mareika pointed to the clouds. "That one looks like a train engine." She plucked a long blade of grass, then another, then another. She knotted their ends together and then began weaving. "I'd like to ride a train. I don't care where."

Ibi still lay without a word. He only looked her over.

Mareika interrupted the silence again. "What do you think people thought clouds that looked like train engines resembled before they were invented? I mean, you can't dream about it if it isn't real, right?"

"I suppose not."

Mareika chewed on a name. She looked at Ibi. She chewed some more. Then she uncorked her thumb. "Ibi, were you that Hutterite boy?"

Ibi stretched. His hand fell onto her hip.

"No, no I wasn't."

"I feel sorry for them."

"I don't."

"But ... she died because they couldn't be together."

"We both can feel their hearts. Here and now. I know the young woman's heart. I know the young man's heart. I know the fear and the torment and the expectation that there will be nothing left without each other."

Mareika's eyes, their blue river highlights crackling around islands of soft grey, slivers of jade, reflected a lacquer of curiosity. Her look washed over him. He rested into his hand and breathed deeply though his stomach as he stared off across Big Gully Lake.

His crow's feet ran deeper than her Foda's. She opened her mouth only to sustain the silence between them. Her lungs withheld the breath she needed to give shape to curiosity, but she felt inadequate, her thoughts unformed, because she could only guess his histories. She sighed.

"You feel it, too." Ibi's thumb followed a salty track from her eye to her temple.

"She loved him ..."

"And he loved her. Sometimes I think about their last night. They only had one last day on Earth together. I wonder if they had known it. I believe that they did, or why would she have hanged herself at the gates? But I feel so lucky to know. Is that wrong? To feel lucky here and now?"

She shook her head. "I'm scared."

"Why?"

"What if I don't go?" Mareika picked and tore at the braided grass.

He took the tattered braid and dropped it aside. "Come tomorrow to see me. I promise to prepare you. And you will go," he said. He folded a hand over hers. He gave it a squeeze.

"I will . . . I will be here tomorrow—I promise. But what if I am left behind Wednesday. I don't know. I can see it in my head, you rising above me, and it feels like the earth is swallowing me up and my stomach hurts, worse than it does now. I couldn't sleep last night. It felt like I was sinking though the couch."

"The Kingdom will open for you."

"But I've never gone to church. I feel so confused." She sat up and stared into the lake. A loon dropped below the lake surface. The afternoon sun burned off the cool spring air. The grasses, matte, no longer glistened with dew. Her eyelids folded her gaze away.

"This is the gift of the Brethren, to take worship out of the church and give it to us here, to let us take it into our homes."

"Mutta used to tell me that . . ."

"Shshsh." Ibi wrapped himself around the girl. "In the waters tomorrow, I will welcome you into God's grace—hand in hand. I will lead you to the gates of His Kingdom. And when they open, together we will rise. Together . . ."

She fell over him. Her arms squeezed. His words felt like truth, and she wanted to roll in them. She felt him adjust as the point of her jaw dug into his earlobe. "Sorry," she said.

Ibi rolled onto her. Mareika looked for herself in his mind through his deep hard gaze. His breath slowed and rested heavy about her neck as his body eased between her knees. Her body followed the press of his weight. Her hips arched. She cradled him now amongst her breath and stare and her other parts.

The calico cat came from the fire. It dipped its chin and pressed a cheek across theirs, its fur soft with warmth. It vibrated with purrs. Ibi shoved the cat aside.

"Don't be mean to kitty," Mareika said.

It huddled again nearer the fire, its paws hidden under its belly of orange, brown, black, and white fur.

"How come he doesn't have a name?"

Ibi's head lowered closer to her, his lips almost touched her cheek, his words cascaded hot from his tongue. "I want you to be with me."

"I am with you." She giggled.

"Corinthians, *If I speak in tongues of men and of angels ...*" His lips fell like rain. The tender pitter-patter pooled liked small, warm meres, levied by her own want. Her cheeks, neck, flushed. Her chest rose. And the heat inside her lungs picked up her body, her hips. She followed the waves rippling from her beating heart.

"But have not love, I am only a resounding gong or a clanging cymbal. If I have the gift of prophecy and can fathom all mysteries and all knowledge, and if I have faith that can move mountains ..."

His hands found her breast, her thigh. She followed their pull into him. His breath filled her lungs as they kissed. When she sighed, his body seemed to melt over her. He filled every space between them that existed. She kissed him back as if she had been thirsty all her life. He rolled with her lead, his separate parts heavy against her. She felt some pressure between her thighs. She moaned, and her hips rose against the pressure.

"... but have not love, I am nothing ..."

His arm reached for her hip. It rode upon his fingertips down the track of her thigh to her knee, circling, circling, circling before it moved up the inner plain to her plateau.

She squirmed under him, inched her hips away from his fingertips.

"What's wrong?"

"Nothing."

His hand came down onto its palm, carrying the weight of his arm and shoulder over her stomach. *"Place me like a seal over your heart ..."* He kissed at her stiffened lip, but kept his whispers falling over her ear. *"Our love is as strong as death ..."* She felt him braid those words through her hair, his lips lingering on her earlobe. *"I burn like blazing fire."*

She untucked the hair from behind her ear, draped it over her cheek.

"What are you doing?" He took up the hair and tucked it behind her ear again. "I like it better that way." He edged over her other parts again and pressed himself against her.

The sharpness plunged against her. She gasped and captured his forearm with a hand. She held him at the elbow. And with her other hand, she pulled at her dress to make sure it still covered her other parts. He kissed for her lips. She gave him her cheek.

"I don't know." She had not wanted to stop, but she did not want to follow his lead. She started to feel more and more under him.

"Let me know your heart if only for one day, as a wife is to a husband—we only have this day, only this day together. Share yourself with me."

"Stop."

"I love you ..."

"Please ..."

"Do you feel it?" he asked. Her hands lifted against the fall of his hips. She held him above but felt a tormented desire to pull him closer. But the feeling was akin to wanting him under her skin, to be inside her heart. She gave his lips a peck, but she held him steady. She felt a spring gale blow between their bodies.

"You feel it, don't you?" he said. Their lips tousled. His fight for passion, hers for tenderness. She lay her head back upon the blanket.

"What is it?"

"I don't know ... I just don't ..."

"*Home. We are a house, complete and strong, braved by a storm.*"

Mareika scowled. Every string of words felt out of context of her feelings. She waited for his words to leave. "I know. I can't."

"Then what is it?" Ibi's hips rocked slowly. His groin got heavier, landing to her as honeybees to a rose. Now only separated by their clothes, he slid against her over her pelvis, pressing the linen and cheesecloth against her. Her arms betrayed the voice in her head telling her to slow down, to stop and pulled him harder into her. Pleasure radiated across her skin.

"I wish to know you." He stabbed into her other parts. Her palms push up against his hips, held him away from her body again. The air colder than their bodies snuck in over her. Goosebumps budded over her entire body.

"Stop." Her legs went rigid. Then she exploded with a push and a buck. Ibi fell to her side. She pulled her knees up close to her chest; the flats of her feet touched the ground. Ibi tried to crawl back between her legs. Her hand met his chest and she held him back with her scowl. "Please."

"What's wrong?"

"We are not married. I am not a wife." She looked for his eyes. Eyes can be tender, eyes can be knowing, and she looked for compassion. His eyes, they draped a gaze over her body under a dozen wrinkles across his forehead. He huffed. Her voice came soft with a quiver. "I may not know the Bible as you do, but . . . I am not your wife."

"But you are an atheist," he said.

"What does that mean?" Mareika hugged her knees harder. "I just told you that I am afraid I will be left behind. And this . . ." Her hands trembled and tossed her fear. "It's a sin, right?"

"But tomorrow, I said I would prepare you." He set upon his knees, hands on his hips. He looked off. His face wrung with disappointment. Then he smiled. He leaned in with a grunt. His lips flecked kisses over her neck and earlobe. She twittered. "Don't you trust me?"

Her downward glanced captured the tenting slacks around his separate parts. Her hand hovered over it, petted down its firm length. But she flinched with retreat.

"You should know how to possess his vessel in sanctification and honour." Ibi grabbed her behind the knees and tugged her against him, the blanket bunching up between her ass and his thighs. He laid all his chest over her behind the weight of a deep kiss. His hips wedged her knees open. He held her shoulders to the ground, his thumbs buried into her collarbone.

"Ibi, stop . . ." Her heels dug and pushed against ground, slipping over the blankets and grass.

His reason and commitment reclaimed his senses. He pulled

back. His face softened, and his eyes looked painted with sadness. He couldn't look at Mareika. The May air got colder, slithered over her bare legs. Ibi huffed before he sat back onto his ankles. He wiped his mouth with his palm, clicked his tongue behind his teeth.

"I'm sorry." He looked at his hand. He ignored her face for Black Gully Lake as he wiped his palm in the grass.

Mareika thought she saw blood on his palm. Her legs recoiled, she crossed her ankles, and then she pinned her feet under her bottom. She looked over his face as she sat up. She fussed with folding and wrapping the gown over her knees and ankles, hopping up off her butt, tucking the loose end under her. He wouldn't look back to her. Her face flushed with shame, and her hands folded over and shielded her other parts.

"I'm sorry," she said.

"You should go back home."

"I want to stay. I don't think—"

"If it gets dark and you aren't home, your family will have all hell with you."

"I can stay a little while longer."

"You should go."

"Okay." She hugged her knees. "I liked it. The kisses felt nice."

Ibi stood. He reached down for her hand. With one arm over her breasts, she grasped his hand, her fingers tightly around his thumb. The yank ended with a sharp pain radiating in her shoulder socket.

She leaned into him. He stood rigid and tipped his chin high to avoid her lips. Her arms grabbed him and cinched him against her body. "I'm sorry," she said. "I don't want to be left behind. I want to go with you." She felt Ibi's body relax. Her chest felt warm again. "Can I still come tomorrow?" she asked.

He held her away, his eyes tumbled down the front of her body. The muscles rippled through her shoulders, rolled them inward, and her chin fell. Still exposed, she folded her arms over her body, tucked her fingers under her chin.

"Please," she said.

A smirk grew over Ibi's mouth.

"What? Don't laugh at me."

He pulled her into his chest. His arms squeezed. "I'm not." He rocked her, his twisting and swaying jaunty. His dejection shed like the last dried brown leaves that still clung to the trembling aspens. A bravado budded, raised his pores. Mareika felt soft and vulnerable. He kissed the top of her head.

"You're beautiful. And I'm sorry. You should go home, but let me tell you about Mutta, my mutta."

"All right." Mareika cuddled up to him. Her ear picked up the pulse of his heart. Her fingers turned from under her chin and found his chest. She played with an ivory button as she listened.

"Everybody called her *Zurechmacherin*. It means she made things right. She had been a midwife and caught babies, but she did more. We still live in this time where it's believed that women just know how to have babies, but that is not Mutta's belief. She started helping her aunt, but she also went to St. Petersburg thousands of miles away from her home. And when my family came to Manitoba, she left for a time to learn more in Cincinnati, Ohio. She saw it as a skill. And she was very good. She must have caught thousands of babies. And some nights, she needed me ... I was there to catch babies myself and to help. I stood and cradled their heads, mopped their faces with cool water. I held their hands for the first time. After the fear and the pain, I witnessed the cries of joy and the wails of life." Ibi stepped back from Mareika but held her shoulders, held his regard. An earnestness emanated from his eyes. "I know your secrets and I know your miracles."

Mareika threw her arms around him. An easy melody rose from the purr of her appreciation. She shifted her ear in search of his heartbeat again. The beats came faster, came stronger.

"Do you trust me?"

"Of course I do." She nuzzled up to his chest.

Ibi stole a kiss. He raised her chin and took her lips. Then he lay his weight over her shoulders and chest. Mareika lay under him, and she began to take his lips.

"Say it again ..." She combed her fingers through his hair.

Ibi whet her ear with a whisper. "I know your secrets ... I know your miracles ..."

She took hold of his arm. Then she neither led it nor followed it. "Please ..."

Ibi understood the tremble in her voice. "I promise," he said, not letting her finish her instruction.

His hand found the lace hem of her dress. It edged under and skated upon its fingerprints over her shin. He turned loops; he traced waves. Mareika's head spun. Her excitement crested, rolled over her other parts, and crashed inside her chest. Her knees fell. She lifted her hip towards Ibi.

He kissed her. He took in her breath as his own. Then he palmed her thigh, kneaded the soft flesh. Mareika's hips rose and fell with the same rhythms of his hands.

His voice, hot, satiny, washed over her. "Does this feel good?"

"Yes ..."

He lifted his palm over her other parts. He paused. He left the weight of his hand over her excitement.

"Don't stop."

He eased his fingers inside her panty, under the padding and cloth. The harmonies of surprise, trepidation, excitement rose from her gasp. Shame tightened her lip. She held onto the gasp as his finger traced the edge of her valley, her other parts. She couldn't feel his lips kiss her hard mouth as an image of her mother's wild scorn flashed behind her eyes.

Mareika opened her eyes. She traced Ibi's features, his petite, sharp, almost feminine nose, the shadow of stubble darkening his square jaw. She touched his face. She looked him in the eye.

He arched her back as his finger eased beyond her Kingdom. She took his lips, her mouth open, and she exhaled all the heat trapped inside that gasp she had held. Her body pressed up into his hand, craving the connection she felt to this man.

"Does this feel good?"

"Yes."

"Do you want me to stop?"

"No ."

Ibi's pace quickened, the pressure and depth of his touch improved. Mareika refused to let go of his mouth, even biting his bottom lip to keep him as close as another layer of skin. Her breath raced with his pace. She held his wrist with both hands, held him closer and closer. She pulled him to her other parts. Her excitement and joy rose and rose. Her heart pounded. She felt as if she couldn't breathe. Pressure rose against her other parts. And Mutta trespassed inside her mind again. Scorn, the sting of slaps about her head could be felt falling over her mind. She winced. The cries of *No* flooded her mind as more pressure flooded her other parts. Mareika felt control slip from her.

"No. I'm going to pee!" She clutched him by the wrist and shoved his hand away. She huffed. She scuttled to her feet. Her eyes swelled over him. She felt so near to him, but she feared her own body. This must have been the power Mutta warned her about.

"What is it?"

Mareika swallowed hard. She ironed her dress with her hands. Her breath plunged out of her, but the image of Rebecca angry, disappointed, lay behind her eyes over her mind. She looked down with the humiliation of a scorned child afraid to lose a parent's affection. A sharp sense of responsibility interrupted the moment.

"Where's Bison?"

Ibi didn't move.

"The donkey! Where's Foda's donkey?"

Ibi, with a shrug, watched her flee. Within seconds she disappeared over a knoll and into the gloaming.

Eastern Reserve, Manitoba

Mustard

1 cup dry mustard
1 cup vinegar
3 tablespoons of flour
sugar

BOIL THE VINEGAR. Whisk the mustard, flour, and sugar together. Add any amount of sugar you desire. Opa liked it sweet, so I used a full cup. But you can add none. When the dry ingredients are mixed add them to the vinegar and whisk. Simmer it until smooth and thick but not chunky. It should pour.

Mustard Plaster. If your chest hurts with sickness, make a paste from mustard and flour in equal parts. Add hot water to get the mix to medium-thin. Use an old cloth and spread the paste over it and save the cloth for another winter. It will be stained yellow so you will know what it is for. Cover the paste with another cloth and place it over your chest. Then layer the clothes with towels and blankets. Take the mustard plaster with tea or hot honey water. Keep under the plaster until you are done your hot drink.

Wapos County

I CARRIED THE full teapot back to the stove. Its contents had cooled while Mutta slept. Its black waters snaked from the spout, slashed into the bottom of the cast-iron pot. I watch it become a disk of muddy waters. I set the empty vessel back upon the dining room table. "Make sure Mutta gets fluids," I said to the kitchen. I squatted and took the coiled handle of the stove inside her apron. The metal pin screeched as it turned, and glowing orange embers that used to be birch hurled heat over my lap. I grabbed a log and tossed it into the hearth, yanked my hand back from the heat. I did this again, this time rubbing the heat away from the surface of my flaring red hand.

A patchwork quilt teeming with matted brown lengths of hair shuffled into the kitchen on naked ankles and bare feet. Mutta raised her neck out of the mound of blankets, her nose blazing red, her eyelashes encrusted with a beige dusting, and her skin washed of light.

"Mutta. Go back to bed."

"Sarah?"

I looked at her. Her hair clung to her forehead, stole the pearls of sweat glistening up through her flush complexion. Her eyelids, hollow, drawn out, and stained dirty brown, looked too small for their eyeballs. She looked rung out, like a laundered blouse draped over the back of a kitchen chair, her skin arranged over the spindles of bones, knuckles, joints and stitched to fingernail buttons and big creamy teeth. Her hands tightened the blankets about her shrivelling body.

"I'm cold," Mutta said.

I yanked my apron over my mouth when Mutta erupted into a coughing fit. I watched her fight to catch her breath, gurgling on phlegm. Then her eyes dropped onto me. It was like her look snuck up on me. I looked away from her. I looked everywhere but at her. I let my eyes rest behind her, to the stove and to the tea warming. Her stare felt heavy. And I asked that Foda walk in from the winter. Maybe he turned around from fetching the doctor. He could take care of her. I just wanted him here again. Her eyes stayed rolling over me, searching through me. I looked at her, ready to plead with her to return to her room.

She raised a dark leather-bound book with her hand from under her shroud.

"Don't cover your face," Mutta said. "You're already sick."

"Please, you need rest." I lowered my apron and used it to take up the cast-iron pot of reheated tea. I poured Mutta a cup. "Foda said you need to drink."

"Oh, what a good man. Foda. Foda John Doerksen. Where is he? I do not see him on his couch with his books." Mutta coughed onto the back of the hand holding the book. She raised the book. Her arm trembled. The book clapped, a thunderous snap, against the tabletop. I shuddered.

Mutta pointed at the book under a burst of energy. "This is the book for him. Full of truth. You tell him to read it."

"He's gone for the doctor."

Rebecca laughed. She held the joke to herself, smuggled it away from her daughter.

"He can't help me. You tell me if I'm able to be saved. Imagine the good doctor, the *righteous led up by the Spirit into the wilderness to be tempted by the devil?* Imagine ..." She stirred a hand into the air between us. Her head lunged with a burp that dragged her tongue to the edge of her lips. She held up that hand. Held it out to me. It twitched before it curled into a shaky pointed finger. "The scuttle."

I looked at her feet, looked every which way—the ash pail. I lifted it to her. She aimed her chin over the rim and heaved. Ash billowed. I turned my eyes and nose from the cloud erupting out of the vessel. It stung with the sour, rennet smell of Mutta's influenza. Heat, intense heat, escaped Mutta through her forearms. I moved a hand to her forehead as she would have done if I were the one who was ill. She felt like she'd been sprung from the stove. The ash pail grew heavier. I had to cling to it and ride its new weight to the floor, where Mutta fell over its brim with her violent heaving.

"Oh, my skin hurts." She let go of the scuttle and flopped back onto the floor with her arms opened. She folded her feet under the quilt. "I asked for my skin to never feel this way again. I made a promise to be good. I married Foda and I promised."

I stayed squatted, still holding the copper vessel, and watched her rise over her knees and fold her face into the pail again. With not a sound, her shoulders lifted, her spine buttressed to her hips foundationed to the floor. She lifted her face, and a line of spit hung from her lip to the rim of the pail. "My kidneys are cold."

I lifted and wrapped the blanket over her shoulders. Mutta tucked the sides under her arms and pinned them to her body. She laid her cheek to the scuttle's rim. "The copper feels nice and cool against my skin." Her eyes glistened with exhaustion. "Oh, you're a good girl. You take care of me. You and Foda. I haven't been good. I was born wrong." She spit into the pail. "And I made you and John pay for it. Can you help me to bed?"

I took Mutta under the elbow and balanced her as she pushed off the copper scuttle.

"It's me, not Foda. It's me who keeps him from our bed. He sleeps in the living room not because he snores like he says. It's because of me and my sickness. He shouldn't have to sleep there alone. I left him away. A man adrift." Mutta laughed. "He is the man adrift." She shook her head.

I kept my eyes on the floor planks, followed the rounded nail-heads moving across the smooth wood surface to the door frame of the room we shared. I eased into a step. And we stumbled backward into the living room on our way to bed. I felt confined by the hundreds of books on their shelves. She pulled away from me.

"Do you know what he's looking for in all those pages?" Mutta didn't wait for me to shrug. "Hope. He's fumbling for hope. It isn't here …" She stared off into nowhere. Her voice began to fall under her weakness. "He lost his hope in other people. There was no salvation. And his hope left with their judgement. Oh, none of us wants judgement, but we need community. So he built himself inside his own little library. All these stories promising us hope. But where are we? Where are we, really?"

Mutta stared at me. I didn't understand her. I didn't understand why her voice was so ladled with hate. Mutta would spank me if I disobeyed her. And it made me angry with her. And in this moment, I remembered a time when I cried to Foda and said, "I hate her." He told me to never say such a powerful word to describe feeling hurt by Mutta or him. He said using hate was as powerful as throwing a stone, and he asked if I would ever throw a stone at Mutta. I felt very ashamed, and I learned that I did not hate Mutta. But she scared me.

And in this moment, I could hear hate in Mutta's tone. I feared answering her question.

"Well?" She tilted a book back on the edge of its spine. She flicked it so that it fell back into place. "I'll tell you. We are all alone surrounded by words. Black streaks splattered over white pages that cease to exist without our eyes."

"Sorry, Mutta."

"No. I'm sorry. I should not curse Foda. He's good. Mareika, believe me. He is a good man. Foda's out there every night, and you have to be in the corner of that room with me.

"Did you know that the pantry was supposed to be your room? It's small—I know—but it was for you. We broke up the crib for kindling one winter. And I made him build me shelves, drawers, coat hooks. In this place, this beautiful house with you growing in my belly, your foda waited for real hope. Maybe a family. Did you know he helped me give birth to you right on our bed."

I watched her feet drag and shuffle, keep up to the weight of her shoulders. I slid my other arm behind her back and eased us into our room. Mutta crawled to the far side of the bed.

"It's cooler over here." She pulled a pillow between her knees before she pulled the corner of another under her chin.

I lifted the sheets over her.

"Don't cover me all the way up, just to my kidneys."

"Okay." I watched her eyelids fall closed. I sniffled. It felt like watching a person die. It kept me awake dreaming of my parents dying. Me alone.

"It's okay, Mareika, I only have a flu. I'll be better in the morning. I promise that I'll be better."

"Did you want a mustard plaster?"

"No . . . I said my skin hurts."

I retreated from her fever. The doorknob felt nice and cool.

"Did you hear me when I told you that you were born in this house? Foda delivered you?" Her eyes opened, looked through the wall of her bedroom into the pantry.

"Yes."

"Well, it's all true. But I didn't love you. I was supposed to be a mother. But I was scared and thought you had taken my life. From out of my body, where I felt you growing from nothing into a tiny person, you came covered in blood and screaming. He tried to put you in my arms, and you were screaming. Your little voice froze all my joints. I curled up like a page burning inside a stove. I couldn't open my arms to take you. I couldn't even look at you. Instead I drowned in tears. For days, for weeks, for months I floated away from you. Foda fetched books, he sought out a *Zurechmacherin*, and he learned how to nourish you. For over a year it was only his arms that you knew. In the pantry he slept with you, and in here I wept. Then one day I stopped crying. You were almost one. It was autumn. About the time the snow flew. I got out of bed. And I walked into your room. I took you from your father's arms. You never cried. I was ready to love you, so I asked Foda to destroy your bedroom. I told him you must sleep with me. I wanted that time back. That's when he began sleeping on the couch. Real husbands and wives sleep in the same bed. They share a bed. It is not right that I gave his bed away."

Mutta let her eyes fall closed again. She rolled onto her back. She reached her hand to me. "I'm sorry it took me so long to love you. I'm sorry." Then she fell quiet.

I backed from the room. I took up the scuttle, led it to the front door. The wind shoved the heavy fir boards open. The snow did not fall but seemed to be pitched from the sky. The slant of the blizzard flakes sliced at my eyes and pores, a million pinpricks. When my feet found the end of the porch, I shook the pail empty. The ash, caught by the wind, swirled up around me. I waved my arms as I backed into the house.

Inside the kitchen I swiped at my face. The sick and ash felt pasted to my skin. My cheeks stung even from half a minute in that cold. I poured myself three cups of tea, each with an extra spoonful of honey, before I could return to our bedroom.

ᕦᕤ

In the night I rose to moans in the dark. I lit a candle. Mutta lay spread-eagled on the bed. Her right foot kicked. Her nightgown had risen, and Mutta's hands rode over her writhing body to hold and rub at the dark, curly hair between her legs over her other parts. I turned the candle away from her. The moans moved nearer my neck. I hunched away towards the door. Mutta's cough sounded wet. So I turned back towards the darkness. I turned back and washed her in candlelight and shadows. She shoved a pillow between her naked thighs. Her hips swayed and ground up against the hand pressing the pillow to her other parts.

"Sarah ..." Mutta bit her own thumb. She rolled to her back, and her body arched, her stomach reaching towards the ceiling. She wailed.

I snatched away a pillow and quilt to escape. I tossed them onto the sofa and scurried into the kitchen to the stove. I jammed four logs inside. The winter howled across the chimney pipe, threatening to burst inside the walls. I ran to the couch as if something in the darkness snapped at my heels. I felt as if it could have had snapping sharp teeth. I leapt onto the couch, twisted the blanket over my head, pulled it taut over my ears, chin, and eyes, and kept only my nose outside the covers. I rolled my back to the door of our room. When my breath calmed and no longer huffed past my lips into the quilt, I noticed the tinge of pine needles on the surface of the couch cushions.

I pressed my nose into the aroma and took in the memories of Foda. Right now, it could have been spring, any day after he was done in the woodpile. Every winter we needed at least five cords of firewood split and stacked. At the end of those days, I would sit beside him on the couch while he read, especially after he'd split the pine or fir. The room would be fresh with the blush of the forest after a summer rain. I'd sit with a book of my own, usually an atlas, and take small samples of the forest sitting next to me. After an hour or so, he would tap my shoulder, hand me his book, which he'd marked with a long slip of cloth Mutta had cut and stitched, and pointed to the shelf where he got it. I would rise and put his reading away and retreat to Mutta's room where I slept on a cot in the corner closest the kitchen.

This wasn't the first night I had retreated for the couch, but the first I could sense Foda. I breathed softly, ignoring the wind rattling the windows, let my head get heavier and heavier as the night's darkness swallowed my cries.

When I arose, I did not find Mutta in bed. And her coat, her chore boots, her scarf, her hat stayed at the door. The wind had stopped. The snow now only fluttered to the ground. I opened the front door. Snow drifted onto the porch. There were dimples scarring the rolling mounds of snow. The dimples held blue shadows compared to the blazing white snow, leading across the banks towards the outhouse.

I closed the door and took to the stove. I patted my fingertips against the coil of steel around the handle. I felt warm. I opened the stove. Then I whistled a breath over the ash. The white and grey flakes whipped up away from six small embers. I used some tinder to poke and corral the embers together, then I cracked splinters of wood and tented them over the coals like Foda had shown me. The blonde wood blackened, and wisps of grey clouds spiralled up towards the stack. I puffed a tiny breath over my lips. The black embers smiled an orange radiance. I added more splinters and more wisps of breath. The wood smouldered and cracked. I got on my palms and knees and with long deep breaths blew the coals. A blizzard of ash rose, some escaping and taking to my hair and pajama collar. Then the twigs and splinters ignited. I added handfuls of tinder, larger tinder, careful not to knock over the tipi of flames. I added branches, the wood crackling from the flames wrapping, weaving themselves amongst the fuel. With a fire burning over again, I stood, listened to the stove hinges screech.

I stepped into the bedroom and put on a pair of Foda's overalls, tucked my nightgown down one leg. I put on my coat, hat, mittens, boots. I pulled open the front door and stared into the blue dimples chasing across the snow. A crack in the clouds poured some morning sun over our pasture. The brightness smoothed the drifting snow.

A scattering of snow blew from off the roof across the yard. I walked through it as the cold snow fell down my collar. I lifted my heavy boots and plunged them into the blue dimples. I followed the path to the outhouse. I wondered if I could pee beside the red wooden shed, do it without dribbling and doing it quickly enough that I wouldn't freeze. The soft snow slipping over the tops of my boots pushed me to the outhouse door. I stomped the drifted snow down and away from the door. I pulled the door half open.

"Sorry!"

I slammed the door. Mutta said nothing back.

"Sorry, Mutta."

I stepped around the side of the outhouse away from the wind. I squatted and leaned. I hummed, not any song or melody. I just hummed to show Mutta I could wait. I stopped. "Mutta? Are you okay?" I knocked on the walls. "Mutta." *Knock knock.* "Mutta." *Knock knock.* "Mutta."

Chickadees chirped and hopped around the Saskatoon berry bush, to snip the frozen, wrinkled purple berries for their bellies.

"Mutta?"

I stretched around the outhouse corner and wedged my fingers behind the door, opening it enough to peep inside. Mutta's head lay rested upon her knees pulled up into her chest, her nightgown tented over them. I saw her bare feet, her toes poking out the bottom. The tips were crimson haloed about the knuckles by a hint of blue. I yanked the door open through the drifted snow.

"Mutta!"

I stepped inside and tried to peek under Mutta's arm and see her eyes.

"Mutta." I poked at her arm. She felt stiff. I pushed on her, but her forehead seemed frozen to her knees.

My mittens slipped off her shoulder. I saw her hair tucked behind her ears. Her ears looked like the colour of Saskatoon berries. I bit at a mitt, pulled it off and touched at Mutta's fever. She felt as cold as the snow. I grabbed Mutta's cheeks, but I could not lift her face.

"Mutta!"

I pushed and shook her shoulder. She was hard and solid.

"Mutta!"

I took off my coat and threw it over her shoulders, tucked it around her sides. Then I stopped and looked her over. I held my breath. Mutta's chest held still, never rising, never falling.

My eyes burned. But the winter stole all their warmth before the wetness seared my cheeks.

I ran from the outhouse, pulled my knees high through the snow drifts. I slammed the front door, kicked and threw my winter clothes off behind me over the floor before I dove under the covers and pillow upon the sofa. I huffed and sucked on the pine memories lingering inside the cushions, trying to trade Mutta for Foda from inside my eyes.

Black Gully Square, Love Faspa

GREY CLOUDS ROLLED overhead. Ibi stood akimbo with a hip against the Jantzen's wagon as he examined the skies. He took a deep breath. He could not smell the mineral tang of showers; instead, a hint of coals, spent campfire, hung over the community. He decided it could not mean rain. Ibi's crowds grew larger on this day. He stood back and watched as the men set out sawhorses and planks to be festooned with tablecloths of greens and whites by the omas. The wives followed with bowls, baskets, platters, pans. One by one the townsfolk approached Ibi and stepped back.

"Welcome, Brother. Welcome, Sister. Peace be with you."

"Peace be with you."

Soon the square filled. An immense harvest or holiday *faspa*. The air lifted on the warmth of chatter.

Mareika approached down from the construction of the railway station. She had risen before the sunrise. She had jolted from her sleep in her attic space. Her surroundings still made no sense. An apprehension crept over her as she peered below half expecting Charlie Gervais and Paul Lee asleep. She wanted to fall back into a sleep where she could reach Ibi. She hugged that sensation, cuddled it as she would a fuzzy ball of kittens.

"Bison!"

She panicked and escaped the house through the attic crawl-space into the barn, where she found the donkey again. He had wandered home and into the silage once more. John had only said: "Don't forget to take that donkey to Paul's boy, Junior."

∼⤿⟡

Mareika kept her eyes towards the square as she turned down Creamery Road. The crowd appeared immense. Ibi stood upon his cart. His arms, his movements pulsed with life. Pride rose through her cheeks. She quickened her pace.

"I greet you in *His* precious name, our Lord and saviour Jesus Christ. And a warm welcome to those visiting us for the first time. Can I tell you all how grateful I am to you all? I am so grateful. Thank you. Look at all this abundance: we have ham, sausage, *kielke* and *schmauntfat, wareneki, zweibach, somme borscht,* and … *Bruderheim.* Brotherhood." Ibi took his time with the words. His cadence held contemplation and veneration. "The sharing. The kindness. This is brotherhood. This is community. Let us thank you …" He bowed his head. Everybody followed with a tilt of a chin and a drawing of eyelids. "I thank you, Holy Father. We are the pitiful sinners en-dowed with the weakest hearts whom you have mercifully endowed with the humility to recognize this. So we pray to you, implore you, to lift us through this struggle, to dispel our confusion and ego. Unify us to what has been divided and make us one again through your glory and eternal truth. Amen."

The word repeated, "Amen," planed off the believer, slipped from every tongue, to fall together before Ibi's feet. He mounted this reverie, stood high upon it and inhaled. The cologne of hearth, that welcome home, wove itself through his pores. He looked past his crowd down the line of homes, smoke rising from chimneys. He took in that hint of burning poplar. And between the rows his ela-tion lifted even higher as he saw Mareika approach the square with that donkey that had pulled her from his arms just the day before. His blood pulsed in his shoulder.

"Please, eat. *Faspa*, Brothers and Sisters." Ibi clapped his hands. Bishop Dyck strolled into the square. With hands clasped behind his back, he said nothing. He waded into the pool of people. Everybody parted as if afraid to splash the man. His wife Sarah trailed in his wake with a babe in arms and five other children in tow. She was dressed in all black, boots matte, save for her starched white bonnet. She minded her toes, followed the ground behind her husband. Her diminutive size and fallen look gave her the impression of being a child herself. But Ibi found the brunette woman attractive, stunning in fact.

He regarded the thorny, briared appearance of the Bishop and thought, *What is she doing with him?* He followed her. Looked at her body. Guessed the curve of her hip and breast. His thoughts turned to disdain. The Bishop's power and money, all churches had money and power. Ibi smirked at the old man. He never saw this many people in the Mennonite church Sunday morning. Then his histories swelled inside his chest. He stood straight, his chin high, confident the old Ibi would have had no problem needling his way into Sarah's sewing circle. Never did a wife, especially a younger wife, dispel his attention or consideration. The folly of husbands was believing wives were property like tools, wagons, cattle, and hens, while the folly of women was keeping themselves hidden inside homes and gardens. Men raised barns. Women quilted. Inside homes, guests never gushed about beams and rafters. Compliments, the acknowledgement of everything beautiful in our lives, were saved for the dried flowers, gardens, and quilts. A roof kept the rain and snow away, but a quilt warmed you. If a husband were the house, then a wife would be the home. Ibi watched the Bishop scowl through his bushy white beard and eyebrows under a black hat incapable of corralling his white hair.

The old man stopped in the middle of the crowd. Everybody rippled around him as if he were a stone. They shifted their toes away from him. He grabbed Sarah by her elbow and pulled her beside him. One of the older boys tried to move in front. He shoved him back. Then crossed his arms and stared dead through Ibi.

Ibi smiled at Sarah. She kept her eyes down. He avoided the Bishop. Paid him no heed. He knew what men like the Bishop needed most: acknowledgement. Like houses, men's lives became about function. That is why some chased power. Power was acknowledgement. Sarah proved this about the old man. So Ibi gave nothing to the Bishop. He looked past the man over the crowd to the edges of the grasses, greener today than yesterday, where, again, he found Mareika. She tied off the donkey at the post office and eased into the square.

"Why am I here? Like Philip, I have travelled with the Word. From the Crimea steppe, I have wandered and I have wondered." He pointed to his temple. "Across oceans, over mountaintops, through deserts and these plains under us. My hands have held the waters, the sands, and the air. And what was I doing? II Timothy 4:5." Ibi took up his Bible and read. *"But watch thou in all things, endure afflictions, do the work of an evangelist, make full proof of thy ministry.*

"I know you all have been doing the same. You held every word close to your heart. It revived you. His Word brings us to life. That's why you're here. That's why I'm here. We all want to find ourselves at His Kingdom.

"Now I'm not perfect. None of us are." Ibi pounded at his chest. "Jeremiah. Jeremiah 17:9. *The heart is deceitful above all things, and desperately wicked.* I wish it was not so. I do. How easy could it be if the babies we bear were as true as they appear? So helpless. But that's our charge. We are not to be helpless. *For the Son of Man is come to seek and to save that which was lost.* Like Luke said, we have a responsibility to Him.

"I used to wake up—every morning I would wake up in a different room in a different town. Foolhardy. I lived like our neighbour, the coyote. Ate like a coyote. Indulged like a coyote. Howled like a coyote. My impulse was for the moment. I survived. But I was not living. Do this; don't do that. As for me and my household ... I so often kept missing *His* true message. In those beds I wondered, *Am I happy now?* How could I be?" Ibi froze on his word. "It was all wrong. The Gospels are not rules, but a reminder of His sacrifice: *justified freely by His grace through the redemption that is in Christ Jesus: Whom God hath set forth to be a propitiation through faith in his blood.* Romans, right? Romans 3:24, 25. It's not a set list of what to do and what to avoid. It's a ... what has He done. His only Son. Into flesh. The Gospels offer a sinner a new heart. Amen."

"Amen."

Sarah's lungs pushed a breath upon her baby. It gathered sound. Her tongue moulded it into an *Amen.* Bishop Dyck spun to her.

"Excuse me?"

"The baby's fussing." She rocked the child. A hush pulsed from behind her teeth. The baby slept.

The Bishop champed. He looked over the crowd. *What are these people doing here?* His eyes sparkled. There she was, Rebecca. She'd come alive again. Her dress, taut, struck him. He took a deep breath and willed his wife to follow his gaze.

She looked at Mareika's lace hem. She followed it to her soft cheek. She breathed in the spring air. Her shoulders rose. Her chest swelled. She took another deep breath. A wispy sigh escaped.

"You go to her. You get that child."

"I ..."

"Woman, go." The Bishop stripped her of the babe and passed it over his shoulder to an older child.

Sarah shuddered and shuffled towards Mareika. She stopped. She fumbled the words, as if she carried too much firewood.

"What do I say?" Her body kept moving away with an obedience, her gaze never promised to meet the Bishop's. That would have been a challenge. She looked from under her brow to understand what her husband had wanted. She had known why. As a teenage girl, he had wanted her. She had been sinful. She was wicked. But this girl, younger than their eldest, she did nothing except be there, to be in the square. She lived as an atheist with John Doerksen, Rebecca's widower. Wasn't that worse? Sarah had never seen this girl at any church services, but now she came. It was not her church. It was nobody's church. Sarah clutched at her collarbone. She traced the soft skin rising over bone. She stared, her mouth watering at the resemblance to Rebecca. Sarah turned from the Bishop and flowed through the crowd towards not Mareika, but back towards her memories of the East Bank. Afraid everybody there could read her thoughts, she tread lightly, not touching a person. She felt light. Like her body didn't exist inside the cloth that covered her body. She looked back to the Bishop for a moment. Their eyes met. And she saw it. Hunger. A ravenous urge. His lip curled with contempt. Yes. He wanted that girl.

She returned to her path towards Rebecca's daughter. She breathed in the warm wood-fire sillage. She needed a sense of home, of safety. In her heart, the draw of this young woman resembled whimsy, nostalgia. It was like holding hands and picking flowers. Never could she recall a better time than when she moved through the corn stalks with Rebecca. She moved through the crowd and through time.

"Here ..." She called to Rebecca. Rattling behind her eyes the old titters and squeals clutched her heart. Holding hands, neither one led nor followed as they fled fields for the glade through the brush before the moment spilt them on the sandy banks of the Rat River. They could barely breathe. That was until their eyes locked. And sharing one breath made more sense than any words could explain. Their lips drew upon each other, their lungs fluid, like in a dream. Sweet butter and preserves brushed pleasant memories over the softest places of their skin for each to pluck and gather. Those dried flowers hung at the furthest corners of her memories. Still brilliant.

Sarah's breath froze as her heart fluttered, leapt from inside her chest. Rebecca came back to life. And Sarah wanted to go to her. But this man, her husband, he wanted to correct her. Correct what? Sarah knew what she wanted to say. It was what she had wished to say to Rebecca after her first visit with the Bishop. She had gone first. She fled from his home and had hated her body for not listening to her heart, angry with her feet as they carried her homeward and not to Rebecca. She deserved to have been warned. She should have protected her. Rebecca, sweet Rebecca, never deserved what they endured. His touch reaching up inside them, turning them inside out, to be left like hides nailed to the cottonwoods and willows.

Sarah seized Mareika's elbow and yanked her to her lips.

"You must leave here." Sarah looked over her shoulder for the

Bishop. She looked for his ghostly beard and prayed he had stayed in his place.

Mareika jumped and stiffened against the pull. She gathered the alarms in Sarah's tone, but with no context, no known history of the Bishop except the shared tension and repressed anger with Foda, she interpreted the tone as belonging to his voice. Sarah echoed her warning.

"You must get away from here."

Sarah became frantic. She mocked a yank and pull at the girl's arm. She thought back to her own mother when she lectured Sarah about not handling butterflies because it killed them. As a child all she had wanted was to hold that delicate beauty for a moment before she set it free. As a small child with opened cupped hands, she eased a breath under the butterfly's glorious wings.

"Go," she said again. Sarah needed to get this girl away. She welcomed her punishment. She needed it to save her memories for Rebecca.

Bison galloped up into the crowd. The donkey in a twinkling, used its prehensile lip to take up and tug the bight in the rope used to secure him to the post, easily solving the slippery hitch Mareika had used instead of a clove hitch. The animal knocked into Sarah. She fell over and hit the grass. Her eyes bulged as the beast reared back, its front hooves poised to crash down upon her. Mareika snatched the bridle and with some quick hard hops tugged the animal away before it crashed down next to the fallen Sarah.

She scrambled to her feet. But the woman stood still, stood apart, and stood between Mareika and her husband.

Mareika gave her eyes to Ibi. Did he see here? She moved away from Sarah, trading her glances between the Bishop and Ibi. She and Bison reached the cart. She tugged Ibi's pant hem.

He glanced down. His words kept flowing. Mareika reached up for his hand. He gave it to her. He had to fall back with all his weight as the girl scaled the wagon away from the confusion.

Sarah sighed. And braced her mind for a punishment. The Bishop would place her face down over their bed. And there she would lie, and the touch of Mareika's skin once again become Rebecca's. The smooth crux, tender and coquettish. She would use that touch to erase his grip when it was to fall upon her and nail her to the cottonwoods.

Bishop Dyck shoved his way to the wagon. Mareika stepped behind Ibi. Bison stood in front of Mareika.

"Brother, Brother, Brother. This *faspa* is about love." Ibi's grin swelled. The forthcoming repression gave his cause, gave him his martyrdom.

"You will shut your mouth! And you ..." The Bishop turned upon the crowd. His eyes scorched the audience. "Blasphemy!" The Bishop pushed those nearest the cart back.

"O! O Lord. What do Ye see upon this green pasture? A false mob spirit threatening to tear a community to sunder. A lamb apart, divided." Dyck mocked the cries of a lamb. "This is how the wolf feeds." He bleeped again. Dashed the noise into the downed look of those he scolded. "Be found among any of us, true prayer. True reverence. Who is this man who has separated you from your flock against your holy will? Let me offer a true prayer. An ancient prayer instead:

"O holy Father, from every type of false doctrine from every type of false living, from every type of guile, false faith, false benevolence, false idea, and—AND—every type of evil opinion, O holy Father, kindly safeguard us. Indeed, graciously, in your kindness, forgive us and deliver us all from false salvation and repair our craven hearts of the damage. Our salvation will be our joy, undivided, so lead us away back to your love and righteousness ..."

Bishop Dyck looked to Ibi, then waved his finger over the crowd. "Or leave them to neglect your holy Word alone with the wolves."

Bison nipped the Bishop's shoulder.

He jumped and stepped away from the *faspa*. With a shove, he ushered Sarah back to the Mennonite church.

In silence Mareika held Ibi's sleeve. Together they watched the crowd leak back into Black Gully, back into their homes.

Wapos County

I COULD NEVER use this book the way John wished. What would I say? The weather was almost always cold. Yesterday cold, today cold. Tomorrow cold. My every day was sweep, wash, clean, sweep wash clean, polish. Weed if it was in summer. And every day your hands will hurt. Your back will hurt. Hurt. I can share nothing helpful. Oma's recipes, take them. Feed yourself. I am a woman. I am kept to a home as an apple or cherry tree, bonded to the ground, expected to bear fruit. Learn the languages of Foda. He has one beautiful gift. He can talk to any person. I became more when he taught me to read and listen. German, English, Dutch, Russian, Cree. Every word gave me more of myself. So leave. Go away. Cities can offer a woman more. Free yourself from this farm. But never take a job with a wealthy family. Never enter an influential man's home. You will remain property. Don't be property. Inside any of the great cities, hide and be a woman.

Black Gully Lake

MAREIKA DIDN'T FEEL the breeze as the evening seeped into the day. It caressed her chin, raised it upon the mantel of the sunset. She listened to the soft percussive purr of the bowed field grass as the fervent tips rattled new against the old. She played with her hair. Each braid relaxed, then dropped adrift over her shoulders. She combed her fingers through them as she thought about the evening she had got her own room, and if pressed, she would admit she adored it. She heard her father laugh and decant stories of camel races back in Russia as a boy. He talked loudly. The stories filled their home with much laughter. He flashed a bony nub on the right of his neck, a broken collarbone racing tribal Nogai boys. Mareika poked at it but recoiled. And at the end of the night, he took the guests over to a stack of books and gave them some to take home. She had never met this version of Foda.

She reflected as the umber-amber greys and browns of forest fires infected and corrupted the skies overhead. The day's incandescence smothered. Shadows befell the exposed face of the Rocky Mountains range. The poplar, fir, spruce, cedar, and birch forests wove themselves into a deep green mat while the hard, grey stone-caps blackened. The foothills seemed to huddle about Black Gully Lake. A single crow hopped and cawed upon the manila rope of Ibi's tent. Its call orchestrated a tremendous murder of crows, which budded about the trees' naked limbs. Their caws muddled the atmosphere of the lake. She looked across the water's opal sheen. Its blackness absorbed what sunlight escaped through the cloud and smoke. The scenery took on a sense of night, a living dream.

As she approached the shores, Mareika spooked a mother loon and her young. The birds dove and darted every which way below the surface, eight silvered zigzags that resurfaced seconds later further from shore and reconvened in a straight line like matryoshka dolls. She turned from the waters, her eye on the skies above.

She massaged her pelvis and hip. Everything under her skin rang as if her body played anvil to an invisible hammer. She scanned the open pasture for Ibi as she strolled back to his camp.

Ibi came out of the brush with an armful of broken limbs. He smiled. Mareika flashed a smile back. As he marched past her, a palm found its way over her hip. She wiggled away, but turned to follow. Her fingers danced up his back to his shoulders, and she rode the pull of his body to the firepit. And once he squatted and dropped the load of wood, she hugged his back. She stole a deep breath of air from off his nape. Her pores rose and danced. She hugged him tighter, cinched her hands under his armpits, and gripped his chest. His hands reached back to tap her hips. He rose, took her hand.

"Thank you."

"For what?"

"For you."

Mareika blushed.

Ibi could have stopped, shared the moment but continued to lay adoration out for Mareika. "The generosity of lending me the donkey." He pointed to the animal. They shared a silence as Bison moved with purpose, its nose in the new grass pulling greens and chewing, pulling greens and chewing.

"Sharing this day with me. And you—What a gift you have been to this soul ..." He took up her wrist and placed her palm upon his chest.

The heat of the fire jumped and slithered, lapped at her shins. She lifted her other palm against his warmth.

Ibi shook her wrists, a thank you, then slid behind her hips and let his palms fall down her back, stroking her ass. Her pores rose once again. Together they sat, shared a silence. From a satchel he scooped up a brush. He passed it through the tussled wave of her hair, his touch light, easing from her temple to her shoulders.

"I want to show you something," Ibi said.

He rose, the horse-hair brush in his hand. He went to the lake, dipped the brush, gave it a shake. Then he jogged to the tent. It was then Mareika noticed a white gown, almost pajamas but more formal with thick sturdy seams about the cuffs, collar, and hem. The outfit waved from the tree he'd been camping under. Ibi took the gown by the hem and brushed it with the damp grooming tool. He dropped the brush, then his shirt and slacks.

Mareika's eyes popped. She looked around. But as they were alone, she returned her attention to the man in front of her. The thickness of his calves and thighs intrigued her—her memory whispered that she had never seen the back of a man's legs. She stole a gulp of air as she looked away towards the open plain, the lake, and then back. She started over again. Slower. She took her eyes off her feet to his, then his legs again. She examined the calves. They were dark like his shoulders. The firm round muscle rippled into a bulge as his tiptoes raised the brush to the collar of his gown. Her eyes hesitated, dashed side to side to still find nobody with them, before they found the curve at the base of his back. Her heart suggested she may be stealing something. Her heart pushed the guilt into her lungs, and she breathed it out her nose. She cleared her throat. She looked around. If she focused, she could hear the chatter of squirrels fighting with robins and the grinding munch of Bison grazing. Her eyes returned to the course, etching the memory of this man.

The western sun fell lower as if to escape the choke of smoke and cloud. The glare got in Mareika's eye. She placed a hand over her brow to shade her eyes. The bush dropped long shadows. They crept across the pasture, patted the meadow, but stopped at her own hem as they stretched to join the obsidian waters of Black Gully Lake. The setting sun's fire raged orange, burnt clouds further. The loons all turned east away from the blazing light before they disappeared in the cattails. The last light kindled Ibi's body.

Mareika's attention swaddled the man. He squatted to pet his calico companion. He pinched it behind the ears. Their every shadow stretched like saltwater taffy towards her. Mareika wanted to grab his and tug him back to her. Ibi seemed to hear this thought.

"Oh, Mareika, I prayed for you to be with me these last days." He faced her, but he looked onward to the sky with shuttered eyes.

She looked at his tight smile.

Mareika smiled, too.

She glanced down. Her heart definitely told her she had just stolen something. The image, his separate parts exposed. She cleared her throat as she looked aloft. The calico pranced to her. Pounced into her lap. Her eyes darted to the cat, interrupted with a push.

"No, Kitty."

When she looked back, Ibi had slipped into his gown.

"I got you an ascending gown. I'm sorry, it's a boy's nightgown. Sorry." He returned to Mareika by the fireside.

The gelding promised to Paul Lee brayed. It jostled and fought with the tether of rope. It munched on pulled-up dandelion greens, three mouthfuls. It followed Ibi with a sideways stare. Then it marched between the couple at the firepit. Ibi pulled taut the length of rope hanging loose from its bridle. The donkey stared at Ibi, one ear forward, the other back.

Ibi froze. He looked back at the animal standing between them. Then he squatted for a brown paper-wrapped package inside his satchel. The donkey folded its ears back.

"Thank you." She pointed at the gelding. Dandelion greens clung to its lip. "That means he's irritated, when his ears do that."

The donkey's ears shifted back and forth in opposite directions before being pinned backwards along its neck. It lowered its head with an eye on each of them.

Ibi stepped between the animal's gaze and Mareika. "Try it on."

The donkey nudged the man at his neck. Ibi stumbled. Mareika rose.

"Hush …" Her palm stroked the beast. Its ears stood up.

She swiped the heat from her lap. Ibi put an arm around her shoulder and offered her the package. The donkey wedged its head between them at his shoulder. The weight of his arm and the animal's head on the base of her neck felt like a yoke. She shoved the donkey's chin into Ibi's chest.

"Stop it."

The donkey lifted its weight from off them. Mareika cradled the brown package. She stepped back. She stepped away. She glanced at the open canvas tented over a line of manila between trees. She looked at the near naked trees merely budding with the promise of green. She pressed the package against her stomach. The paper crinkled under the pads of her fingers. She took a deep breath as the damp pressure against her groin cooled between her legs. She slapped the donkey's butt, and it scooted off towards the brushline where the spring rye grass and dandelion greens grew lusher.

"Where do I put it on?"

"Here." Ibi smiled with a nod.

Her face twitched almost into a smile.

"Well … Only Mutta …" She looked at her feet. She held her body.

Mareika thought back to Rebecca, *What's this?* The little girl had placed a small black dome critter on six whiskery legs on the table. Mutta pressed it under her thumb. The unmistakeable crunch of death didn't come. When the insect sprang back up and tried to scuttle away, Rebecca trapped and burned the critter with a match before she stripped Mareika down and searched her body for more of the parasites. They found no other ticks.

"I don't know," Mareika said.

Mareika had spent the last couple of days thinking about Ibi. And now, she had seen more of him than she fathomed. Behind her anxiety, she revelled with it. He was a wondrous distraction to the blood and pain seeping from her body. She envisioned him as a husband. In some far-flung home, he would sit across from her at their dinner table. He smiled under his quilted eyes. He would thank her for the bread that was still warm. They would later lay together on the floor by the fire. He would read from his book, *Heimweh*, because she would not be able to read German. His translation would be perfect upon her ear. She would watch his perfect, smart lips.

But inside this moment, her dreams, her thoughts did not cross enough time. She hugged her body, her arms over her clothed breast. She looked away. Only she and Ibi stood upon the pasture at Black Gully Lake. She thought of his prophecy, as only a day remained before she would either rise or stay upon this earth.

"I'm scared," she said.

"I know. You told me. So am I." His lips left a moist shadow upon her temple. "I wish we had more time. But after tomorrow we will have more than forever."

"Are you sure, Ibi?"

Mareika looked for that mother loon and her trail of seven chicks. One little loon darted under the surface of the lake, side over side outside the soft wake of mamma loon.

Ibi's arms squeezed her into his chest. She sighed and let her head fall onto his chest. Her ear searched for his heartbeat. It raced. She sighed again.

He reached for the front of her jacket, unbuttoning it. She stood straight and stepped from under the coat as he tossed it to the ground.

"You're beautiful," he said.

Her shoulders rolled forward under his reach again as he came to her vest and blouse.

He freed the first button. He slid his arms under her elbows for more buttons, the third, fourth, fifth ... His fingers, nimble, moved fast. His hands had learned the tight eyelets needed a twist. His fingertips scaled down her blouse, freeing every button and letting in a supple breeze that pulled at her flesh.

Mareika's shoulders quivered; her knees trembled. She crossed her arms when he took her collar with his hands. He peeled everything down but got stopped at her shoulder.

"Don't you want to try it on?"

"I do …" She looked away.

His eyes stayed to her chest as he unwrapped the packaging. The gown unfurled down to her feet. He moved behind her. She felt his separate parts press against her ass. Then his fingers fumbled for her collar again. His thumbnail scratched her shoulder. He leaned closer. The shadow of a coming beard pierced the crux of her neck as he peeked over her shoulder.

"Is this better?" His breath fell on her earlobe.

"Sorry." She rubbed each stiff forearm with a straight smile.

His voice, warm behind her ear, slid over her against the breeze. "You're beautiful."

Mareika trapped her arms, kept them from crossing with a pinch of the seams of her skirt between her thumb and finger. Her shoulders relaxed when she thought about his lips again. She breathed out of her mouth when his hands took the open face of her blouse, his thumb knuckles traced upon the curve of her breast, stopping at her firm nipples. She closed her eyes as he dropped her blouse. Her pores tightened against the breeze. She sighed, and promised to remember how this man gave her a new kind of goosebumps.

She took a deep breath. Then she unbuttoned her own skirt. It fell. She backed into Ibi.

"You're amazing …"

The weight of the wool skirt warmed her feet as the open air kissed her skin.

"I wish to wash your flesh," Ibi said.

Mareika eyes darted to her panties, the edge impressing the round of her thigh as it rose into her body, stained an earthy clay colour. Her hand crossed over them. And her cramps, further away from her body than the night before, still rattled behind her stomach.

"Can I have the gown?" She looked down at her breast. She watched Ibi's hand swing around to the front of her thigh. A glance over her shoulder saw him look up upon her naked body.

"You're beautiful," he said.

Mareika looked across the lake, followed the edge of the opposite shoreline to where the field grass grew tallest as it crawled up a divide of thickets. Between the separated clusters of trees, a meadow rolled over a hillock where the moon rose into the night sky. The grass bent down upon this opening that created a path. She knew that that was the trail the deer took to the lake to drink.

"We should let the gelding drink."

"Hush . . ."

His hands played with her shoulders, his fingertips massaged her tension free. She felt him try to influence her to turn to him. She anchored her heels. He stepped around her. His eyes followed her chest. He held out the gown, level to her eye. She had to lift her hand from her panty to take it. He knelt and took them down, her panty. She went rigid. But she watched his face. The edges of his eyes, turned up, looked excited. He showed her a smile as his eyes met hers. She smiled.

He held her gaze as he stood before lowering his eyes to her breasts. His hand met their edge. He cupped them inside his firm palms. She looked down.

"May I wash you?"

"Okay."

He kneeled again, slid his hand over her ass down behind her ankle guiding it out of her skirt, then he took her other ankle. Mareika balanced herself with a hand on the top of his head. His fresh-barbered hair felt soft and smooth.

"Oh, you're bleeding," he said.

Mareika's hand folded over her eyes.

"Stop."

"No, Mareika. It's okay."

"No, it's not." She dropped to her skirt and picked it up over her breasts. Ibi tugged at it.

"No."

"You're okay."

"No, I'm not. It's all my fault."

"What?"

She felt the air move about her hair and chin as he stood.

"It started Monday. I kissed Jonah Wiebe. Then my stomach

exploded in pain. He was kissing me back, his hands pressed against me, under my dress. Then the pain pierced me. Jonah ran off. And I won't stop bleeding, and my stomach feels like there are buffalo running from thunder inside. And I keep bleeding. I don't know why. It feels like everything is ending, and I think I'm being punished, and, and, and ... I won't be allowed to follow you."

"Who's Jonah?"

"I told you. He's just a stupid boy."

"And ..."

"No."

"Don't interrupt." Ibi stood and took Mareika by the shoulders. "Look at me." Ibi stood taller, more immense. She looked away.

"Were you with him?"

"No."

"Really?"

"I promise."

"Oh, Mareika ..."

She felt his lips dance over her knuckles, climb her chin, then dash over her eyes. He returned his kisses to her hands. The moist tip of his tongue graced the skin over her ring finger.

"You are an angel. I promise God would never leave you outside the Gates." He stepped into her. His middle finger traced the edge of her lips. Her mouth parted. He slid his finger over her tongue. She wrapped her lips around his knuckle. His finger tasted the way cut grass smells. He pulled his moist finger from her mouth. His smile looked like a dragonfly balanced on a wild rose. He pressed his mouth to her lips as his finger traced the length of her body to her other parts. She did not let go of his mouth. Her eyes held to his eyelids. She took his forearm, but his hand continued. He traced the edge of her kingdom, graced the soft folds before he followed them inside.

Her lungs filled like they needed all the air that hung over the pastures and off the lake. His middle finger curled and massaged inside her. She pushed against his forearm.

"Stop."

"Doesn't it feel nice?"

"Yes." Mareika did not lie, but she still held his forearm. "Please …"

"It's okay." He removed his hand. "I told you. It's only God warning you of the Rapture. His rebirth. You're not dying. He has chosen you to share His message. You are a messenger as I am His messenger. You're not going to hell. He chose you. You are one of His angels. The pain you feel is His second birth. He lives through you. He chose you because he needs you."

"No …" Mareika's head fell into his chest. She hugged him.

"I need you," he said.

Mareika, her hips and chest tingled, so she released his forearm. "Please put my gown on."

"If that's what you want." As he dropped the gown over her, Ibi tracked her body with kisses. He paused at her nipple with his suckling lips, then dropped his final kiss at her bellybutton.

"I'm sorry," Mareika said.

"No, I'm sorry." Ibi fussed with the gown over the girl's body. "Do you like it?"

"It felt nice."

Ibi pulled up a blade of grass. He placed it between the thumbs of his cupped hands and blew. The green reed squawked as he kneeled. His hair was tussled by the breeze. He traced the blade of grass over the corner of his lips.

"You travelled deserts and mountains and rode camels in caravans. Foda used to race camels." Mareika pulled her arms to her chest. She leaned in, taking Ibi's hand to wrap around her.

Ibi pulled her down over his body, so she lay beside him.

Her conversation kept her mind away from their physical proximity. "In Russia. He told his friends that when he was a boy in Russia, Opa Martin used to take him to race against other boys."

"Other Mennonites?"

"No. He said they were like our friend, Charlie. He's Métis. But he said they were nomads."

"The Tartars?"

"No. No-something."

"The Nogai."

"Yes! Do you know about them? Were there any in Central Asia?"

Ibi sat up. "Your father came from Molotschna. There are no Nogai there."

"But Foda said that he raced with them and his foda would bet money."

"Gambling." Ibi tossed his blade of grass away. "I think he's a storyteller."

"No."

"The Nogai left the Molotschna probably a couple generations before we were born. There was a great exodus. They all were forced back to Turkey."

"Foda wouldn't lie. He said that his family paid to come to Canada from the winnings."

"I doubt it. Not against any Nogai."

"He did." Mareika stared off over the lake. A crane stood in the cattails with a perch that fought against the clamp of its bill. "Foda does not lie."

Ibi sat up and wrapped his arms around her. "I didn't come from Molotschna. Maybe some of the Nogai stayed, and I bet he raced camels. If that's what he told you, then that's what happened."

"He did tell me. And he wouldn't lie. He's a good man. And him and his friends, they built me my own room, and they ate and drank, and they laughed and told stories. Charlie told a story about Charles Dickens, the famous writer, and his son. Did you know his son lived in Saskatchewan before it was Saskatchewan?"

"Drinking, eh?"

She scowled with a slight groan before biting at the corner of her thumbnail. She sat up and hugged her knees. Mareika dropped her head, shook it for an answer, the way a person would shake the last coin through the slot in an upturned piggy bank. She needed to buy back her confidence. She felt like she was in the schoolhouse.

Ibi's hand left a swatch of heat over her back as he rubbed it against her, sliding down the ripple of her spine. He groaned as he squeezed the edge of her hip. "I didn't mean—"

She swallowed and chomped at her knee. "He seemed so happy. He laughed. He told stories. He was smiling and laughing."

"Those kinds of things are important. But I wasn't trying to judge him. It isn't my place. I worry. I worry for those men because of the drink. Indulgence, that kind of indulgence, it instigates departure. It leads men away from the Kingdom."

"He's a good man."

"It's not your choice."

She turned into him. She pinned his wandering hands to his thighs. Her eyes looked for some kind of fun in Ibi's dark eyes. This moment fell heavy. She wanted to feel a tingle in her hip from a tugging she'd see in his eyes. "I don't want to talk about him."

Ibi stood over her. His body eclipsed the setting sun, and his body under his white gown turned dark, like a shadow. The ripple of the material made him seem to hover there. "Envious, murderous, drunkenness, revelry, and such like: of the which I tell you before, as I have also told in time past, that they which do such things shall not inherit the Kingdom of God. Drunkenness. I know the dark places drunkenness takes men. I should think that your mutta taught you better. But I guess she kept a home with an unholy man."

"He is a good man." She rose. "And she did teach me. She told me drink no water, but use a little wine for thy stomach's sake and thine often infirmities. My father broke no sin. He is hurt. I can see that. He has never worn a smile in so many years. I saw his spirit lifted. He may not have time or patience for the *Word*. But you will not call him a bad man."

"*For he shall be great in the sight of the Lord.*" Ibi threw his arms up and spun. He hopped on a foot. He stopped and pointed a finger between her eyes. His lips parted, ready to cast another line. "*For he shall be great in the sight of the Lord and shall drink neither wine nor strong drink; and he shall be filled with the Holy Ghost, even from his mother's womb.*" He nodded and crossed his arms. His face looked like stone, his figure, rigid, was only missing a sword for him to lean into, the tip buried between his naked feet like a sentinel for God. "Don't quote me scripture. For that one lesson in Timothy, I can find a dozen more that warns there is no room for drunkards in heaven." He pointed to the sky.

Mareika looked up to the darkening atmosphere.

"I am here now for you. For your salvation. If you wish to stay on these plains and face the wrath of the red dragon to suffer in the Holy War that will rage and destroy not just men, but tear down those mountains into rubble, then go away from me. I am here to rise to His Kingdom. I do not want to lose you. But if you are asking me to make a choice between you and *His* glory . . ." Ibi stared through Mareika. His head turned the slow side to side of disapproval.

"You insulted me."

"No, I did not. I warned you. Do you not think I don't know about the revulsion caused by the drink? Who hath woe? Who hath sorrow? Who hath contentions? Who hath babbling? Who hath wounds without cause? Who hath redness of eyes?" He fell upon his knees and lifted his palms to his face. He stared into the wrinkles, the valleys and peaks of fingerprints etched through his skin. He showed his palms to her. His eyes now reddened. "I know. I know." His hands trembled. "Thine eyes shall behold strange women, and thine heart shall utter perverse things. At the last it biteth like a serpent, and stingeth like an adder. I was only a boy and I was lost. I left the West Reserve like Claas told me. And I waited. I waited. And I waited. And he never came. Just like before. I had turned against my household: the Prodigal Son. I was lost. Somewhere on these prairies I went where anybody would take me. I was a boy no older than you. I worked in the forests, I worked on the rivers and lakes. I have been beaten. I have been robbed. I have had nothing but the clothes on my back and this beating heart." Ibi punched his chest three times.

"It was a French couple . . ." He stopped and dropped his head to the grass. "You should go. This is not a story for you."

"But Ibi . . ."

"Go!"

"Tell me what happened."

"It doesn't matter ... I cannot help you."

"Please tell me."

Ibi lifted his face. His eyes, puffed and ruddy, held a silence between them. The intensity blocked out the sounds of birds, bees, and the rattle of grass and budding tree. His gaze bent around Mareika.

"The French couple, atheists like you, they took me in as a boy. As a boy ... They believed in wine and food. I built fences and cut barley. They were wealthy farmers on the lands of antelope. They grew their own grapes, taking them into their home in the winter. Like a boarder, I stayed on for almost three years. And one evening they invited me to share their wine. The missus was beautiful. She was like a mountain bluebird amongst magpies. Her singsong, fluttering captivated me. That place felt so beautiful to this heart." Ibi massaged his chest as he would his calico companion. "She was a shoot of fireweed rising out of the black charcoal of a great fire. I have seen a forest decimated by flame, and after the heat has gone, these long, slender stems rise above the ash bearing soft violet petals. Their beauty brings the return of the honeybees, the hummingbirds, the butterflies, to drink nectar. Madame Dubois—she smelled of cream and honey." He laughed, and with a swipe of his wrist across his eyes he continued. Mareika stood back, collected his words. "I laugh because her name, Dubois, means forest. She and Mr. Dubois. We imbibed the grapes of their harvest. They filled me with wine and rich food. She stared at me only from the side. She smiled. And Mister he saw this. And with a drunken heart, a clouded mind, they invited me into her bed." He shook his head and turned his eyes away from Mareika. "To eat and drink with the drunken. I was taken away. She was so beautiful and tempting, and she beckoned to me. He ushered me to her inside their bed. And ..."

"I don't understand," Mareika said.

"I was with her as she was my wife. I was lying between her legs. She lured me between her thighs. She held my face. Her hands were soft. But I was a boy. I was not older than you. And I had not known these things could happen. It was all so intoxicating ... and inglorious ... *For he is cast into a net by his own feet, and he walketh upon a snare ...*" Ibi took his face in his hands and wept. "Then the Mister ..." Ibi could not turn his gaze to Mareika. It would bend and move around her like the wind moves about the trunk of a powerful birch. His voice rattled as the leaves would. "*Woe unto him that giveth his neighbour drink, that puttest thy bottle to me, and makest me drunken also, that thou mayest look on their nakedness!* I know what the drink does. It takes souls. But I am here to save yours."

"Did he hurt you?" Mareika offered her arms as wide as she could hold them.

Ibi looked away. Shame dragged his eyes down into the earth.

"Please. Let me hold you?"

He walked upon knees into her arms. She cinched him to her breast. She felt his breath fall over her head. It pounded out of him. His arms moved around her waist. A hand took the small of her back. His pinky fell over the crest of her ass. He received her embrace with a draw of breath.

"I'm sorry they hurt you."

"It's okay. *God shall wipe away all tears from their eyes; and there shall be no more death, neither sorrow, nor crying, neither shall there be any more pain: for the former things are passed away.*" He rose, and as he did, he took her by her face, lifted her chin up, and kissed her.

"I like kissing you," she said.

"Don't be ashamed." Ibi reached and lifted her gown above her thighs, where his grip took her hips. Then a hand roamed to her ass while the other took the inside of her knee. He lifted and pulled her nearer.

"Can't we just kiss?"

She threw her shoulders back, lifted her chin up, but tossed her glance and hair behind her shoulder. Ibi pulled her by the ass into him with a deep kiss. A downward stroke of his middle finger raised her gown and her arms. He freed her. Her hands fell to her sides. She stood naked. She watched a smile inch over his face. His eyes turned up, his eyebrows, too. The wrinkles about his chin, they were all turned up high like a thousand smiles.

She rose higher to him upon her toes, offering her mouth to his. She exhaled every ounce of breath, and her heart pounded out of her lungs. Ibi's biceps and forearms rippled as he took her weight in his arms. His lips escaped but found her forehead to sketch a soft line that fell down the bridge of her nose to capture her lips again. She held her breath as his tongue slipped over the edge of her lips. His breath carried the sweet tinge of raspberry tea. It mingled with hers as she inhaled. Her lungs rose and pressed her chest into his tight body. She reached for his hip, pulled him nearer. His touch rolled off her breast to her hand. She spread her fingers, and they tangled with his. He pulled back. He freed his fingers to fold his grip over her wrist. He guided her hand between his thighs. She pushed her lips for a deeper kiss. He turned his head and folded her fingers around his separate parts. She followed his lead, followed his hand away from his body then slowly back.

"Faster," he said.

She listened. She drank in his face. His eyes, down, took in her body.

He reached for her hand. "Not so tight."

She loosened her grip. She kissed his neck. She kissed his chest. His hand wrapped around hers. They sped up. She watched their hands sliding over him.

His hand rose and as the pads of his fingers, wet, slid under her chin to lift her eyes to his. He begged her, "Faster."

His lips missed hers and pressed to the corner of her chin. Saliva crept out his mouth and ran down to her chin to her breast. Her shoulder and forearms muscles burned with effort. He palmed her breasts, kneaded them like dough. With the other hand he took a handful of her ass. His voice pumped out groan after groan, each one louder, each one warmer as spit dripped onto her neck. His body at his hips and shoulders shuddered. He shook like a wet dog.

"I love you." He exhaled. He kissed her like he had not eaten in weeks. "I love you." He kissed her. "I love you." He kissed her more.

She wrapped her arms around him. He hugged her back with one hand. She let his strength lift her to his chest, and she held her breath to search for his heartbeat with a pressed ear. It fluttered like a bird inside a cage. She wished to join him inside that cage.

"*Defraud ye not one the other, except with consent for a time, that ye may give yourselves to fasting and prayer; and come together again.*" Ibi kissed Mareika once again, but held his lips to hers.

"Will you baptize me tomorrow?" she said.

"I promise ..."

Wapos County

PAUL LEE RODE upon his horse under a smudged-out sky. The spring chinooks dragged the evidence of the forest fires Charlie Gervais mentioned days earlier, from the burning northern forests, over Black Gully.

Paul dismounted and led his horse into the open barn. "Hey, John, looks like our ol' friend Charlie was right about them forest fires."

John's head fell from the loft. He saw only the man's shadow.

"Did you see it out there? It's practically night. I feel like a Christmas ham in the smoker box."

"It's thick."

The sweet aroma of charred birch, willow, poplar felt like a scarf wrapped too tightly around a person's mouth and nose. John crawled down a ladder with a bag of seed over his shoulder. He coughed.

"How's the gelding?"

"Well, that's why I'm here." Paul's hand swallowed John's whole, but his grip was as delicate as if he was collecting roses. He followed John's lead and let go after two pumps of his elbow. "I know you said I would have it Monday before I got home, but my boy says your girl took it back."

"She did what?" John, halfway back up the rungs, moved down the ladder like a daddy-longlegs.

"Yeah, she came with it to the schoolhouse Monday, but then she left with it."

"Well, she never brought it home with her."

"Junior said she headed towards Black Gully Lake."

"What?"

"And Glenda was at the post office yesterday, sending an order to Eaton's for some sweaters and things, and she said she saw your girl helping that strange fella up in the square."

"What strange fella?" John wiped his hands off on his thighs. He moved back and forth around his barn listening but not hearing Paul. His mind raced back to the Bishop and his smirk after their tussle, *He does have your daughter.*

He picked up a pail of oats. He set it down. He grabbed it again then lifted it over a pen gate and hooked it to a timber.

A castrated donkey came from out of the corner for the pail. Flies buzzed about its wound, trekked along the rows of coagulated blood upon its fur. Its prehensile lips pinched at the grain before a pink mound of tongue flopped over the side of the creature's mouth into the treat. Its teeth ground and champed. John scratched the beast under the jaw.

John shook his head.

"The Rapture guy."

"Say that again."

"The Rapture guy—Glenda said your girl was helping him up in the square. There's a big to do off at Black Gully Lake tomorrow. She said he was an excitable man."

"And Mareika was with him?"

"Yeah."

"You're sure."

"She said she was right up beside him, holding his hand while he preached about the coming end. That's what she said."

"No, no. That Gietz fella—you're certain."

"Yes, I think that's his name. Yeah. Tall guy. Glenda said he looked like a stoat to her. She didn't give him no attention, but said with certainty that she was with him."

"No. Mareika wouldn't. She's never set foot in a church—we're atheist."

"Sure. But Glenda saw what she saw. She's been hanging out with him in the square where he's been preaching and singing, playing his piano for days now. I heard he's been camping out on Black Gully Lake, and, I guess, tomorrow he's having some sermon. And everybody is expecting to rise up into heaven."

"No." John paced between the pen and Paul. He wouldn't look at his visitor. He scrubbed at his chin. His stare narrowed, and he began to mutter. He turned and marched into his home. He moved about the kitchen, took stock of her breakfast dishes. He took the stairs into her new loft. She had made her bed like she always did, her patchwork quilt folded, laid across the foot.

He marched back to Paul. He had a hand inside the pen, where it stroked the gelding. John shook his head. He took a scowl out the back of the barn into the muffled daylight. He stared across the plain. The daylight felt like dusk through the stained skies choked by smoke.

"Are you sure?"

"What?"

"Are you sure Glenda saw her with that man?"

"Why would she make that up?"

John nodded. "All right." He went to Paul and shook his hand. "I'll talk with Mareika later and ask her about your donkey. My apologies."

Paul's giant mitt found John's shoulder. He gave his neighbour a squeeze and his eyes. The silence he shared with John, though only a moment, promised this conversation stayed with them only.

"By the way, where is that Gietz now?"

"Black Gully Lake."

John tipped his hat.

As the rest of the day drained away from John, he kept to his duties as if normal but kept an eye out for Mareika.

When he gathered firewood, which he did not need, he carried it around the house to the front door instead of through the barn. He dumped several loads onto his porch throughout the afternoon, and every trip he gave his eye to the horizon, followed the ruts from his yard to the gravel roads until everything rose over the knolls and disappeared into the brushed smoky sky.

He returned to the barn. He brushed the dried blood from the gelding. He sprayed its wound with mix of water and vinegar. Then he released the gate latch inside the pen. The gelding bounced out the barn to the fenceline. John stared over his shoulder to the road again. He followed after the animal as it reunited with its mother. She nuzzled the gelding. She gave it a sniff. Then she nuzzled up again. John looked over the field. He counted the head of cattle—every cow and every calf—he counted all of them.

He opened the gate, and the gelding turned its haunches to the jenny. She licked at his hindquarters before she nipped at the top of his tail. He gave a playful buck and scampered off amongst the cattle. John returned to the house, again walking around to the front porch.

He moved inside. He compared his watch to the clock. Nothing was off. He moved to his stacks of books, looked but didn't see anything. He moved up the stairs, looked over Mareika's made bed before he moved to the smoker box in the chimney. He pulled the crispy bits from chickens and hares. He took that handful into the kitchen and dropped them into a pot. He ladled enough water to cover them and stewed the parts well past supper, adding a ladle every so often to keep the pot stewing. He dumped the meal into two bowls, set two places at the table, cut some bread, and ate half of his bowl alone. He sat with his eyes to the door and listened to the crackle of firewood inside his stove. Soon his home fell dark, and still, no Mareika.

SATURDAY, JULY 30, 1892.

Eastern Reserve, Manitoba

Somme Borscht

1–2 ham bones with meat. Fill stock pot and boil the
    bones all day. The stock should be in half then add:
3 onions
2 pounds of potatoes
1 pint of buttermilk
5 sprigs of parsley
few sprigs of dill
1 tablespoon salt
pepper
Cook until vegetables are tender, add:
1 cup cream
1 tablespoon flour
1 egg
When serving add vinegar.

I FEEL SO rushed to share so much in this book that boy has given
to me. This is the last recipe. I know it is your favourite. In the
garden at the end of Somme, we collected everything we needed,
didn't we. I shall always hold this time with you inside my heart,
Rebecca. Remember it's the time we share … Ich liebe dich.

Black Gully Lake

IBI BROUGHT ME the gown. It felt heavier than the day before. I had reservations about whether I could float off into the heavens with it on. I couldn't let him see my doubt, so I looked down.

"You will wear this for your baptism. And we shall hang it near the fire so that it can dry for tomorrow."

"It's beautiful. Thank you."

He stared at me. He seemed to see everything about me. I wanted to turn away.

"Go ahead, put it on."

I unfolded it and went to put it over my head.

"No. You have to remove your clothes."

My heart leapt into my throat, and my stomach fluttered. I hugged the gown to my chin.

"You have to look away."

Ibi folded his hands behind his back and turned from me.

"No peeking."

I peeled back everything. The cool of the spring night kissed my skin. Goosebumps raced over me. I stared at Ibi. He stood tall and true. He looked into the sky.

"Do you see those clouds?"

I looked to the heavens as I removed more clothes. "Yes."

"Do you smell the air?"

"Yes."

"But the fearful, and unbelieving, and the abominable, and mur-
derers, and whoremongers, and sorcerers, and idolaters, and all liars,
shall have their part in the lake which burneth with fire and brimstone:
which is the second death. Revelation 21:8. You can smell the world
on fire already. Can you smell it?"

"It's scary."

"Only for the fearful."

"It's so smoky. I have never seen it like this before. It's been almost night all day."

"The sun shall be darkened in his rising, and the moon shall not
shine with her light . . ."

I pulled the gown over my nakedness and examined the skies.
Through the chalky brown haze of cloud and smoke, the sun was as
orange and large as a harvest moon. It glowed like an ember. It was
perfect and round. Below it, I could see sunlight smouldering on the
eastern horizon.

"I'm ready."

Ibi turned around. His smile filled the air between us. I stood
taller, rocked upon my tiptoes. And as he stepped to me, he wrapped
me into a hug, his movements soft and smooth. I felt as light the air
around us.

He led me into the waters. The cold pinched my flesh. I froze.
But he took me deeper. The gown became heavier even as it floated
up around me, my calves, my knees, my thighs. The cold shook me
as it rose over my other parts, yet it soothed the ache still haunting
my hips. I checked the water for blood. When I saw none, I fell into
his arms. He cradled me.

I stared off into this bizarre reversal of day into night under the
false harvest moon. My ears filled with water shutting his prayers out.
Then, with a hand over my heart, I took what felt like a last breath.

He plunged me under. I kept my eyes open. Peering up through
the rippling waters, I spotted through the glassy surface the gigantic
orange glow of our sun breaking through sky and cloud and smoke
and water. Its light rode the rippling surface. The wrinkles radiated
orange and black, orange and black. The green algae floating under

the surface stole this glimmering and sparked into fiery embers all around me like a million tiny stars.

As my throat constricted following that last breath seeping out my pursed lips, I watched the rolling silver orbs float up and burst against the surface, rearranging the glassy lake surface from orange and black to black and orange. It was like Black Gully Lake was on fire, and I had escaped under the water.

But eventually I ran out of breath. The cold rushed deeper inside me. And my toes, fingers, and lungs began to tremble. I calmed as I still felt his hands upon me. He held me weightless. I let my eyes close as the weight of my arms began to sink.

Ibi yanked me from the waters. I gasped. Then I cried. He scooped me from the water, the weight of the ascending gown a hundred pounds, like I'd been buried. He lugged me to the shore and let my toes touch the sand. My knees wouldn't work, and I collapsed. The air stung colder than before.

He followed to his knees. His lips just off my breath. The thin space between our gaze warmed.

He kissed me.

No. I kissed him ...

He kissed me back ...

Then my arms reached for him and pulled him not into the sand but into me. I can't explain my actions that followed, because they came from love, a love unfamiliar to me. I felt safe, and I felt saved. His words, his prayers before had not resonated, but in those moments he pulled me from the water, between the gasping and the moment I stole his breath for mine, I felt saved. I felt safe. I ceased feeling temporary. This man had saved me. I had been trapped nowhere. And now I was alive. And his lips and his chest pressed to mine felt like the best place for me to be in this moment. My stomach and hip stopped aching. And I forgot the world might end.

We took a breath, and I saw the stars flash and sparkle between our eyes.

The air felt warmer as his hand pulled my wet gown up to my waist. I let my legs part for him to rest between me.

"Are you sure?" he asked.

I didn't understand his question, but let my body answer, pressed up against him. I kissed his mouth. I felt his hot skin against mine. The pressure of his lips against me, and at my other parts, I felt him. Everywhere I felt warm. I pulled him to me.

I gasped. My lungs felt as if I had inhaled the entire sky. I pulled every star and the moon through the clouds and smoke. We ceased being two. I brought my knees from off the sand, drew them up, and spread my hips. Ibi pressed against me. I gasped again.

"Are you okay?"

I combed my spread fingers through his hair and directed his mouth back to mine. "Perfect ..."

But the moment seemed fragile ... I had never felt so close to another person, but removed, pulled away. I feared everybody would find out. I could not stop what had happened. I did not want to stop. But what would Foda think of me? Is this what Mutta feared? It felt so right. But in every blink, her memory stole the tenderness. Ibi's hair sprang long into cascading brown curls tangling me. My skin stung from her wooden spoon. Then the cold of the oncoming night reminded me I was very wet. The sand of the shore reminded me I was very naked and very outside.

This time belonged to me, to us. I wanted to take control of this moment.

"I'm cold."

He lay still inside me, grunted and lowered his lips to my ear. "Let's go to the tent," Ibi said.

I slid from under him, stood, and reached for his hand. We laughed as we rushed to the tent, pulled off our wet clothes and let our flesh warm us again under some covers.

"It's going to be late soon ..."

"Don't." I reached for his other parts. I held him, massaged him. "Say something ... beautiful ..."

"You're beautiful."

"Don't mimic me."

He pulled me on top of him. I sat easily over him. His hands followed my hips, gripped them.

"But it's true."

I felt in control again. His face looked so handsome. He seemed to see me. I rolled my hips as I bent to kiss him. His moans excited me. I wanted to hear more of him as it chased everybody else from my mind. Every part of his body and his movements felt exaggerated, felt fierce. I balanced my palms upon his chest. I controlled him. I controlled me. Overwhelmed, I started to feel angry. Angry that I saw Mutta scowling at me if I closed my eyes. I wanted to scream at her to get out of my mind. I pushed harder and deeper to chase her away. This was my moment. I didn't want to feel ashamed. It felt good. Why did it feel so good?

That's when Ibi grabbed me, rolled me over, and groaned as his strength melted over me. He groaned with every tilt of my body.

"Stop," he whispered. "Sorry ..." fell from his lips upon my ear.

"Why are you sorry?"

"I yelled in your ear. I didn't mean to. You just make me feel so amazing."

"I love you ..."

"Thank you." He rolled off me and stared off.

"I want to stay here tonight. With you." I snuggled up to him, traced my fingertip about his skin.

"I want you to stay, too."

I squeezed him.

"What about your foda?"

"He doesn't even know where I am. And if this is the last night we will see, I want to be with you."

We pushed the rest of the world away. Nothing else felt so important. We didn't even eat. But we did sleep. I fell exhausted beside him, warm, safe, free.

Everything that followed, I cannot say if it was a dream or not. Woven amongst the brattle of new leaves a grunting stirred me. I sat up and stared out over the camp. Ibi lay lost in his sleep. I rubbed his shoulder, but he rolled away from me. I tipped my ear to the breeze. I heard a twig snap. The calico bounded into the tent upon my lap.

"Hello, Kitty. Was that you making that noise?"

His purrs could not overtake the grunts, now almost a muttering, a deep tone, too human not to be words. I listened for them. I cradled the cat to my bare chest and strolled into the open pasture. I eased forward towards the brush. The grunting got louder. And now heavy breathing filled in the space between those grunts.

Wrapped in the darkness I felt the Bishop.

I scoured the brush for him. I couldn't be certain, but a flicker, almost a glare, captured me. The weathered white and burnt bark of the paper birch and white poplar turned into a thousand pale bearded faces. The rustle and rattle of wild grasses and naked branches chattered distain.

"Whore ..."

I stepped back from the thicket.

The quickened shuffle of cloth rubbing against cloth grew louder. More grunts. Then I heard a whispered monotone.

"Hail Mary full of grace ..."

Then a soft but forceful grunting, crescendoing into a moan, a pain-riddled moan. I looked across all the thousands of faces for the real Bishop. I knew his shimmering glare had to be inside that darkness.

"Go away from here, Bishop!"

I stared deeper, past the trees. The image of an old man came into focus. I knew our eyes locked.

"Go away from her!" I said.

He opened his coat and unbuttoned his shirt. Built from years of hard work, his muscular naked chest also looked withered as his skin barely clung to his body, falling away in soft wrinkled ripples of flesh at his joints. He held his hat in one hand and pawed at his separate parts with the other.

"Whore ..."

I turned and ran. Back inside the tent, I buried myself under

Ibi's arms. I squeezed my eyes shut trying to wring the image of the Bishop from inside my mind.

"Huh, what is it?"

"I heard the Bishop. He's in the bush."

"What? No."

"Listen."

Outside a crash of underbrush, the snap of branches, and a boom of heavy hooves pounded the ground all about us to fade off in the direction towards town.

"Shshsh ... It's probably just a moose."

Black Gully Lake

THE GREY CLOUDS overhead, too high to promise rain, looked smudged together. The hand of a manic artist could have thumbed umber and amber through a slapdash swipe of charcoal and white. These clouds filtered all sunlight through a burning wick, as if the world had been cauterized by candlelight. The entire county smelled of campfire. The odour, though pleasant, gave way to the ominous ashy haze, which pulsed with the fears that blew in with severe storms. Mareika watched the sun rise. It appeared for less than an hour on the eastern horizon before the smoke and cloud smuggled it away. Mareika could still see it glow as a solid, matte, orange disc searing through the woolly heavens weighing down over them all.

She moved about the pastures that morning holding Ibi's hand.

"Do you think they'll come back?"

He prepared his words to blame the Bishop for smothering his oration. Instead Ibi rationalized his disappointment. "I am no longer worried for them. Like the Church belongs in our homes and our hearts, we do not have to be here to rise." He squeezed her hand. "I am glad you are here. If I have done only one great thing in my life—it was to save you ..." He bowed to her.

She smiled.

"I imagine Claas and Elizabeth are back in Ak-Metchet readying themselves. And I imagine the others, too, are ready. If it's us, then it would make the most magnificent wedding day overseen by our Lord and Saviour."

"I'm scared."

"And I will give them an heart to know me, that I am the LORD; and they shall be my people, and I will be their God: for they shall return unto me with their whole heart. You will rise. I know your heart. And your heart knows *Him*."

Fewer than twenty followers came to Black Gully Lake. The Jantzens never returned. Mareika knew none of them. Her heart felt sick with so few people arriving. She felt sicker as she watched the plain for Bishop Dyck, but he never returned.

Some of the parishioners took out breads and meats as an offering to Ibi.

"No. Brothers and Sisters today should be about fasting. Soon enough we shall all have our hearts' content." He took Mareika's hand. He reached out his other for another follower to take. Then each and all linked together. Ibi bowed his head. "O please *Father*, we ask your grace and mercy and protection. We draw upon these blessings and cares and ask you not to divide us. Our unity represents *You* and the one true Lord Jesus Christ in the Holy Spirit. Amen."

Ibi, Mareika, and the small fraction that remained stood in the pasture allied, hand in hand. They shared hymns and prayers, and they offered themselves to the burnt-out skies above. The minutes became hours. The morning became noon.

~∞~

"There's your donkey, Paul." John pointed at the animal dipping its nose into the waters of Black Gully Lake. "And that looks like one of Jantzen's carts." He squinted into the tent hanging between trees. His eyes looked over the edge of the waters around the pasture to its ends as it rolled out from under the foot of the trees foresting the west. He looked through the clearing. Children ran inside the meadow.

Paul pulled the reins to stop his wagon.

"Thanks for the ride."

"How are you getting back?"

"I'm going to take your donkey and Jantzen's wagon."

"Oh."

"Yeah, I have to go talk to that Gietz." John hopped down and walked beside the path of fallen grass into the next clearing.

Gietz sat on a stump, a book opened on his lap. Mareika on the ground leaned against his legs. Even from his position coming from the brush into the neighbouring field, he saw an admiration sparkle in her eyes as she looked up at the man. She stood and turned her back to him. He watched the doomsayer rise and look over his daughter's shoulder. Several families and townspeople stood or milled about. Most held hands, sang hymns. They all looked like they were wearing their bed gowns. John shook his head.

"Mareika Lynn Doerksen! We're going home now!" John ignored everyone's eyes turn upon him. "Come on. Get your clothes back on."

"I'm glad you're here, Brother Doerksen."

"I am not your brother." He took his daughter by her arm. "Where are your clothes?"

"Sir." Gietz put his arm on John's shoulder.

"Yeah, you can remove that," he said.

He bowed to the demand. "Join us for *His* glorious return." Gietz reached his hands to the sky.

John's eyes focused on the spine. *Jung-Stilling* and *Heimweh* flickered with golden lettering. He remembered the book from when he was a teenager back in Samara. It was the fuel for Claas Epp Jr., taking up hundreds of his neighbours and cousins into Asia looking for the Rapture. His father read the novel and shared it with him. He read it as nothing more than a romanticized notion of Mennonites. In fact the book, the paranoia Epp stirred, they spelled the end of John's faith.

"Did you miss Epp's Rapture?"

Ibi Gietz thrust the book out near John's nose.

"This is a testament! This shows us our salvation after our folly."

John snatched the book. Gietz lunged for it, missed. He huffed and turned to Mareika to make it right.

"Give him his book back," she said, avoiding her father's eyes.

John's eyebrows slammed together, but his lips did not curl. He sighed, lowering his stance only slightly, but Ibi caught this softening, so he stepped toward the donkey farmer. He now held some of John's personal space. He puffed his chest out without touching John.

John shook his head at his daughter's alliance with the chiliastic transient and lowered the book.

Ibi Gietz again snatched for it.

John flinched. He stepped to Mareika, an attempt to shepherd his daughter from Ibi. He opened the book.

Ibi followed John and reached around him with a hand to Mareika. She took it. He looked down at John. His voice vibrated deep below his throat. *"Come, thou Almighty King/help us thy name to sing,/help us to praise ..."*

The other women and children joined in the hymnal.

John shook his head and spoke over the singing.

"This is a story, a novel, an imaginary world." John closed it and passed it to his daughter. She turned the book over to Ibi. "I have read that book. I know all about this man's mentor, Epp. He came from Samara, same as me and Martin."

"You came from there?" She stopped humming.

"Yes. And that book is not a book of the Bible."

"What is it?" she asked.

"That is ridiculous," Ibi said. "Is the black elm not a work of our Lord? Just because it comes to us from a seed ..." Gietz slid the book into her hands and knelt at her feet. "This is another one of God's seeds. He planted it in the mind of a great man, where it flourished with fruits that fed our people. And that fruit gave us strength and courage."

"Get up!" John grabbed the doom-monger's arm. "This book

was written by a Swiss eye doctor who had a pathetic, romantic idea of who we Mennonites were. But he was no Mennonite. He was an aristocrat who looked down upon us whilst he sang our virtues."

"Oh, you do not understand—he does not understand our path."

Mareika walked backwards holding her father and Gietz one view. She looked to each, then the other and again.

"Mareika, it's only a story. It's about a prince of a large empire who meets and marries a Mennonite girl. This prince then leads his believers into Asia where he expects them to be taken to the Kingdom of our Lord," John said. "Oh, Mareika, this man thinks he's Eugenius. So did Claas Epp Jr. Don't be fooled."

"A prince who marries a Mennonite girl?" Mareika looked at Ibi.

"I am no prince," Ibi Gietz said, putting his book back into his pack, shouldering it, and walking away.

"Foda, please stop." Mareika stepped to follow Ibi, but she stopped at her father's shoulder. The western sun fell in the late afternoon. Blurred through the haze about them, Mareika chased after the vision of Ibi, the man. She tried to focus on his gown.

John looked back to the lake. He looked along his daughter's shadow as it stretched three times longer than her true height.

"We will not be in this clearing come sunrise. Our destiny is to meet our Lord at heaven's gate. Will you be joining us?" Gietz said.

"I have fields to till and seed to plant. I'll have to catch the next Rapture."

"This is not funny, donkey cutter."

John watched his shadow join into his daughter's as they warped over the budding prairie.

Gietz bent over his satchel for another book. He moved upon the stump and read. "It says in Matthew 24:32, *Now learn this parable from the fig tree: As soon as its branch becomes tender and sprouts leaves, you know that summer is near. In the same way, when you see all these things, recognize that He is near—at the door! I assure you: This generation will certainly not pass away until all these things take place. Heaven and earth will pass away, but My words will never pass away.* We saw the buds, and these leaves—the floods, the famines, the wars, the disease—are falling from this tree. We all see it. This young woman feels the end inside her insides."

John watched his daughter's face flush red. She hugged herself, refusing to look at the other followers.

He scowled but squinted with a deep examination of his daughter. She turned her back to his eye. He held his hand up to Gietz. He passed his Bible to John. He found the passage and read it silently. He stopped and looked at Mareika. "You never read the whole passage."

"It's all there, donkey cutter. Why do you deny this work? He is coming, and He is coming to mend and repair this sick tree."

John frowned shaking his head.

"What?" John didn't know what to say to this stranger. He sounded ridiculous. He looked at Mareika. He examined her. He made no sense. Yet his daughter stood by his side. He stopped and let the man speak. He needed to hear more before he could continue.

"You—like of many other men—think you are a god, cutting the sex away from the beasts in a feeble attempt to hold dominion over them." Ibi walked an arc out of reach of John. He darted in and out like a rabbit escaping a fox. His words and streams of thought were just as darting and errant. "It is *all* there ..." He turned to his crowd. He started a hymn. *"It may be at morn, when the day is awakening...."*

The women and children again follow Ibi's lead.

"Hallelujah! Amen. Hallelujah! Amen."

John wiped his mouth and gave a polishing cough to his vocal cords. That natural frequency chimed out with that cough and called out to his daughter's attention. She tilted her ear up towards her foda. But she crossed her arms.

"*'No one knows about that day or hour, not even the angels in heaven, nor the Son, but only the Father.'* Matthew 24:36." He snapped the book shut and handed it to Gietz. "So when was it supposed to happen? This morning? Tonight? When?"

"Maybe tonight when the comet can be seen to our eyes. That is when we shall ascend."

John looked up at the sky. Clouds cluttered the blue with billowing greys and whites. He looked to his daughter. "When this doesn't happen, will you come home?"

"She's not one of your beasts, donkey cutter."

"You keep calling me that. What's that supposed to mean?"

"You can't expect to cut her off from this world and *His* word. She is a Lamb of God. Neutering those beasts may draw them into subservience, but pretending she isn't a woman under *Him*—"

"You bastard. What did you do?"

Mareika stared into the grass. Her tremble more than shook a no from her body. She did not need to use words to reveal the intimacy shared with Ibi Gietz.

"Mareika?" John stared at the man who looked identical in age to himself. He stepped to his daughter, then lunged for Ibi.

Mareika shielded him.

"No!"

"Did he hurt you?"

"I said no!"

John's eyes slammed like hammer and chisel into the man, an attempt to carve his ignorance away and expose the truth he didn't wish to imagine.

"Jesus Christ, what's wrong with the men in this town?"

"Don't take the Lord's name in vain."

"Excuse me?"

"You swear, and you finish his name."

"You don't get the moral high ground here. No. You …" He pointed his finger in the face of the parishioners. None looked his way but continued their hymn. "You used …" He looked over Mareika. She did not look harmed in any tangible way. The splinters deep in her back days earlier, John could see it. But what damage had he done? This false narrative of salvation. This larceny. John nodded. "Who has taken the Lord's name in vain? You've fooled all these people to follow you. *He* doesn't speak through you. You used a false narrative to convince these people that the end is imminent. Why? What are you gaining from peddling lies?"

"Look around you. This world is ending and about to pass."

"Forest fires, plain and simple." John pulled up at his pants. "And for the record, swearing is not taking the Lord's name in vain. Misrepresenting the Bible for your prosperity, that's what it is to take his name in vain. This man has deceived you all for what?"

"I have gained nothing."

John threw his hands up. Mareika pushed John back again.

"And my daughter ... She's not anyone's wife. That's two commandments downed."

"There's nothing here for you, donkey cutter. *The devils also believe, and tremble!* Seek salvation, and ask for forgiveness. There's still time."

"From whom, you? You are not saving a single soul."

"You doubt me? Everything I am here to offer is in tradition. Do you wish to plant seeds of doubt and regret? They will sprout. The shoots will twist and curl, reach for you. You will become ensnared. Held to this earth. Overcome. Overwhelmed. Then what? There is a war coming. Look above us. The skies are smudged with soot and ash. *Upon the wicked he shall rain snares, fire and brimstone.* Do you stay and fight? Or maybe you become his vessel again. You were once holy. You can be again. Open your heart and let *Him* in. We are his vessel."

John sauntered back and forth, ripped a tread between Ibi and his daughter. "Tradition? Tradition makes a man—and women for that matter—forget how to think for himself. Don't you have questions?"

"No. For *He* is the answer."

"That's ... that's nothing. You have said nothing. You aren't a vessel. You're a colander. In fact, we are all colanders. We would like to think of ourselves as a vessel, carrying our loves and our pains. But really we are more like colanders. Life washes over us, and we filter these experiences and keep the biggest parts. We want to pick only the sweetest bits. But we are all so different that what those parts that remain saved will always be different. That's what forgiveness is for. What it really is for. It's when we turn ourselves upside down and shake the bad filtered through us out. Forgiveness for the most part is for ourselves. Trespass? I've been afraid to leave my own property. I've shown my little girl that the world is some place to hide away from. I thought I was teaching independence. She can read and write. She can use a compass and map. She can feed herself. And she can castrate a beast. She can ..." John looked at his daughter. "I'm sorry. I forgot to tell you. You can do anything, Mareika. This world doesn't think so. But I've watched you become one of the smartest, most capable people I have ever met. I'm proud of you. This, whatever this is ... I won't judge. I can't. All we have to do is wait. Then you'll see he's wrong. I'll wait with everybody else. I'll wait for this Rapture. But when it doesn't come, I ask that you come home." ·

She stepped behind Ibi's shoulder. She dropped her eyes from John, but with no shame. Her chin refused to fall. She huffed. John waited through this resistance. Then she bowed her head twice. John tucked his thumbs behind his suspenders and took to Ibi Gietz's other side.

⁓⁕⁖

Hours passed. John's impatience fell out as questions and sniggers tossed at Ibi.

"I heard you came from Winnipeg."

"I did."

"Why did you leave? I imagine there's way more people there that would need saving than here."

"There was no hope for Winnipeg."

"What does that even mean?"

"It means I found hope here." He looked into Mareika's eyes.

John rolled his. He walked to Mareika's other side, excused the child holding her hand, and joined the circle there. Mareika refused his hand, reaching it across her body to close it around the top of Ibi's.

"Do you know how I think you found Black Gully? You ran out of track." He stepped inside the circle of parishioners. He took off his glasses. He pulled the bottom of his shirt loose from his pants and cleaned them. When he replaced them on his nose, his smirk was washed in earnestness. "You got run out of Winnipeg and every other town."

He looked at Mareika.

"Do you have a wife?"

"No." Ibi scoffed at the path John chose to follow. "I have always served *His* ministry."

"Oh. So you are just that devout."

"I have been called. Mark said, *Go ye into all the world, and preach the Gospel to every creature.*"

"Is that why you have one of my donkeys? Is he one of your converted?"

The gelding strolled about the open field, its head down while it nipped and pulled the new grasses. It looked up at John and chomped the greens.

"Why do you choose to mock us, the Believers?"

"I'm not the one standing in my bed-gown in the middle of a field in the middle of the night. There is nothing happening. *He* is not coming. And I have to tell you, I cannot wrap my head around how you've been able to convince these good people to join you like this."

"You can't dream about it if it isn't real," Ibi said. He smiled at Mareika and wrapped his arm around her. He looked to the remaining families. They kept their eyes to the ground.

"What? Yes, you can. It's called imagination. It's called insight. It's called inspiration. It's called art. Man's greatest inventions started with necessity before it became a dream. And then ... ultimately reality."

Ibi shook his head as he took a breath to feed the words that would come. John put out a hand. He walked the circle as he addressed the followers.

"Who is this man? Ask yourselves, *Who is he?* And *how did he get you here?*" Everybody looked over themselves and the field.

"We are a culture capable of asking for hands and shoulders to raise our barns, our homes. We build up communities. But if we whisper upon your ear that we cry, that we hurt, that we feel differently, you turn your voice upon others' ears and decry us weak. You point and cast stones. But did we not just ask you to help us raise our lives upon a stronger foundation when a wind has knocked us down? Do not be another gale. Be the hands that cements brick. Be that hand that feeds. That's the truth. There is pain, when you decide to be honest, not to hide behind the shawl of any society. People will judge you. They will talk about you behind your back and use your confessions as evidence of weakness, when patience, empathy, honesty comes from strength." John looked forward searching for eyes to meet with his. Even Gietz looked only to his shoes. "I am not trying to shame you. I want to prepare you for tomorrow and the days after. Maybe today was about community. You got to share the day. But tomorrow there's work to get done. This man's promise is hollow. His own Bible told you that. I believe it was in Mark—that day, that hour knoweth no man, no angel in heaven and not even the Son. Just God. And this man is no god." John nodded to the people. Each rose an eye to him.

One by one the wives muttered with their husbands. Scowls speared Ibi. He kept true to the skies as dusk dimmed the landscape. His voice repeated silent prayers until they remained inside. The followers became fewer. Then soon he held only Mareika's hand. John watched the last family move off the plain and disappear into the night.

≈

The sun fell away. John on Mareika's side with Ibi inside her hand, they all watched the sky all through the night. Gietz kept his head up towards the clouds, swaying back and forth from one foot to the other. He stole looks at Mareika and John. If a cloud parted, revealing any glimpse of sky, he would open his Bible. After several hours John went to Gietz's tent and took several blankets. Mareika curled up in one and fell asleep in the grass. Gietz refused the one offered him. He shook the sleep out of his legs and kept swaying. John laid one out and sat on the ground. He looked east, confident, as the sky turned from black to navy blue.

"The sun is coming."

"The Son," Gietz said.

With the full sun rolling over the still waters of Black Gully Lake, John crouched down and heaved his daughter up in his arms.

"Did *He* make it yet?"

"No."

She put her head on his shoulder, still belonging to her sleep. Then her head snapped up. She kicked her legs. John set her on her feet. She pulled the blanket taut.

"But I felt it, Foda. I felt the end coming. God told me. Everything inside me hurt and turned into the weight of lead. And I bled his blood, the blood of the Lamb. Tell him, Ibi."

John closed his eyes. "What do you mean?"

"I bled." She waved her hand over her stomach. "Tell him, Ibi. I felt his rebirth. I hurt like a woman in childbirth, and I bled."

John's head snapped into a nod. He caught up to Mareika.

"Did you tell her that?"

"He didn't have to, because I felt it. I was bleeding his blood. Everything Mutta told me about the Bible when I was a girl. I felt it." Her hand came free from the blanket, and she pointed to her other parts. "From where he was born, I felt his return. I thought I was dying, but I didn't and yesterday it stopped. And he's coming. Ibi, tell him."

John looked around the clearing. He found relief in its emptiness. They remained as all other followers had given up and returned home under the limited moonlight the overcast evening allowed. The gelding promised to Paul Lee roamed at the glade's edge where it still tore at the tall grass. In the silence amongst them all, they heard the grinding of its teeth.

"That isn't a warning." John said. "It's not the glory of his god or any god. He's twisted it. He's twisted something normal to . . . to use you."

His daughter shook. "No. He wouldn't do that. I felt something . . .

A change. I hurt and the bleeding. And I didn't know what it was. And Ibi, he was the only one who would listen."

"No, Mareika." John pulled down his face with a palm. "Just come home."

"No, Foda. It's real. It's coming. Tell him Ibi."

John said, "Yes, you are going through *The Change*, but it's not what he's told you. It is normal. Tell her."

Ibi stalked the grass in front of his tent. He chewed at his thumb wicks and kept his eye from John.

Mareika looked back to John. He stared hard, critical. She didn't look at him as a daughter, but as an adult. "Then you tell me. Why am I bleeding? Why is the blood of the Lamb staining my skin? I feel pains of this world aching though my skin and bone."

"No, Mareika."

"I feel his rebirth! He's coming back."

"No. No. It isn't any of that, believe me."

"No, Foda."

"Yes. If Mutta were here, she would tell you. And it has nothing to do with any Bible or god."

"You don't understand. I am bleeding. Every day the blood comes. It's not like the fence—He's coming back."

"I know where you were bleeding." John looked the field. He washed his face again with his palms.

"But Foda. My other parts—"

His mouth opened, and a grunt tumbled into primal shout. "No!"

Mareika shook. Her head fell to the side, and she squeezed her eyes into a squint to corral the pain. She had never heard him raise his voice. The cries stuttered out of her. "Why don't you believe me?"

John looked at Mareika. Then he looked to his hands. He remembered she fit into his palms, not so long ago.

John lowered his head and moved to her. She stepped and turned away.

"Mareika, let's just go home."

She looked back. His gaze felt desperate. The tension held a scowl under his sadness. She saw his irritation erode with the breeze. He looked like he did when she was a girl asking him questions about grasshoppers that stole his grain.

His voice came like the June showers. His words washed over her. "It's normal, the bleeding. And I'm telling you all women bleed from there." John looked at Gietz, who stood with his back to them. "You're a grown man. She seems to want to listen to you. So why don't you tell her what's happening to her." John watched Gietz's stand alone. He seemed to stop moving, even breathing. He almost disappeared into the background.

Mareika reached and took Ibi's hand. "Tell him, show him that *He's* coming back."

The blanket fell from around her shoulders. Gietz pulled his hands free. Mareika kneeled and gave the blanket a swirl around her shoulders, pulling it tightly. Ibi looked at the grass, his feet turned away from his tent; they pointed the way out of Black Gully toward the western horizon past the mountains. He shook his head.

"Tell him, Ibi." Mareika's voice came with a lash. "Tell him."

"Tell me, Gietz," John said.

"Foda, stop! Mutta told me. She told me she was sick. She felt God."

John sighed. "We are standing in the middle of a field in the dead of night." He shook his head. "Tell her now."

Ibi's mouth opened only enough for words to fall out between his lips like decayed teeth. "It means that God wants you to have a child." Gietz said. He turned to her and held her shoulders. He kept his eyes locked to hers, trying to keep any doubt from creeping inside her heart. "Women are the transgressors. It was Eve who was deceived, not Adam. And it's in Timothy, Mareika. You have to believe me. It's in Timothy, *She will be saved through childbearing*. Please believe me. He is coming."

"I believe you, but . . ."

"Tell her it happens to all women."

"Ibi?"

"It's natural, Mareika." John said.

"Ibi!"

Ibi let Mareika go and turned his back to her, turned his feet back to the mountains. He couldn't rearrange John's words to spin and weave for his last follower. Ibi felt like the distraction he seemed to have been his entire life. "It happens to all women."

"But you said …" Her mouth stayed open. Her eyes narrowed. She looked at the back of Ibi's head. The muscles in his neck relaxed. His head fell under its weight. He turned to Mareika, his eyes to the ground beyond where her father stood. She followed his contemplation to her father. John stood straight, arms crossed, and the muscles in his face were drawn taut over their bones. He, too, looked way beyond the moment they all shared. Ibi shifted on his feet, turning on his heel, his back to Mareika, once again.

She huffed, pulled her blanket tighter. Then she huffed again.

John broke his gaze and gave his eyes back to her. The ripple of his jaw rolled away, dropping the corners of his mouth. His eyes, Mareika would remember, were like canes. The look he offered kept her standing. She stepped towards her dad, away from Ibi. She hesitated, waited for Ibi to explain. He kept quiet. He kept his distance.

"No. I felt it." She looked to the sky, then to the grass bent and pressed from the feet, the wagons of those who had come for the Rapture. She marched to Ibi, who knelt, his forehead in the dirt. She saw the orange glow of embers at his camp stretch and blush. Ibi stood, still away from her. The flames followed his rise, lapping at the air, twisting around fresh kindling. He dropped to his knees again and crawled into his tent, a small dark shadow followed over his back.

"Ibi …"

"Did he touch you?"

She looked at John. Her lips folded inside her mouth.

John shook his head and stared off through the blackness. The sound of a hundred thousand budding branches rattled with the passing of a gale.

"I want the girl!" Marching from the edge of the brush came Bishop Dyck. In his hands he gripped a long rifle. He followed the natural curving path along Wapos Creek towards them. He leveled the rifle. "I want the girl!" His scream came reckless, desperate as a yelp from a hungry den of coyotes cursing a full moon.

"Foda?"

John stepped in front of Mareika facing the rifle. His shoulders widened. He held his hands up, too. John made himself as big as he physically could. Mareika never imagined him as a large man. He was usually unimposing. He moved through every day like a leaf falling in autumn and twisting, turning for any passing wind. Today he felt like the tree, a cottonwood.

"No."

Bishop Dyck pointed the gun to John's face.

Mareika looked for Ibi. Even after his confession, she still felt that his arms around her, holding her, could shield her from the Bishop.

"Where is that false prophet?" He looked into the tent. "Get out here, Gietz, and do what's right." The Bishop turned his attention again to John. "I said I want the girl."

Ibi crawled from his tent. Wide-eyed and trembling, he looked around the pasture, from Mareika to John to Bishop Dyck. But with the Bishop's gaze held upon John, Gietz tore off. He fled with the speed of a whitetail. He sprinted through the glade and bound into the brush. For several tense moments of silence held amongst them as they stared hard into one another—a mere rifle distance apart— they all heard the snap and cracks of Ibi fleeing, stumbling, tripping through the brush as fast as he could.

Mareika's heart felt heavy. It sank into her stomach. She looked all over the meadow. She looked above. A sheet of stars twinkled inside a gap in the smoke and clouds. Then she looked again to John but saw only his back. Fears of losing Foda crawled over her spine, sank inside her. She wanted to say, *Don't take Foda*. Her jaw froze. But a whisper escaped: "Foda . . ."

"It's all right, Mareika. The Bishop isn't going to hurt us." John quoted the Bishop, as per their argument days earlier. "Thou shalt not kill. You want dominion. And I won't let you have it."

The Bishop spoke through his teeth, "I will shoot you dead, John."

"No. No you won't. You are a beast but not a killer."

"I want the girl. You two have harmed her enough."

"Put the rifle away and go home, Bishop."

"Why should I? If I am already condemned to hell as you claim, what is stopping me?"

"Forgiveness."

"What did you say?"

"I forgive you."

"What?"

"You were right. I can't let you rule my heart. I gave too much of it to you. I paid it over, hoping it would save Rebecca. But while I did that, I forgot to give it wholly, completely to the most important person in my life, Mareika. Through my mistreatment of her heart, I have served to push her away from me. I thought I was showing her how to be independent. There is going to be nothing for her here. She works beside me every day. As a girl, she learned to break soil, plant seeds, pull calves, and castrate donkeys. But can I give her any of what she has worked for? No. The lands we live can never be legally permitted to her. And why? Because she's a woman. I have no sons to own what should be hers. It's as if she doesn't exist. But I know she's real. I just didn't notice she didn't feel that way ..." John stepped to the Bishop.

He stepped back. "You are harming her! Your ungodly, unholy life. I can save this angel from your corruption."

Mareika's hand, as if under somebody else's control, rose and found John's back. She felt his heart beating. It rattled his rib cage.

John took another step towards the Bishop.

The rifle trembled. She peeked around John. She saw the Bishop's hands wring the gun's stock with his fingers. But all of them clenched about the butt. John had been right. The Bishop had no intention of harming anybody.

"I mean it, John!" He poked at John's chest with the barrel. If he were to pull the trigger it would have travelled through his heart before piercing Mareika's hand.

"My daughter will not disappear like Rebecca, like her oma, who became a few notes and recipes inside a journal. I saw more for her. I see her going off to far-flung schools, using her skills in the corrals and pens of our farm and studying medicine. I imagine her lifting a community up the way only a doctor can."

"Woman cannot be doctors."

"She can. And I won't let you stop her. Mareika, I'm sorry. I buried my head alongside Mutta. I took for granted what she was teaching you every day. I'm sorry. You're a woman. And I missed it. Do not believe this man or any other who will proclaim he knows better than your heart. That includes me. You did not come into this world to serve a master ..."

Then from behind the trees, while the three remaining stood at the banks of Black Gully Lake, the gelding tore in, chased down the Bishop, who had no time to register what was happening. The animal reared up and punched the Bishop with one, then another hoof. The old man fell back. The long rifle fell to the ground. John turned and grabbed Mareika and moved her free of the attacking animal. The donkey stomped at the Bishop with rapid successions of kicks. One after another dropped heavily upon his head. He stumbled. He rolled. He could not escape the donkey's attack. He finally collapsed onto the grass, his face chewed up, his beard and hair stained red.

John stroked Mareika's hair and hummed the song he purred so long ago when she was a baby to ease her to sleep. His hand felt large and heavy as it gently cradled her head. His other hand patted out tiny beats like a heart above her shoulder blade.

She viewed the Bishop as he lay still, bleeding into the dusty ground, a lifeless husk. She pried herself from John and went to the old man. She squatted, her hand frozen at bay. She ignored his bloody masticated face. His crystal blue eyes looked at her. His pupils narrowed, and the corners of his lips perceptually rose, though hidden inside a mess of beard and blood. She watched an even stream of vapour push one last breath from between his lips to be lost amongst the cold night air.

She palmed her mouth. Not in dread or horror or sadness but

with a regret. Her sorrow was a wish, a wish that in this moment as he fell away from life, that the last image he had seen would have been that of Sarah, his wife. She looked up to John.

He moved with purpose. He moved with efficiency. She saw no guilt. He grabbed the donkey's harness and moved to the Jantzen's wagon and hitched the animal.

Her eyes and mouth fell into a frown. She couldn't look at the man who once menaced her. Her eyes glistened but did not shed a tear. His death placed there at her knees as they soaked up the cool dew from the evening grass left her torn.

He should not have been smiling upon her. His family deserved to hold him. A muddle of emotions, shame, and disgust. In the violence—though she would never confess—for a moment, only a glimmer, she had felt what could be best described as joy. His fall meant he could no longer harm her household.

"Sorry," she said to his body.

But a man now lay, his pupils relaxed, his chest fallen and still, a pod of bones, blood and tattered black linen. He died angry and desperate. And he had looked upon Mareika for his last moment on these prairies before he slipped out of this world.

She looked for Ibi. He did not reappear.

John moved to Ibi's tent, and with a snap, he shook the canvas tarpaulin free.

"We'll put him down in this."

She followed his voice, and her body followed his instructions. Together they wrapped the Bishop and heaved him into the wagon.

"Let's go home."

On the seat of the wagon, Mareika saw their quilt. She graced it with the pads of her fingers as if it shimmered.

"I thought you could use it," John said. He threw it around Mareika, then helped her into the wagon. The smell of evergreen, cedar, jack pine took over as the wagon moved forward. "I promise to take the Bishop home to his family."

Black Gully Lake

IBI'S EYES FLUTTERED open. His eyelids, rusted from his defeat, closed. He squeezed them until his whole face wrinkled. He wrung all the sleep out of his mind, and he let the burn of sunlight bleach his stare. His pupils pulsed and shrivelled. The world rose from outside the blur. His stare captured a caterpillar as it wriggled its way along the long brown manila rope. It crawled the twisted and oil- and dirt-stained fibres that had once supported his canvas tent.

"Why did she steal my tent?" Ibi asked the caterpillar.

He tipped his head as if he were to be looking up, pointed his eyes towards the verdant shores of Black Gully Lake. Upon its waters, loons scooted, dipping under its surface. He rolled and eased to his knees. He reached for the manila rope and used it to raise himself to his feet. This tug catapulted the caterpillar off into the brush. He looked through the meadow. He looked at his feet. Blackness stained the creases, wrinkles, and nailbeds. He shook his head. He clicked his tongue against the gap between his teeth five times.

His calico friend jaunted over and gave the yarn pinned at his hem a clawless smack. Ibi scratched at its cheek with his middle finger.

"Why did you let them steal our home?"

It pushed its face and rolled its head against his finger, then it headed around one leg, its hip and tail rubbing his shin before it rubbed a cheek against his other shin. They walked together to the shore.

Ibi took a breath. He filled his lungs, and a pain like a knitting needle stabbed between his shoulder blades. He held to that pain, looked skyward. His cheeks swelled with the breath. He wanted his lungs to burn with poison. The chirp of wrens, blackbirds, chickadees, robins filled the air. He looked around, through the pussy willows, the cattails, back over his shoulder to the poplars, jack pine. Everything was green, every branch, reed, and blade of grass hummed with life. Today looked like yesterday, which looked the same as the day before. He let go of the breath.

He dropped to his knees. His hands fell into the lake water. "Many men died of the waters, because they were made bitter." His eyes followed his forearms to his wrists, his palms. He drew his cupped hands from those shores. Inside his hands a face looked back at him. He looked over the eyes, the mouth, every bit carried a falling expression. He saw parts of his parents. His father's eyes and forehead, his mother's nose and chin. That apparition he held passed through his fingers. The lake water rained over the same face hidden below the shore's surface, and every drip rippled, warped, twisted, and changed his reflection. He sat onto his heels. A sigh passed his lips. He turned his head to the calico.

"Claas..."

The cat crept over the brown sand. It lowered its nose to the black skin of the surface. Its whiskers doubled and branched into fine hoary lines scratching the onyx surface. Pinkness darted over and over into the waters. The surface wrinkled. Silver rings radiated from the calico critter's thirst.

Ibi's voice thundered. The crush of sound fired the cat's defenses. Its long body arched like an accordion and splayed its fur all the way down its spine as it danced big away from the bellowing wail. Its tail curled over its genitals, and it froze wide-eyed. He scooped the animal into his arms, pressed it to his chest, and marched to where his tent once stood. He fell inside its memory onto his belly. His feet reached past his bedding into matted grass. He rested his cheek over the cat.

"Sh, sh, sh. Sh, sh, sh."

He pushed his chin into the cat's face. He felt the hard edge of its fang as it pushed its face against his. His friend smelled of wet grass, full and sweet. He rolled to his back. The cat crawled upon his chest. Its paws lifted and kneaded at his chest. He rubbed from its cheeks to its back hip. Drool pooled at its lips and dripped onto Ibi's neck before it disappeared into his collar.

When Ibi's eyes opened again, the cool hold of the morning air had been burnt off by the afternoon sun. The calico lay balled up beside him. He raised his hand and rested it just against its fur. Its lungs lifted its body against his palm. He sighed. He sat up and returned to the water. He dropped his pants and peeled off his shirt. He stepped into his reflection and let it swallow his body until the lake took them both. Ibi burst out; water splashed. A mallard and his mate flapped off the surface into the air, their feet dragging a line through the water, before landing thirty feet farther away. Ibi swam across the surface with his mouth open as wide as a whale. He swished it and spit it across the lake. He took another mouthful and swallowed. He rose from the waters and marched past his clothes to the dying fire.

He blew on the coals. A blizzard of ash swelled, and grey and black freckles clung to his glistening body. He pulled a twined bundle of dry grass, bark, and twigs and dropped it all onto the coals. He reached into the flap of his satchel. He took two matches and struck them over a soot-stained stone. It sparked, and a stole of heat wrapped around the match head. The bundle accepted the flame. Ibi tossed twigs, branches, and then logs over the flames until the dancing, flickering flare disappeared. A grey smoulder rose out. He blew at the pile of wood. He blew and blew and blew again. The wood crepitated, and a slither of energy, orange and white—all with a halo of blue—leapt free over it.

Ibi reached for his satchel. He shook it upside down letting his books and scarves fall out. He balled up all the purple scarves and tossed them over the flames. They wilted, the threads crowding back together and disappearing into flame. He took up *Heimweh* and tossed it onto the fire. He took up his Bible and opened it. He turned to Revelations. He held his thumb at the beginning of the book, flipped the pages to the end. He pinched all the pages together, slid his grip to the top corner, and pulled the pages from the spine. Threads and glue hung from the sheets like entrails, glossy. He chucked them into the fire. The flames rose around all four sides, the edges blackened, and then the top page shrank under flames before it lost its glow. The pages, now ash, lifted into the air by the heat and blew away. Page by page rose until a flurry of soot rode the winds past Ibi's naked body.

Eastern Reserve, Manitoba

MIX *1 OUNCE of beef gelatin with 2 tablespoons of cold water. Boil ½ cup of milk. Cool. And skim the fat from the top. Boil the milk again and let cool skimming the fat from the top. Take about 3 tablespoons of the skimmed milk and boil again.*

Stir the dissolved gelatin into the hot milk and mix.

Use the liquid to mend dishes or glassware.

Black Gully, The Café

FODA AND **I** put the day away for both of us. It would be a day of nothing. We promised not to talk about the previous week. And at home on the kitchen lay *The Wonderful Wizard of Oz*. It represented the last book he ever started to read to me years earlier, but inside a diamond of cloth kept the place where he ended. This day would be just for us. And later we would go back to re-start and finish this book together.

We headed into Black Gully for lunch. The sheer pink curtain skimmed sunlight which gave the Café a succulent radiance. Nancy came to the table.

"Morning, Doerksens." She rubbed Foda between his shoulder blades. She nudged him with an elbow. "This girl of yours is nearly a woman."

He nodded. Then he gave me a smile.

I lowered my head with a wrinkle of my nose. Foda pulled his slim round wire glasses on, wrapping them around behind his ears.

"I see the world kept going," Nancy said.

"I think it began all over again," Foda said.

I smiled after his words.

"I bet it did, John. I think you should get the pork loin chop. It's a big cut." She held her thumb and index finger as wide as she could.

"Want to split the pork chops?"

"Yes, please."

"Anything else?"

"Can we have your fried potatoes, the hash?"

"Of course. Cream gravy?" Nancy disappeared into the kitchen.

Foda looked slim this day, clean and neat. He also didn't feel as tall. His bald head appeared dull even with the sunlight falling onto it. And he kept his lips tucked away. I noticed his eyes, too. Their corners no longer draped, neither weary nor miserable. He looked poignant. I sighed. Then I caught myself inside the frames of his glasses. I saw my mouth and eyes were being held the same way.

"Reflective," I said.

"Reflective?"

"I can see myself in your lenses." I liked the way my face captured the sunlight, the way my face felt, and the smile shining back at me.

"I can see you in my eyes," he said. "Do you remember when you were a little girl and I read to you on the couch until you fell asleep?"

"Yes. My favourite part was being all tucked into a blanket and watching you read because I could see myself in your glasses, and it felt like I was there in front of you. And I felt like I mattered. I used to wonder if you could see me there in your glasses."

"No, but you were always in my mind."

"How come you stopped reading to me?"

"Because I thought you were old enough to read on your own." He seemed to shrug at his honesty like he'd just stained his shirt. Then Foda cut to the heart.

"I left you alone, didn't I?"

My lips folded over my teeth, and I eased a nod, careful not to tip that hurt over the brim.

"I thought if I raised you to be independent that I was doing my job. I'm sorry."

"I want to tell you what happened. But I'm scared."

"I'll listen."

"It was the fear of a god and Mutta. She created this unknown. She impressed it upon me. I felt a responsibility to be afraid of my body because it would ... I don't know ... betray me. She made me afraid of myself. And there was supposed to be this great force watching me for when I did. It felt like I was always being wrong. Then I felt this dramatic change. Everything inside hurt and began draining from me. And I was afraid to go to you, because then I'd have to admit or confess ..." Mareika couldn't pull her eyes from the tabletop. She picked at her fingernails. "I felt so many things. Fear and guilt mostly ... Then he came around."

"Ibi."

"Yes. And he said I wasn't wrong. He acknowledged my confusions and fears. He listened. And it felt easier to accept an authority greater than me, but maybe it was because all my life I've been a child, doing what I've been told." She looked at John. She looked over his entire face, measured every muscle for his true response to her confessions. His eyes tipped a sadness down his face, and he bowed his chin with a long blink, an apology and an encouragement. Her tight lips loosened to bloom into a rosy smile. "It was easier not to ask why. I thought maybe Mutta had been right. Maybe there was something out there bigger than us. And I honestly— when I found that blood—I honestly thought I was dying. I can't tell you how scared I was. And I didn't understand why. But I knew it had to have been my fault. Mutta had said it was going to be my fault. But Ibi told me it wasn't. He had been very kind and tender with me. And I thought, where did he come from? It all had to be everything Mutta said."

Foda reached into his satchel and took out a dark blue book. "This is the book you found when you cleaned out Mutta's room after she passed. Do you remember?"

"Yes. I was afraid of it. I found it under a drawer hidden."

"It's her journal. She wrote in it while she was alive. It explains and expresses who she was. I want you to have it."

He placed the book onto the table. I kept my hands on my lap but stared at the crackling leather cover.

"You don't ever have to read it."

I nodded.

"I mean it. You never have to read it, but it is here if you want."

He reached his foot out under the table and pressed down on my toes. A laugh flapped out from inside me towards the beige ceiling of the café. "It exists because she did. And you deserve to know her, okay?"

I nodded.

"I want you to take it home and put it into our library. I could have put it onto the shelves, but you would not own the physical presence to remember where I put it, so if you put it on the book-shelf, then you will know where to go when you need it. I'm sorry, but I tore some of the pages out. I wanted to burn them when I read them the first time, but I couldn't. They were Mutta. If I took them away, then she could disappear. So I glued them back inside to some of the blank pages."

I turned the book in my hands to catch the misaligned edges and bulky pages that had been placed back inside. I nodded. I almost couldn't swallow. I felt afraid to confess to Foda I could not remember Mutta's face.

"I find it hard to remember what she looked like. I remember how she feels, but most days, I struggle to see her face." Tears rolled down my cheek. "I'm sorry."

Foda took the book up into his hands and opened it to some pages he had bookmarked. "There is so much around us we do not see. Secrets. When the winter overtakes the poplars, turning summer's last breath into white fuzzy shards clinging to every trunk and branch, holding the trees captive, seemingly dead, know that the earth is merely holding its breath before the buds of spring's song burst forth, with the croak of a million frogs rising from the frost to join with the returning birds of summer."

"Did Mutta write that?"

"Yes, she did."

"It was pretty."

Foda turned the square he used to bookmark that page. It was a photo of him and Mutta on a bench in a house. He held it, pressing it against his lips.

"I thought there were better things for you inside all those other books outside away from me and this." He tapped the diary with his finger. His nails were clean and trim. "I wanted you to draw inspiration from the art of those who observed beauty, not pain."

He handed me the photo. Inside my mind the faded shadow burned off in the light of her image, and inside my mind she returned. "There she is …" I felt saved.

"I am sorry I never allowed you access to her. She …" Foda choked. "Plain and simple, I wanted you to be able to depend on yourself. I wanted you to be your own hero inside your own story."

"Why can't I want you to be my hero?"

His eyes fell away. He held onto what I had said for a moment. I can admit I knew his answer before he said it. And I knew what I would say. I had had this conversation inside my mind before. I never thought I would actually have it with him in person. But there he was in front of me, listening. Then his words came faster. "Oh, I've made too many mistakes." He laid his palm over the journal, edged it closer.

"But that's what heroes do. Inside all those books you built our home upon, every protagonist made mistakes. It was their response to those moments of error when their heroism rose. And I've watched you rise every day I can remember. Alone, you always made a choice based on what was best for me. You were there. You were present. Yes, I have felt excluded from your life. Yes, I had been feeling like you were pushing me away. But here you are again. With me. If this was my tale, this is how I'd write my hero." I tapped my finger against the leather cover.

Foda rose. He took up the book and placed it upon my lap. I hooked my fingers around the spine, pulling it into the warmth of my tummy. I watched his arms rise, where in a twinkling, I found myself against his chest. My toes lifted me harder into the cradle of his arms. I felt his weight wrap around my shoulders. It was never inside the walls of that house where I found home. It was his heart. Foda's drive, inspiration, and motivations had always been for me. He wanted me to be strong and independent. He wanted my mind to flourish and strive for higher expectations. My nose found that old fragrance of chopped wood in his shirt I had so looked forward to as a child while curled upon his lap when he read. I knew it was not possible, but my grown body remembered this had to be the way he had held me when I first came into his life as a helpless baby. And once he let go, I knew I was welcome back whenever I needed. But until then, I let Foda hold me.

Acknowledgements

IT TAKES A village. And I believe my writing career is no exception. It does come down to whom you choose to surround yourself with. There have been people in my life who have told me to "quit" or "get a real job." But they are the few. I have always chosen to not just follow my passion but to work on it and improve upon it. I could not have done so without the support, encouragement, or gifts of those who have reinforced me for more than two decades. Admittedly, this page has been the most difficult to write. I need to get it right. I owe it to my village.

Firstly, I wish to give thanks to Guernica Editions and their family of editors, designers, and artists who toiled to pull together this novel. I'd like to acknowledge David Moratto for including me and respecting my vision while designing the book cover, Julie Roorda for endeavouring to make this manuscript shimmer, and Michael Mirolla for trusting and believing in my manuscript. It has been a pleasure to work with everybody to bring this part of me out into the world.

Secondly, I want to thank Vivian Zenari, who helped edit and prepare my manuscript for submitting. I encourage any writer to seek her services. I met Vivian years ago when I volunteered at *Other Voices*. Thank you, Vivian.

Thirdly, I'd like to thank the Alberta Foundation for the Arts, but especially the Banff Centre for Arts and Creativity and The

Writers' Guild of Alberta and their Mentorship Program, for their financial assistance. The book started at the Writing Studio and came to fruition with the Mentorship Program. Thank you. I hope someday that I can return what you have gifted me.

Fourthly (who says fourthly?), to the egg-tooth writers, I encourage you to look into writer-in-residence programs at the nearest libraries, universities and colleges, or writing programs. They are a wealth of information and experience. Along the path leading to this novel, I had the joy and privilege to be in a room with many mentors, who shared their wisdom and nourished my growth as a writer, which cannot be quantified. So to you, the selfless Canadian (and some American) writers, I bow. Those most inspirational, in no particular order, include: Joselyn Brown, Lynn Coady, and Marina Endicott (you know why you're grouped together), Minister Faust, Omar Mouallem, Shani Mootoo, Erín Moure, Andreas Schroeder, Fred Stenson, Gail Sidonie Sobat, Richard Van Camp, and Tim Bowling and Theresa Shea.

Next, I wish to acknowledge the Writing Department at the University of Alberta when I studied there. Do not mistake this as a nod to the UofA. With only half of a semester left to gain my Combined Honours Degree in Creative Writing and Linguistics, I became ill and had to pause my studies. The bureaucracy and greed of the institution made it impossible for me to continue, even years later, when I became well enough to do so. To them, I say shame on you. But to the glorious staff who worked there, thank you. Those include Rebecca Cameron, who encouraged me to pursue creative writing; Kristjana Gunnars, who first believed in my voice; Mary Elizabeth (Betsy) Sargent, who taught me how to truly read; and Rob Appleford, who, with great joy and enthusiasm, led me down the path of great and fascinating Canadian theatre and film.

I'd like to circle back to the Banff Centre For Arts and Creativity's Writing Studio. It was there that I swam in a well of talent and made incredible friendships. I would like to acknowledge those friendships and talented writers: Sarah Mian, Sandy Pool, Leigh Kotsilidis, Lindsay Bird, and Daniel Kincade Renton. You all made me laugh until I peed. I will forever look forward to the gift of time and conversation with you. I would also like to say thank you to the mentors who gifted me their energies and talents: Michael Crummey, Padma Viswanathan, and Kristín Ómarsdóttir. You are all such incredible talents and so generous.

A short intermission …

I would like to thank the Provincial Archives of Alberta not only for the snazzy white gloves but for the hours of research. I wish to extend the same thank you to the Mennonite Heritage Village, who actually learned a couple of tidbits from me, including identifying a nutmeg rasp, the Mennonite Heritage Archive at the Canadian Mennonite University, and the Centre for Mennonite Brethren Studies in Canada. My time in all your archives gave a depth that is immeasurable to my manuscript.

I want to doff my cap to my friends and family, including Coach Barb, Janine, Kelly and Michael, and Barb and Sheldon, for believing that writing is a viable way to make a living and for sharing your encouragement and pride through the years. Coach Barb, you will never know how meaningful it was when you encouraged me to "push." It was not just that first conversation, but how you cared enough to follow up and check in. Thank you. I want to also give an additional thank you to Michael's Uncle Fred and Barb for reading my work in its infancy and giving honest feedback. And thank you, Michael, for introducing me to Edmonton's Raving Poets. The atmosphere and community breathed life into my work when I had doubts.

Further acknowledgement for my family needs to be extended to Uncle Steve and Auntie Jenn. Through the years, you both have always been a comfort and pillar, keeping me up. When I went through my divorce or accident, you listened. In regards to my writing, you have always given me support, whether by reading and editing my work, just talking about writing and novels, providing me with work, showing up for my readings, or actually organizing a reading for your book club. You have never wavered in your support for my endeavours. I love and admire you both so much. Thank you. Go Roughriders!

A special acknowledgement needs to be shared about my ex-wife and her family. They are the Mennonites. They all shared their family histories and recipes and answered openly personal questions without batting an eye—or changing their opinions of me. On a personal level, this book began with you as a way to learn about and comprehend your personal histories. So to Stefanie, Sara, Shane, Shiela and Robert, Cousin Kory, and Grandma Sarah Klassen (Fehr), Thank you. And, Stefanie, you took me to Manitoba and toiled in many archives to help me exhume the skeletons for this novel. You gave breath to Mareika's voice. I will be forever grateful for the trust and belief you gifted me with your family's culture, heritage, and histories. Danke Shine und Ich liebe dich ...

Mom ... Thank you. You taught me to read, write, research, and love and respect literature. This notion now feels esoteric, but I have never been so scared or more intimidated to share my writing with you than with this book. So much of your strength is in this book that I needed your approval. If you had told me to hide it away in a drawer, I would have. I cannot express my relief or gratitude for your enthusiasm for it. Thank you. I love you.

Continuing, I want to recognize the incredible time and energy MWG Ink put in for not just hours but weeks and months. Years ago, you started with an idea and 9,000 words before you poured over individual chapters and three revisions. You had this manuscript at its worst, but you saw its end and brought it to a polished finish. I could not have done this without you all. I always look forward to our time together, whether we're editing, writing, or just talking. You ask the hardest questions. But most importantly, you keep my writing honest. Thank you. Keep an eye out, dear reader, for the publications of other members of MWG Ink: Laura Barakeris, Amanda Lim, Melissa Morelli Lacroix, Brett Sheehan, Michael Sheehan, and Nikki Stalker.

If anybody reading this knows Greg Hollingshead, you know what an immense presence he has been not for only myself but for innumerable Canadian writers for decades now. I first met Greg when he graciously took on my Write Tutorial project at the UofA. You had decided to only take on one grad student that semester—competition was fierce—so when you actually read my portfolio as an undergrad (submitted late, I might add) … what a privilege! Those hours spent working one-on-one for a semester on my short story collection fertilized not only my writing but also my resolve to continue with this dream. Then, a decade later, to spend another 5 weeks with you at the Banff Centre, it's impossible to quantify what you've given to me and others across Canada. You are a national treasure.

Jill Robinson … I cannot say enough about your support for this novel. What an immense pleasure it was to work with you through the WGA's Mentorship Program! You got it as a short story and helped it become a novel. Then, years later, when you had no obligation to, you read it again. I cannot wait to read your next novel. You have an incredible talent, and *More in Anger* is still one of my favourite novels of all time. Thank you, Jill. I will treasure what you brought to this novel, especially the energy and spirit you helped infuse into a fully realized teenager, Mareika.

I cannot conclude without anybody reading this knowing how pivotal Paula has been to the final drafts. You opened up about your teenage years, answered challenging questions, and addressed complicated feelings. You gave Mareika's character her sinew and muscle. You also believed in my work. You believed in me. Thank you. Forever, I will admire you as a partner, woman, and mom. You make me a better man. I promise to always say, "Thank you." I love you, Doll …

And finally, Isa—my Isa Bär. Since the day I knew you were going to be a part of my life, I have never felt a stronger love. Happiness and joy were merely concepts before. Then on that day I met you, tiny, ruddy-cheeked, and fitting merely inside Mommie's two hands, I promised to always care for your heart. And what a huge heart you have! It has been incredible to watch you grow and mature into the most unbelievable young woman. You see hearts everywhere—in the shape of stones, clouds easing through prairie-blue skies, water stains on drying sidewalks after a cleansing rain. You are what flutters inside me, giving my lungs the breath I need and the resolve to be better every day. This book belongs to you now. I love you!

About the Author

See the life I've had can make a good man bad.
—The Smiths

BORN AND RAISED at the periphery, the intrigue and inspiration of those who crossed lines blew Gregory around the Canadian Prairies like a jewel spider orb. He landed in Edmonton with his daughter after a crippling fall while building his passive solar home. However, that fall gave to him not only permanent pain but his greatest gift—staying home to raise his indubitable daughter. Those closest might say he's passionate—not temperamental—quietly empathetic always looking out for his family and neighbours. When not writing or editing, you'll find him in his kitchen either improving his culinary skills (not without a wine or local craft beer), dancing (was beer and wine mentioned), and/or filling the nights with games, music, and laughter with those he loves.

So for once in his life . . .
He got what he wanted . . .

Printed in January 2023
by Gauvin Press,
Gatineau, Québec